THE FOSSEWAY LANTERN

Also by the author

Crossing Over the Bridge

THE
FOSSEWAY
LANTERN

REBEKKA CARROLLE

Tudor Press (London) Ltd

Published by
Tudor Press (London) Ltd
27 Old Gloucester Street
London WC1N 3XX

The Fosseway Lantern
Copyright © 2013 Rebekka Carrolle

ISBN 978-1-874514-28-2

Front and back cover illustrations by Virginia Whiting (watercolourist)

Design and artwork: Santoshan (Stephen Wollaston).

Printed and bound by CPI Group (UK) Ltd, Croydon, CR0 4YY

Contents

Dedication

This story is dedicated to my dear friends Joy and Les Borrer, of the Isle of Wight. To Les for his continuing inspiration from the Higher Realms and to Joy for her encouragement.

1 Looking back on corollary, we are all merely travellers of time!

BRIGHT SUNLIGHT SHONE through chinks in the curtains. Ellie turned over, landing on her stomach, relishing the smell of freshly laundered bedding. The early morning air was cool and fresh after a night's heavy rain. Turning onto her back, she stared at the ceiling, studying many diverse shapes created by dappled sunlight and deliberated on the unforeseen turn of events.

Half asleep, bleary-eyed, she glanced at the clock, snuggled deeper into her bed, curling and uncurling her lithesome frame as she did so, thankful for a good night's sleep and vowing to conceal her painful secret for another day.

Her feet always stuck outside the duvet in the morning. She never understood why or which side they would appear. Every morning was a surprise! Wriggling her toes, her feet felt cold. She brought them sharply under the warmth of the duvet, where she could retreat from the world. The day could wait another ten minutes.

The early morning mirror reflected painful memories. Her long thick mane of untamed hair resembled a frightened chicken. With careless abandon, she resigned her fate to a mask of make-up, reluctantly accepting that expensive salon sessions had failed to control her unruly locks.

Rolling over, cuddling a pillow for comfort, she deliberated before greeting a new day, mulling over what to have for breakfast. Having decided on quick and healthy one, she pondered what the day would bring and what her diary would reveal.

"My social diary is so very full," she chuckled. "I just cannot possibly fit in another engagement ... I wish."

Turning recent events over and over in her mind – unexpected meetings, unexplained happenings and bizarre conversations – led her to question once again the weird and wonderful synchronicity of life.

Sliding easily out of bed, Ellie peeled back the curtains of her luxurious bedroom which, with its soft creams, pinks and white, guaranteed a good night's sleep. It was a sanctuary she was always glad to return to after being on holiday or stopping over with friends.

A light, sunny room cleverly built on above the garage, it overlooked meadows, woodland and the river beyond. Part of the early morning ritual was to look out of the window. This day lit up the green and gold of the fields, the farmer's diligence in stacking corn sheaves in symmetrical patterns carved out by the baler. Momentarily, she watched various birds flying high and heard the shrill sound of the lapwing, or she presumed that's what it was.

Ellie waited, eventually hearing high in the sky the sound she loved best – Canada Geese enjoying intense morning conversations before swooping down on the field to feed and rest. They would be migrating soon. She would miss them. Watching a while longer, she listened with delight to their constant honking as they prepared for the long journey ahead. Her body tingled with excitement, amazement, witnessing this wonder of nature, emotions bubbling to the surface.

Instinctively stirring in unison, before they took flight. On a still day, you could just hear the beat of their wings as they soared higher and higher, then silence.

Descending the familiar staircase, Ellie's cold feet sank into comfy old slippers, reminiscent of her beloved Nana Jack, she sleepily wrapped a long towelling dressing gown around her slim frame. The huge family kettle was warm, thanks to the perpetually lit Aga, a friendly morning welcome. Automatically, she made hot coffee, adding spoonfuls of sugar, sploshing milk, sitting close to the range, relishing warmth on her back.

The old pine kitchen table had been lovingly bleached and scrubbed over the years. "It has character!" her mother had remarked lugging it into the kitchen for the first time. The wood was warm and friendly to lean on, especially first thing in the morning before surfacing fully into the world.

Sipping coffee, remembering it was Saturday and no work, Ellie's spirits lifted. Hooray! The day was hers. Declaring it was an Ellie Day, her feet now warm as she wriggled her toes into pre-shaped slippers created by morning feet. Grinning with delight and stretching, she suddenly remembered she did have something in her diary. Ellie jumped up, grabbing a small blue book from the shelf beside the Aga, decorated haphazardly with self-adhesive flower stickers, believing it was easier to find.

Methodically flicking pages, scanning handwritten scrawl, her impressions, her mind buzzed, questioning recent events, while she made another mug of coffee. What really was to be done?

A successful freelance journalist, it was a role she fell into by chance. Despite her university course of accountancy, she was unable to focus or decide what she really wanted to do with her life. Ellie was a natural mathematician, so why not?

The subject was a soft option and she passed exams with flying colours, without much effort. She had found the chapter of university life unfulfilling, unchallenging and a bit of a chore. Fresher's Week was interesting, where everyone got drunk and lost their inhibitions, only to regret it later. A total bore. There must be more to life. Not a complete out-and-out rebel though admitting to being disgruntled, she was fed up with trying to understand who she was and what to do with her life.

Fortune shone in the form of a placement with a highly respected accountancy firm, with a whopping big salary and perks offered without any effort. Yet Ellie felt unable to sign the contract. Even the sweetener to pay her student loan failed to sway her, as she stubbornly knew she could not commit to staying with the firm for five years, accepting that she was – and always had been – a "free spirit." Despite financial and parental pressure, in her mind there was no contest, so she declined the offer.

In quiet moments, she suspected many regarded her as a fool. A people's person, sitting in an office nine to five, poring over pages and pages of figures, meeting clients with more money than they knew what to do with! Ellie needed to be out and about, meeting people. People fascinated her, as they always had a story to tell. She knew she had the tenacity and patience to listen which, unfortunately, got her into trouble more often than not. "Stop talking. Get on with your work!" was a frequent comment voiced by previous employers.

Accepting she could talk for England, while chatting on the phone, she was often told, "Time is money. You miss valuable sales. Clinch the sale, keep the conversation short and move to the next customer." Eventually, she acknowledged that a role in marketing/sales wasn't for her.

One day, out of the blue, she bumped into Grant, a post-grad student she had enjoyed chatting to over endless cups of coffee at the uni refectory. He, too, appeared to be a bit of a maverick, sharing common ground. Over a welcome dark rich café latte, Grant announced he was moving right away to Australia.

"I just need to get away," he voiced to Ellie. "My family are driving me nuts. If I don't go, I will definitely be swallowed up in the family firm. I could not stand that."

"I thought you enjoyed the prospect of taking over the family business," Ellie asked surprised.

"I did at first, but I have met someone, a physiotherapist, who is mad about surfing and the outdoor life, so we have decided to take a risk and move away."

Shifting from one side of the chair to another, obviously a little agitated, Grant continued by saying, "I know Dad is upset and disappointed, as he put all his hopes and dreams in me wanting to run the farm for him when he retired, but believe me, Ellie, looking after 200 acres of farmland, and a large dairy herd, isn't for me."

"What about your sister Lucy? Didn't she adore animals, spending hours and hours with her beloved horses?"

"I am not exactly sure," muttered Grant quietly. "I suppose it all depends on her future plans and who she decides to marry. Sadly, it is not Dad's wishes, but Jayne and I feel that if we are to take the plunge, we should do it now. The decision is made. Who knows what's around the corner? There's one good thing, though; Dad and Mum have agreed to spend next Easter with us in Melbourne. That really will be something."

Grant's face relaxed a little. "Mum has never flown before and is more than a little terrified of flying," he added. "I told her to have a stiff drink, a double gin and tonic during the flight, relax and sleep!" He chuckled at the thought.

"How have your bosses taken your news? I presume you are working? You were absolutely brilliant at English, if I remember, and romped the Student of the Year Award."

"Yes, I am working. They are disappointed I am leaving, yet at the same time, wish me well, which is great. They knew at some point I would spread my wings. In a way, I am sad as I love the job, though changes are inevitable in every area of our lives. Nothing stands still. I have in fact been offered a fab position in Melbourne. I feel so lucky to have met the girl of my dreams and to clinch a job with the 'Melbourne Times.' I can't quite believe my luck! Life is simply, as they say, absolutely fabulous." Grant's face beamed in anticipation of a new life.

More interested by the minute Ellie asked, "Who are you working for at the moment?"

"The 'Torchester Times,' but only as a freelance journalist. I suppose it is a bit risky, but well worth it. I dictate my salary, and the harder I work, the greater the payout. The pressure I put on myself encourages me to excel. I thrive on deadlines, the adrenaline rush, especially when working on intriguing chunks of info that refuse to dovetail together."

"My fiancée and I are flying out at the end of the month." He whooped proudly, "We have accommodation arranged and I have one week to get organised before taking up my new job in Oz. I am beside myself with excitement at the prospect of what Australia offers us."

"Wow!" Ellie shrieked with delight. "I always knew you would do something with your life, but moving to Oz is awesome, pure genius. Hey Grant, you deserve the opportunity. You were definitely Bristol's brightest student when we were there. What did old Mrs Harrison say? 'Grant Whittaker, you are nothing less than *crème de la crème*'."

Grant and Ellie giggled in unison, reflecting with pleasure and satisfaction the endless hours spent poring over old exam papers.

"Yeah, overall we had a great time and made some really good mates there!"

Grant proceeded to stir his half empty coffee cup. He was lost in thought, reminiscing on happy, carefree days.

"Before you go Grant – just a thought. Is there any possibility there could be an opening for me at your paper? Not to take your place, I couldn't do that, but an opportunity to contribute as a freelance writer, news-based articles on my quirky, zany perception of events. I have had so many hit-and-miss jobs since I left uni. I am being pressured by my old tutors to study for my Masters, but to be honest I am heartily fed up with the studying bit. Like you, I want to see life, live a little, stretch myself and be fulfilled."

"Well, although it can be rewarding, I cannot call it exciting," replied Grant. "The job can be very mundane. You have to ferret out stories and make them as interesting to the reader as you can, such as following up a lead on, say, a succession of stolen horse-boxes, fired and damaged beyond repair, or vandals demolishing a children's play area. It's not all fire and brimstone!"

Ellie sat deep in thought. "I suppose being a journalist is about sniffing out throwaway comments potentially leading to a winning coup?"

"Come to think of it," said Grant. "You always were a rebel and hated routine, doing everything in your power to stir the pot."

Grinning from ear to ear, their shoulders shook with laughter, enjoying the merriment of the moment, recalling many of the pranks and situations Ellie often found herself in, her wicked, feisty streak seemingly getting the upper hand.

"Tell you what, for old time's sake I will make a phone call and see what I can do," answered Grant thoughtfully. "Give me a call; say tomorrow afternoon after four. Must fly now."

"Fingers crossed!" Ellie called out, laughing.

"I will be in touch."

Ellie stared at her morning mug of warm coffee, reliving that conversation five years ago with Grant. Acknowledging she could be temperamental and a little rebellious, thriving on freedom to make choices, she was honest enough to admit she was ambitious, needing to succeed, intelligent, sensitive to other people's problems and feelings. She was her father's daughter after all, strong, determined, charismatic and attractive.

"It's those eyes. They will get her into trouble one day, mark my words. She will break many a young man's heart!"

Ellie pondered on Nana Jack's comments, a family tale retold many times. They had shared a special bond, a stirring of the heart. She used to say, "From the day I set eyes on her, just a few hours old, I knew I loved that girl!"

Ellie enjoyed her new role, as every assignment was a challenge. She patted herself on the back for a successful two-month stint in Scotland profiling for a low-key holiday organisation's "All inclusive activity weekend breaks" at various Highland locations. The project turned out well and secured some very good contacts. A few short stories were accepted by a weekly girlie magazine, so her funds were okay. Occasionally, niggles were raised. "I could do with more pennies... if I worked as an accountant I... but this is much more fun."

Now she was just home a week, returning from a break in the Channel Islands which had proved restful, therapeutic and invigorating. Ellie was refreshed, ready to face the next challenge, missing the adrenaline rush. In buoyant mood, jumping up from the chair she headed for the bathroom, chuckling, "Bring it on!"

2   Promise of light

THE BOY CROUCHED LOW, manoeuvring his small, trembling frame into a tight ball, silent sobs of distress echoing throughout his tiny body. He was fearful of being discovered and of the cruel reprisals should he be found. Silent tears streamed down his face.

He recalled meagre portions, being beaten unmercifully, scolded for being in the way – for existing. He revelled in the silence, a peace he found at the copse, a scraggy group of overgrown shrubs and discarded fruit bushes concealed behind derelict sheds in the left hand corner of a run-down allotment.

The den, built in the spring, was nothing more than the centre of an enormous blackberry bush hollowed out and carpeted with bracken and fern. Here, he created his own world, a solace of imagined warmth and love.

He wished his heart would not pump so loudly. It echoed in his ears like a bass drum, and he was convinced anyone passing could hear the beat. Trying to hold his breath, he took sharp intakes, attempting to control his breathing, praying any passers-by would be unable to detect his silent emotional outpouring of isolated unhappiness.

The palms of his hands were clammy; his curled up frame drenched in anxious cold sweat. Trickles of perspiration blended with salty tears, staining pale dirty cheeks, creating clean abstract criss-cross lines. The sound of footsteps and chattering people drew closer and closer. His legs ached, becoming painful. He needed to change his crouching position yet he dare not in case any movement gave away his position. His school uniform was creased and grubby, but it was vital to remain still.

This was his special place. He dare not let anyone discover his hiding place. Fighting back heart-wrenching tears and desperate to control irrational breathing, he closed his eyes tightly, wishing to become invisible.

The movement of people and the sound of voices grew closer. The urgent, fragmented interchanged chatter seemed to get louder and louder, the volume rising with a mixture of concern, frustration and anger. Consensus of annoyance and frustration gained in momentum – "How dare this boy run away and cause all this unnecessary fuss!"

The ground vibrated as the running feet moved closer. He tried to stop breathing, praying they hadn't thought to enlist the help of Mrs Lacey's dogs.

"Where is that boy?" He recognised the voice of Mr Partridge, the Maths teacher, one of the teachers he liked. He enjoyed his lessons, feeling safe in his class.

Putting hands over his ears, he desperately tried to shut out the impatient raised concerned angry voices.

"I saw him at registration, Sir!"

The boy bit the sleeve of his jumper preventing him from uttering a sound. He recognised that unfriendly tone. It was the voice of the classroom snitch, a real teacher's pet.

"After assembly, he said something about going to collect a book; we haven't seen sight of him since."

As the voices faded away, he shuddered and sobbed, hearing the tired, disappointed voice of Steve Partridge. "Thank you boys, I will sort this out. We'll find him. He can't be far."

The boy sat up a little, wiping tears from his face. He hated bunking off school, knowing he should be working hard in his final year, but couldn't face it. Closing his eyes, he wished Ma was here with him. Ma loved him; he loved listening to her stories of heroes, angels and fairies.

Ma told him, "Remember that someone always hears you when you call, when you're really scared."

This was a time of need. She made it sound so convincing; he wondered if this was indeed true or just a load of hokum, made up like Super Dan stories. He knew he would get a beating and no supper if Jake discovered the drama before he got home.

Feeling wretched, his eyes red-rimmed with crying, his wet, clammy, trembling body ached with sobbing. Feeling a total wreck, he dare not leave his hiding place until the area was quiet. He couldn't risk being discovered and re-positioned his cramped legs.

He shut his eyes tight. His lips mouthed words silently, asking for help. He was strong. Ma had told him so, putting his hands together, he prayed. Nothing happened, so he asked again. Nobody appeared! He sighed. Drawing his jumper tightly around his neck and face for comfort, he drifted into peaceful warmth.

Emotional tiredness enveloped him. His frame relaxed. Emotions quelled, he drifted deeper and deeper into a soporific awareness of peace. With intermittent waves of fearful sighs, emotional trauma calmed. Peace dissolved tension in his physical frame, and subtle rainbow colours merged with the sun's rays. He relaxed into exhausted acceptance.

Colours of every hue, iridescent, vibrant colours, swirled around and surrounded him, bathing him in a cloak of wondrous rainbow light. Sensing tinkling bells and wistful pan pipes in the distance, and a soft, clear, gentle voice singing far off in the distance.

Searching for Ma, he realised he was alone in a field of flowers. Close by woodland and stream, sitting on a bank, his hands played with the cool water as he watched the crystal clear droplets running through his fingers. Music gently resonated with his being. He relaxed, listening to the melody, the words echoed over and over again. "Open your mind, expand your possibilities."

Consciousness absorbed emotion, a peace message of soothing musical chords. Sinking deeper and deeper into the moment, his day-dreaming continued through the rest of the day.

Illusion of Woe

Moonlight sporadically illuminated the landscape, creating a soft light intermingled with hidden dark places, interspersed with menacing dark shadows. Dampness filled the cold night air with an eerie silence, which was forbidding and uncomfortable, apart from an occasional screech of barn owls and foxes on the prowl. There was movement overhead as the high pitch sound of bats zoomed in and out of the woodland, a sound almost inaudible to the human ear. Woodland night air stirred gently, rhythmically, absorbed in drama and sound.

Forest density masked the road threading through the open countryside, relatively straight with a few winding curves. Drivers needed to treat it with respect and care. The moon's movement, hiding from time to time behind a criss-cross of heavy clouds, revealed a picture of misty moonlight markers. Woodland silhouettes created a black darkness, a feeling of menacing intent against a backdrop of bright moonlight and starlight sky.

The Mercedes smoothly took the turns, eating up the miles

as easily as a sledge moving through the snow and ice. It purred, performing effortlessly, like an enormous cat on the prowl. High performance wheels spun, humming as they ate up the miles, creating a soporific droning sound as tyres met the road surface. The driver, oblivious to the travelling speed and scenery, was lost in a world of his own fabrication.

In what appeared to be a split second decision, the car inexplicably screeched to a halt, leaving a trail of smoke and tyre tracks imprinted on the road surface. Lights on full beam appeared menacing, as if trying to stalk unannounced bewildered prey. Silence was destroyed in a single thoughtless unprovoked action.

Profuse sweat drenched the lone male driver, who dared not explore the explosive energy boiling and swirling deep within. It was a frightening unexplored depth of destruction waiting to unleash its fury on the world. The driver's eyes were wide open, pupils dilated, face puce, lips tight and teeth clenched. His hands trembled with a mixture of fear and apprehensive anticipation of what was to come. Inexplicable fury had begun, the volcano of energy erupting from an unexplored secret place deep within. Fear had taken its grip – the pressure was building. Eruption was nearing its pinnacle of power. Then it began – a powerful outpouring of unresolved anger and built up frustration.

A tirade of emotion followed, layer upon layer of hurt, guilt, distrust and misery – "The fucking bitch. I hate the world, hate the fucking world. I hate it, hate it, hate it! I'm going to kill myself; I do not want to have to exist in this pit of humanity any more. I hate it, hate it, hate it! I am going to kill myself, kill myself, kill myself!" The tears flowed; the shoulders shook with uncontrollable sobbing, like a lost child who had fallen, cutting its knee.

Screams and cries of unresolved fear ricocheted through the trees, the echo bouncing off the inside of the vehicle, through the frame, to the tops of the trees and back again. The car shook, rocking violently as the driver continued to allow the outpouring of rage to continue. The flow of forceful anger had to have its way. The car continued to shake as the rage continued. Demons had to be released. Doors hammered relentlessly; feet pounded the floor as the driver desperately tried to release the pattern of rage needing to be expressed. The vehicle was used to this rampage – it was nothing new, occurring on average every three to four months. Moonlight and woodland witness to this release of unwelcome energy, silently watching and waiting for it to be expelled, for the emotion to be quelled.

Silence resumed as quickly as it had been disrupted. The explosive volcano of emotion spent, for the moment feelings subsided. The driver put his foot hard on the accelerator and sped off, leaving a wake of jagged energy to dissipate in the remainder of a bemused woodland night.

3

Ellie loved living in the family upside down house. Originally an old terraced tied cottage, built about 1890, it was located less than five miles, as the crow flies, to the west of the Jenkins Estate, home to numerous families over the years.

The family enjoyed living in the countryside, waking to the sound of the cocks crowing and hens clucking softly, patiently waiting for their morning corn. At times the sound of silence! The house had been extended over the years, with bits added on.

"Not bits," her smiling mother corrected her. "Additions, my darling daughter, done in the best possible taste."

It was unique, special to the family. Visitors commented, "Your home has character and charm."

Ellie described herself as quirky and was fascinated with the past, grasping every opportunity to view properties steeped in mystery or secrecy. Anyone looking at Nestledown from the road found it incredibly difficult to describe the interior layout or living space. Cleverly created through artistic design, the family affectionately referred to it as "Our very own Tardis."

Nestledown was built on the edge of the village at the end of a long, winding lane, close to the old blacksmith's forge. Although sadly no longer in use, according to Ellie it maintained a brave reminder of its purpose. The village population had expanded since she had moved there at the age of seven. It was surrounded by wooded hills where sheep grazed, with dairy and beef herds painstakingly nurtured for milk and meat. Fewer than one thousand residents called the village their home. Over the years, property prices had escalated due to excellent commuter roads to nearby Torchester and the South West. Many of the younger generation were forced to set up home elsewhere, although there were mutterings that the parish council was devising a scheme to enable young families to stay, ensuring the village's survival.

"The young 'uns need to have a choice," old Bill Prentice continually spouted from his soap box. "If we don't do summat, the little school will close. We need to keep it filled." People chuckled, agreed and understood.

When her parents moved to France three years ago, they asked if she would like to stay in Nestledown and look after Truffles and Wynchester, the two fiercely independent Siamese cats. Her parents' long-held dream was to set up their own business when her father retired from the Army. They had close ties with France, so when life-long friends suggested they jointly run a patisserie and café in Deauville, a seaside horse-racing town on the Normandy coastline near Le Havre, they jumped at the chance. Deauville was considered an ideal location for a business venture with easy travelling distance to the UK an added bonus.

Her parents adored the French lifestyle and were enchanted by Deauville from their first visit. Tourists, equine visitors and trainers, drawn to the many surrounding stables, were captivated by the early morning sight of racehorses galloping on the sands, frolicking in waves to end their exercise regime. Initially deliberating about what to do with Nestledown, it was eventually agreed to keep it as a family home for future generations. A perfect solution.

A wealth of village charm, being located ten miles from

Torchester was a big deciding factor in choosing a family home. Four or five small clusters of houses were grouped in a country setting, its inhabitants forging a community. It boasted The Carvers Arms, a beautiful thatched eighteenth century pub set alongside a mill stream. Many happy hours could be idled away, drifting, dreaming of nothing in particular while frequently downing a glass of strong local cider.

From the pub doorway to the left of the village green stood dilapidated stocks from years gone by, a talking point for visitors and used for fun at the annual Summer Fayre. Raised monies maintained the green and duck pond, the heart and soul of the village, where children played, fed ducks and visiting wildfowl. It was also a place where Mums gathered to chat before and after school. Two carefully positioned well used wooden seats faced south west, many older residents stopped to rest and while away time.

Although most of the villagers shopped monthly in Torchester, the village store-cum-post office was proudly supported, and always well stocked, a trade of excess local produce on display. It was a unique system that worked well. No one went without, especially elderly villagers surviving on a meagre pension. A box of fresh produce, carrots, cabbage, eggs, home-made cakes and jam or chutney appeared as if by magic on their early morning doorstep at the beginning of each month. Not one person was willing to admit to being the benefactor. "It's the little people!" the children chanted mischievously. "It's the little people!"

In carefree mood, Ellie donned jeans and blue striped tee-shirt. "Smart casual," she smirked, tying shoelaces and buckling a favourite brown leather belt. Flamboyantly throwing a long cashmere blue scarf around her neck and over her shoulder, she ran downstairs. A beautiful day, she felt good. It was a day for power walking to collect monthly magazines and the local newspaper.

Ellie passed the ruins of the old village church, stopping to watch birds flying overhead, a gentle breeze moving through the trees. She glanced with sad incredulity at the remains of what must have been a beautiful medieval church, once the heart of the village. Venturing inside the shell, she could just make out the shape of the nave, vestry and chancel, with dedicated inscriptions eroded by weathering. Before going to university, she had spent time researching the 1911 demise of the old church. As far as anyone could ascertain, the horrific fire had been a tragic accident.

Quentin suddenly appeared one stormy night, seemingly from nowhere. The Rev John Hardacre bumped into him late one evening as he left the vicarage on his way to the church. He did his best to help Quentin, showing true compassion, offering food and shelter.

Quentin stubbornly refused to stay at the vicarage, stating, "Your home is too good for me, but God's house, that's different. I promise I won't take anything. Never have and never will."

Despite misgivings, John Hardacre allowed him the sanctuary of sleeping in the small vestry on the strict understanding that it was only for a few nights until he was strong enough to move on to Torchester, where he prayed he would receive long-term help.

Quentin stayed around the village for nearly six weeks and was no trouble. In fact, people warmed to him and became accustomed to him being around. A polite gummy smile greeted everyone with a hearty "G'day!" Even though the villagers of Carvers Green took him to their hearts, he steadfastly refused to sleep anywhere but the church vestry, surrounded by prized tobacco tins, smelly blankets, and two tatty coats safe in a collection of carrier bags.

Sadly, one bitterly cold night, records read "11th January, 1911 – Church Tragedy." As snow lay thick on the ground, it was surmised a mixture of meths, bedding and cigarettes sealed the fate of the old church. It transpired that only the Rev Hardacre heard a cry for help when Quentin became disorientated, screaming, shouting and scared out of his wits through too much booze. Tragically, when the alarm was eventually raised, it was too late. Both men became trapped by falling masonry and debris and perished. The ugly charred church roof was now open to the sky. Tapestry hangings, pews, lectern and altar were burnt beyond recognition. Likewise, the church was also beyond repair. Large segments of the thick stone wall were demolished for safety. The only salvageable items were a fragmented stained glass window which had once graced the altar, a distorted altar cross and the blackened stone font, now safe under lock and key until the church is rebuilt.

Quentin Sandler, a wastrel, a wandering, hopeless alcoholic, originated, it seemed, from Cumbria. Despite in-depth searches by parishioners, it appeared he had no family and was an intrepid loner, although everyone mused he had parents, and who knows, perhaps a family somewhere. Despite everyone's best efforts, all avenues of tracing them drew a blank.

The graveyard was still in use, lovingly well tended. Services now held in the village hall until sufficient funds were raised to rebuild the beloved church. A service of remembrance was held every 11th January in the ruins in memory of Reverend John Hardacre who lost his life helping a needy soul, reminding everyone of the wealth of love and compassion he proffered to all who sought solace. This tragedy heralded an enormous outpouring of emotion, so much so that it spurred the villagers into action, lest they forget. In memory of two men from vastly differing background, the villagers grouped together, vowing to rename their village Hallows Rest. It remains so to this day.

Ellie enjoyed her jaunts into the village, especially on lovely sunny days. Everyone seemed friendly, had time to chat and were eager to discuss local events. She was always amazed at the information she gathered from impromptu meetings. Although still considered by some as a bit of an outsider, after spending years at boarding school then university, she was always glad to be back, renewing old ties, absorbing local gossip.

Her mother believed the family was destined to live in Hallows Rest, a village locked in a gentle time warp, seemingly oblivious to the fast pace of the rest of the world. "People don't give themselves time to live or breathe," was her famous stock phrase. "Here in Hallows Rest, cradled by surrounding hills, we choose when to dip in or dip out of life." Ellie found these expressions out of sync in today's world, although she understood her mother's ethos.

Strolling past the pond, Ellie chuckled at the never-ending collection of ducks jostling for best position to gobble food as excited children fed them sparingly. "What a real difference the sunshine makes to everyone's mood," she thought, patiently waiting in the queue to collect her weekly magazines. She was tempted by a large bar of chocolate convincing herself she deserved a treat.

A large group of ramblers had assembled outside The Carvers Arms. "Obviously their morning pit stop," she mused. The noise level of laughter and chatter was so infectious; she crossed the lane to greet them.

A wiry young man with ruddy cheeks caught her attention. He stood proud from the rest of the group. His hobby was obviously an obsession as she glanced at his array of gear, gadgets and cameras. "Why does he need more than one camera?" she wondered. "That rucksack must weigh a ton!" They looked an unusual group, all shapes, heights and ages, dressed for serious walking. "I wonder if they all possess the obligatory bobble hat?" she grinned wickedly.

A bossy one, obviously the leader, built and equipped for passionate walking, beckoned her over. They turned out to be a friendly crowd, who walked regularly and obviously knew each other well. They invited Ellie to join them for coffee.

"'Tis a twelve-miler today, good for walking, as long as the sun don't get too hot." The guy spoke with a slight twang. "When the sun is high, we get too hot. Gets uncomfortable. We prefer it when it is cooler, as we don't sweat so much."

Ellie discovered that he originated from Canada and was here on a five-year work contract. He introduced Ellie to everyone and they all acknowledged her with a ready smile, their names forgotten as soon as spoken. She was interested to know where they had walked from and what brought them to Hallows Rest.

"Interesting countryside. We enjoy walking through new territory, somewhere none of us have visited before."

"The hill's a piece of cake compared to some we have climbed," added the wiry youth.

"I thought you only walked on the flat," replied Ellie.

"Sometimes we do. None of us have been this way before, so we thought we would try a new route, and we're glad we did. We discover what people are really like when we walk. Some are friendly; others greet us with suspicion." The group chuckled in embarrassed agreement.

"Some see us as threatening. Crazy, we're only out enjoying ourselves." The group nodded.

A small middle-aged lady with curly grey hair swept back behind her ears, sitting precariously on the collar of her anorak, chipped in, "The people here are so nice and seem quite happy to chat with us. You are so lucky to live in such a beautiful place. Most of us live in the city, so we relish our walks."

Ellie glanced towards the green in appreciation.

"Yes, the village certainly has a heart and history. We all love it."

The relaxed, friendly group proceeded to bombard her with questions. Ellie was in her element, revelling in revealing local knowledge acquired over the years. They listened in silence, absorbing every word. She began to grasp their fascination with rambling, their excitement in unearthing unexpected historical gossip and stories peculiar to the area.

"Tell us more about the beautiful house behind the high wall." The wiry youth raised the question they all had on the tip of their tongue.

Ellie thought for a moment, racking her brain. "Which house are you referring to?"

The bossy one opened the flap on an enormous pocket on the side of his trousers, producing a well worn, neatly folded map. "This one," he said pointing. "You can't miss it. You catch sight of it as you drop down into the village, high on the ridge, bathed in sunlight. We all noticed it."

Ellie thought before answering, "The only house I can think of is the big main house on the Jenkins Estate. I haven't been up that way for a while. I believe it is empty and boarded up."

The group grinned as if they were at cross purposes. "No matter," chipped in the leader. "We must make a move. Who knows, we may meet again? You can tell us more then."

The group gathered their valued possessions, map and

compass at the ready, and followed the leader in crocodile fashion. "Bye," they shouted, waving. "Nice to meet you!"

Ellie sat perplexed, doubting memory and integrity, and slightly annoyed, muttering, "Someone has definitely got their wires crossed."

4

ELLIE WATCHED THE RAMBLERS disappear into the distance, words, comments swirling over and over in her mind, resulting in muddled bewilderment, convinced she misheard the conversation. The last sentence continually buzzed through her brain – "magnificent house bathed in sunlight."

"Someone must be completely off the wall... and it certainly isn't me," she muttered in annoyed frustration. How dare the impromptu meeting with the ramblers turn her peaceful day into a whirlwind of frustrated confusion?

"What planet are they on?" Ellie thought. Her rational mind tried to make sense of throwaway words – a casual meeting. She felt hot under the collar, uptight, uncomfortable and inexplicably challenged. She turned towards the pond, feeling grouchy and conscious of muttering out aloud, "What a strange conversation!"

In robotic mode she journeyed home, recalling the brief comment made by the lead rambler, or as much of it as she could remember, feeling utterly puzzled. She knew the area and surrounding hills, having explored as a child, and recently walking old Mr Beck's two black Labradors while he was recuperating from a hip operation. She enjoyed conundrums, if there was a solution. Lost in her own world, she increased her pace, unintentionally ignoring courtesy greetings by local children out on their bikes.

Ellie prided herself on being a brilliant diplomat and problem-solver, but the confused outcome of this somewhat inane meeting left her mystified. She mentally embarked on a heated two-sided argument as if she was legal counsel defending a client, thinking to herself, "I know there is only one big house overlooking the valley, roof, chimney pots just visible in the winter months— Fosseway Hall, the Jenkins's Estate. It's been empty for years. Talk about mixed messages. They've definitely got crossed wires." She continued grumbling, "They're crazy! It's a ruse, nothing more than a bad joke. End of story!"

Tutting in annoyance as she walked, her riled emotions quelled. "I know the answer!" she whooped. "What they saw was a trick of the light, an illusion of sunlight!"

Now strolling gently, she reminisced about happy childhood memories in the estate grounds; of balmy summer picnics and noisy uplifting Summer Musical Evenings. Chuckling, giggling to herself like a chastised naughty schoolgirl, she recalled gigantic firework displays against a backdrop of an enormous roaring bonfire, scrummy food, happy faces singing, jostling in the heat; the noise and excitement of Guy Fawkes Night. Out of the blue, her mood inexplicably changed, the reality of the moment giving way to unexpected melancholy as she recalled lost childhood years.

Slowly and purposefully, Ellie continued her journey home, clutching magazines and papers tight in the crook of her arm, stopping briefly at the old forge, emotions swirling deep within. Choosing to ignore raised nagging uncertainties, she threw her head back in defiance, tossing swaying hair as she welcomed the warmth of the sun on her face and neck.

Leaning against the lichen-covered wall, her eyes closed with the heat of the sun, Ellie momentarily delved deep into memories of happy days – the emergence of adolescence; childhood camaraderie, climbing trees, exploring woods, streams and rivers close to Nestledown. Sauntering home muddy, dirty, content, a child's idea of heaven, a safe, tight knit community where everyone and everything appeared perfect.

Recalling never-ending talk of the Jenkins problems, how villagers supported one another during a time of despondency. How they buoyed up estate workers' reluctance to seek work outside the area prior to the estate being wound up, respecting the immeasurable support given to tenant farmers, fiercely defending the Jenkins name from interfering busybodies.

The Jenkins clan were not the *nouveau riche*. The estate was founded on old money, built by entrepreneurial enterprise and allegiance to the Crown, though no-one discovered exactly who was involved and what had taken place. They knew how to treat people. Life had not always been kind to past generations, who had suffered alongside most families, enduring more than their fair share of heartache and tragedy. Yet throughout it all the family members retained their dignity, fulfilling expected responsibilities and duty with imbued pride. They lived the family motto, "Trust God, respect your fellow man."

Ellie suddenly laughed out loud, feeling stupid for getting so knotted up over a casual throwaway remark. She knew she was right. The villagers of Hallows Rest were fully abreast of the sad Jenkins saga. Her step lightened and she ambled home lost in thought.

Over the years, the workers on the rambling Jenkins estate were given the opportunity to become agricultural tenants and an estate manager was appointed. Cottages were built to house them and a community was forged, established in the village, and now known as Hallows Rest.

During the war years, the Hall and Estate were commandeered by the Army, deemed an idyllic location as a cottage hospital for sick and invalid servicemen. It was quickly established to administer comfort and care to wounded servicemen, staffed by Red Cross volunteers, as most of the regular nursing staff were commissioned overseas. A bronze plaque set high on the east wall listed all who convalesced and recuperated. It was a testament to a slice of history and to the Jenkins contribution to the war effort.

Many servicemen fell in love with local girls during this time and stayed, so the village grew. Shortly after the war, the estate settled into a prosperous routine.

Fosseway Hall was built in 1886 by Sir Rufus Jenkins, a successful hard-working, high-spirited sociable character, with a determined stubborn streak and a remarkable visionary for his time. Renowned for being fair and just in all business dealings, he couldn't abide fools or shirkers, thus earning loyalty and respect from people of all walks of life. Tragically, his eighteen-year-old twin sister drowned while holidaying with family friends in Dartmouth, after which his younger brother Stephen followed a calling to join the ministry.

After a privileged upbringing, as the eldest son of a wealthy landowner, his officer progression had been cut short by being invalided out of the army at the age of thirty-five. This enabled him to pursue his hobby and passion for writing philosophical poetry and Spiritual Naturalism, a loose title given to studying philosophical/religious global views from a naturalistic spiritual perspective, a private belief shared by many. Fosseway Hall became an inspirational haven for many. Rufus's prolific writing reflected spiritual experiences based on nature, which he studied with ease. He became a popular debater and speaker, sharing his views with anyone interested enough to listen.

His passion and later obsession to purchase land and build a family home for future generations led to a search for the right location, which took many, many years. He eventually chose 550 acres of agricultural land in the heart of Somerset, twenty-five miles west from the Vale of Avalon.

During his long search he uncovered with delight many surprising spiritual truths and myths, finding undisclosed medieval holy sites in the process. Geographical and historical maps led him to identify a crossing point of magnetic earth energies, as prehistoric man had instinctively done in the past. His acquired knowledge fuelled a determined fixation to choose the right location to build his visionary Hall, his life's purpose.

His brother shared his spiritual leanings. An agreed site was carefully chosen, pedantic plans dictating layout, with windows and entrance positioned in relation to the rising sun. Water to the Hall was to be supplied by natural springs uncovered under the watchful eye of Bill Anderson, a local revered man of the woods, who by dowsing identified the earth's magnetic key energy points, between "negative and positive" water lines.

In later years, Sir Alf Jenkins followed his great grandfather's philosophy, adding personal findings to family archives and penning his own personal spiritual experiences.

Acquiesce Lament

The weeping woman sank heavily into the shaped shingle dip created by hoards of happy children. Tears streamed down her cheeks, her tiny frame rocked with sadness and regret. Sobbing silently, with remorse, she yearned to love and be loved. To belong; to feel special; to feel wanted!

She drew her exposed knees up to her chest, resting her aching head on them, releasing heartfelt tears. She was aware that people were watching her every move, yet she didn't care. It wasn't important. Nothing really mattered any more.

She was fully aware of furtive glances seeking answers as to why she was there. Anger welled deep within. People had no comprehension of the pain and distress she was in. They saw what they chose to see, a tearful thirty-something unhappy woman.

"I wish they would mind their own business!" she screamed inwardly. "Can't they pretend I am not here and leave me alone?" She hurt so much she felt her body would snap, quaking uncontrollably with waves of deep-seated unhappiness. Deliberating how far she would get if she walked into the sea, she guessed some smart arse would wade in and save her.

She ached for peace, happiness and a joyful past, wishing she could turn back the clock. She questioned over and over in her head her rash, hasty decisions. Did her motives have a hidden agenda? Caring for her family wasn't the issue. She loved them so much that it hurt. How could she reveal her undisclosed past, her painful secret, the raw truth? She was a victim of her own deceit, a weak coward, unable to face and deal with gnawing repercussions of the past, with her future beyond comprehension.

The sun danced on a gentle calm sea, the incoming tide effortlessly creeping up the shore line, following its own motion and energy. Each wave lapping the shore created soothing whooshing sounds, caressing the shingle, a sound she found strangely reassuring and comforting. Her eyes searched the towering formidable granite cliff face for imaginary faces, protecting and cradling her much-loved island cove.

Slowly, sounds of the seashore calmed her frustration and pacified her needs. She resisted the need to plunge into the cool inviting water. She swam as often as she could before winter's chill merged with cold frosty mornings. The seagull cry reminded her of childhood, rock pools, collapsed sandcastles and pebbles. The herring gulls' piercing cry momentarily took her back to a time of carefree bliss.

Looking down at her feet, she suddenly noticed her shoes were now sopping wet. The tide was creeping up relentlessly, but she did not care. Jumping up, she suddenly realised that her latest acquisition, an expensive green corduroy autumn skirt, was watermarked, ruined as the in tidal water crept closer and closer. Her shoulders closed inwards, her throat ached.

"Why do I hurt and ache so much?" she thought. "Cutting one's finger is one kind of hurt, but loving someone so much, or maybe too much, really hurts, especially when your words cannot reach them or they won't – or cannot – listen."

A man and young boy dressed in black rubber diving suits clambered onto the beach, dragging a bright yellow rubber dinghy behind them, laughing, enjoying the winter sun, probably father and son. She wondered what right they had to be so carefree. Did they not realise this was her patch of shingle where she could unburden painful tears and grief, where she could cry like a baby if she wanted to?

She watched them push the little dinghy into the water, the boy climbing in first, the father pushing it further out into deeper water before jumping in. They sat facing each other, the paddles expertly manoeuvred by the father. When they realised she was watching them, they waved, acknowledging her existence before paddling effortlessly and purposefully out towards the mouth of the cove.

With ingrained politeness, derived mainly from her paternal grandmother, she gave them a wry wave. They were happy. Why could she not be happy? Her body ached with pain. Deep-felt tears continued to flow, as endless sobbing continued. Her eyes stung, her throat ached. She felt as if she had the sadness of the world on her shoulders, then in a split second realised how selfish she was being. After all, there were people in the world who really did need to shed tears. People were struggling to survive, desperate for food and water. But it was *her* destructive pain, *her* tears. She could cry if she wanted to.

After a further bout of sobbing, her mind momentarily cleared, bringing her back full circle to how she truly felt and the source of her unhappiness. Slowly, her emotions began to quell. Her erratic breathing settled into a more normal rhythmic pattern, as the emotional strain she put her body through eased. She found a core of strength to face the day.

Unnoticed by her, the water had crept further and further up the beach. Now her knickers and slip were wet through. Feeling more in control, she stood up, shaking her now sodden shoes, and turned to face the small flight of stone steps leading to the sea road and car park beyond.

Raising a pathetic smile, she squelched to her shiny red sports car. "I suppose I will just have to put my soggy clothes in the boot," she thought. "I can't possibly get the driver's seat wet." The thrill of being outrageously naughty, perhaps being discovered in a state of undress, raised her mood just a little. "I suppose I must display some sense of decorum."

She grinned at her wicked thoughts. Reaching the car, opening the boot and replacing the soggy shoes with sandals, she discreetly peeled the wet lingerie from her equally wet lower torso and with great difficulty struggled to put on a pair of dry jogging bottoms, throwing the ruined wet skirt into the corner of the boot in annoyed disgust. "What a waste!" she muttered. "Still, in the scheme of things, who really cares? I don't." But she did care. She cared a lot. Composure restored, she jumped into the driver's seat, fired the ignition and drove effortlessly away.

5

Nestledown's comforting welcome raised Ellie's spirits as she approached the front door, kicking off her shoes. She was happiest in bare feet. Next, her favourite doorstep sandwich of ham and cheese, washed down with a large mug of strong coffee.

Lunch balanced on a tray, she headed for a huge squashy comfortable deep red Chesterfield. The room was dominated by a large picture window, the rolling Torchester hills just visible in the distance. The window overlooked the front garden, which was bounded by a privet hedge, picket gate, front and side path to the back of the house, and a lawn edged by a wide herbaceous border.

A wild garden lay to the right. Three Silver Birch trees offered sanctuary to numerous birds and cheeky grey squirrels. A small alpine garden close to a large fish pond completed a landscaped garden of interest. It was regularly maintained by Jason, a young enterprising gardener whose knowledge and hard work reflected everything he touched. Ellie was happy for him to fulfil this role.

From this position she could see callers, ignore the telephone at the far end of the hall and settle to focus on matters in hand. Grabbing a pen and pad, she eagerly began scanning collected national and local papers for possible follow-up news stories. She snuggled into the deep luxury cushions, curling her legs beneath her.

The sun slowly moved position, settling on her face, enveloping her in soporific warmth. Ellie was struggling to stay awake. Sleepy heaviness was winning, and resisting no longer, she dozed. Instinctively curling into a foetal position, her mind drifted, as creased discarded newspapers fell to the floor in a crumpled heap.

Fosseway Hall had become a sad talking point over the months and was often referred to as a white elephant. Now a neglected shuttered mansion, it solitarily sheltered from hostile howling winds that seem to tear unmercifully through winter hills. Dark menacingly scary shadows lurked around every corner. Nature's vengeance on man's once tended lawns, specimen trees and flowering shrubs was clear to see. The enchanted cherished house was now neglected and dingy, with dirty, weather-beaten windows and doors. Its silence was deafening.

The circular turning of the sweeping drive was uninviting and barely visible, hidden beneath a tangled mass of straggly ungainly growth. Formerly gleaming paintwork, coloured wash masonry and brickwork was dank and mucky with lack of care. Creeping overgrowth invaded every window and entrance. The huge solid oak entrance door blistered with seasonal elements. A build-up of leaves and rotting debris concealed magnificent semi-circular marble steps whilst the walled garden was so overgrown that it might never have existed. The deserted, formerly productive vegetable garden was lost in a thicket of brambles, now indistinguishable from its original concept.

Cleverly crafted hands of the stable block clock tower stood motionless at five past six, rain having halted time and corroded the mechanism, now hanging precariously. Narrow steps to the hayloft, witness to many clandestine meetings, were smothered with lichen and rotting debris. The picket green wooden gate to the empty chicken run stood wide open, swinging dangerously at a peculiar angle, exposed to the elements. The arboretum, apple and pear orchard stood abandoned, fruit rotting where it fell. The famed Sun Pavilion, designed for entertaining, was home to a variety of vermin and a nightmare for arachnophobics. Outbuildings devoid of purpose, many in total disrepair, boasted discarded rusty machinery lying idle.

Sprawling Fountain Hill Downs covered a distance of nine miles, the rolling green hills a source of pleasure to many. Horse lovers cantered, exercising their steeds. Villagers competed in their unique rustic form of summer rounders, winners and losers picnicking in a sheltered copse. Dog owners and walkers strolled leisurely, oblivious to the monotonous hum of endless streams of traffic on the busy dual carriageway snaking its way to the north. The peaceful downs unconsciously participated in the master plan. The frenetic daily hubbub was mentally exhausting.

The inexplicable inhospitable energy surrounding the perimeter of the Jenkins's Estate was sensed by many, so much so that the locals chose to walk on the opposite side of the long high stone wall on their way to the Downs. Huge hoardings mounted on stout wooden posts, located every half mile along the wall, warned, 'NO TRESPASSING. KEEP OUT. DOGS ON PATROL.'

This strong message was adhered to by everyone, including older lads, who delighted in taunting younger ones to play the dare game. Youngsters would rather be called a cowardly custard or chicken than risk clambering over the wall. Villagers knew that the notices were to deter poachers and would-be vandals. Locals dared not venture inside the wall, as the estate had taken on a forbidding gloom over the years. The towering magnificent entrance, graced by two majestic wrought iron gates, secured with four forlorn large rusted chains and padlocks emitting a sinister air. Shadows lurked in the menacing atmosphere, brooding for a lost life. The pristine drive, dressed in warm shingle, once giving a warm welcome to all who visited, was now obscured by the collaboration of overgrown shrubs and weeds, victors of a long battle.

Ellie knew the estate well as a child, often accompanying her mother in organising various Women's Institute events. Total shock and disbelief was voiced by villagers when they realised that rumours were in fact true: the estate was going to be wound up and abandoned. The unbelievable waste! How sadly the repercussions of a tragedy resulted in so much unhappiness. In consequence, a thriving successful manor and its grounds were intentionally deserted for nature to invade.

Ellie stirred. The sun had changed position from warming her face to falling on the back of the sofa. Sensing the warmth had disappeared, she woke with a start. The rambler's description of the "magnificent house bathed in sunshine" was still very much in the forefront of her mind. Repositioning her legs beneath her, she settled against the back of the cushions, as if seeking reassurance.

Inexplicably disturbed and in a drowsy state, she turned the morning's events over and over in her mind. Used to reliving happy childhood memories in her sleep state, meeting people she did not know, she was seeing images that made no sense. More fully awake, the provoking comments occupied her thoughts. She knew the estate's staff had been dismissed, grounds and house left unoccupied, and no one left to maintain it. So far as everyone knew, it had been closed and boarded up since Lady Lillian moved abroad.

Ellie understood why no one dared enter the grounds,

believing the trite comment that some terrible mishap or dreadful curse would befall them if they did so. It was a tale fuelled by fear, festering and fermenting in people's minds. The estate, as far as she knew, had been deserted for years, apart from the monthly visit by Torchester police. The ramblers' incident she thought extremely odd.

Villagers knew that the gardener – "Old Dippy Pippy" as local children called him – had stayed on for a while, but the locals were under the impression that he left to live with his sister in Torchester. No one had seen him for years. People avoided walking past the estate. Everyone said it was eerie. Ellie continued her silent debate. "Doesn't make any sense," she deliberated crossly, wondering if it was worth asking Ruby Knox for answers. Ruby helped out with dog-walking and was the village know-it-all. Persisting niggles eventually got the better of her. Ellie ran to the phone and dialled Ruby's number. No one was at home. She felt cheated.

Going back to the sofa, she suddenly stopped, her eyes shining with excitement and expectation. "Well, Ellie May, you call yourself a journalist, so investigate! Discover the truth behind that crazy rambler's comment otherwise you will never have any peace."

With new-found enthusiasm, she quickly took her empty mug and plate to the kitchen, ran to the loo, and threw on her coveted journalist's shoulder bag, which was furnished with a voice-activated tape recorder, torch, bottled water and chocolate. She locked the door behind her and sped down to the path on a mission. Confused emotions of annoyance, confusion, frustration were now firmly dealt with.

Walking quickly past the old Blacksmith Forge, she stopped to adjust the uncomfortable bag cutting into her shoulder. "I should have remembered to bring my old scarf with me as a shoulder pad," she scolded herself, she had been in too much of a hurry. Debating whether to go back for it, she decided against it, saying to herself, "Use your initiative Ellie! It's a little hiccup you can easily solve."

As she paced the long winding lane it appeared to be shorter. Unable to explain why, she felt compelled to follow this questioning. With no clear idea of what she might discover, if anything, she just knew somehow this journey was important. Ellie giggled to herself, recalling the time she pretended to be one of the Famous Five when she was in Miss Gibson's class. The rest of the gang followed her lead, laughing at planning escape routes and imaginary dangerous escapades, where baddies always lost the plot and the goodies always won.

Ellie wished she had a companion, someone to share her thoughts and feelings, and to offer encouragement if her courage failed. She felt nervous tension building within her, wondering what she would encounter and how she would deal with it if she met someone on the way.

Suddenly common sense took over. Stopping in her tracks, wondering if she was wasting time, she knew she should be working on her next assignment. Was there any tangible purpose behind this impetuous jaunt? Was she on a fool's errand after all? The child within easily took her back in time, when life had been exciting and exhilarating.

Continuing her journey to Fountains Hill, stopping momentarily to adjust her precious bag, her nervous system settled. "I don't know what Mum and Dad would say," Ellie thought. "Probably think me crazy. Hey ho, no matter. I've started, so will finish. I will enjoy today."

Her philosophical head reminded Ellie that each new day is

an adventure, a challenge with unexpected elements thrown in for good measure. With rhythmic stride, the bag now comfortable, she passed groups of mums chatting. Their offspring tormenting each other in fun, oblivious to her presence, as the pull of the duck pond was as strong as ever to people and wildlife. Grinning inanely as she approached The Carvers Arms, firmly deciding not to get caught up in conversation with a small group of bikers enjoying cool beers in the sun, by avoiding their gaze (another puzzling *tête-à-tête*). But they were too quick for her and waved, smiling. Ellie returned their courtesy, sheepishly glancing at a row of six black biker helmets lined up on the wall by the side of the table, like treasured crystal skulls, prized leather jackets in a careful pile beside them. Avoiding the bikers' stare, she politely returned their wave.

Maintaining a comfortable stride, she reached the bottom of Fountains Hill's famous winding contours. The clear warning of a one in five gradient was treated with respect by most drivers. A footpath to the left closely followed the angled corner of the long high wall. On the right lay a newly laid tarmac footpath banked by hedging and thickets. The footpath, maintained by the local council, narrowed after fifty yards, curving with the contour of the road. Many young mothers complained, stating it was dangerous for people pushing baby buggies, but that's the way it was. Ellie didn't care.

The seven-foot high wall on her left appeared to snake on and on. Built of granite, stone and flint, it was truly inspiring, a feat of hard graft and ingenuity. Ellie clambered up the hill, her breath slightly laboured and the bag a nuisance. Suddenly, in the distance, silhouetted in the blue summer sky, she saw the two familiar concrete pineapples standing proudly on top of the huge stone gate pillars, the main entrance to the Jenkins estate.

Her steps quickened, and suddenly she achieved her aim, facing the magnificent gated entrance to the famed Fosseway Hall. Ellie stopped, swallowed hard, and swaying uncontrollably, put her hands to her mouth in total disbelief. Her bag slid awkwardly down her left side, landing face down on the ground. Her eyes welled with out of control tears.

Looking around for reassurance, she found she was alone. Opening and shutting her eyes in quick succession, daring not to breathe too quickly, she pinched the flesh on her arm hard. Ellie had reached the gates of the Hall yet somehow everything was different. She couldn't comprehend what she found.

Staring into space, steadying her balance, instinctively wanting to run, yet unable to do so, a well of courage reaffirmed the reason she was there – to investigate! Slowly retrieving the bag from the dusty lane and clutching it tightly to her chest, she silently sought answers that refused to come.

Ellie stared in sheer amazement and total disbelief, glancing side to side and top to bottom of the huge gates. There was no hint of the heavy rusty chains and padlocks that held the gates firm. Their intricate wrought iron had been freshly painted and the overgrown shrubbery cut back. New buds and growth was forming, with ground-covering plants in full bloom and grass borders neatly cut with gleaming white marker stones. A clever mix of pea shingle dressed the sweeping drive. Clean, fresh and reflective in the sun's rays, with no hint of weeds or unsightly growth. Trees to the side had been pruned, creating a canopy of soft green as far as the eye could see.

Ellie's feet froze her body numb. Tears fell as she wondered if she could accept what her eyes were revealing. She felt strange, weird, yet not fearful. Shutting her eyes tightly, she opened them again slowly to check she wasn't lost in a time warp of years gone by.

Looking around, everything was as she remembered childhood summers. Silence was broken only by the persistent monotonous sound of crows, high in tree-tops. Furtive hidden movement occurred in the undergrowth, with occasional melodic birdsong plus the odd distant drone of soaring aeroplanes high above her head. Again she questioned, "Is this real?" Was she the only witness to a seemingly special event?

Checking to see if she was alone, Ellie gently pushed the gates. Surprisingly, they swung open easily. Heart in her mouth, Ellie took courage in both hands. She slipped inside, closing the gates behind her. She desperately tried not to make a sound, but her footsteps announced her arrival as her feet crushed the shingle.

She edged her way forward, checking from time to time to see if her movements were being monitored, glancing furtively from side to side to see if she was being followed. Ellie edged her way slowly to the house, which she could just glimpse in the distance, a gleaming cream masonry building, with numerous sash windows glistening in the sun and bright blue shutters fastened back.

Looking at the house from the front, Ellie could clearly see the turret shape in the middle of the building, gently curving to the sides. The recessed porch, intricate moulded canopy, soft cream semi-circular marble steps and enormous heavy oak door, radiant in the sunshine, completed the illusion. Glancing to her left, the vista took her breath away. The grounds rolled away far in the distance, a brilliant canvas of colour. The sun pavilion was reflected in the waters of an immense sparkling lake. Home to a myriad of water fowl, its surface danced in the sunlight. Witnessing this indescribably wonderful splendour took her breath away. She sank to the floor, unable to grasp the reality of the moment.

Ellie did not want it to end, knowing that the visualisation was real yet somehow she was unable to comprehend how this could be possible. Her breathing slowly settled to a gentle rhythm as she absorbed the peace and incredible beauty surrounding her.

6

Entranced by the peaceful beauty surrounding her, Ellie collapsed in a heap where she stood, the scenario before her bewildering. Everywhere was familiar… wildfowl on the lake, manicured lawns and abundant coloured borders. It was an inexplicable conundrum, knowing she was where she was meant to be with a role to play yet unable to comprehend exactly how or where she fitted in.

The events of the morning seemed to belong to a different time zone and place. Ellie looked down at bare feet, shoes tossed aside. Feeling warm and safe, her eyes eagerly flitted from side to side observing and memorising every colourful detail like a long lens camera mimicking movement.

Time seemed to stand still, the sun creating shadows, slowly absorbing the magnificent vista all around her. Suddenly, her reverie was broken by distant ethereal strains. Ellie stood up, scanning furiously towards the direction of where she sensed the sound. She was alone. Still the haunting sound persisted. Perplexed, she moved to the top of the steps leading down to the lake. No one was there. She turned back to the house and for a fleeting moment, out of the corner of her eye, she thought she saw movement. Turning to focus, there was nothing. The sound continued, seeming to come from the direction of the front of the house, an angelic, magnetic monotone

Turning towards the house, Ellie believed she glimpsed a slight, almost transparent figure standing slightly to the left of the entrance porch. The huge oak door was now slightly open. She wondered if the figure would disappear if she moved towards the door. Deciding to chance it, she moved slowly, silently, closer and closer to observe the figure in more detail.

Viewing a slender, beautiful adolescent girl, dressed from head to toe in a flowing pale blue translucent gown, drawn in at the waist by a deep periwinkle blue sash edged with gold. Soft folds of iridescent fabric draped her tiny frame and brilliant light reflected her fragile silhouette, shimmering in the sunlight. Her hair was golden, like sheaves of corn, tumbling in soft curls below her waist. An encrusted golden pin was at the nape of her neck. Her feet were encased in gold open-toe sandals decorated in intricate woven design. Her skin was like porcelain, her eyes deep blue, like a cornflower in bloom. She smiled, beckoning Ellie to join her.

As Ellie drew closer, the girl gestured her hand in welcome. "I knew you would come," she said softly. Ellie struggled to control a sickening mixture of joy and fear.

"Do not be afraid," she continued. "My name is Avani, I am an earth angel. I was the one who called you." Silence reigned.

"I don't know what you mean; I don't understand." Ellie's words tumbled out in a confused babbling mumble. Her legs felt like jelly, as if they would give way at any moment. She felt sick and faint. The figure sensed her fear and apprehension.

"Come and sit with me," said Avani, "and I will explain."

Ellie followed the figure into the house, silently questioning, "An earth angel? I must definitely be off the wall." Wrestling with the accepted definition of reality and fantasy, she was having great difficulty in acknowledging or accepting she was in the company of a real angel. Indeed, she wasn't sure that she believed in angels.

"I must be dreaming," Ellie said softly. Her heart was thumping and her head hurting, bursting with trying to make sense of everything.

Ellie wanted to run, to leave this place, frightened of the unknown, of not being in control, experiencing a feeling of dread she could not describe, but one she did not enjoy. She froze.

The figure reached out to her. "We will talk in here," Avani said. Reluctantly, Ellie took her hand.

They moved through a long hall with a high ceiling and a succession of doors either side. A door at the far end on the left led to a small room at the back of the house, overlooking the orchard. The room, although small in comparison to the rest of the house, was cosy and welcoming. Window seats had been fashioned at the base of two wide full-length sash windows. The gold tapestry drapes were simple yet effective; the blue silk festooned blinds a clever contrast. A huge gilt mirrored wall mantel dressed the wall, reflecting light from the windows back into the room. Three cleverly chosen blue Chinese porcelain artefacts graced the tall mantelpiece to complement the room. The hearth gleamed; the copper log basket was highly polished. Two lines of miniatures were positioned to the right of the fireplace whilst books and family photographs were assembled on two small mahogany tables. A large, rare hand-woven Persian carpet graced the centre of the room, completing the scene of warmth and comfort.

They instinctively sat opposite one another. From this vantage point, Ellie could see the beautiful figure in finest detail. The angel proffered reassurance, so Ellie relaxed.

"Do not doubt or be fearful of me," said Avani. "I am an earth angel of the heavens, bringing a symbol of awareness and love. My purpose is to bring a source of inspiration where dreams and wishes can become reality."

The angel pointed to a small leather book bound in red and gold lying on her left – a book of awareness and knowledge.

"Trust me, Ellie," she said. "Everything is happening as it is meant to be. Look past the veil of illusion and see underlying order. Rest assured, as there is angelic energy working behind the scenes. Positive thought can speed the process."

Ellie felt tears welling in her eyes. Her throat ached. She swallowed hard to regain her composure.

Avani continued, "The spark of life has ignited your imagination, stirring creative gifts, instilling a strong desire for change. You have shown courage to act upon your impulses in order to initiate new beginnings. Trust your inner desire for change. Commit to new ideas and follow your heart. The divine will give you strength to understand your doubts and fears, and give you courage to commit to new ideas. The elements of your success are in place. Take that leap of faith to what you truly want. Act with confidence. You will not fail."

Ellie felt her eyes brimming with tears. Her heart raced and she wanted to run. She was her own person, a free spirit. Why was she listening to such rambling? The tears began to trickle. She felt a fool, unable to move. Ellie could do nothing but allow the tears to fall.

Avani continued, "You believe no one hears your cries for help, your frustrated mutterings. Believe me, thoughts are registered and all prayers eventually answered. That is why I am here with you now. Don't allow periods of inertia to win. Clear away blocks. Now is the beginning of creating your dream by putting one foot firmly in front of the other. Rekindle your inner light – allow change to manifest."

Ellie sat speechless. She didn't comprehend what had brought her to this place or why she was here. Yet although reluctant to admit it, the words this figure spoke made complete sense. Ellie had been on a rollercoaster to nowhere in particular, a situation she found easy. She knew she was capable of more. The lazy, negative side of her personality allowed her to coast.

"What do I do now?" she asked.

"There is someone who wants to meet you, but first you need to balance your energies," Avani replied. "Make yourself comfortable, be still and close your eyes. Trust."

Ellie did not question. She relaxed into the high backed chair, closing her eyes.

Venerate Pledge

Pip, a few weeks over the age of sixty-three, the longest serving member of the Jenkins staff, was totally devastated when Lillian Jenkins informed him and the rest of the household and estate of her plans.

The once happy house and grounds now held painful memories. She wasn't impetuous, but just felt unable to stay any longer, so arrangements were put in place to close the house and secure the grounds until a time when she felt able to return.

She was a gracious, elegant lady who suffered greatly in her life, losing people she dearly loved. After her husband died tragically, she lived for her only child and for charity work, fulfilling all social, family and charitable commitments with dignity and pride. She was distraught and heartbroken to discover her beloved son David suddenly left one night without any warning or hint of his plans. She was inconsolable, finding it impossible to meet people's expectations and live at the Hall on her own.

Her failing health necessitated recuperation and a move

overseas to live close to her sister. It was a temporary answer. This solution broke the desire to be reclusive, hiding from the world, grieving for the loss of a soul-mate, for a son she loved, fearing they would never meet again.

The opulent security she once enjoyed with friends and family was now totally meaningless, with the Hall now nothing more than a magnificent mausoleum.

Putting misgivings to one side, Pip felt he owed allegiance to the family. They gave him hope and compassion when their paths crossed when he was an angry, unhappy, homeless young man. Generations of the Jenkins family trusted their gut instincts. Over time they were always proved right.

Pip arrived on the estate late one bitterly cold afternoon as a rebellious, broken seventeen-year-old, seeking shelter in return for casual labour. They took pity on him, offering him a month's trial with food and lodgings. In time, he gained their trust and over the years graciously repaid them with loyalty and hard work. Pip often reflected on their kindness and perception of giving everyone a chance, of bringing to the surface the good in people. Overjoyed with his new life, he made a silent vow always to stand by them, and somehow, at some time, to repay the debt he knew he owed them.

Despite protestations, after in-depth discussions Lillian Jenkins and her legal team in London eventually agreed that Pip could stay on the estate, living in one of the smaller cottages until he felt unable to cope. It was muted he would find the experience lonely, as he would be the sole person living among acres of gardens, lake, rivers and woodland.

Over the years, Pip became a valued retainer, an unspoken, unannounced adopted member of the family. He had witnessed first hand the value of trust and truth, and knew that one day matters would turn around. They always did.

Private arrangements were made with James McGoonan, the family solicitor based in Torchester, and the legal team in London, for Pip to occupy the little cottage. He could hardly contain his excitement and joy at the decision. Pip knew every square mile of the estate during his forty-five years' service and was unable to consider living anywhere else. The letter of the law dictated that he had to report to the family solicitors every three months, and Torchester Police every month, with any perceived concerns. Matters were settled.

Pip and Nanny Su, an affectionate nickname for the housekeeper, became great friends over the years. She was the one who encouraged Pip to stay. "You love it so much," she said. "It's been your home for so many years you would be lost and heartbroken to live anywhere else." Pip agreed.

James McGoonan turned a blind eye to proposed legal issues raised by the London lawyers, especially as Pip had been given special permission by Lillian Jenkins to stay on the estate. He, like the Jenkins clan, trusted Pip, knowing change was inevitable and unavoidable, although he was secretly dispirited, witnessing a viable prosperous estate being wound up even as a temporary measure, creating a temptation to would-be vandals. Somehow he rested a little easier knowing that someone of merit was on hand if anyone dared to trespass, steal or damage property.

James McGoonan and the legal team had no alternative but to abide by some issues, especially under the conciliatory pressure of Lady Jenkins.

Su Marsh, a sprightly seventy-three-year-old, lived in a tied cottage on the North West side of the estate, close to the hamlet of Welham, enabling Pip and Su to keep in touch in a secret discreet manner, as requested by the family. They were adamant that they did not want outsiders knowing about or interfering in family matters. Although Nanny Su could no longer handle heavy physical work, she was always on hand to support Pip with emotional worries. The mutual respect built up over the years forged a working partnership of friendship and trust.

It saddened Pip to see the estate disintegrate, unable single-handedly to turn the tide of neglect, devoid of day-to-day maintenance. He kept buoyant by ensuring his little cottage garden and vegetable patch was neat and tidy, producing an abundance of soft fruits, herbs, vegetables and flowers. He appointed himself honorary caretaker of the estate, a self-imposed disciplined post as he mentally divided the estate into manageable zones, which he covered systematically on his reliable Honda, "Blue Boy," with Jess, his beloved Collie always in hot pursuit. Pip covered the vast estate grounds over a period of six weeks, methodically recording changes in a little notebook.

In his role as Head Gardener, he watched David grow from a shy little lad into a popular social character. Their relationship grew into an odd friendship of trust and fun. "You can talk the hind legs of a donkey, m'lad," Pip used to say.

From an early age, David expressed appreciation for the wonder of inner and physical beauty. He was a gentle soul, one who couldn't abide aggression in any form, hated cruelty and lies, and treated friends with importance. David was fearless, very sensitive and easily hurt. An unpredictable daydreamer who failed to conceal or control meaningful emotions, he was also extremely smart and, like his great-grandfather, didn't suffer fools gladly.

Pip and David spent time together when David was home from Prep School, especially traditionally planned Guy Fawkes celebrations. He later boasted to half term boarding school friends that he had single-handedly built the guy and organised the huge bonfire. Although a private person, respecting his position within the family, Pip was delighted and never surprised when David took great pains to find him whenever he was upset or worried about a decision he needed to make. Pip became a valued listening ear.

David was a well-liked bonny lad, quick-witted, academically bright as a button, who sadly never came to terms with the loss of his father and the stark realisation that he would never truly get to know this wonderful man of whom everyone spoke so highly. The absence of his father's presence left him bereft and despondent. Everyone was shocked and saddened when he suddenly took off, fearing for the health of Lillian Jenkins.

Pip prayed that one day David would make contact – and when he did, he made a promise he would be there waiting for him.

7

ELLIE WAS ONLY TOO HAPPY to sit down, to collect her thoughts and relax into a deep, peaceful state of awareness. Even though this scenario was new to her, she was grateful for the opportunity to allow her nervous system to calm. The day had been long, though starting normally enough, yet what she was experiencing was anything but normal. Questions kept reverberating in her mind. Could this experience be a figment of her imagination?

Opening her eyes very slowly, peering through heavy lids, she secretly hoped the figure would still be with her. Yet she was hesitant to look in case the experience was nothing more than a hypnotic fantasy, expecting to find herself on the Chesterfield at Nestledown. She glanced across at the slim figure facing her. Their glances met. The angel smiled, acknowledging her thoughts.

"I am still here. Do not concern yourself with anything. Do you feel refreshed?"

"I do, strange as it seems," came Ellie's reply from deep within.

"If you are ready then, it is time."

Ellie straightened her crumpled top, as if she was about to meet a royal visitor.

"I would come with you," Avani spoke reassuringly. "However, I am confident you can do this alone." Ellie looked up at her, trembling.

"When you go out of this door, turn left and follow the hall until you come to the main staircase. Climb the stairs, turn left and knock on the third door on the right."

Ellie rose and gestured thanks to Avani. "Will you be here for me later?" she asked.

"If you wish," Avani answered with a smile.

Purposefully, as if avoiding a trap, Ellie opened the door, looking back for encouragement. Her mind was spinning, her heart pumping and her head pounding. Her muscles ached. Yes, she could do this.

She turned left, following the long hall, glancing at a parade of doors to the left and right, eventually confronting the foot of the staircase. The flight of stairs was wide and deep, the elegant carved mahogany banister smooth and warm to the touch. The stair carpet, rich in traditional reds, blues and gold, enhanced a luxurious texture only the very wealthy could afford. Ellie counted seven treads to the first landing, the intricately carved banister curving to the upper staircase.

She gauged the landing to be as big as Nestledown's study. "What a house!" she mused, counting another seven steps before reaching the top landing. The walls were painted soft creamy gold, like spring crocus, a perfect carpet colour match. The top landing was wide enough to twirl with arms outstretched. One long landing led to the left, with a shorter one to the right.

Avani's clear instructions resonated in her head. "I am sure you can do this alone. Out of this door, turn left, follow the hall, climb the main staircase, turn left and knock on the third door on the right."

Light at the top of the staircase illuminated the landing whilst a prism of colour projected from a magnificent stained glass window depicted three gowned figures in white at the water's edge surrounded by a garden of flowers. Three doves appeared in the top right corner with a radiant sun in the top left hand corner and a lamb in the bottom left corner. The bottom right was a thatched cottage with a small circular window of a tiny white rose. The panes of coloured glass sparkled in the sun, illustrating a meaningful story. Ellie wondered what message the window was portraying.

Confirming Avani's instructions, she silently muttered, "Knock on the third door on the right." She felt nervous, aware that perspiration was winning. "Third door on the right!"

The oak panelled doors were sturdy and heavy, a magnificent testament to bygone carpentry skills.

As Ellie quietly crept passed the first door she encountered a pulsating glow creeping under the crack of the door, a spectrum of oscillating colour creating a haphazard glow on the carpet. "Very strange," she thought. As she gingerly crept past the second door, she sensed vibration, a soft light just visible. She felt weird, wanting to turn back, but carried on.

"Meeting Avani was a surprise revelation. I trust her!"

She approached the third door, stopped, hesitated then knocked softly. There was no reply, so she knocked again. Ellie waited, then very slowly turned the handle and pushed open the door to see a gowned figure sitting.

"I didn't mean to intrude," Ellie stuttered with embarrassment, suddenly inexplicably aware this intrusion was planned, somehow meaningfully different.

"Come in my child. I knew you would come. Please be at peace and sit with me for a while."

The essence of the Being was almost transparent, emitting light, a pulsating shimmering white luminosity that resonated with warmth, a continuous musical wavelength of stillness and peace. Ellie desperately tried to make sense of what was happening, wondering if she was in some kind of trance. Was this real?

She swallowed hard, pinched herself on the arm, shut her eyes tightly and then slowly opened them. The Being was still there smiling, the face soft and gentle, with skin like porcelain. Fine blonde hair with a few wispy strands lay close to the cheeks gently caressing the face while resting softly on the shoulders. The eyes, a beautiful deep periwinkle blue, mirrored a spiritual knowing of truth and wisdom.

She thought, "If the saying is true 'The eyes are the mirror of the soul,' this entity's soul is pure."

Still trying to make sense of the meeting, she continued to scan his raiment, a description more appropriate than 'garment' or 'clothes.' It was a soft cream, edged with blue and gold. The sleeves were full, like a Mandarin's coat, of a fabric beyond earthly explanation. It was finer than silk or muslin, not of this earth. A slashed neckline enhanced a graceful neck, free from any shadow or stubble. Peaceful, radiant and etheric, the chin-line was strong and resolute. The perfectly formed feet were encased in open sandals, lacking the trauma of having walked many miles.

Ellie swallowed, feeling wobbly, not sure whether to smile, laugh or cry. She felt bewildered as to how she happened to be in this room. Again she opened and shut her eyes in rapid succession for reassurance that this was not a hallucination. Conscious awareness once again confirmed she was in the presence of someone not of this world. She slid awkwardly into the chair positioned just behind her.

"You are safe. Do not be afraid. This meeting had to be!"

Ellie fought back excitement and fear. Her prayers were being answered in a way she could not possibly have known or comprehend.

"Why am I here?" she blurted out. "Why are you here with me?"

"You have been screaming for answers, and your thoughts and prayers have been heard. I asked if I could come because I was curious as to why there seems to be so much unhappiness and unrest in your world. I was given special permission to visit your earth plane. I am only here for a very short while."

Ellie recalled restless nights, bad dreams, scary nightmares and occasional depths of black unhappiness words could not describe.

"Why me? There must be many others who have been searching and seeking for answers."

Ellie swallowed hard, realising this meeting was more than a journalistic jaunt. She silently acknowledged she had been questioning life and its meaning, thrown off balance in the knowledge that somewhere there was a possibility her thoughts were registered. This she found more than a little scary.

"Be still," he answered gently. "Take a sip of water. I will try and explain."

"You may, or may not, have heard of the Akashic Records." The beaming Being spoke with conviction.

"I'm not sure," Ellie answered, bemused but slowly recovering her composure. "Yes, I'm certain I have heard the name or read about them somewhere, but don't truly understand their significance."

"The Akashic Records, to give them a name, are spiritual records of the Higher Realms, recording thoughts, words and deeds experienced by the soul (spiritual body) from the moment of creation to the present moment of time and beyond by the Heavenly Divine Spirit, referred in your world by many names.

These records document each soul's many journeys, meticulously recording every extreme experience a soul chooses to take."

"A lifetime is merely a physical journey through time and space – a spiritual journey transcending many lifetimes and incarnations. A spirit never dies. It exists for all time. You are so much more than a physical reality. Existence on this earth plane is merely one brief moment in a soul's journey. As your very famous playwright, I believe his name was William Shakespeare, wrote, 'All the world's a stage, and all the men and women merely players. You all have your exits and entrances, and one man in his time plays many parts.' He was a very gifted wise old soul, whose legacy illustrates clearly the many complexities of humanity – their actions and reactions to a situation live on and on."

"Remember that whatever culture or creed, we are all merely players, electing to play a different role in a never-ending cycle of situations and experiences."

Ellie's eyes grew wider. She questioned whether she really wanted to listen any more. Yes, it made sense, yet the content of the conversation made her feel awkward and uncomfortable.

The Being acknowledged her thoughts, saying, "Although this concept may be new to you, the words will resonate with your unconscious Self. Be patient a little longer."

Ellie squirmed in her chair, feeling uneasy, reluctantly accepting that his words made sense.

"When a role is chosen, the lesson contained therein is also agreed," the Being continued. "Be mindful that you do not embark on a journey alone, but are accompanied by an assigned and nominated spirit entity who can inspire and guide when sought with the right intent."

"Memories of past incarnations are shrouded in vapour, or erased for a life journey, to ensure that the soul achieves maximum learning. To that end, every soul carefully selects parenting, culture and circumstance to give them the best possible opportunity to achieve their chosen goal to provide a strong foundation stone.

"However, during a life journey many negatives become attached or deeply embedded through unwise choices, some affixed by others. This can happen during many lifetimes. Negative energies lodge deep in the subconscious mind, colouring reactions to actions or circumstances.

"In essence, they leave tendrils and blockages. Removal is possible through a genuine willingness to search deep within, accepting that deep-held truths lay behind those harmful, destructive negativities. It is a painful process. Letting go, de-cluttering and cleansing the subconscious mind of negative traits and energies accumulated during a soul's journey enhances the soul's purpose. Holding tight to harmful negative experiences because they become familiar creates an unstoppable chain reaction. The relief and joy that souls sense when this is dissipated is truly wonderful!

"From our standpoint it seems relatively easy for negativities to become deeply lodged in the subconscious mind. In large measure it is responsible for many negative reactions in your world today. Remember Ellie that every action has a reaction."

Ellie swallowed hard, now calm and more relaxed, sensing more and more the crucial importance of this meeting. She found her voice, asking, "If this is so, how can we remove them, especially if they are doing us harm?"

The Master continued, "Their removal allows the soul to move forward. Souls benefit greatly when they are removed. Negativity is then no longer instrumental in reacting to situations. Removal allows the soul to move freely, unencumbered on the chosen pathway ahead."

Ellie's drowsy head drooped. Mesmerised by the hypnotic soft, dulcet tones of wisdom and truth, she sensed healing vibrations travelling through her body, gentle rainbow colours surrounding her. She felt bathed in a light vibration of powerful love. In that moment, she knew and understood that this Being worked through a gateway of wisdom, love and light.

She asked again, "Please tell me why you have come. I feel privileged and honoured being here with you yet I know there is a far greater purpose for this moment in time."

The Being settled into the huge high backed chair that seemed to dwarf his tall, slender frame. His eyes lowered. The sun's rays moved through the leaves of the Silver Birch tree caressing the window outside, creating moving dappled patterns of light and shade on the highly polished wooden floor. Each pattern magically intermingled with streaks of blue and green shining through the tiny stained glass window set high on the wall behind him, depicting a simple white rose with a stem of three leaves.

He continued, "We have watched your planet over eons of time and marvel at its unfathomable synchronicity, and how every living form has a purpose and interlinks with each other. We see how the animal kingdom kills to survive, protects their young and instinctively responds to the order in which they find themselves. It is an intricate, incredibly fine balance of procreation and survival. You humans often voice the saying that "Life is a battle for survival; the strong and fittest win through." Mother Nature echoes this in an amazing way, maintaining a unique, intricate progression that works. Some pockets of humanity conduct their lives to a completely unconnected agenda.

"I was curious to understand why mankind appears so unsettled and so discontent when sharing such a beautiful, rich planet with such fascinating instinctive creatures. Why does aggression rear its head in all areas of their lives? Why the need to exhibit spiteful anger, jealousy, cruelty, greed and envy? I fail to understand the careless abandon and loveless regard for their fellow man, which, in consequence, taints their world."

"If only mankind could witness the harsh reality of all the negative and harmful energies bombarding their planet, I know they would be mortified. At a meeting with the Supreme Intelligence Higher Realms, I requested a brief opportunity to sense these energies and to report back my findings. I feel privileged to have been allowed this gruelling, arduous, but very vital mission."

"It appears that throughout evolution man has sadly ignored the purpose for their very existence and lost sight of the quintessence of humanity. They must renew this vital aspect, so crucial to their fellow man. No human being is an island. They need the support, in whatever way it may appear, to enable them to respect and consider one another. If it were not for the female form, there would be no procreation. Mankind fears one another."

"Belief in their fellow humans is essential to their very existence. Even what you term matrimony is merely a structured guideline for mankind living on earth. It is disregarded, swept aside, ignoring this simple teaching, with many people systematically and purposefully preferring to pursue their individual egotistical way."

"The Higher Realms are saddened by recent events, created to a certain extent by mankind's folly. Throughout eons of time, the Higher Realms have watched with sadness humanity's progression gravitating towards power, status and wealth, which are their icons. Yet throughout, mankind has absorbed skills and learned, eventually realising that material trappings are in essence worthless when balancing the final account."

"Throughout history, cultures have worshipped what they perceive as inspirational direction from the galaxy, the sun, moon and stars. At that point in their evolution, the wonder and majesty of these planets were important, and still have a place in your world today. In essence, they were worshipping the cosmos in all its powerful glory."

"Humanity is now wiser. Men have acquired knowledge, though cannot define a scientific answer for creation, the intricate complexity and wonder of how every living form interconnects. Many cultures now believe in Divine Intelligence, referred by many names, a perfect power of divine love, to all that is true and wondrous."

"Mankind is heading towards an abyss, perpetuated by selfish, arrogant greed. The desire to be content with their life pattern is lost somewhere in the mists of time. The desire to emulate what they perceive as role models is misguided. They are heading in the wrong direction. Deep within they know the journey ahead is empty and barren. Yet they persist on this collision course of destruction, mutilating and annihilating this planet for selfish means."

"We have watched from the Higher Realms with great sadness, establishing that many wise old soul teachers have been ignored or vilified. Rest assured: we have heard prayers from many devoted souls – humans who observe the sanctity and miracle of life, those who understand how life and synchronicity beautifully interconnect and intertwine with each other. So there is hope!"

The Master's eyes glistened as he voiced his thoughts. He continued, "Although mankind will soon witness the mighty and majestic power of Mother Nature, divine power will ensure that some pockets of humanity are protected and shielded in order for species to continue, alongside designated wildlife and fauna to sustain the chosen inhabitants."

"Humanity will witness the destruction of its so-called 'modern technological world' reflecting the incredible evolution of the human mind. Again, this is something that scientists cannot quite fathom out."

"We say, 'Believe in the power of love.' Love is the only truly sustainable emotion. Ellie, love the creation that is you, your family and friends. Appreciate and respect the majesty of your planet. Greed and poverty on a vast scale has been regurgitated by man. If mankind had allowed nature to be the master, you would not be in the situation you are in now. Belief, love and trust are the key."

Ellie felt cocooned in a soporific cushion, hearing truth in its jagged raw form. Feeling guilty and uncomfortable, she understood the teaching, recalling intuitive feelings and situations. She silently questioned why some people appeared to glide through life while others struggled. Perhaps lives can simply be changed by looking back at past life's patterns. Ellie sighed deeply.

Lost in a meditative state, she imagined how truly magical it would be if by looking back on life, the distorted betraying patterns of energies could be unmasked, and persistent fears and blockages revealed, then dissolved.

She sat mortified by the experience. The Being was truthful. She felt saddened, angry and helpless. "May I ask why me? Why did you choose me to sit with you today?" The Being gestured for her to relax a little.

"Because you have been questioning for some time, deeply dissatisfied with aspects of your life. Yet it is a good life. You have everything you could possibly need."

"I know I do," blurted Ellie, embarrassed, her cheeks and neck deeply flushed. "I do want to know more. There are so many questions for which I need answers."

She suddenly took the initiative, "Can I help in any way?"

"My dear, you have helped by acknowledging my very existence. Be mindful. Not everyone will be given the ability to see or sense my presence."

In that moment, the desire to share this experience with others overwhelmed her. Clenching her fists hard, digging fingernails into her palm until they hurt, Ellie checked that this meeting was really happening.

With welling emotion she did not fully understand, she asked, "I have gained so much by spending time with you, but I sense you are tired. May I come again?"

"I feel that is enough for one day. I will be here for a little longer. Go and see Avani. She will look after you."

"When can I come and see you again?" Ellie asked eagerly.

"Avani will arrange this." The Being smiled at her impatient enthusiasm.

"When I return, can you tell me more about the other rooms? I spied light under the door of one and the other one appears to vibrate light." She laughed at the nonsensical babble.

"All in good time. I promise all will be revealed. I will be here for a little while yet and will remain until I have achieved my purpose. I wonder if it may be possible for you to help. I expressed my concern at the depth of depravity, depression and unhappiness here on Mother Earth. I am protected in this great Hall and gardens, which have been especially prepared for me. The energy is harmonious for me to exist. It would help me greatly if my task was based on actual cases. Do you know of anyone who would benefit from my help and be open to receive?"

Before he could finish, Ellie's thoughts were racing.

"Yes, yes and yes! I have a very dear friend who is always uptight, unhappy and angry with life. His name is Sam. I will talk to him. How will I be able to let you know?"

"I will know. Speak with Avani. You will enter the house as you did before, but this time, please knock at the door gently." He smiled with a twinkle in his eye. "Thank you for coming."

"Oh great! I do beg your pardon. I forgot myself. May I come tomorrow?"

"You are most welcome."

"Great!" replied Ellie with new-found confidence. Fear dissolved, she acknowledged how lucky she was. Jumping to her feet, she tried hard to contain her exuberance.

With a smile that lit the room, a wave gestured that the meeting was at an end. "We will meet tomorrow."

8

THE MASTER LINKED IN to disturbing waves of energy, wishing to understand human misery. Lost dreams rivalled with antagonistic cold indifference, edging on cruelty. It all raised the question, "Why?"

His thoughts focused on a young soul, as he continued his daily morning saunter of contemplation. Restorative deep peace was heightened by fragrant flowering shrubs and vibrant herbaceous borders. He paused frequently to absorb colour energy, an accolade to Mother Nature and to man's endeavours.

As he turned a corner, he came across a shy young man, looking younger than his sixteen years, absorbed in his work, tending flowerbeds with a passion the Master had not witnessed for some time. His thoughts focused once again to the deep unhappiness surrounding the youthful figure.

"Hello young man. How are you?" he asked. "I have been enjoying the beautiful garden on yet another wonderful sunny morning. What may I call you? You seem lost and so sad. Your unhappiness camouflages the beautiful peace all around you. Whatever has happened to you in your young life to make you feel so wretched?"

The Master spoke gently, with an inquisitive overtone.

"Me Sir?" replied the boy with a slight Somerset nuance. "I'm fine!" But his eyes turned away, a well of emotion frantically trying to bubble to the surface.

"Are you really?" The reply was soft and gentle.

The boy turned. Their eyes met. "Why do you want to know?" he asked. "No one has ever asked that question before."

The youth glanced downward at his dirty boots and shabby trousers. Then again the eyes met. The young man's shoulders shrugged, his thoughts lost for a moment in time as he instantaneously re-lived episodes of his young life, recalling memories and feelings of deep-seated pain and cruelty that he would rather forget.

"I am not really sure what my name is, Sir," he whispered.

"Do not call me Sir, young man. I greet you as one friend to another."

The Master's voice was calm but firm. "Please stop for a moment. I would like to talk to you. I have all the time in the world to listen."

"Why?" replied the boy, his eyes glistening with uncontrollable rising tears.

"Because I want to understand," replied the Master.

The boy's feet shuffled from one to another, his body tending to curl inwards and upwards, as if he was struggling to catch his breath.

"I don't know what to say." He stared at his feet, aware that the stranger was standing still, looking at him. He felt strangely safe, but then started blubbering uncontrollably.

"Well it is like this – I'm classed as a bad 'un, full of badness, not worth bothering with."

The boy turned away, salty tears trickling down his cheeks, the rim of his eyes slowly turning to red.

"I've cried so much, I thought all my tears had gone!"

The boy choked on his words, his chest and shoulders heaving with the painful outpouring.

"You see, I never knew my real Da. I's frightened. I hate Jake, the man I thought was my Da."

The youth looked sad, somehow out of sync with life, forlorn in the beautiful garden he tended with such passion. His enthusiasm was fuelled by instinct. He knew where to sow plants and had an inbuilt knowing of where shrubs grow strong and foliages blend, harmonising at their best. Each planted flower, shrub and tree was a perfect colourful fusion of shade and flora, a triumph of nature's splendour.

"Tell me all about Jake," the stranger asked.

"I hate him!" replied the boy, his body and face contorted as he remembered. "He's huge, a drunken brute, big – much bigger than me. He always smells funny, of stinky sweat, bacca and booze. I hate that smell."

The boy looked as if he would retch, then he sank to his feet by the side of the path, willing himself to stop shaking yet somehow relieved to share his heart-wrenching pain.

"He has mean eyes," he continued. "He scares me with those eyes; they turn black when he is off on one. He's just a huge lumbering giant. You can always sense him coming towards you. He has long matted hair too thick for a comb, so he uses an old nail brush, when he bothers." The boy's body relaxed as little.

"Me Ma is gone. Her heart broke when I left, but I had no choice, honest. I couldn't stand the rows and beatings any more. You see, me Ma told me I was a love child, whatever that means, and that no matter what scrapes I find myself in, I should believe in angels. I knew I was a bad 'un. I was different, and it was my entire fault. Everything my fault."

He looked up at the stranger, pleading for understanding.

"It was me that had to do the chores, me that had to do

the errands and me that had to take the blame. The other two were horrid, blaming me for their mischief. They picked on me, pinched my things. Nothing I had was mine to keep; nothing was ever safe. They liked hurting me and getting me into trouble. Even at school it was the same. Though they were five years older than me, I always got the blame. Everything was my fault."

"I hated school 'cos the teachers didn't like me. Said they couldn't control me. They wouldn't listen when I said I'd done my homework. Likewise, they wouldn't listen when I said the boys had torn it up or when I said I wanted to change my seat in class 'cos the boy behind was always flicking things at my ears, prodding and pushing me in the back till I nearly cried." The ramblings continued.

"In the end I gave up. I pretended to go to school, but hid instead." His eyes shone with victory.

"I found a special hiding place. No one knew where it was. So I would run, run real fast with my jam sandwich and hide. They never knew where I was. Teachers didn't care. They gave up. Jake didn't care either. Me Ma never found out. I knew from a little 'un that I was different. The other two got big pressies for birthdays and Christmas. Mine was always a little 'un with torn paper. It didn't matter. I really didn't care."

The boy's outpouring was full of hitherto undisclosed anger, pain and resentment. He frantically tried to wipe tears from his cheeks with the cuff of his grubby sweater. His voice grew louder as he screwed up the tail end of his open neck shirt.

"I did care about their pokes and prods, putting mustard in my jam sandwiches and kicking me under the table at mealtimes, so I squealed, got into trouble and had to leave my supper. Everything was always my fault."

"I was really angry and sad inside when they were horrid to

me Ma. I was always being sent to my room without supper and wasn't allowed out even to use the John. I got used to sensing what was going to happen. I would drink and eat only a little; I had to be prepared so I didn't get a beating if I made a mess, if you know what I mean. I hid a special jar under my bed just in case."

"Your mother loved you though?" asked the stranger, crouching down at the boy's level. Now in full flow, he continued his outpouring.

"Me Ma told me one day, when we were alone, giving me big hugs, that I was her special gift. She told me one time, when Jake was working away, that she and Aunt Josie used to have fun and went out dancing. But then she never went anywhere."

Tears rolled down his cheeks, landing on his grubby shirt. "I can see her now, crying, sad, exhausted, cooking, cleaning, washing and ironing."

"It was as if she was invisible to everyone. No one seemed to notice her. She was always tense, not knowing when the next row or hollering would come. When Jake was away working, visiting pub pals, she was different. Warm, soft somehow, with a beautiful smile."

The boy's face softened as he visualised her face. "When Jake was around, she looked unhappy and never laughed, except when we had time together without the others."

His face lit up as he added, "Then she would sing, laugh and be happy again. Throwing her head back, her blue eyes twinkled with happy thoughts and memories. She would hug me tight, as if I would break. Then I knew, deep down, that she loved me. That made me feel strong, and helped me to face Jake and the other two."

"One day, Jake hit me Ma real hard. I tried to fight him off. His hands were tight around my throat. I couldn't breathe. Ma ended up on the floor in a pool of blood. Her white apron was smothered with red."

His body shook. "She was hurt real bad. Ma slowly eased herself upstairs and got into bed. After this, she became really sick. The doctor said it was touch and go, and wouldn't be long."

The boy straightened his back as he recalled every heart-breaking detail.

"She was so poorly; I knew it wouldn't be long. I couldn't stand it any more. I ran upstairs, held her hand, kissed her, told her that I loved her, then ran and ran."

"I didn't care where I was going; I just ran. I ran to my special hiding place, where I cried and cried. No-one knew I was there. I didn't care about anyone. It was good to be free, out of the house, and not to have Jake and the horrid bullies yelling at me, calling me names."

"I thought I would join the Army, but I was too young. I didn't care; I wanted to die, like Aunt Josie. We used to visit her on the farm when I was young. She was cuddly, soft and warm. Her home smelled of cooking – bread, bacon, biscuits and cakes."

His eyes brightened at the happy thoughts. "The hot range in her kitchen was always full of food. The cooking smells made you feel real hungry. She gave us eggs from her hens to take home and scrummy chocolate cake. Oh, I loved those visits! Ma and I never wanted to leave."

The boy's shoulders dropped down, a softness returning to his face as he recalled pleasant times.

"Ma was very sad when Josie went. She was alone and lost. I knew, but Jake and the horrors didn't care. Poor Ma."

The boy settled onto a nearby stone, pleased at having a willing audience. He was feeling more composed, eager to continue.

"Anyway, I decided I would die, like Ma and Aunt Josie. So I ran and ran, making sure no-one knew where I was. At first it was quite exciting, like being in the Army hiding from the enemy. I pretended I had a gun, ready to shoot anyone who would hurt me. I reckoned I could have been a good shot. I enjoyed that part. It was like being in the real war. I was very careful not to be seen, so no-one knew where I'd come from or where I was going. I pretended I was incognito, like being a Territorial. I was used to hiding, being quiet and still."

"I was so quiet I watched rabbits moving in and out of their burrows. They weren't frightened of me. I ran and ran till I was tired and hungry. Time to die. For my plan it was important to find a safe place to die. After walking for miles and miles, I eventually came across this enormous high stone wall that went on and on."

His face lit up with excitement. "I remember thinking it would have taken men a long time to build it. It went on and on. I followed it for ages, deciding it would be a good place to die behind this wall. No one would ever find me."

He shuffled. "I got cross as I couldn't find any good footholds in the wall to climb over. It was much too high for me to jump, even if I stood on a pile of stones. Then I found an old oak tree with huge branches. It must have been growing there for years and years 'cos the trunk was so wide. I hugged that tree – it was my way over the wall. I fell several times, but managed to climb it. I scuffed my school shoes, but I didn't care. I cut my knee as well, but as I was going to die, it didn't matter, so I was brave and didn't blub."

"It was great climbing that tree. I was proud of myself, like feeling on top of the world. I could see for miles and miles. The trees in the distance looked like a sea of green and gold, like

Aunt Josie's patchwork quilt. I cheered! Then I remembered why I climbed the tree."

The boy stared at the stranger in the hope that he was still listening. He continued, saying, "It was a long way down. Even though I was going to die, I didn't want to break a leg and die in pain. I wanted to die in peace without hurting!"

The stranger smiled at the boy's rendering.

"So I took deep breaths, like Ma told me to when I was scared and in a scrape. Asking Ma's angels to help me, I closed my eyes and jumped. Like a Territorial I knew I could do it, but it was a very long way down, so I planned to jump and roll, like we were taught at school in one of the PE games."

"When I fell, I rolled into a ditch full of bracken-type stuff, which broke my fall. I lay still, waiting. I wasn't dead. My legs and arms didn't hurt, and my head was okay. I made it. I did feel proud. I'd found a good place to die."

"I was surrounded by a copse of trees. I spied some cobnuts, so I ate some. I wasn't going to die hungry. I found myself in a world of nature. I sensed movement around me. I knew I was safe. I thanked Ma's angels for not breaking my legs." He beamed with pride."

"I remember thinking, 'Perhaps they do exist after all.' Ma and Aunt Josie always said 'God's angels come when we call.' I was so thrilled that I managed to get over that huge stone wall."

The stranger then suggested they walk further down the path. The boy agreed. "Shall I continue?" he asked.

Putting his hand on the young boy's shoulder, the stranger smiled, saying, "Please continue. I am anxious to find out what happened next."

With lightness in his step, eager to recount his escapade, the boy proceeded to share the end of his tale.

"I decided to make a comfortable little shelter, like my special hiding place at home, to lie down to die. I was dirty, tired, thirsty and hungry, but free. No more yelling, shouting, arguments, beatings and everything being my fault. I was free and could be me. I closed my eyes and shouted out loud, so she could hear me, 'Ma, I do love you.'"

"After making a shelter in the thicket with bracken, broken twigs and small branches, I felt safe. Time to die. I thanked Ma's angels again, curled up into a tiny ball, like I did in bed, wrapping my dirty torn sweater under my chin. It was something to hold on to. It smelt of Ma's washing powder, Ma's smell!"

"I was frightened and cried a bit, but I was free. I was so tired. I closed my eyes, then heard the honking sound of flocks of geese flying. I wondered where they were heading and wished I could fly with them, then snuggled down into my little hideaway to die, free at last."

"I thought I was dreaming because I woke to see a very old man standing over me, shaking my shoulders. In a sort of gruff kind voice, he wanted to know what I was doing and how I got there."

"I began to shake and to cry. I was scared for what he might do. He was dressed as if he belonged to the woodland. He wore laced up boots and thick cord trousers, which were held up with a wide, worn brown leather belt just below a big, round stomach. He had a thick checked shirt and a dark green quilted jacket, patched at the elbows. His face was kind, and he had brown eyes, like cow's eyes."

"He said, 'Don't worry, young man. I am not going to hurt you. Let me help you up. Come with me.' The old man helped me up, holding my arm. We walked and walked. 'Do you know where you are?' he asked. I said nothing; I had no idea. I was busy planning my escape."

"'Does the name Jenkins mean anything to you?'" the man asked as we jumped a small running stream. "'No Sir, it doesn't. Please, please let me go. I am here to die.'"

"'Well, we'll see about that, but first shall we get your knee cleaned up?' he asked. 'I'm sure you do not want to die with a bleeding knee.'"

"I looked at my knee, shocked at the deep, gaping wound and dried blood. It did not look a pretty sight, so I gave in. I was too tired to argue. I was surprised he noticed my knee."

"We walked and walked through dense woods, over turnstiles and fields, finally coming across a beautiful lake where ducks, geese and swans were busy feeding. We walked over a little bridge and I remember looking back at the wood."

"Where are we going?" I asked. I was planning my way out, hoping to find a more suitable place to die.

"We're nearly there," replied the old man. "Just a little bit further. I know you can make it."

"Suddenly, we came across an enormous house in the distance, like you see in the movies. It had soft cream coloured walls, and windows shut tight with bright blue shutters. Two gigantic dog statues stood either side of an enormous oak front door. I thought I was in heaven."

The boy glanced at the stranger with tears of joy in his eyes before adding, "I remember telling him I'd had never felt such kindness from anyone, never been on such a wonderful walk or seen so much space – only in the films.

For a moment, I was glad to be alive. Everything was so different from everything I had ever known. I couldn't believe I'd escaped to this from a grotty two up and two down terraced house in Osmond Street, ten minutes from the engineering factory."

"We walked around the side of the big house. A side gate with a bolt and handle ran alongside a tall fence with climbing roses and clematis. To the left was a small thatched cottage. It had a green front door and tiny oblong windows. A brass plate next to the brass knocker read 'Welcome.'"

"I spotted another door, a possible escape route. As if reading my mind, the old man said, "That door gives access to the big house." Turning sharp left, we faced the little thatched cottage. He whispered, "Welcome to my home.""

"I took off my shoes. Ma always told me to be polite. I sat on a footstool close to a roaring wood burner. I'd forgotten how cold I was. As I snuggled close to the fire, a cup of lovely warm sweet cocoa was put into my hands. "Drink and get warm," the old gent said, "then we'll talk.""

9

As soon as Ellie left the Hall, Avani checked on the Master. The light power energy bright and steady, he was resting, replenishing his energies, communing with the Higher Realms. She silently bade him good night, leaving him in peace. Quickly going downstairs, she checked the front door was closed.

Resting in a little armchair in the small blue and gold room, she remembered with a smile how the powerful light energy came to be here in Fosseway Hall. She marvelled with admiration at the wondrous Mother Earth, the complex mystery of cultural and religious beliefs, and in particular, the geographical locations of historical significance.

Ellie respected the old and new believers in Earth mysteries who identify and recognise certain global locations to be "sacred," accepting mysterious spiritual "energies" that remain active or dormant, patiently waiting the vortex of power to be triggered into action.

Avani understood that time and history is nothing more than a continuous passage of existence where events pass from a state of potentiality to probable future events, knowing that sometimes the past and present inexplicably intertwine.

Preordained Intent

Early one heat-hazed September morning, with the sun high in a cloudless sky, a group of six excited children, eager for the day, stopped to play by a dammed stream, a project they completed earlier in the summer. A mix of ages, the youngest was a girl of six, the eldest boy eleven going on forty-two, with a devilish yet responsible streak, always daring his siblings to challenges, yet mindful of not putting anyone at risk of harm.

Living in a small farming community set in a hamlet surrounded by fields of corn and barley, with grazing sheep and cows contentedly chewing the cud, the children were happy, boisterous and robust on a diet of fresh produce.

Maisie, the youngest, a dainty six-year-old with a mop of dark, curly hair, huge eyes and a look to melt even the coldest heart, was frequently lost in her world of make believe, with an aversion to dirt and wet feet.

While the others played, absorbed in an imaginary water world of drama, splashing, climbing trees and jumping into water from overhanging tree branches, Maisie would play happily by the side of the river bank watching sticklebacks, delighting in clouding the clear water with sticks. Contentedly, she filled her hand-made leather pouch with small stones and pebbles, additions to her growing collection. Oblivious to her passion, the older children continued fooling around when she announced that her pouch was full, she was bored and walking home.

Once in the garden, Maisie proceeded to wash her carefully chosen pebbles and stones, thrilled at the various shades of colour, texture and shape. Her imagination revealed intricate images, pondering how far the pebbles had travelled to the river bank. She slept with them neatly arranged on her bedside table, her spoils for the day sandwiched between two floppy rag dolls.

The following night, her sleep was disturbed by a soft whooshing sound. As Maisie glanced at the moonlight peeping through a chink in the curtains, she noticed the light highlighting a small pearl white stone, which was round and smooth to the touch. She loved looking at the moon, remembering stories of the Man in the Moon, as told by Uncle Walt when she visited him in the city.

Her bed alongside the window enabled Maisie to creep underneath the curtains. She did this often, silently and without waking Amy, gazing longingly at the moonlight lighting up the garden and fields beyond. She grabbed the little creamy white stone in her hands, showed it to the Moon, then crept back under the bedcovers and fell asleep, leaving the little stone on the windowsill. When she woke in the morning, Maisie noticed that the stone had moved. It had changed colour and shape, and was now emitting a soft glow. Her face beamed with delight when she noticed that the stone had grown in size and was now a dark grey with flecks of white.

Maisie was excited with her find, which was a real treasure. Over the following nights, the stone glowed so much that she hid it under one of the doll's dresses. Reluctantly, she shared her find with Amy, who instinctively knew that the stone was different and special. After many whispered discussions Amy decided this was their secret. Mum and Dad would not want to see or know about the stone. As they were older, she felt they were too busy working the farm.

Maisie and Amy agonised what to do, worrying that the stone might grow too big for them to handle, so it was decided to show it to Syrus, a man they met by chance one afternoon when collecting cobnuts in the woods.

"People don't like Syrus because they do not understand him," said Maisie. "I like him. He's kind and heals animals. When I twisted my foot the time we met in the woods, he made it better. People don't understand, but we do, don't we, Amy?" she announced proudly.

Syrus's home was nothing more than a ramshackle shelter in the densest part of Emblems Wood, close to the river at its highest point, undiscovered by most who ventured deep into the wood. In essence, he was a harmless lonely old man who preferred a life of isolation, avoiding contact with people, preferring the company of animals and nature.

Their paths met when Amy and Maisie, playing hide-and-seek, became lost late one afternoon. Syrus heard Maisie's distressed cries for help as the frightened, bedraggled girls tried to find their way back to the path. Although initially a little scared at the sight of a scruffy, bearded man wearing a battered old hat, enormous smock coat and old odd boots, they found him fascinating. The girls were enchanted to discover that he would spend hours and hours watching otters play in deep water close to the river bank. It was agreed that Syrus would be their exclusive forest friend, one to be shared with no-one, especially the boys.

The girls knew the stone wasn't bad, but could not understand why it glowed and felt hot to the touch, so agreed to take it to Syrus. He was a man of the world; he would know what to do. One afternoon when everyone was busy, they set off, telling the boys they were going to the woods to pick flowers.

Syrus was a kind soul with a big heart. He was unkempt and a prolific hoarder, who had lived by his wits since leaving the employment of Ruben Jackson, a local wheelwright. When he was seventeen, Ruben said he was "Thick in the head and too damn slow."

Syrus was so hurt and upset by these degrading remarks that he picked up his tools and left without as much as a goodbye, going to a place where he knew he would not be ridiculed. He adored the pulse and peace of the forest. Animals trusted him. Syrus respected and admired all wildlife, so an unspoken agreement was forged. Even the badger and fox became accustomed to his presence, never, ever fearing for their safety.

When Maisie and Amy arrived in the glade, he was nowhere to be seen, so they waited, sitting patiently on a log he called "Syrus's seat." Eventually, he arrived from seemingly nowhere and they relayed the tale of Maisie's find. As Syrus held the small, glowing stone in his enormous grubby hand, tears filled his eyes.

"Do you know what you have here, little 'uns? You have found something very few humans ever get to see let alone hold in their hand."

The girls gazed at him in awe, silently approving, and admiring his knowledge.

"This is a rare portal stone, a very precious, powerful stone," Syrus added. "You must keep this safe. Now is obviously the right time for it to be found. It has a purpose, you know."

The girls listened, wide eyed, trembling with fear and excitement.

"What is a poddle stone?" asked Maisie huskily.

Syrus laughed. "Poddle tone? You mean a portal stone. As far as I can remember from teachings as a young 'un, I believe it is a link between two worlds."

He scratched his bald head. "Yeah, I am sure. I know this 'cos when I was little, when my Ma couldn't look after me no more as she was ill, the monks did. They told me a lot about mysteries like this. They read to me, telling me stories of the myths, legends and history of the old earth."

The line of his shoulders softened. Syrus glanced up at the wide eyes of his captive audience. "I remember them telling me a story of the placing of these stones around the earth to be fired into action when the time is right."

Syrus's hands shook as he held the stone in the cup of his grubby, rough hands and his eyes filled with tears. "Methinks," he said, "you'd better leave this with me." Muttering quietly while scratching his head, he repeated over and over, "I do wish I knew what powered this to life."

The girls nodded in agreement as he proceeded to wrap it carefully in a dirty cloth he pulled out of his right hand trouser pocket.

"Isn't Maisie clever to have found it?" whispered Amy. "Yes, she was," Syrus answered deep in thought. "She was obviously guided by an unseen hand."

He smiled, softly touching Maisie's tousled locks. "You are clever girls. I will tell the monks it was you that found it."

"Me did!" said Maisie excitedly, seeking praise for her find.

"I mean you," said Syrus smiling.

"So we did right to bring it to you?" Amy chirped in excitedly.

"Most definitely," said Syrus. "Without doubt, this stone has a purpose. I don't know what it is, but the monks will."

The girls sat still, their cheeks glowing with pride.

"Thank you, Syrus. Can we come again so you can tell us what the monks say?"

"Of course," replied Syrus whistling through a gap in his teeth. "It will be my pleasure. Off you go now before you are missed!"

The monks were delighted to see Syrus again, showing no surprise at his unannounced visit as they opened the heavy battered old oak door at the side of the dedicated building the monks called home. The iron ring door knocker was still as awkward and stiff as he remembered. Brother Peter beckoned

Syrus to join him in an adjacent room. He was directed to sit on a heavy wooden bench, a seat well worn and shiny. Syrus watched the monk, but was saddened by his frailty, loss of weight and tired eyes. His once dark brown thick thatch of hair was now white, thin and wispy, but Brother Peter's smile was still warm and welcoming.

Syrus was heartbroken to discover that since the dissolution of monasteries and religious orders by the Crown, many monastic buildings had fallen into disrepair, their artefacts destroyed or stolen. Fearing for their lives, many monks fled to a brotherhood order in France, their simple spiritual life of prayer annihilated.

Bad news travelled fast. After devout contemplation, the fear of death or possible incarceration became so great that a group fled early one October morning, carrying only a handful of precious holy items they could safely conceal while travelling. Brother Peter recalled the monastery's final act of defiance, hiding valuable holy items from aggressive, greedy prying eyes.

The carefully chosen hiding place was a natural small cave, deep in the heart of the forest in the Vale of Avalon, with cavernous dry crevices ideal for protection and concealment. The entrance was cleverly devised in such a way that passers-by spied nothing more than a shallow underground hollow. Over time, it blended into nothing more than a high bank close to a fast-running stream. Surrounded by brambles and thicket, obscured from scrutiny its contents were safe to be unearthed when timeless energy dictated.

Syrus was saddened to understand that only four monks remained, eking out a meagre existence, refusing to leave, and devoted to their spiritual values. Choosing not to flee because of poor health, knowing they would hinder their brother's progress, they agreed to stay for propriety and visible normality.

"We are too old to start again – we would be a nuisance," admitted Brother Peter sorrowfully. "I love this building and will remain here until I die. The powers that be have given up on us. We are no threat. We just live quietly and peacefully, and are content. We hear from our brothers in France from time to time. They are well, rejoicing in their new-found freedom. We wish them well. We continue to help those unfortunates where we can."

Syrus gave him a huge hug, then realised his own natural powerful force as the monk winced. "I do hope I didn't hurt you. I forget my own strength sometimes."

"Not at all," smiled Brother Peter. "It is a joy to see you again. How can we help you?"

They walked slowly towards the ruined cloisters, Syrus recalling happy memories as they did so, checking to see if the fig tree was still standing proud in the middle of the open space. He was pleased to see it was, amazed at the growth, height and girth. Syrus reached deep in his torn worn smock pocket, producing a grubby piece of cloth.

"What do you make of this?" he asked. The monk took the cloth, gently revealing the content and gasped, looking Syrus straight in the eye.

"How did you come by this?"

Syrus relayed the story with a measure of self-importance and responsibility.

"Am I right in thinking it is what I think it to be?" he asked.

The monk's eyes filled with tears. "My son," he said. "I cannot thank you enough for sharing this with me. You are right. This is precious, so very precious it is priceless. Only those knowing souls who seek the truth will have an understanding of how rare and precious it is. I guess that somehow a pure human heart and moonlight activated its power."

"The question now is what we do with it? I am certain it has a purpose yet I do not feel the purpose is now."

The two men sat in the shade of the fig tree with a dilemma on their hands. The monk continued, "If the powers that be heard of its existence, we would certainly all be killed. The power of the stone would be misused for dominance, greed and ill-gotten gains. It is vital it does not fall into the wrong hands. Come into the chapel with me. We will pray and then we will know what to do."

Quietly and purposefully, they walked towards a small decaying stone chapel, where one single candle lit the small limestone altar. It had been a long time since Syrus prayed. It was alien to him. He felt emotional and humbled entering such a spiritual place yet did not question the need to pray, knowing this contemplation was important. He knew – and accepted – that he had somehow become a vital link, a connection with something he did not understand. Syrus trusted the monk. He must find the courage to see this through and abide by what Brother Peter felt was right, so they fell on their knees and prayed.

The light shone through the small high altar window. Trembling, glancing at the altar candle, then with heads in their hands, the two men prayed for protection and answers. Silently, the men were locked in truth and devotion. As the skies darkened, they rose in unison. Brother Peter smiled at Syrus, shook his hand warmly and beckoned him to join him outside in the cloisters.

"This stone was deemed to be found by an innocent child," he said. "You were right to bring it to me. It is extraordinarily powerful and has a unique special purpose. You will be pleased to know our part in its journey is nearly over. It is to be taken to the small cave, where it will be safe and protected. Its pulsating energy will wait until the time is right for it to be discovered, activated and used. It will not be in our lifetime dear friend, but we have been an essential linkage in its journey."

Syrus's emotions, which he felt had deserted him, flooded his being. "I feel so proud and humble," he said.

"I have to say," continued Brother Peter in serious mood, "to tell the girls they did well, but do not disclose the whole truth. It is too big a burden for two young people to carry. Just tell them it is special and safe, and how clever Maisie was to find it."

"But I did say something. I am sure I did," replied Syrus urgently.

"No matter," replied the monk earnestly. "The importance of the words will not register with them, for they are too young. What is important is to tell them they were clever to find it and it is special and safe. They will understand and in the fullness of time will forget the content of the conversation."

"I will, I will. Leave it to me."

Syrus left feeling as if he had been to heaven and back again. Suddenly feeling once again part of Mother Earth, he kissed the ground in gratitude for having come alive.

10

ELLIE CLOSED THE DOOR quietly, in fear of upsetting The Master. Excitement pulsed through her veins as she ran along the top landing and down the flights of stairs. Her head thumped, and her heart was beating faster now for a different reason. She felt vibrant, desperately trying to contain an exuberance she hadn't experienced before. She had the bizarre feeling that she was playing a part in a play with an unrehearsed script presented to her every few hours. Ellie felt ten feet tall, mastering the stairs as if floating on a cushion of air. As she reached the bottom step, Avani stood waiting to greet her.

"I knew you could do it," she smiled.

"It was incredible," replied Ellie.

"I can't explain why, but it was mind-blowing."

Her face beamed, eyes sparkling with renewed vigour. She had the voice of a happy animated child.

"He spoke for ages about matters of a vital nature yet I can't quite understand. I have so many questions needing answers. Explain to me, Avani, how can this house possibly have been transformed so quickly into something so beautiful, and why me?"

Avani took her hand. "All will become clear in the fullness of time. Be patient. Allow the essence of this meeting to unfold when the time is right."

"Oh I will. I promise." Ellie squeezed her tiny hand. "The

Master said you could arrange for me to come again."

Avani looked deep into Ellie's eyes. "Would you like to come again?"

"Oh yes. Oh yes please."

"Very well. I suggest you go home now and relax. The Master will need to rest. Would you like to come tomorrow morning?"

"Yes... yes, please! What time?"

"Say ten o'clock, after his morning meditation?"

Although Ellie's breathing eased, she found it extremely difficult to restrain her enthusiasm. "That would be great. Thank you so much."

Unsolved crazy thoughts circled her mind. This day was unlike any other. No one could have predicted the outcome when she left Nestledown for Fosseway Hall.

Ellie waved to Avani and then ran down the drive, her head buzzing with questions. Looking up at the clear blue sky, she thought how beautiful everything was. Then she suddenly stopped, glancing back at the now distant house to check she wasn't dreaming. The cloudless sky was still deep blue, and the shingle drive pristine, borders ablaze with colour. Stopping as she reached the pillared wrought iron gates, Ellie examined the paintwork. Yes, they had been recently painted and there was no evidence of heavy chains or rusty padlocks. Whatever she was part of, wherever she was, she was happy, eager for tomorrow and hungry to know more.

The gates silently closed behind her. Ellie stood puzzled, then with a flurry of hop, skip and jumps ran all the way home, waving madly to those she passed.

Approaching Nestledown, she stopped to gaze at her little Tardis with fresh eyes. Truffles lay underneath the garden gate as if waiting for her and she scooped him up, nuzzling her face into his fur. "Oh, my darling Truffles," she exclaimed. "Today has been a truly extraordinary magical day!"

* * *

Joe resumed his tale with gusto to the old gentleman who, it turned out, wasn't that old after all, and disclosed that his name was Harry Parsons, known as Pip to his friends. He gave permission to the lad to call him Pip.

In full flow the boy continued. "The man, he asked me my name, you know. I had to think. I am used to being called 'Imp,' but my proper name is Joe after my real Da. He was in the Navy, you know. I never knew him, but me Ma says I look just like him."

"Well, young fellow," volunteered Pip. "Let's give you something to eat and then we can decide what to do with you."

"Just let me go, Sir. I want to die. Please, just let me go and I'll run and run, I promise."

"No can do," said Pip. "You were found on the Jenkins Estate, so I reckon I need to decide what to do with you. How old are you?"

"Fifteen, sir...I mean nearly sixteen. My birthday is next month."

"Really?" replied Pip. "You are very small for your age. Let's not be too hasty, but think about this."

Pip sat silently in deep thought. "Umm," he mused. "Umm..."

"Lady Lillian Jenkins is a gracious lady, m'lad, who suffered greatly in her life. Her beloved only son is missing. No one knows his whereabouts or has heard from him for years."

His expression changed to one of reflective sadness.

"She became a recluse in that mausoleum of a house, beautiful though it is, grieving for a son she loves, fearing never seeing him again. I have an allegiance to her, m'lad. I reckon you might be the very thing to lift my spirits and perhaps give renewed hope to the estate, which sadly is now nothing more than an abandoned shrine to her lost husband and son."

"Sit comfortably, drink up your cocoa and I will share with you how I met Lady Lillian."

The boy fidgeted, warmth having thawed his negative emotions. He faced Pip, fascinated and entranced.

"Lady Lillian's family showed me great kindness when I needed help," Pip began. "She was a beautiful young woman, an only child, a true blue aristocrat. She had big brown eyes, a sunny nature and was always laughing. Her brown hair was tied back in a pretty neat bun at the base of her neck. Slim as a reed she was, charming and sophisticated, always able to put everyone at their ease."

Pausing before continuing, he chuckled. "Always the height of fashion, she loved shoes," he giggled. "Everything had to match. Lady Lillian adored animals, especially dogs and cats, and was always feeding lost strays. It's strange really. Wildlife must sense compassion. They never feared her presence."

Pip poured himself another coffee before adding, "Her husband was a real gent, one who studied the stock-market and was incredibly shrewd. A highly respected lawyer based in London, he had an inbuilt desire to help the underdog. He was honoured quite young for his charity work at home and abroad. Sadly, he was tragically killed in a car accident a few days before David's seventeenth birthday."

Pip swallowed hard, wiping a tear from his eye.

"Davy was a bonny lad, bright as a button, who took the death of his father really hard, never coming to terms with the realisation that he would never grow to know this wonderful man whom everyone spoke so highly of. He was the spitting image of Sir Alf, his father."

"The community was devastated and divided after that tragic event. Investigations revealed that a local twenty-year-old girl was involved in the collision. Luckily, she survived with only minor injuries. Although no charge was brought through lack of evidence, the blame was left, sort of in abeyance. No proof, you see."

His voiced trailed to a whisper. "We may never find out the truth about where the blame lies. The incident happened late one January night in the depths of winter on an unlit country road close to the far estate boundary wall."

Joe squirmed on his stool, remembering his adventure with the wall. Lost in memories Pip continued. "Many villagers found the news difficult to grasp and how such a seeming minor accident had such a far reaching catastrophe for many. How could such a tragic event possibly happen to such a highly respected God-fearing family, and so close to the estate?"

"The local girl left the area shortly after the event, distraught. She was fortunate in only suffering minor injuries, though scarred mentally. I believe she and her family left the area after all the trauma. Distressing for the family who had worked and lived in the locality for generations, the overriding need to move away from the area dominated their lives. No one knows where they live now."

"It was a difficult time for everyone. Sir Alf and Lady Lillian were, in a way, the heart and soul of the village. After her husband's untimely death, Lady Lillian devoted time to the numerous charities her husband supported. With a special sympathy for the homeless and elderly, she often helped volunteers manning the Midnight Soup Run in Torchester. She became a respected magistrate when young Davy was seven, a lady of great standing in the community, the essence of warmth, integrity and kindness."

"In keeping with family tradition, Davy was schooled at Keyhaven, a boarding school on the Devon coast, where honour, truth and self-discovery were big chunks of the strict curriculum. He was a likeable lad, not particularly tall for his age, a little shy and self-contained, possibly because he lacked his father's ability to charm people. From chatting to him, Davy gave me the impression that he felt completely overwhelmed by the authoritarian educational system he became part of. He often played truant rather than buckle down to studies."

"When he was nineteen, after many arguments with his mother, Davy rebelled against following in his father's footsteps and going to Oxford, stating he felt suffocated with every aspect of his life. We believe he was hurt at his mother's lack of understanding of how he truly felt. Late one evening he emphatically refused to continue his studies at Oxford or any university."

Joe sat wide eyed, mesmerised.

"After a period of being withdrawn and morose, without giving any hint of his intentions to anyone, even close school friends, he packed some things and left in the middle of the night. He left a brief note for his mother on the sitting room mantelpiece. As far as I can recall, it read: 'Sorry. Have to get away. Much love always, David. X'."

Joe sat with his hands on his knees, absorbed in Pip's rendering of the estate's history.

Pip continued as if reliving the moment. "As you can imagine young Joe, Lady Lillian was inconsolable when she discovered he'd gone. Her private grief was compounded by being constantly in the public eye. Within the space of a month, she cancelled all engagements, gave her private secretary leave of absence, set up a series of meetings with her solicitors and fled to be near relatives in the Caribbean."

"I met her when I was twenty after getting into mega trouble with the police. I was to be charged with assault for punching this guy senseless. Thankfully, it transpired he hadn't sustained a broken nose after all. Poor man, he didn't do anything wrong. Unfortunately for him, he happened to be in the wrong place at the wrong time at a moment when I needed to explode to vent my frustration with life."

Joe sat perfectly still, a little afraid of Pip, as this story line echoed his own young life. Enjoying an appreciative audience, Pip lit his pipe, puffing slowly as if re-living the episode.

"Steve Wright was his name. He was out socialising with a group of lads, chatting up girls, out for the night, having fun. Having just been sacked from my job again, I was in a filthy mood, bored and hostile. With hindsight, I was rebellious and angry, without a purpose to my life. Kitty, my grandmother, was the Head Cook when the Estate was running at full tilt with a full social diary, charity events, hunt dinners, etc. Nanny Su, the Housekeeper, and Kitty got on really well. Nanny Su, under the watchful eye of Lady Lillian, managed the Hall like an oiled clockwork spring. They understood one another so well that many instructions were unspoken. Nanny Su knew what was expected and always delivered 'first class service,' as Sir Alf would say."

"A very wise young Lady Lillian gleaned from the odd titbits of information from my grandmother that my home life was pretty dire, although I have to say it was never mentioned when I visited as a young boy. I firmly believe that Lady Lillian's compassion for the underdog was the main reason she opted to be a good character witness for me when I stood in the magistrates' dock. Like you, no-one had time to listen or come to my aid. Sadly young Joe, my childhood was similar to your own. My father belted me every night out of habit, fuelled by an old war injury and too much booze."

"I, too, ran away, first to my grandmother. So young man, my heart reaches out to you. I understand." Joe looked at him, struggling to contain his emotions.

"Although I left the estate for a time when I was about twenty-two, believing life would be better outside the confines of the estate, I had to return. It was then I realised how much I loved the estate and what it stood for. I felt safe. I learned with sadness when I returned after nearly three years that old Pete, the Head Gardener, had died. He loved the grounds. He'd worked on the estate since a young lad. I felt I belonged, knowing Lady Lillian would be happy for me to walk in Pete's shadow, and care for the grounds of the Hall."

Puffing on his pipe, and with Joe now settled on the floor in front of the fire, Pip reminisced.

"Prior to going to the Caribbean, Lady Lillian shocked the staff by giving them notice. It was agreed I could stay on and live here in the old cottage till she returned. Nanny Su said she would look out for me, so arrangements were agreed with solicitors for me to stay here for as long as I wished. The house had to be shuttered and the utilities turned off. I was to keep an eye out for any squatters or vandals. So trust me, young man, I do understand. I believe you were guided to this estate for a reason. Rest assured, you're safe. Give me some time to decide the best course of action."

Joe relaxed, pleased to be warm, with a full stomach. Pip continued his story.

"Lady Lillian, bless her, gave me hope and belief in a future when I desperately needed it. She gave me a purpose and helped me to belong. It's very strange that I found you because I don't usually visit that part of the estate this early on in the month. It was Jess, my old Collie, who took me that way. She must have sensed you were there."

"I was truly blessed to be allowed to stay on. Over time, I felt secure as my anger dissolved and my fear of folk eased. Pete, the old gardener, shared so much with me. It was through him I grew to love and respect nature. I now feel in tune with wildlife and trees. People let you down and always seem to have a hidden agenda. Animals and plants never do. They reward you for the time you give. Time spent with them is repaid threefold."

Joe's face glowed with understanding. "I adore furry, cuddly animals," he said. "I always loved holding the school hamster. Auntie Josie showed me how to plant seeds."

Laughing, Pip touched Joe's tousled hair with friendly warmth, assuring him, "You'll be all right, young man." Joe smiled back in gratitude.

"I am happiest in the open air in the garden," said Pip. "It's my domain. Every border, rock pool and shrubbery has been created by my hands knowing that God is by my side."

"Do you really believe there is such a thing as God?" Joe butted in.

"Without any doubt," answered Pip quickly, recalling the harsh challenges he had confronted before living on the estate. Obstacles were overcome and he mastered the creation of a natural flowing garden, eventually making it a surge of colourful glory.

He recalled feeling safe after childhood memories of fear, indifference and cruelty. In that instant he vowed to assist this vulnerable, determined young man, to help him find the same sense of peace and purpose he had discovered on the Estate.

Suddenly a flight of geese flew over head, honking as they criss-crossed the sky on their way to the lake. They always flew over the estate at this time of day. It was a sound he grew to love and marvel at. Joe swallowed hard, and then with soft reverence uttered, "Is there something more than 'us' Pip?"

Sharing thoughts, Pip replied, "No doubt at all in my mind, young Joe." Looking at Joe in delight, he grabbed his arm, pointing to the window. Both eagerly peered through it, gazing in sheer wonder at the magnificent panorama of colour, leaf canopies in the distance, rich woodland surrounding the estate and the birds flying high. "No doubt in my mind, at all!"

Eyes glistening with admiration for the young lad's courage, he looked directly at Joe. "I know what I'll do." His face beamed. "Little imp!" he said, laughing. "I have an idea!"

11

ELLIE FELT TOO EXCITED to eat. She grabbed a large mug of sweet coffee, crashing heavily on the Chesterfield. Truffles and Wynchester followed, sitting patiently at her feet as if sensing something was amiss, aware Ellie was finding it difficult to settle in one place. Her head buzzing with the day's events, Ellie thought, "I really ought to make notes, but where do I start? I know – I'll contact Sam!"

She dialled his number with nervous anticipation of what the outcome would be. The tone persisted, but there was no response. She tried his mobile, becoming infuriated when the call went to voicemail. "Sam! It's Ellie from Nestledown. Long time no speak. I really need to talk to you. I've left a message on your landline. Please call me back when you have a mo – have some news for you. Hope you're well. Speak soon."

High spirits soothed, she sipped her coffee, curling up on the sofa with knees under her chin, gazing at the garden as if in a trance. Occasionally, she glanced down at two pairs of eyes staring up at her. Scooping up both cats together, depositing them on her knee, she hugged them both at once, comforted by their feline presence. They purred in unison, nuzzling into her lap, relishing the loving warmth.

Ellie told herself, "Calm down and breathe deeply. You are not regarded by others as being emotional, but considered to be totally balanced, so control yourself."

She chuckled at outsiders' perceptions, moved the cats and went to the window, glancing at the late afternoon sun creating shadows. "If I was a painter," she began to sing, "I would create a truly wonderful masterpiece."

Brimming with energy and at a loss where to channel it, she fidgeted like a cat on a hot tin roof, singing out loud. Ellie decided to make contact with Sally, a friend down the lane she baby-sat for on occasions when Gary, her workaholic husband, was home. His expertise necessitated him spending most of his working life flying between Dublin, Aberdeen and Heathrow. Ellie fulfilled the friendship role perfectly, being reliable and trustworthy.

She dialled Sally's number. A disembodied voice answered, "Hello, we are not available now. Please leave your name and telephone number after the bleep and we will return your call." Ellie returned the phone to its station feeling annoyed and frustrated.

Grumbling in bad grace, she resigned herself to a quiet evening, annoyed she had no-one to share her news. Feeling the need to share her adventure with someone who would understand and be excited for her, Ellie was irritated that all her best efforts had been thwarted. Unenthusiastically settling in the middle of the Chesterfield between two good-natured cats, she flicked through the channels on the "goggle box," as her father called it, with the remote control. Eventually, Ellie chose to watch a foreign documentary on climate change, which she found depressing and dispiriting.

Tired after a long day and frustrated there was no call from Sam, she fed the cats, secured the house and went to bed with a book, which she tossed aside after trying to read a couple of pages.

Ellie woke early to a warm bright morning sun, with the hens noisily clucking to welcome the day and two contented outstretched lazy cats sunning themselves on the garden path. Dressing casually, she was anxious to receive answers to the many questions ricocheting through her mind, so Ellie checked her mobile and landline, but found no response from Sam.

Although hungry, she didn't feel like eating breakfast. A large mug of coffee would suffice and keep her alert. With a sense of urgency, Ellie set off in the direction of Fosseway Hall, choosing to go the long way around in the hope of avoiding people, as she was definitely not in the mood for small talk.

Striding out, she reflected on yesterday's events – meeting Avani, the amazing transformation of the Hall and the mind-blowing interlude with the Master. Slowing her pace a little, she felt wobbly and light-headed yet Ellie knew she had to continue the journey.

In what seemed only a few minutes, she was back on the high bank opposite the meandering high wall of the Hall. She slipped, sliding down the bank, soiling new jeans with dirt and grass stains. Brushing the excess grime off her jeans, Ellie jumped the final foot onto the path, then walked quickly towards the huge gates, determined to find answers.

As she approached the vast stone pillars, the wrought iron gates slowly opened just enough for her to walk through, as if operated by an unseen hand. Ellie shivered, realising she was alone. Whenever she faced the gates, she was totally alone. How weird! The abundance of flowering growth welcomed her, the fragrant heady floral perfume somehow reassuring. Feeling a little more confident, she sauntered towards the house, her arrival announced with every foot impression on the pea shingle.

This time Ellie was here by invitation and could make as

much noise as she wished, so she did so, enjoying the moment. The impressive sweeping drive with its wide turning circle was pristine as if it had just been laid. Melodious birdsong and a gentle breeze caressing the leaves and branches gently swaying overhead broke the stillness.

As if being seen for the first time, the Hall stood proud in the sunlight. An imposing building, with its sparkling windows and gleaming paintwork, it had an extraordinary sense of peaceful beauty and uplifting energy.

Approaching the semi-circular marble steps leading to the huge front door, she heard her name called in the distance. Turning left, then right, finding it extremely difficult to detect the direction from where the sound was coming, Ellie realised that Avani was calling her from the stone steps leading down to the lake. She waved, running down to meet her.

"Hello Ellie!" said Avani warmly. "How are you? Did you sleep well?"

"Strange you say that," answered Ellie. "I found it very difficult to settle when I got home. I didn't want to eat or do anything. I just couldn't concentrate yet when I went to bed, I slept really well, remembering nothing until I woke this morning, much earlier than I usually do."

"Excellent!" replied Avani. "You experienced the effect the Master has. He is aware of everyone's needs, especially where emotions are concerned."

"Will I be seeing him soon?" asked Ellie impatiently.

"Later," Avani answered softly. "He is resting after his early morning walk. He will tell me when."

"May I ask you something that has been puzzling me?" queried Ellie.

"Of course," Avani smiled. "How can I help?"

"The burning question is this – how and why Fosseway Hall?"

"Take it slowly," Avani laughed. "One question at a time, although I am sure they are all connected."

Ellie took a deep breath explaining the conundrum posed by the ramblers. She explained how surprised she was that no-one else had noticed or mentioned changes at the Hall, why she didn't believe their story and how she felt compelled to find out if there was any truth in their remarks. Avani smiled, her sweet face beaming with delight.

"Ellie come and walk with me. Let's sit by the lake and I will try and answer your questions and put your mind at rest. Don't look so tense. Remember that life is merely a projection of our thoughts. Also be mindful that in life nothing is ever as it seems."

Ellie felt a little awkward, wondering if she was moving into a realm out of her depth. They ambled towards the lake, where wildfowl seemed to have multiplied since their last visit. Avani read her thoughts. "The warmth and water attracts them," she said. "They know they are safe."

Eventually, they reached a stone seat facing the lake, where a small willow tree's branches draped the water's edge. The Hall lay in the distance, glistening in the sunlight, reflecting warmth. Avani allowed her fingers to make a movement in the water and then stopped, beaming at Ellie.

"I will begin," she chuckled softly, touching Ellie's hand for reassurance. "The Higher Realms have been searching for a suitable place for the Master to reside during his stay on the earth plane with the right location and energy field as his visit is of vital importance.

"Fosseway Hall was built on land witness to a myriad of historical events, aggression, cruelty and compassion. Landlocked

109

with high magnetic energies, magnified by ley lines and a fine portal, it is one of the few undisturbed places on the planet today. The portal stone uncovered on this land was originally concealed by spiritual beings unafraid of the truth and was a light beacon. Over time, modern man unravelled secret mysteries previous civilisations fought hard to protect."

"The energised active portal here is magnificent. The Higher Realms see the light source clearly. We had to be patient and wait until the timing was perfect and the house was empty. Although from your perception it is sad the owner is abroad, rest assured that everything is happening exactly as it is meant to be. Trust me when I say that all will be well in the end. Everything that has happened and will happen in the future is as it is supposed to be."

Ellie swallowed hard, feeling queasy, unsure if she wanted to continue listening yet knowing she needed answers. Avani continued, "You have a saying in your world, 'When a job needs doing, ask a busy person; they always find the time'."

Ellie laughed.

"Another prolific saying, 'I will make time,' is used by busy people when asked to slot an urgent request into a tight hectic schedule. We chuckle over this flippant comment. You have no comprehension of the powerful significance of this statement."

Ellie felt silly at this string of words used quite often when under extreme pressure struggling to reach deadlines.

"We have the ability to stretch, stop or shrink time!" Avani giggled at Ellie's blank expression.

"It is true!" she laughed out loud. "Believe me: one day with acquired knowledge, and all the intricate technology you have on Mother Earth, man will be able to do the same. We have simply found a way to stop and suspend time. I only exist in an environment of balanced harmonious energy."

Ellie's eyes opened wide. She stood up, arms outstretched, gesturing all around her, and blurted out, "How did you change all this?"

Avani touched her hand gently, saying, "I will try and explain, although I know you are struggling to believe what I am telling you."

"Once the perfect location was identified, our priority was to transform the house, which sadly, as you know, had been neglected. We energise in harmony. Neglect attracts disharmony. It was vital to ensure the energy was free-flowing during the transformation. The spirit controller of time worked his magic. We had just fifty-six hours to complete the task, as the Master had already agreed the date he would visit Mother Earth."

"It was imperative to have no disturbance of energy flow by human beings during the process to guarantee that the energy surrounding the perimeter of the estate was not compromised in any way during the transformation."

Ellie swallowed hard. Avani continued, "You may recall the Grand Summer Fayre and open market in Torchester a few weeks ago."

"Yes," replied Ellie. "It was quite something. Jugglers, clowns and farmers' markets all came together to celebrate the fifteenth Torchester Carnival. The Carnival Queen's Maid of Honour was Lucy, a villager's eleven-year-old daughter. The procession was fantastic and the town packed. The event was so well publicised that people flocked from miles around."

Avani grinned. "As most of the villagers focused on Torchester, it was equally important to ensure any thoughts of visiting Fountains Hill were disrupted and dissolved."

"I see," said Ellie, now fully engaged in the story. "But how did you deal with the through traffic from the main road to

Fountains Hill leading into Hallows Rest? Surely there would be the odd cyclist, local vehicle and delivery vans taking that route?"

Avani laughed again at Ellie's blank expression. "Can you recall the local news a few weeks ago?" She was teasing, enjoying every moment. Ellie's face remained blank.

"Let me refresh your memory – 'Flood water causes havoc on local roads'."

Ellie's face remained expressionless. "Forgive me, I am teasing," said Avani, her face beaming with light-hearted mischief.

"Ellie, can you recall the media warning residents they would be without water for the day due to a fractured water main located half a mile from the main road?"

Ellie looked lost. Avani continued enjoying the banter. "Despite the water board's best efforts, the fault could not easily be detected. The problem was difficult to resolve. The drop in water pressure and disruption to local residents necessitated roads being closed. The road block included Dorcas Mill Lane leading to Fosseway Hall and Fountains Hill. Police monitored the closed roads for safety until the repair was complete which, if you remember, took just over two days."

Ellie's eyes shone. "Wow! How clever."

"Not really," replied the angel. "It was an essential simplistic way to keep the energy flowing around the estate for the transformation to be complete in the time allowed."

"Who did the work?" Ellie quizzed still open-mouthed.

The angel laughed in delight. "Spirit helpers, of course, although they needed human form to do the work. They did a brilliant job too, although, as with all plans, we overlooked one person – Pip the gardener."

Ellie gasped. "I thought – I mean we all thought Pip had

passed away. No-one has seen him for months."

"Really?" replied Avani. "He is safe and well. In fact, he has appointed himself the caretaker of the Hall, taking a young man under his wing, so to speak."

Avani laughed, enjoying watching Ellie's expression change from a state of disbelief to one of confused frustration, unable to grasp all that was being revealed.

Avani squeezed her hand gently. "It is okay. We resolved the oversight."

Ellie smiled. "Of course." By now used to asking, "How?"

"Well, Pip and Joe, the young man, both animal lovers, were made aware, via a supposed casual remark from Su, the retired housekeeper of the Hall, of a badger set that had collapsed and caved in on the far side of the estate. Early one morning, they left with shovels, netting, hammer, nails and wood – in fact everything they could carry – to inspect the damage and try to repair the entrance. It is well known that Pip respects wild animals, especially badgers."

"Yes, they always seem to get a bad press," chipped in Ellie. "I echo his sentiments."

"Well, they arrived on site, spending all morning clearing the fall of earth."

Avani grinned as she recalled the mischief created to resolve the overlooked problem. "Dorcas Wood, as you know, is named after the Dorcas Stream Mill owned by the Dorcas family."

Ellie's thoughts momentarily drifted. She recalled reading an article whereby before the huge water paddle was silent, a young lad clambered onto the ledge above the wheel to retrieve a girl's hat. Sadly, as he leaned through the open window above the enormous moving paddle wheel, he slipped, lost his foothold and fell, his arm getting badly mangled in the machinery. He survived, though his left arm was so badly crushed that it had to be amputated just above the elbow. The poor fellow was never the same again. The mill closed for safety checks. The Dorcas family was guilt-stricken on discovering that the young, fun-loving lad was a worker's nephew from the States. It transpired that he was tipsy on cider and showing off to a local girl."

"How sad," mused Ellie. Her attention returned to Avani.

"Well," the angel continued, enjoying herself. "They had lunch and fell asleep under the trees for what they believed to be about half an hour. In fact, they had been asleep a whole day, twenty-four hours."

She giggled. "They woke, continued their work and completed a safe new entrance. Then they hid, watching the badgers until sunset when they returned home and slept." Enjoying the moment, Avani giggled again.

"I see," said Ellie. "So in effect, during that block of time, anyone in the vicinity of the estate was locked in a time warp."

"Yes, I suppose that is it," replied Avani, jumping off the seat, twirling and enjoying her role. "I am glad you asked."

Ellie glanced around her, absorbing the colour and nature's unspoken order. She looked towards the Hall, astonished at how wonderful and perfect everything seemed. Words failed her and her questioning thoughts disappeared.

"It is time," Avani said gently, looking at Ellie's puzzled expression. "Let us walk back to the Hall. The Master is ready to see you."

12

ELLIE AND AVANI SLOWLY made their way back to the majestic Hall, which was immersed in bright sunlight. Ellie glanced back at the lake. The conversation with Avani had touched her heart in an unexpected way, leaving her feeling content, yet disturbed. She was here willingly. Feeling a little fearful, in her heart she knew she had no reason to feel this way.

Avani sensed her apprehension. "Don't be afraid. You are simply overwhelmed by the wonderful energy surrounding you purely due to the love of beauty you feel in your heart."

Blinking back tears, Ellie swallowed hard, conscious of the wistful music leading her to the Hall as an uninvited guest. Acknowledging that she was here by invitation, Ellie willed her mind to be calm. As she breathed deeply, her head slowly cleared.

The warm sunlight followed as they entered the inner entrance hall. As they reached the middle of the long high ceiled hall, Avani stopped, touching Ellie's hand.

"I will wait for you in the little blue room, the room at the end of the hall, where we talked the first time we met. The Master will tell me when the meeting with him draws to a close. I will be waiting for you. The Master is in his room. You know the way?"

Avani's smile was graced by beautiful blue eyes shining like polished sapphires. Ellie felt reassured, gave her a spontaneous hug and slowly turned to climb the stairs. This time she vowed to recall every thought and feeling as remnants of the last meeting merged into a frustrating blur of nonsensical amazement.

Quietly tiptoeing past the first door, she stopped, remembering the pulsating glow of sporadic coloured light just visible under the door. Crouching down and staring at the chink of light, Ellie was mesmerised by the array of coloured lights moving, merging and separating into a myriad of coloured patterns. She needed to know about them. She was sure the Master wouldn't mind if she was a few seconds late. After a few seconds of silent debate, her curiosity won. Though decisive, she found this proposed action uncomfortable and awkward. Recalling Avani saying that all would be well, Ellie still wondered if she should pry. Would it do any harm? She was convinced that if so, Avani would have warned her.

Glancing down the stairs, along the landing she saw and sensed no-one. Inquisitiveness got the better of her. Taking a deep breath, placing her right hand firmly on the round brass door handle, which turned easily, she pushed the door open. As Ellie did so, her heart skipped a beat and she almost forgot to breathe, completely unaware she was being watched. She stood transfixed, unable to believe what her eyes were showing her.

A room ablaze with vibrant coloured energy faced her – an energy she could sense, feel and touch. The ceiling and walls were alight with interacting and dancing swirls and patterns of coloured light of every hue. In her excitement, Ellie momentarily forgot her meeting with the Master. Tears of joyful bewilderment trickled down her cheeks.

Leaving the door slightly open, she moved further into the room noticing the space and the absence of chairs, apart from a small wooden high backed chair in the centre. Ellie's eyes circled the room, viewing plinths of what appeared to be gleaming black granite. Each plinth supported the weight and splendour of huge blocks of shining luminous crystal, some smooth, others rough hewn. Each block measured about three feet in length by two feet in height. Each one emitted a similar magnetic metaphysical vibrant energy.

Conscious of foot imprints on the thick pile of a luxury carpet, Ellie felt light-headed as if floating on air. Fear, anxiety and doubts dissolved. Closing her eyes, she wished she could record how she felt, what she could see and sense. She felt mesmerised as waves of vibrating energy emitted from each crystal block, leading to a crescendo of powerful healing light. Still unaware of being observed, her eyes continued to search the room. Ellie counted seven plinths, then spied a small wooden box full of tiny crystals to the right of the small chair. "How strange!" she thought.

Captivated in this world of vibrating colour, she felt a pang of guilt, slightly nauseous as she remembered the Master and her invitation to a meeting. She turned to leave, suddenly realising that the Master had been watching her every move.

"I knew you would not be able to resist," he spoke softly.

Hopelessly embarrassed, Ellie stuttered, "I am so very, very sorry, I do apologise," praying she had not offended him. "I did not mean to stay. I just wanted to peep. I was being nosy."

"No matter," answered the Master. "I knew where you were. I read your thoughts."

Ellie looked down at her feet, completely ill at ease, wishing she hadn't succumbed to curiosity. The smiling Master sensed her discomfort. "As you are here, would you like me share with you the importance of this room?" he asked.

"Oh, yes please!" replied Ellie. "And I am truly so sorry. I didn't wish to be discourteous."

Wishing her heart would slow down and her head stop thumping, the Master's gracious kindness reinforced Ellie's discomfort. She was wrong to intrude.

"No matter," answered the Master. "Be still now. This is a Healing Room of hope and light orchestrated by the Higher Realms."

"It is awesome... magnificent!" exclaimed Ellie excitedly. "What is it for?"

"It is a blending of powerful mineral energies, earth's energies. Your world may regard it as an experiment. We gauge its power when it is used for the purpose it was intended."

"What is that?" asked Ellie enthusiastically.

"To heal those I will guide while I am here." The Master beamed. "Join me in my room and I will try and explain."

Ellie followed him, sitting opposite in the small blue padded tapestry chair she had earlier occupied in awe of the essence and presence of this wondrous being.

"As you know Ellie, healing is a mechanism to restore and repair by natural processes. Your physical body is merely a reflection of your consciousness. Unknowingly, past tensions and difficulties affect emotional responses, which can build up in the body and affect the physical frame. Sadly, some diseases can be the result of unacknowledged issues and unresolved tensions from difficult relationships with parents, siblings or unrequited love. Sometimes, it is helpful to understand how one's forebears' lifestyle and attitude influence generations."

"When you delve back in time, you can discover you are merely in part a product of your parents' teachings and beliefs. This unleashes an unconscious drive to receive, recognising misunderstood complex connections with, say, your mother or grandfather. The only prerequisite is a desire for truth, to feel complete and the courage to search deep into the unconscious mind, exposing repressed questions and feelings."

"The unconscious mind and chakra system is a remarkable key in the pursuit of a closer connection with your father and mother's ancestors. As you know, in the chakra energy system, the major centres of spiritual power in the human body are located along the spinal column. Recognising a balanced chakra system is vital for optimum wellbeing. Many now accept that problems arise when the chakra system is out of alignment."

"Unfortunately, when this happens many are completely unaware of the detrimental effect this has on emotions, mental agility, physical fitness, spiritual awareness and their perception of life. This can easily be brought back into balance by bursts of pure white powerful light energy, plus a willingness to believe. The mind is vast. No mystical symbols or tools are necessary to release and dissolve the many debilitating symptoms the body exhibits and the mind controls. Barriers between the two dimensions do not exist. Barriers are not solid, and the mind creates its own limitations."

"The fine balance of energies in this room has been orchestrated very carefully. Each block of crystal emits its own metaphysical element, which together creates a strong magnetic energy of healing, lifting repressed emotions to the surface, so healing can take place. It is the first step to awakening the potential of the heart and mind."

"We watch with disbelief the layers of repressed limiting emotions absorbed into the fabric of mankind and blockages formed over many lifetimes."

"Humanity has always searched for happiness. How individual entities define happiness differs. Happiness to one may not be the same definition to another. Each has to search for his own personal triumph and accolade."

"The unsettlement and restlessness within nations is about human consciousness moving into another direction. You have an earthly saying, 'No pain no gain.' That is also true of the expansion and shifting of the universal consciousness that slowly and purposefully is shaping your planet today."

Ellie sat still, absorbing every wise word. "'Why then talk to you this way?' you may ask yourself. If you haven't recognised it, there is a very profound reason for your visit. It is to shake your beliefs in such a way that you will expand your horizons, share your truth and understanding with others wishing to listen and learn. There are many enlightened souls living in all corners of your world patiently waiting for the right time and place for the unveiling of a new blueprint for mankind."

"Unbeknown, you are a key player, your visit crucial to a new awakening. Your choice to enter this room was not chance. It was pre-planned, as is the rest of your visit, so do not be fearful. Be humbled and privileged. You take responsibility on your shoulders well, but need to examine deep-seated emotions. The energy in this room is only the beginning. So, my child, you are special. Do not cry. The Higher Realms are fully aware of your limitations."

Ellie sank deeper into the chair, not sure whether to laugh, cry or run. "Chosen? Me? It cannot be so."

Yet being with the Master, Ellie sensed a change within her thinking. Yes, the Master spoke truths. She hadn't dealt with emotion, desperately concealing fears from everyone, especially her family, to the point of deceiving herself. If this journey was worthwhile, the outcome to find true happiness, she surmised, would all be worthwhile. Ellie swallowed hard, her face crimson with embarrassment. She felt foolish believing she could conceal her deepest doubts and fears from such a highly advanced being.

The Master continued. "Let me briefly share with you the powerful properties of these crystals, then when I have finished I would like you to sit in the Healing Room in the little wooden chair and close your eyes, allowing your being to absorb all the wonderful uplifting energies. When you feel invigorated, just before you leave, select one of the crystals in the small wooden box to the right of the chair. They are merely smaller versions of the crystal blocks. Keep it with you. It will remind you of this room and be a constant reminder of the healing experience. When you feel fearful, hold it in your left hand, close your eyes for just a few moments and you will be able to link with healing energies."

Ellie sat wide-eyed, her body shaking with a release of tension she did not understand. She sobbed like a baby deprived of food and sleep.

The Master gently touched her on the shoulder. "Be still, my child. Crystals can transform and harmonise energy for healing. The huge hewn block of clear crystal quartz on the left of the door focuses energy precisely where needed, enabling the higher self to attune the physical body to repair and balance itself. Blending the earthly and higher self, it aids clarity."

"Next is the beautiful deep purple amethyst, which is renowned for activating the crown chakra. It cleanses the aura, balances energies, enhances connection between earth and the Higher Realms, and aids peace and calm."

"It is followed by the burnt amber of Citrine, which helps to resolve problems on physical and spiritual levels. It balances energy, the root of who you are and connects with subtle energies. This aids dissolving negative energy."

"Next is the magnificent deep blue Lapis Lazuli, which

enhances knowledge and the acceptance of esoteric ideas, wisdom and awareness. It brings light to dark recesses of the mind and aids creative energy."

"Shimmering energy blending with the milky sheen of Moonstone cleanses negativity from chakras and heralds new beginnings. It renews confidence, understanding that difficulties can be overcome, increases general wellbeing and rejuvenates. It aids willingness to change life's configuration on physical, emotional, mental and spiritual levels."

"This is followed by the lustrous volcanic glass of Black Obsidian, which is a grounding energy. A powerful protector against unwelcome psychic energies, it reflects character flaws, stimulates beneficial changes, enhances insight, acceptance and promotes forgiveness of self and others. It aids dissolving of self-limiting barriers."

"Finally, the soft pink warmth of Rose Quartz opposite the Clear Quartz balances all the chakra energies. It activates loving energy of the heart chakra to give and receive love. As well as healing emotions and relieving stress, it assists in dissolving emotional blockages and enhances the synthesis of love and spirituality. This crystal aids the safe release of trapped emotions."

As he finished speaking, Ellie studied him, noticing his gentleness, warmth and kindness. She felt honoured to be in his company yet unsure of exactly what role she had to play. She waited patiently as they sat in silence.

The Master closed his eyes momentarily, and then opened them slowly. His bright blue eyes showed a warm exuberance she had not witnessed before. His voice softened almost to a whisper, so much so that she had to really concentrate for the words to register. Ellie sensed tiredness overshadowing him.

"Go my child," said the Master. "Spend as much time as you

wish in the Healing Room, for you will feel the benefit when you sleep tonight. Avani will meet you before you leave. I would like to see you again and will explain the contents behind the second door."

Ellie's eyes fell to her hands, which lay loosely on her lap. She felt as if she had been caught out. "He read my thoughts," she said to herself. "I must be careful. It's a good job my thoughts are honest!"

She smirked and the Master responded with a smile, a gesture it was time to leave. Ellie rose, bowing in reverence, acknowledging that she was in the company of someone extraordinarily special.

"Thank you... thank you," she spoke softly, recognising his exhaustion.

"You may touch the crystals," he beamed. "They will enhance your awareness. I will see you at the same time tomorrow."

Ellie closed the door carefully behind her. With lightness in her step, she entered the Healing Room. The powerful crystal energy danced, bouncing off the walls and ceiling in gyratory patterns. The crystal blocks glowed with an effervescence she could not fully comprehend, being transported to another world. Breathing gently, touching each crystal mass in turn, powerful magnetic energy pulsated through her body. Sitting on the little wooden chair, she realised the blocks appeared to fuse together, as if she was encased in a circle of vibrant coloured brilliance.

Comfortable, with her feet firmly on the floor, Ellie allowed her eyes to close. Selecting a crystal from the little wooden box on her right, she drifted into another world, a world of enchantment.

13

Ellie's mind drifted in and out of unchartered realms, completely entranced by the powerful pulsating energy. She shivered with anticipation, sensing subtle physical chemical changes. Her dry hot hands trembled with joy as the small crystal vibrated in her cupped hands, the texture resembling quivering jelly.

Allowing herself be transported to an unfamiliar place, she became increasingly aware of unseen healing hands rapidly replenishing and invigorating every bone and pore while moving deeper into an overwhelming contented peace. She sensed the build-up and momentum of swirling coloured power moving faster as the energy encompassed every crystal block. Then with a final "whoosh" of heightened power, the energy slowed and stopped. Patterns now danced to a different pace, a gentler movement, until they too eventually slowed and stopped.

Ellie's heart slowed to a gentle rhythm, welcoming the stillness as she sat, allowing the energy to settle around her. As her eyes opened, she noticed that the blocks were pulsating, although the tempo had changed, as if the power source was idling, recharging for the next wave of pinnacle power.

She smiled at the little crystal clutched in her hands, recognising its essence and colour. Her choice, the Black Obsidian, was the stone of protection. Respectfully running the tips of her fingers over the smooth glassy surface, content to sit quietly and still, she deliberated when to leave, then slowly stood up. Tip-toeing towards the door, she was unable to resist touching the Rose Quartz, which was hot yet cool. Breathing deeply, she sighed and relaxed, accepting that the crystals were vibrant, mysterious and powerful.

With the precious stone clasped in her right hand, Ellie slowly made her way downstairs. A smiling Avani was waiting. "You look radiant," she said.

"Oh yes," Ellie replied. "I cannot possibly start to explain or describe what I have experienced. I just feel amazing. I cannot believe how incredible it is to be here."

Avani laughed, her face shining as she gave Ellie an angelic hug. "Go now; make your way home and rest. I will see you tomorrow."

"Oh yes!" replied Ellie finding it difficult to contain her exuberance.

She left the Hall in a stupor, feeling on a wonderful high, exhibiting the heights of a hypnotic drug. As she twirled with her arms outstretched, her voice broke free, exclaiming, "I am happy! I am so happy!"

At the top of Fountains Hill, Ellie stopped for a moment to scan the horizon, where it was said on a clear day one could see a glimpse of the sea. Grinning, she recalled that visitors actually believed this bit of nonsense. From here she could see for miles and miles – green fields, woodland, clusters of homes, shops, spread-eagled small-holdings in and around Hallows Rest and the sprawling growth of Torchester far in the distance.

Squinting, she could just make out the roof of the Carver's Arms, where all this began. Although longer in distance, she preferred this route, encountering less people who would unintentionally break the enchanted spell of mysterious uplifting energy by inane polite chatter. Ellie increased her pace, hurrying all the way home. She awarded herself smug congratulations on avoiding face-to-face contact with another living soul.

Reaching Nestledown, she ran upstairs, flopping down on the bed, her mind vague, but aware for once that the cats could look after themselves. The bedroom window framed scudding white fluffy clouds against a blue sky. Intermittent laughing, crying and uncontrollable tears of pure joy brought her back to an overwhelming tiredness, unconsciously curling her exhausted frame into a foetal position. Ellie wrapped the comforting duvet tightly around her exhausted frame, staring up at the ceiling, motionless for explanations. Involuntarily, she fell into a deep sleep until dusk fell.

Early morning silence was shattered, broken by a persistent unexpected monotonous ringing sound in the distance. "Oh buckets of bright blue blood, go away!" she muttered in annoyance, burying her head deeper into the pillow. "Leave me in peace."

Pulling the duvet over her head to shut out the sun, sleepily glancing at the clock, reality setting in like a sledge hammer, realisation dawned it was nearly nine o'clock and she was still fully dressed. Momentarily recalling recent events, Ellie sat bolt upright in the middle of a sea of bedding, anxiously searching for the little black stone, guessing it had slipped beneath her as she slept. Panic set in as she failed to find it, her heart missing beats, and then relief on finding it safe under the pillow. Kissing it, Ellie was delighted it was real and safe.

She showered, dressed and had breakfast in record time. Absent mindlessly, Ellie robotically replenished the cats' food and water dishes. Side by side, the pair of them sat bemused, looking up at her as if she was slightly unhinged. She stopped, laughing at their expressions, imagining they were talking to each other like two elderly ladies chatting over a cup of tea. "Wonder what she is up to today, my dear? Do you know that she missed supper and didn't even undress? Shame on her! It's all a bit odd. Do you know she didn't even think of us once."

Ellie glanced at their bewildered faces, shouting as she locked the backdoor behind her. "I am quite sane cats, just enjoying unrivalled fabulous adventurous fun." Too busy eating, the two cats ignored her.

The sun bright and warm, flocks of birds flying high in the sky, Ellie enjoyed the summer sunshine, running all the way to the Hall via a short cut she recently discovered. With hopes high, her step quickened as she saw sight of the Hall, but the intimating wrought iron gates blocked her progress. For a moment, she felt sad and disappointed, wondering if she was on a fool's mission. As if by magic, the gates opened slightly, allowing her just enough space to slip through, then silently closed behind her.

Glancing back at them, in disbelief Ellie tutted, "This place is really quite weird," buoyantly convinced she was on an incredible unbelievable journey as she ran up the drive, enjoying creating big hollows in the pea shingle with her feet.

As promised, Avani was patiently waiting, sitting by one of the large bronze dogs, as if posing for a photograph.

"You made it then?" she asked with inquisitive mirth.

Ellie's face flushed with excitement, at the same time feeling slightly pushy. "Oh, I wouldn't have missed this for the world."

Avani touched her hand gently. "The Master has nearly finished his walk. Sit for a while and rest. You seem out of breath."

"I just ran and ran," replied Ellie.

They sat in silence, watching the wildfowl and geese on the lake. Avani gestured, "He is ready for you." Ellie jumped up, asking, "Is it all right for me to go up?"

"Why yes," replied Avani. "You will enjoy today."

She laughed, tossing her golden curls in the process, her delicate wise face creamy white, her hands perfect and petite.

Now surer of herself, Ellie ran up the stairs. Sunlight lit the landing, patterns of the Healing Room creating coloured streaks on the carpet. Gingerly making her way to the door of the second room, Ellie grew more and more excited, her heart beating faster and sounds in her ears resonating like a base drum. Animated, she felt somewhat strange.

"I sure am on a mysterious unimaginable journey," Ellie thought, tiptoeing to the second door. She sensed throbbing, noticing a soft light which was barely visible. Suddenly feeling keyed-up and overwhelmed, Ellie wanted to turn back, but decided to carry on. Stopping abruptly at the second door, suddenly unsure of what to do, she silently debated, "Should I venture in or wait for the Master?" Thankfully, the decision was taken out of her hands, as the door slowly opened wide, the beaming presence of the Master greeted her. "Please come in."

He ushered Ellie into a square high-ceilinged room, two small circular windows set up high close together facing the door. The highly polished wooden floor mirrored sunshine shapes. The Master pointed to two small high-backed padded chairs facing one another, which were upholstered in the same beautiful tapestry fabric she remembered seeing before. "Please sit down," he asked softly.

She obeyed and they sat opposite one another. Ellie swallowed hard. "You are now in the midst of true power!" the Master whispered.

Ellie's body shook. She hoped the Being would not notice, blinking furiously to prevent tears betraying her emotion.

Breathing deeply, she gradually restored her equilibrium.

Her eyes quickly scanned the room. "How could anything be more beautiful and powerful than all I have experienced since visiting the Hall?" she wondered inwardly.

"We are now moving to the heart of the matter," said the Master, smiling with reassuring warmth. "Do not be afraid. I bring you hope."

Ellie blinked, closed her eyes momentarily. Opening them again, she clutched the small obsidian very tight in fidgety hands, which, strangely, gave her comfort. "Tell me what you see," the Master asked.

Ellie wriggled further into the seat of the chair, her back leaning against the high back, her feet not quite touching the floor, legs dangling to one side. The chair seat was wide and long, too big for someone of her stature yet surprisingly comfortable.

"Tell me," asked the Master with warmth. "What do you see? Take your time."

"Well," said Ellie. "It is strange really. The walls are soft cream like the rest of the Hall. The wall's full of pictures yet somehow they are weird."

"Tell me more," asked the Master enjoying the moment.

"Well," answered Ellie, feeling a little more relaxed. "They appear to be merely blocks of coloured canvas set in magnificent gold patina frames. Just pictures of colour."

"Really?" the Master continued. "Study them more closely. Tell me what you see."

Ellie sat bolt upright, opened her eyes wide and looked around the room, trying hard to concentrate.

"Take your time. Describe one picture at a time in detail."

Ellie took several deep breaths and began. "I see seven pictures about 26 inches by 18 inches and a small square one about six inches by six, all beautifully framed in gold patina frames."

"That is correct," said the Master. "Now continue. Relax, my child. Enjoy. Relax."

Ellie became aware that the Master wasn't scolding her, but just having fun. Once her breathing settled into a rhythm, both ears inexplicably popped. Smiling in mutual amusement, she looked up at him.

"Well," she responded finding her voice, "I will begin to the right of the door and work my way round the room."

"The first is a magnificent red, not a blood red, for it's somehow richer and deeper. As I look deeper into the colour, it seems like the colour of red poppies, yet the colour is moving and swirling. I can see crimson, a soft red, with tendrils of very dark red. The more I look, the more I see. It truly is beautiful. What I thought initially was one block of colour is in fact depicting all shades of red."

The Master smiled, explaining, "This represents the base chakra, depicting energy, enthusiasm, anger and aggression – the now."

Ellie's eyes glistened with amazement.

"The next picture is a block of orange, like a beautiful sunset, ripe orange fruit and the bright saffron robes of Tibetan monks. As I look deeper, the colour changes – it's swirling and moving. The density of colour is very dark and then becomes lighter with tendrils of deep dark orange. It is rich and bright, like a golden bronze chrysanthemum in full bloom."

The Master echoed, "This represents the sacral chakra; potential and the future."

Ellie now felt more in the swing of the Master's expectations.

"The next picture houses a block of yellow, like the sun at

the height of summer, delicate trumpets of daffodils blowing in the wind or newborn chicks. Again the colour changes as I look deeper into the picture. The shades change from very soft – a little like the colour of Avani's hair." The Master smiled. "The hues of colour change from deep, deep mustard to the pale golden yellow of corn in the field."

"You are doing well," the Master smiled contentedly. "This represents the solar plexus chakra, angelic guidance and wisdom."

Ellie turned towards green, one of her favourite colours. "This majestic, strong colour reminds me of woods, trees, nature, the many varying shades and textures of leaves, plants, stems and an evergreen backdrop to Mother Earth. I find this colour gentle, soothing and calming. Others avoid it, yielding to superstition that it is unlucky, yet all shades of green surround us at all times. As I gaze into the centre, the colour deepens and softens, the pattern swirling in never-ending patterns of light and dark, with tendrils of extremely dark green. It's almost black."

The Master continued, "This represents the heart chakra – balance and trust."

Ellie curled her legs together, enjoying her seemingly insignificant contribution. "The next is of a beautiful blue yet as I look more deeply into the colour, the shadings move and the picture depicts all shades of blue from the many colours of the oceans to the skies."

Ellie became excited realising this wasn't just an exercise of concentration. Allowing her mind to drift, looking deeper she excitedly shouted, "I can now see hieroglyphics!"

"Continue," motioned the Master.

"They are so incredible, the blues merge and then change patterns," shrieked Ellie. The Master beamed, "This represents the throat chakra – honesty and truth."

"The next," said Ellie joyfully, "is the magical mix of the visionary Indigo, the colour of the enlightened and the wise referred to by many as 'The third eye' – the seer, the mystic, the knowledgeable one. The tiny violet-perfumed flower mixed with the beauty of the creamy white snowdrop echoes hope after a dark, cold winter."

As she looked deeper, Ellie's eyes glazed, moving further into the picture, unaware that it was drawing her deeper and deeper into the hypnotic power of the colour. The Master interrupted her gently. "You have done well: you are nearly there. This represents the brow chakra – knowledge and insight."

Ellie yawned with tired relief. "The last but one," she said excitedly, "has a radiance of colour which is difficult to describe. It is an effervescent, luminescent blend of purple and deep purple, swirling and whirling around in complete harmony. Known as 'The colour of royalty,' it is regal in its own right and worn by many in ecclesiastical and legal circles to indicate power. Very few flowers can match its warmth, richness and intensity in colour and purpose, although the lilac, gladioli and pansy make a brave attempt. It is a powerful, strong, majestic, high spiritual colour."

Ellie again unconsciously felt drawn into the centre of the block of colour, struggling to resist the vibrancy and intensity of the swirling shades. Again the Master came to her rescue. "This represents the crown chakra – eternal truth and enlightened thought."

Ellie's gaze returned to the Master, her eyes slowly recovering after the intense concentration.

"You did well, my child," he reassured her. "You can relax now."

"Thank you," replied Ellie. "I wasn't sure exactly what you

wanted me to do. It is strange. I found some colours hypnotic and others calming. Some made me feel quite agitated."

"I know, but you did well."

"But I forgot to describe the little brown one," stuttered Ellie.

"Okay," replied the Master. "Tell me what you perceive about the little brown one."

"Well," responded Ellie, "it is brown, quite a flat contrasting colour to the others yet has density. It's quite small in comparison to the rest yet I am sure it has a purpose."

The Master smiled with twinkling eyes, "It represents the earth – being grounded."

"Oh, I understand," replied Ellie pensively, although she didn't understand at all…

14

Ellie remained still, her heart beating so fast she was sure he could hear. She glanced at the peaceful being. His eyes were closed. She, too, closed her eyes, guessing this was all part of the meeting.

As her senses drifted, she began to see in her mind's eye a mix of swirling shapes, a mosaic of colours, some brilliant, others dull, moving, whirling at an alarming pace, like fireworks shooting in unison into the sky. Feeling as if her head would explode, her mind swam as she struggled to maintain some kind of equilibrium. It was as if she was suddenly imprisoned in an enormous kaleidoscope. Waves of nausea overwhelmed Ellie's disorientated body, as her clammy hands gripped the crystal hard. Remembering Avani's advice, she began to breathe deeply, slowly achieving a natural rhythm. Calm overtook fear as the swirling manic colours settled into an agreeable, meaningful pattern.

Relaxed and moving into the moment, she was content to watch the patterns change until a picture emerged from a palette of greens, blue and purple. As she focused on the colours and moved into the experience, a picture suddenly evolved, instantly recognisable as the beautiful rugged Quantock Hills. Sharp intakes of breath relaxed her, allowing Ellie to move deeper into the moment.

She saw a small child sitting by a stream surrounded by clumps of heather, happily playing with the water. An uncontrollable squeal of delight came from her lips as she recognised the figure as herself. All sense of panic and fear deserted her. Aware of Ellie's meditative journey, the Master looked directly at her. Ellie felt his gaze, slowly opening her eyes.

"How do you feel?" he asked softly.

"Oh!" replied Ellie surprised, realising his eyes had been on her all the time. "It was…" she trembled. "It was like nothing I have every witnessed before."

"That is good. How do you feel?" the Master asked again.

Ellie struggled to find the words. "A little light-headed, a bit spaced out. I suppose… good… okay… a little scared."

The Master smiled reassuringly. "I am pleased. Rest assured that you will not experience the bombardment and onslaught of power in that way again. You will learn to control it."

Ellie's eyes widened. "I have to say it was truly amazing. I never knew I could do that. It really was an incredible experience."

"You will learn in time," replied the Master smiling.

Finding composure, Ellie sought answers. "Is this what these rooms are all about?"

"In part," replied the Master gently. "Share with me your impressions of the first room."

Ellie thought long and hard before answering. "Well," she said thoughtfully, "I guess it is all about healing. I say that because Avani told me I would sleep after spending time in it and by golly gosh I did!" She chuckled out loud and recalled sleeping many hours fully dressed, something she had never done before.

"You are correct. And this room?"

"I am not sure," replied Ellie. "It too has energy, but a different kind."

"Correct again. What do you sense?"

Ellie grew silent, emotions welling up inside her, eventually burbling out, "A completely messed-up mixture of feelings. When I glance at one of the pictures, I feel a bit tearful, wobbly almost, for no apparent reason. I have no foundation for feeling that way and yet there are some colours which make me feel good, happy, content and peaceful."

"Right again," said the Master. "So what do you feel is the connection? Be mindful: I said feel." As if emphasising the point, he placed his right hand across his heart. "Feel with your senses, your heart. I want you to talk to me about feelings and emotions. Put your analytical mind to one side for a moment."

Ellie swallowed hard whilst struggling to disconnect her rational mind. She was, after all, a journalist where logic, questioning, reasoning and analytical skills were essential to succeed. They sat in silence. As she didn't feel at all pressured, Ellie sat still and closed her eyes.

The image of the rambling Quantock Hills appeared on the screen of her mind. Words tumbled out as if they had a life of their own. With heartfelt affection, Ellie recalled the happy hours when she was about eleven visiting Aunt Sadie in her small terraced house in Bridgwater, close to the foot of the hills. Aunt Sadie was her father's eldest unmarried sister, a retired head teacher who proudly ruled her school with a rod of iron tempered with a wicked sense of humour. She fervently believed that discipline and respect were essential to mould the young generation. Although strict, she could also be fun. Ellie recalled the memory as being happy and free, with no conscious cares to speak of.

"I felt good and at peace," she said.

"So," continued the Master, "every time you recall that image you feel good, taking you back to happy childhood memories."

"Yes, that's right."

"So with that in mind, tell me more about this room."

Ellie's eyes scanned the room for clues, viewing each picture in turn, recalling her unexpected meditation. "Well, I suppose it can highlight memories."

"That is correct," answered the Master, "but be mindful that memories can be happy and sad. Some we choose to bury or conceal and pretend they never happened."

"Yes," replied Ellie, her face betraying withdrawal and awkwardness. Her mood was now a little flat. Feeling slightly downhearted and despondent, she whispered, "I suppose you are right."

The Master looked deep into her eyes. "The mind can play tricks and easily distort the truth."

Ellie felt flushed and hot, aware that this conversation had a hidden meaning which made her feel uneasy.

"What else do you see in this room?" the Master continued.

Ellie's eyes searched the content of the room, recalling briefly her description of every picture. "Nothing apart from pictures, two chairs, wooden polished floor, door, two small high windows, you and me."

Insistently, the Master said, "Look again!"

Ellie felt more uncomfortable by the second, aware that her clammy body was reacting badly to what she perceived as invasive persistent questions. Sighing and clasping her hands together for comfort, she looked at the Master for direction. He was smiling, so obviously wasn't disappointed in her.

She relaxed, her gaze scanning every detail of the room, counting the pictures, recalling her spontaneous interpretation of the colours. Her eyes settled on the little brown picture, seemingly so insignificant, yet she knew instinctively it was important. Ellie glanced up at the high ceiling, focusing on the two small circular windows, carefully positioned to let in just enough natural daylight to brighten the room.

She studied the Master's serene face, his wispy, fine blonde hair glinting in the shaft of sunlight effortlessly moving around the room, framing a face of gentle, loving wisdom. His frame was draped by a soft cream robe edged in blue and gold. The simple open neckline sat easily on his shoulders whilst wide sleeves graced hands of porcelain and his feet relaxed in openwork brown and gold leather sandals.

Then she saw it! The Master smiled as her eyes rested on the object she had missed. She sighed with relief and delight. On a small wooden table set neatly in the corner to the right of the Master stood a small lantern.

Ellie's eyes sparkled. "It just looks like a battered old lantern, a bit like the ones they used years ago, hooked onto the back of horse-drawn carriages taking passengers to the cities. The flame was surrounded by a metal-type arrangement preventing it from burning the wood."

"Continue..."

Ellie's excitement grew as she studied the little lamp. "It appears to be about fourteen inches high, with a small flame encased in some type of material, with a small handle on the top."

"And?" continued the Master.

Ellie stared at the lamp, wondering what else she was expected to see. Suddenly, she saw sight of a small bright flame or was it a light? She wasn't sure. What she was sure about was the colour – its core blue and the outside white edged with pink. The flame grew in size as she stared at it, continuing to grow until it filled the glass interior. The brightness reflected into the room, lighting every corner, each picture taking on a different mood, as if they were all the same block of colour.

Ellie sat mesmerised. "Oh, how beautiful, how absolutely incredible!"

She sank back into her chair, overawed and a little ashamed. The flame continued to burn bright and high. Ellie had been so overcome by the enormity of the pictures that she had forgotten to search the room for all it had to offer. Then came a realisation that she noticed big things, forgetting the importance and value of small things.

Settled into the chair, Ellie's eyes riveted on the flame, which continued to burn brightly. The Master smiled with deep satisfaction. He had achieved his aim. They sat in silence.

Eventually, Ellie could stand it no longer, asking, "May I please ask?"

The Master interrupted with a twinkle in his eyes. "Certainly, my child."

Ellie continued, "Can you please tell me the significance of these rooms?"

"Of course. I was not teasing. I just wanted to see, and understand how much knowledge you had acquired during your lifetime and discover how observant you are. You did well."

"As I explained before, I have been granted a mission, which I gladly accepted. Let us move to my room where I feel protected and comfortable."

The Master gestured Ellie to follow him, sweeping past her slowly, the lantern in his right hand. Once settled, he continued.

"You see, Ellie, this room was prepared especially for me. It is where I can commune with the Higher Realms and they with me. As you have seen with your own eyes, this house and land has been transformed from a soulless place to one of harmonious beauty. I cannot exist where there is chaos, unhappiness and neglect. To achieve my aim, certain conditions had to be fulfilled to enable me to understand and guide my chosen charges."

"People you mean?" asked Ellie.

"Yes, I suppose, but I prefer to call them 'invited charges.' The Healing Room is where their energies will be replenished and fortified in a manner of their choosing, as you experienced. The Chakra Room is where they will gain insight into their present life, their existence prior to this lifetime and the potential ahead of them."

Ellie gulped and swallowed hard. Her throat was dry, her voice a mere whisper. "The lantern?" she stammered, pointing.

"This little seemingly insignificant lantern makes everything possible," answered the Master. "This is why I said to you earlier, this is 'true power'."

Ellie flushed in embarrassment, listening to words refusing to register. Ignoring Ellie's discomfort, the Master continued.

"This burning light was transported to planet earth many, many years ago, programmed to wait for the right time to be unearthed by someone with intentions of pure innocence. It was to be placed in the hands of wise spiritual human beings, unknowingly pre-programmed to know what to do. The brilliance comes from the power of the portal stone, where energies of earth and the Higher Realms merge, an etheric bridge between two dimensions. It reminds me of home."

"Yes, yes…" replied Ellie, desperately trying to justify her discomfort. "I did not notice it at first, possibly because the flame was so tiny yet when I looked hard at the light just now, the flame grew. Why?"

The Master smiled. "It was merely assessing and attuning your power," he explained. Although not really understanding, Ellie nodded in agreement, musing silently.

"The power is a small stone, not a naked flame. Although it looks like a living flame, it's a power house beyond man's comprehension, one so powerful it can accomplish anything."

The Master's voice broke her train of thought. "Do you now understand why it was hidden so carefully, away from anyone who may consider profiting from its power? Unbeknown to mortals, if it fell into the wrong hands, it could destroy those who stole it."

"In other words, the light burns bright on purity, love and trust. You are here because you trust your thoughts, which, most of the time, are honest and pure. As a human being, you would not let anybody down or intentionally hurt them."

"Brother Peter carefully concealed the precious portal stone inside the shell of this lantern, so that if it was found before the timing was right, thieves would toss it aside as being worthless. Over aeons of time, an angel has been guarding it, awaiting my visit. It was removed carefully during the transformation. The lantern was buried on the land surrounding Fosseway Hall. Hence, that is why we are here."

"Oh, I see!" commented Ellie in a daze.

She sat dumbfounded. Words failed her. They sat in silence, looking at one another with a deepening understanding passing between them.

"Now I know the connection of the rooms," asked Ellie, "does that mean I cannot come again?"

"Would you like to?"

"Oh yes. I feel so good when close to you. I just know I need to see you before you go back to wherever."

The Master chuckled quietly. "Of course, my child. I will be pleased to talk with you at any time."

As Ellie jumped up to leave she blurted, "Oh, I forgot to tell you, Sam called. Sam is a friend, the one I told you about. He desperately needs your help. He has been a friend of mine for years now. We met briefly when I was attending a seminar in Birmingham and then somehow I lost track of him. He contacted me out of the blue about six months ago. Apparently, he had been working in the Middle East for a while. He rang to catch up on local news and things."

The Master thought for quite some time. "Why yes, I do need to see him."

"How will he know how to contact you – that is if he is willing to come? He can be obstinate and stubborn. How will I or he know?"

The Master smiled with overtones of exhaustion "Speak to Avani. She will arrange."

Ellie's spirits lifted as she jumped up. "Oh thank you, thank you! I will see you again."

The Master waved her to leave. "Speak to Avani," he repeated. "She will arrange everything."

Beaming, Ellie moved towards the door with a thoughtful, "Until next time…" At that, the Master pulled his robe closely around him and closed his eyes.

15

THE MASTER MET the boy the following day during one of his early morning strolls. Deep-seated unhappiness exuded from the boy's despondency and hopelessness, which was firmly etched into his young face. The Master recalled the boy's heart-wrenching story of how he felt loved by his mother, but was tolerated with disdain by his stepfather and half brothers. The Master decided to report back that this young person was going to be one of his charges.

Walking through the fragrant alpine garden, he spied the youth crouching down weeding, totally absorbed in his own private world, oblivious to the fact he was no longer alone. The Master waited patiently for the boy to sense his presence.

"Hello young man!" he called. "Do you remember me?"

"Yes, sir," said the boy getting up from his knees.

"I have been thinking about you since our last meeting. I would like to get to know you and to spend some time with you. Would you like to come up and see me at the Hall later today?"

Staring in disbelief at the stranger's request, and feeling awkward, unprepared and self-conscious, the boy fiddled with his trowel while looking down at his feet. After a pause of uncomfortable silence, he looked up, finding his voice.

"Why do you want to see me? Have I done something wrong?"

The Master smiled, shaking the boy's limp, clammy, grubby hand, saying, "Avani will show you the way. Till later then…"

The boy stared into the distance watching the Master walk slowly past the recently completed intricate alpine garden. Suddenly, Avani appeared, as if from nowhere, introducing herself as a loyal friend, so as not to alarm the lad.

"Do not be frightened or apprehensive, Joe," she said reassuringly. "The man you met is very, very special and would like to get to know you better."

Wiping tense, dirty hands on the pocket of his jeans, the boy gulped, whispering, "Me?"

"Yes, you."

Avani's eyes twinkled. "You are special, too, in your own way."

The boy stared at her with panic in his eyes. She responded by giving him an angelic hug of warmth and reassurance. He sighed with unquenched emotion. The last hug was from his Ma. Tears flowed. Avani smiled, touching his grubby hand.

"I will come and collect you later," she said. "Don't worry. Everything will be fine." With a smile and flourish of her soft gown she was gone.

Once out of sight, the boy dropped his trowel sobbing, running as fast as his legs would carry him to find Pip. Immersed in dust and gloom, Pip was cleaning out the hen house. He emerged on hearing Joe's anxious cry. He looked up, agitated when he saw the state of him. The lad's words tumbled out in uncontrollable spurts.

"I am good, Pip… really I am. I am… good!"

Pip locked the run, greeting Joe with a huge bear hug, drawing him close. "Now, calm down laddie," he said with concern, "and tell me all about it."

Pip recognised an inexplicable wave of uplifting righteousness encircling the estate. For the first time for many years, he felt vibrant, alive and in great physical shape, with looks belying his age. Not daring to question why, he accepted that something indefinable, beyond human understanding was unfolding, and somehow he was caught up in it. As long as it was good, he was content and happy to go with the flow.

The weird happenings in Dorcas Wood reinforced Pip's investigative findings – his inability to focus on the job in hand, the time frame jolting out of sync, speeding up, then slowing down to a standstill, mislaying time. Privately, he dared to believe his prayers would be answered and that one day David and his mother would return. His priority for now was to pacify a frightened young man, a lad he had become very fond of.

"Come, Joe," he said with his arm on the boy's shoulder. "Let's have a nice cup of tea. Tea always tastes much better after tears."

They sat together on a rickety old bench close to the hen run, where they watched the hens' antics with amusement. "You wouldn't believe how different in ways they are if you didn't see it with your own eyes," said Pip.

"Them townsfolk know nothing!" responded Joe, a little annoyed.

He felt better after washing his hands and face, but needed to cry. Then Avani appeared.

"I didn't see or hear you coming," spurted Joe, with soapsuds on his jumper.

"Come on," she smiled. "The Master is waiting, and it is okay with Pip?"

"The Master?" The boy shied away from her.

She laughed. "That is what I call him."

"Oh, I see," replied Joe somewhat unconvinced.

As they walked towards the house, Joe looked at the building with fresh eyes. "It really is awesome," he uttered wide-eyed.

"Yes, I suppose it is," she replied smiling.

They climbed the steps to the huge front door. Joe brushed the backs of the huge bronze dogs with the back of his hand, checking that they were really solid.

Avani accompanied him to the Chakra Room, where the Master was ready to greet them, the lit lantern in the middle of the wooden table, to his right. Joe's eyes nearly popped out of his head.

"Wow, I never did! I never ever seen anything like this!"

The Master beamed. "Thank you, Avani. You know when to return."

Nodding, she left, knowing that Joe was safe in the company of the Master. He turned to Joe with a radiant smile, ushering him to sit on the little chair.

"I am so pleased you are here."

Joe's head buzzed with questions, unknowingly absorbing calming energy, soon feeling reassured.

"Joe, I asked you here because I know I can help you," stated the Master, in a kind authoritative manner.

"In what way?" asked the puzzled boy, easing his frame into the middle of the chair.

"Where shall we begin?" asked the Master. "You love colour?"

"You bet!" replied the boy enthusiastically. "I love the borders when the flowers are out in full bloom. The mix of colour can be seen from the other side of the lake."

The Master smiled approvingly. "I agree! Joe, you seem to be so unhappy, carrying a heavy weight on your shoulders for such a young person. Would you say your life has been difficult?"

Joe looked down at his feet. Silence reigned, then awkwardly he uttered a muffled "Yes, I suppose so. I never knew my real Da."

He shuffled his feet, twisting the edge of his jumper into tight knots to avoid bursting into tears, recalling images of heartache and misery. As he stared at the Master, tears welled in big brown eyes and his shoulders tensed.

"Joe, listen. Close your eyes, breathe deeply and remain quiet and still until you feel able to continue talking."

To the right of the wooden chair, carefully placed by Avani, stood a little wooden box brimming to the top with semi-precious stones. They sat in silence. When the boy looked settled, the Master asked, "Joe, please choose one of nature's gems from the little box."

With hesitation, Joe reluctantly did as he was asked, sensing the density of the rocks between his fingers, finally selecting one which he withdrew with surprising confidence.

"What did you choose?"

As Joe looked at the crystal in his podgy hand, the Master identified it as Rose Quartz. The Master smiled and they sat in silence.

"Tell me Joe. How do you feel?"

Joe swallowed hard; this was an unfamiliar question. "Well Sir," he spluttered, a little tongue-tied.

The Master interrupted. "You have no need to call me Sir. Please let me be your friend. I would like to help you."

Joe stared back at him in confused amazement. His body was contorted with pain, as if a knife had been stabbed through his heart. He guessed that the Master was waiting for a reply.

They sat in silence for a while longer and then Joe spoke. "I feel sort of empty and painful, like there is nothing in me. Even when I work, eat and sleep, the pain still hurts."

Joe stared at the Master, tears trickling down his crimson

cheeks. The Master's glance revealed the essence of the meeting.

"I know Joe. Have you courage?"

The boy's posture changed and was now upright and alert.

"Oh yes. I wanted to die, you know. That's why I ran away."

Joe's frame crumpled as he glanced at the Master's expressive gaze. "I know. You must have been very unhappy. Joe, please listen to me. In order to dissolve the emptiness and find contentment, you need to accept and understand that you have done nothing wrong. You are not responsible for your unhappiness."

"'Course I understand," said Joe fiercely. "It's that Jake's fault. He hates me and..." he stuttered amidst a deluge of tears, "Ma would still be here..."

"Hush! Joe, listen to me, I mean really listen. It is important that you understand."

Joe shrugged his shoulders in unquestioning acceptance of his plight. Silence reigned. The Master continued. "Joe, look at me. Do you trust me?"

"I suppose so, though I don't know you," stammered Joe.

"Will you allow me to help you?"

"Yes, okay," replied Joe grudgingly, looking down at the floor, mindlessly turning the warm smooth stone over and over in the cup of his hands.

"Hold the stone in your hands. Feel its warmth, smoothness, facets and vibrations."

Joe did as he was asked, sensing its beauty, shape and energy.

"Now," said the Master, "look at all the coloured pictures surrounding you. Which one are you drawn to? Which do you like best?"

Without any hesitation Joe answered, "The red one!"

The Master beamed at Joe.

"Now I would like you to really look at the picture and tell me what you see."

Joe wriggled in his chair despondently uttering "Just red!" Then suddenly frustration and impatience disappeared as an expression of excitement filled his face, his eyes alight with joy. The Master looked on approvingly.

The young girl, immediately recognised by Joe, seemed to be identical to a precious photograph of his mother as a young woman, which he squirreled into his trouser pocket when he ran away from home. As his focus became more intense, the block of red slowly changed into a series of moving pictures.

"It's Ma! It is Ma! It is like being at the cinema!" Joe swung his legs to and fro in excitement.

"Keep looking Joe," said the Master, delighted at the reaction. "Relax. Watch."

The picture revealed a pretty, happy, slim, blonde, carefree young woman, arms locked tight with a fresh-faced young man by her side. He looked a reliable, lovable lad with a mop of thick dark hair, determined to enjoy the fun of the fair. Joe noticed that the girl was wearing an 18th birthday badge.

He became enthralled as he followed the excited couple amble around the fairground, trying their luck at the coconut shy and hoopla stall. Joe laughed watching the antics of the young man keenly trying to win a prize by throwing ping-pong balls into empty goldfish bowls, eventually succeeding and winning an enormous bright yellow teddy bear, which he passed to the girl with excited hugs and kisses. He saw them walk hand in hand, enjoying enormous toffee apples, laughing, joking and teasing each other as their teeth got stuck on the gooey toffee.

The young man confidently manoeuvred dodgem cars, bumping into rival cars with a wicked determination, cleverly avoiding being knocked. The girl clutched him tightly as they emerged from the Haunted House, arms wrapped round one another as the car entered the Tunnel of Love. Joe sat transfixed, enjoying the bright lights, movement, noise and action of the fair. His hands and feet moved with excitement as he became caught up in the whirling motion, noise, craziness, screams and heady movement of the carousel.

Settling into his seat, Joe silently wondered how the Hall could have a film of his Ma when she was young. He continued to watch the young couple, who were obviously head over heels in love. He followed their weekly routine at work, home and planning their marriage.

With little squeals of delight, he watched the planned summer wedding, which was attended by a small happy gathering of friends and family. The bride was dressed like a fairy princess in a full-length white dress, with layers and layers of chiffon and tulle. His heart reached out to the nervous groom waiting patiently, grinning, proud and deliriously happy.

Suddenly the picture accelerated. Joe blinked, his hands and feet still. The picture changed to a hospital ward. The girl was in a single side room, with bleeping equipment and flashing monitors. The young man and family were waiting outside excited. Doctors and nurses surrounded her tiny frame as twin boys were safely delivered, the proud parents ecstatic. Joe sighed, wiping away a wayward tear.

As the years sped by, he saw the family move from a small one-bedroom flat to an end-terraced house with a small garden at the back, overlooking sprawling grassy fields and shops close by. He admired the young father's disciplined work routine at the local engineering plant, following his father's footsteps, though taking on a different role.

Wistfully he saw the father play with the boys, pleased

with his young wife's contribution to the household budget by working part-time in a local grocer's shop.

Joe squirmed as he watched the young man's nervous pride and embarrassment as the workforce noisily elected him Social Club Secretary, a role he fulfilled with enthusiasm. Joe warmed to the natural born gregarious organiser, whose social hours revolved around organising works' events and – more recently – coach excursions for families to enjoy.

Joe sat glued to his seat, completely at ease. Suddenly the picture accelerated. Joe's posture altered as the mood changed.

The snow fell thick and fast, covering the ground as far as the eye could see. It looked like a typical bitter November winter afternoon. Joe saw children on their toboggans, cars marooned in snow drifts, people busy with shovels clearing paths. He watched sheep, cattle and horses struggling for food and shelter as farmers laboured to reach their livestock. As far as he could tell, the landscape for miles around was blanketed in deep snow, reminding him of Ma's favourite traditional Christmas cards.

He saw the young father on the phone, slightly agitated, and groups of people chatting together. As he continued to focus, he noted an air of concern. Then as if by magic the young father took control and the group disbanded.

Three coaches pulled up outside the works main building. After excited families boarded, the vehicles slowly moved away in tandem and noisy excited children on back seats waved madly to their friends in the following coach. The young father and family in the first coach were relieved, but mentally exhausted now that the ambitious trip was finally happening after unexpected trauma and hiccups due to unpredictable weather.

Joe watched with pangs of envy as families alighted from the coach and rowdily entered the foyer of a West End theatre.

Suddenly, without any warning, the picture accelerated again. He sat silently, annoyed and thinking, "I wish it wouldn't do that!"

Happy people shopped until they dropped. Laughing and chatting, they made impromptu purchases which were concealed in brightly coloured store carrier bags, then wearily trudged to an agreed vantage point to board their coach for the homeward run. The coaches slowly moved in convoy, converging on a comfortable family-orientated country hotel for evening supper. The children were animated, but some were so exhausted they slept in their mothers' arms. Joe sighed wishing he was there.

As darkness fell the coaches left for the long journey home. Joe chuckled as lubricated by alcohol some passengers sang at the tops of their voices. Some sat quietly whilst others dozed.

The picture accelerated again. Joe sat motionless, wishing it would not do that, when suddenly he sat bolt upright in horror as he watched coach one and two turn off the motorway onto a slip road. Then, as if in slow motion, coach number three swerved, lost control and flipped over. With hands to his mouth in shock, he witnessed the horror of people being thrown out of windows like rag dolls. Some lay motionless. The engine reeled precariously and squealed as the coach's wheels began spinning eerily.

Joe spied wisps of black smoke tinged with orange curl from the engine. He saw that the driver was trapped. People were screaming out the names of loved ones. Suddenly, there was an explosion and a fireball lit the sky. More screams were followed by silence.

Joe stared at the Master in revulsion and shock, silently questioning what could possibly be the point of watching this terrifying development. Feeling agitated, emotional and uncomfortable he could contain his words no longer.

"Why did you encourage me to watch this?" he asked.

Looking into his eyes, the Master said gently, "Please Joe, keep watching."

Joe scuffed his right shoe in annoyance. He was upset, choosing not to see any more, but reluctantly his gaze returned to the picture, which accelerated. Joe sighed with relief to see the young father and family were safe after being miraculously thrown clear from imminent danger.

Bewildered groups stood aimlessly; families were crumpled in shock; wailing pierced the night air as shaken, frightened lives were broken and destroyed. The young father stood shock stilled, mortified, distraught and enveloped in a cloud of guilt. The meticulously planned outing had ended in tragedy. For some, life had changed for ever.

Joe witnessed heart-wrenching funerals. After the longed for inquest, the result was an open verdict. He cried uncontrollably as he watched helpless groups of bereft families speechless, sobbing and huddling together for comfort. Feeling uncomfortable, unable to look any more, Joe picked at his fingernails, the horrific scene revolving around and around in his head.

He saw the young family safe at home. The young boys were shaken, but otherwise unhurt. The mother cried inconsolably, nursing a fractured right leg. Incredibly, the young father suffered only superficial cuts and bruises.

Joe cowered into the chair as he watched the young father's amiable mood change to one of uncontrollable anger, punching the air with unresolved emotion, hitting the living room walls with clenched fists in incandescent anguish. Joe winced as the man sat with his head in his hands, inconsolable grief eating away at the person he once was, now riddled with guilt. The loss of friends, work colleagues, beloved parents, an aunt, a twin sister and his unborn child, created a stinging grief, which was raw and transparent.

The black cloud descended unmercifully as nothing consoled or eased the wall of anger. The distraught father screamed into the ether through heart-wrenching tears.

"It was my fault, my fault … my decision!" he shouted. Torment reverberated in his skull. Joe's heart went out to the now unshaven, unkempt, broken-hearted man, the burden for loss of life too heavy to bear.

The police report read: "Accident. Cause – black ice." Joe felt the young father's pain. Twisting and turning the edge of his jumper into a tight ball, anguish affected his solar plexus. Instinctively, he wanted to comfort the young man, as he menacingly questioned out loud, "Whyeee…?" over and over again.

"Why did the first two coaches drive safely off the slip road? Why did the third coach lose control, roll over and burst into flames? Why?" Joe screamed words of comfort out loud, as he buried his head in his hands, weeping.

Despite approaches from colleagues, the young father refused to accept the Accident Investigation Team's report, which read: "Coach tyre tracks show the driver a little too far over to the right, driving blindly into the path of a five-metre stretch of invisible black ice. In treacherous conditions, hazard increased by sudden drop in temperature."

Tears filled Joe's eyes. He wished he could ease the young father's pain. The man read the accident report again and again, refusing to believe that he had been vindicated, blanking everyone who tried to reach him. Obstinately refusing to listen, he was unrelenting in the belief that the accident was his fault.

Joe saw him rudely decline professional help, refusing to discuss the tragedy with anyone. His temper frequently became volatile. With the burden of guilt growing daily, he believed he deserved to be persecuted and punished. In consequence, family life became fragmented beyond repair. Sadly, the twins grew fearful, their mother enduring the trauma in silence. She was sucked into a dark void, unable to give or receive solace from the man she loved.

Stinging tears streamed down Joe's face as he witnessed the father's pain and drunken bouts of alcoholic temper. Tantrums were fuelled by impassioned guilt. His immediate family was safe, but workmates were bereft. Watching helplessly, the young father was unable to face his own reflection. Hating work, home and detesting everything and everybody, he became aggressive and distant.

Joe's throat ached with misery. The once jovial mild-mannered man's hard-working personality changed to one of anger, aggression and cruelty. A close-up of his face revealed a man in torment and pain.

The picture accelerated again. Joe watched the fast-track scenario of a guilt-torn wretch of a man unable to sleep, drinking to blot out memories. Joe understood. The father's thoughts transcribed into the words: "Why was his coach last? How did he, Rose and boys, fast asleep at the back of the coach, survive by being thrown clear? Why did only eleven people escape? Why did the others burn to death?"

Joe's heart and head ached with crying. He felt sorry for the man, beginning to understand how a burden of guilt and grief could destroy a family, leaving an isolated mother, now a solitary lonely figure pining for a lost baby girl and the man she once knew. The man she adored, unable to receive her love, now impotent. Feeling lost and helpless, she was unable to find solace in his company, becoming incapable of consolation. Watching her beloved husband drink himself to oblivion, she retreated to a private lonely world of emptiness.

With hands shielding his eyes, Joe blurted, "I don't want to see any more. Please, please, please turn it off!" As he spoke, the depth of red changed, softened, swirled and whirled until it settled into a dark crimson.

"I wish I hadn't watched that, it was horrid," said Joe, wiping his eyes with his sleeve, dredging deep suppressed emotions to the surface where they could do no more harm.

The Master got up from his chair, putting his hand on Joe's shoulder to give him comfort. "Look at me Joe," he said. "What did you see and understand?"

Wailing and stamping his feet in annoyed disgust, Joe exploded, "Was that me Ma?"

"Yes, my child. It was the best way I know to help you understand why Jake, your Mum and the twins reacted as they did towards you. Sadly, they absorbed so much deep-seated unhappiness that it became part of them, creating a deeply embedded unhappy furrow of enraged grief. They never found the courage to explore their feelings."

"But they looked so happy at the fair," Joe responded.

"Yes," said the Master gently. "But you see Joe, in life every action has a reaction, sometimes resulting in unexpected consequences. Sadly, Jake will never come to terms with what happened that November night until the day he dies. Your Ma was grieving for the loss of her unborn baby and the cruel indifference of the man she loved. Children unknowingly look to their parents as role models. The twins grew up in a household of antagonism, aggression, indifference and spite. That is all they knew. Happy times were a distant memory."

"But why hate me?"

"As Jake kicked against love and kindness, the twins did the same."

Joe sat still. His unhappy face was stinging with tears as he rocked to and fro for comfort. Silence and stillness filled the room. He relived the scenario, sadness replacing hate.

"But he was so nice. Everyone liked him!"

"Yes, he was," replied the Master smiling. "Remember, Joe, that life is all about decisions and consequences. How you handle them is the key."

"So Jake isn't my Da?"

"No Joe, you were conceived with love. Your father showed Rose warmth and comfort when she needed it most and her natural body rhythm responded. Although not planned, the pregnancy was meant to be, to give her hope, to continue living her life. You are the result! She loved you with every fibre of her being. You were not tainted with an unhappy past."

"Your mother unknowingly sought comfort. She needed someone to love and care for. In you she found pure love. You were not contaminated by the weight of guilt."

"But…Jake…" interrupted Jo, probing further.

"Jake did not need to carry the burden of guilt. The accident was nothing more than a tragic unavoidable misfortune. The Investigation Accident Team proved it."

The Master sat back in his chair to allow his breathing to settle before adding: "There are two tragedies here Joe. First is the horrific coach crash, which occurred due to a series of unfortunate circumstances. The second tragedy was more complex. Jake rejected all offers of help, preferring to wallow in a life of desolation and misery. Sadly those close to him suffered, so the circle of unhappiness reached out to many."

Joe swallowed hard.

"You, my young man, brought immeasurable joy and love into your mother's life. Don't ever forget it. When you think of Jake, feel sad for him. He needs kind thoughts. The twins need to learn that compassion and kindness achieve far more than spite, aggression and bullying."

Joe sat still, his eyes swollen and red with crying. His sobbing subsided. He recalled life at home and the special bond he shared with his mother. He also recalled the unexpected friendship and kindness he found with Pip, sharing the beauty and magic of all living forms.

The lad shivered as his mind turned to Jake's energy, the hopes and dreams he had as a young man and the wretch he had become. "I don't hate him," he snivelled. "I feel sorry for him. He needs help."

"That is how it should be," replied the Master softly. "Remember Joe that kindness is always returned. You may not be able to help Jake, but perhaps one day, someone will."

They sat in agreeable silence. Joe scanned the room, his heart beating like a drum. "I don't understand," he said. "I got really upset, angry even, yet somehow I feel better."

The Master beamed. "Joe, you have learned a valuable lesson today – to look beyond what you see. You will be fine now. If at first you do not understand someone or something, look deeper. The answer is clearly there! Remember that there is always a reason why. Look forward now, young man. You have your whole life ahead of you."

Joe wobbled as he got up to go.

"Before you go Joe, would you like us to meet again?" asked the Master.

Joe's eyes widened. "Promise you're not going to show me anything horrid or scary?"

"No, my child. I just want to take this opportunity of exploring all your doubts and fears."

The Master escorted Joe to the crystal room, beckoning him gently to the little chair, ensuring that the crystal was still in his hand.

"This is a wonderful healing room. You are safe and protected. Relax and sleep. When you awake, all the frightening visions you have just experienced will be nothing more than distant memories. You will fear the past no more."

"I will ask Avani to come for you soon. Rest a while. Sleep, my child. I will see you tomorrow."

Joe yawned, his body relaxing as the crystal energy began its work. His eyelids closed and he slept.

16

Joe woke to find Avani patiently waiting for him. She smiled, gently saying, "You look rested." Joe stretched sleepily. He returned her smile. "Are you ready?"

"Yes," said Joe yawning. Quietly they made their way downstairs into the bright sunshine.

"Do you know your way from here?" Avani asked.

"Yes. Thank you."

"See you same time tomorrow" called Avani as she disappeared into the little blue room at the end of the hall.

Joe ran so fast all the way back to the cottage that he bumped into the back of Pip, who dropped the wheelbarrow in surprise.

"You look good!" remarked Pip. "Are you glad you went?"

"Yes, I do feel good Pip. Why, and what happened, I cannot rightly say. I feel sort of spaced out."

Pip laughed, scratching his balding head in surprise.

"Right young 'un. Grab a fork and let's get this border complete before teatime."

Joe felt lighter. He ate his tea in silence, pushing the peas and cottage pie round and round his plate.

"Thought that was your favourite," noticed Pip.

"Yeah it is, but don't want any more," Joe responded. "I think I will go and sit by the lake."

Joe sat by the lake, watching reflections dancing on the water.

Looking up at the house, which now held a meaning for him, he questioned why he didn't feel angry and hurt. Unnerving thoughts focusing on the day's events flooded into his mind until Joe decided, "Perhaps he did help me after all!"

Avani arrived at eleven as before. She always appeared on time, as if from nowhere. She truly was beautiful – magical, gentle and fragrant like the beauty of a full-blown rose. She waited patiently, caressing the tops of flowers with barely a touch. When Joe was ready, Avani took his hand.

The Master was waiting for them in the Chakra Room. He beamed, delighted to see them, saying with delight, "I knew you would come."

Joe gave a sheepish smile and without being asked sat in the little chair. Avani disappeared with a flourish, smiling and leaving behind a heady floral fragrance, which Joe found pleasing. He knew nothing about perfume, recognising only flower fragrances.

They sat in silence, smiling at one another. "Do you remember much about yesterday?" asked the Master.

"Not really," replied Joe, "except that I feel different and better somehow. I have been thinking a lot about Ma and Jake; they just remind me of being sad."

"You have done well young Joe."

The Master adjusted his robe, stood up and asked Joe to stand. As they held hands, he continued, "Do you really understand the reason for our meeting?"

"To make me well," Joe gulped.

The Master chuckled. "You are extremely healthy, young man. Dare I say robust?"

The Master put his hand on Joe's shoulder and looked directly into his eyes before continuing, "The reason for our meeting is for you to understand who you are, how far you have travelled as an entity and where you are heading. You have a marvellous future ahead of you young man. In order to reach out and achieve your full potential, it is important to completely understand who you are and why you react to some situations whilst choosing to ignore others."

They dropped hands. Joe returned to the little chair. Looking around the room, Joe tried to remember the contents of yesterday's meeting, finding it incredibly difficult to do so.

"No matter," the Master replied tuning into Joe's thoughts

"Joe, yesterday we explored the here and now. Today, I would like you to explore a past memory, a life-time that colours your everyday thoughts and feelings. Are you happy to try?"

Joe glanced around the room, the sunlight glinting on the pictures to his right, highlighting the patina frames. Taking the little crystal out of his trouser pocket and holding it tightly in his hands, he sat deep in thought.

"There is no rush," reassured the Master, who sat quietly with his eyes closed. Joe followed the sunlight, seeing for the first time the wisdom, warmth and fragility of the Being.

He waited until he stirred. "Please, will it hurt?"

The Master opened his eyes. "The only thing that can hurt you, Joe, is fear of the unknown, of what tomorrow will bring."

Joe felt foolish. He looked down at his feet, the crystal in his hands, then suddenly sat upright saying, "I am ready!"

"Good. Then we will begin." They sat smiling, a bond of trust forged.

"What colour are you drawn to today Joe?" queried the Master.

Joe's eyes circled the room in apprehension. "I like the yellow one. I don't know why, but the yellow one."

"That is fine," acknowledged the Master. "Now Joe relax,

remember to trust and all will be well."

Joe sat transfixed. He thought of heady, hot, sunny days as he focused on the bright yellow block of colour, which softened, brightened, darkened, swirled and moved gently with images appearing and then disappearing.

Joe repositioned his stance to enable him to focus more intently. He allowed his eyes and mind to drift. The image revealed golden sandy beaches, with waves lapping gently against smooth shingle, which created a wonderful soothing whooshing sound. He watched a balloon seller trying to tame a huge bunch of balloons – mainly red, orange and yellow – struggling to hold them against a wilful breeze. With delight, he spied some of them breaking free, floating away high into the sky. His gaze observed a mix of people busy, content in a world of relaxed enjoyment. He struggled to keep awake, his heavy eyelids eager to close.

The Master watched over his charge with loving care. "Joe," he said reassuringly, "talk to me and tell me what you see."

"I am at the seaside. I can see a sandy beach full of people. There is a fair in the background. People are laughing and chatting. Some are swimming, others paddling. I am looking out to sea. I'm high on a building over the sea. Wait; I am on a pier. I'm standing on the pier. Hey it's great! I can see the sea crashing beneath me. I can see it through the slats of the walkway."

Totally absorbed, Joe's face lit up with joy. He heard the Master's soft voice way off in the distance say, "Joe, listen to me. Allow your mind to drift. Become part of the picture. Tell me, what you see, sense and feel."

Joe allowed his mind and senses to drift, moving into the heart of the picture. "I am nineteen years of age, twenty in July, an idealist, waiting to go to university to study law. I am here in Brighton with Jack, a great pal I met through Mum's work in

Scotland. We have good fun together. The sun is hot, a little too hot for me, as I have blue eyes and fair skin. I burn in the sun."

"We are exploring the pier entertainment and have just come across a bunch of lads, laughing, joking and flirting with a group of girls. I guess we have been on the pier for almost an hour, trying the slot machines and generally mucking about. The boisterous lads keep chasing the giggling girls, who in turn chase the boys, like a crazy game of hide-and-seek. It is getting hotter; the sun's bright in a cloudless sky. We sit on a bench facing the sea at the end of the pier, the sun on our face as we share a bottle of ginger beer."

"My Mam tells me I am good looking, diplomatic, a good listener, strong minded and adventurous. I guess she is right. After all, she knows me best. Jack and I had the chance to visit while his father holds business meetings in London. We travelled down with Bert, a chauffeur of very few words. His remit was to deposit us safely into a small hotel and collect us at three o'clock precisely the following day."

"Jack and I laugh a lot. We watch the other lads in disbelief, as they are cheeky and almost rude whereas I suppose you could call us shy. We were brought up to respect girls. The sun is very hot, so we remain on the seat as watching the others got boring. We notice a couple of the girls hang back from the others and give us the eye. We giggle. Suddenly one of them trips and like gentlemen we come to her aid. The others laugh and jeer, but I do not care. She is nice. We all sit on the seat talking and looking out to sea."

"Her name is Dorothy May. She is just about five foot tall, with a cute nose, big blue eyes and an amazing smile. Maureen, her friend, hangs back until we persuade her to join us. We chat and laugh, and the four of us get on really well."

The picture accelerates as Joe added, "We are all together in the ballroom of a small hotel with garish wallpaper. A noisy live band is playing. The loud music is simply amazing. We dance and fool around to the music. It's great fun! I like Dorothy as she is brilliant company, and oh boy, can she dance! We enjoy a late supper together in the Dining Room, explaining that we are only down for a couple of days, returning home tomorrow. We promise amongst lots of hugs and stolen kisses to keep in touch, as everyone does in the excitement of the night."

Joe's face creased in annoyance as the picture accelerates. "I am in sitting in the highly polished sitting room of Dorothy's home. Her tall, thin, spectacled father is totally engrossed in today's newspaper, looking lost and uncomfortable in an enormous armchair. He fails to notice us while her rounded, nervous mother fusses about. Dorothy and I sit silently on a worn out settee waiting patiently for afternoon tea. It is difficult as her father seems reluctant to engage in conversation, which creates an atmosphere of discord. Feeling awkward, I politely look at Dorothy, waiting to be seated for tea."

"Tea is served in the best room. A crochet white lace tablecloth graces the table. The heavy brown teapot sits on an obviously handmade trivet. China cups, saucers and plates are strategically placed around the table. A folded white cloth hides the teapot, which I am politely told is to keep it warm whilst the tea brews. Despite shortages due to the war and economic uncertainty the spread is fabulous. There are delicious egg sandwiches, laid by faithful hens, fish paste – my favourite – and scrummy homemade cakes. Her parents are country folk and eager to please. On the whole, they made me feel quite welcome."

"Jack continued to write to Maureen, then the letters tailed off, but he wasn't upset as he met someone in Norfolk, who hunts, fish and shoots. Although great fun, Maureen would never have fitted in, as she wasn't in his social class, but Jack is pleased for me. I really like Dorothy; she is in my thoughts every day."

The picture accelerated yet again. "Although a little cloudy, the September day is warm, the sun breaking through now and again. I see a small country church and hear bells ringing. Dressed in white, the bride emerges happy and glowing, her arm on a proud, bewildered groom. The dress is perfect for her frame, with every bead and pearl hand-stitched with love. Looking happy and a little embarrassed, the Matron of Honour is dressed in a long satin gown of blue."

Suddenly Joe shrieked, "The groom is me!" The Master smiled, saying, "Continue."

"I don't believe what I am wearing. It looks like a skirt!"

"Look again, my child. Relax and move back into the picture." The reassuring voice settled Joe.

"I am wearing a kilt, a tartan of pale blue and green. I recognise it as the Mackenzie tartan. I am in a group walking to a nearby pub a few hundred yards away, where we are greeted with shouts of 'Hooray! Congratulations!' Everyone is so happy for us, apart from Dorothy's parents, who seem sad. We eat, shout, sing and dance. Everyone is enjoying a real Scottish hoolie of a celebration."

Joe's eyes filled with emotion. Tears trickled down his cheeks. "What a crazy, perfect wedding day. No honeymoon is planned as the war overshadows everyone's plans."

"I joined up when I was twenty, volunteering to do my bit for the country while young and fit. Dorothy reluctantly understands. The lads at university all agree that the country needs young men and feel it is our duty to serve, especially as there is talk that the war will be short-lived. To do my bit, I enlist as a proud Seaforth

Highlander before settling down to law studies and family life. We plan to have five babies. Dorothy is very keen to have a big family, as she is an only child."

"Dorothy and I spend two wonderful days of bliss together. Free from army and family pressures, we talk, walk and share special intimate moments. We realised how precious every second, minute and hour is of every day. We talk long and hard of the future when the dratted war is over and people can get on with their lives. We spend our last evening together enjoying a pot roast, especially prepared by the pub landlord. It was a perfect evening."

"Lying in the stillness of the night, we draw close. We share hopes and dreams for the future, praying for peace. Locked in one another's arms, amid bursts of tears and laughter we spend the rest of the night declaring undying love for one another."

"Dorothy tenderly cuts a tiny curl from the nape of my neck to place into a gold oval locket, which her grandmother gave her for her twenty-first birthday. I bite my lip hard to hold back tears. With a heavy heart, I tell her that if the unthinkable happens, 'Promise me you will love and live again.' We cling tightly to one another. Dorothy whispers, 'You are my first love and only love. I will love you always.' We kiss, hold each other very tight and sleep."

The Master glanced at Joe, pretending not to notice tears tumbling down his cheeks and silent sobbing.

"Continue Joe. You are doing great."

"Well," said Joe desperately trying to compose himself. "The picture has accelerated again. I do wish it would not do that."

The Master replied gently, "Lives are nothing more than a series of experiences, changeable chapters. Joe, be patient for just a little longer."

Joe wriggled until he felt more comfortable. "I have rejoined my battalion at Shorncliffe Camp near Cheriton, Kent. My combat uniform is heavy and uncomfortable. Despite training, I feel unprepared and have a bad feeling, which is shared by many of the lads. We joined keen to do our bit, eager to thrash the Germans and to show them what the Brits are all about. What started off as bravado to our friends and family has disappeared. We are all really scared of what tomorrow will bring."

"We are lined up like sardines in a can waiting for a boat to take us across the channel. Some are so scared that they cry until they vomit. We found out that one soldier who falsified his age is only seventeen. He has never left Yorkshire before and is shit scared. Reality has dawned. We start to board, heading for France. We duck as planes fly low overhead."

"I am surrounded by solders. Some I know; others I don't. As I look around, we seem to have lost our identity. We do not appear to be people any more, but just human robotic bodies in uniform. I touch my inside pocket and close my eyes just for a second. Dorothy's smiling face looks back at me. I have one of her tiny white hankies close to my heart, so I know she is always close to me."

"The Captain has just informed us that we are expected in France as part of the British Expeditionary Force. Our mission is to support the French in pushing back the Germans. We are to be deployed initially in a conflict near Le Cateau, Marne and then make our way to an area surrounding the River Aisne. Words cannot describe how cold, tired and dispirited we feel. We all just want to get this war over and go home. This is not at all as we imagined!"

Yet again, the picture accelerated. "We are exhausted, disillusioned, frightened and angry at the waste and hostilities of war, the need to survive kicking in when faced with a German bayonet. I cannot possibly express or describe the blood, gore, fear and terror of war. A small group of us have forged a network of friendship, vowing to support and encourage one another if one of us gets wounded or homesick."

"We trudge en route to the River of Aisne. We have been told that the Germans have the upper hand, holding one of the most fordable positions on the Western front, between Compiegne and Berry-au-Bac, where the river, which is about one hundred feet wide and very deep in places, winds westward."

"Our training prepares us for the low-lying ground, which extends a mile on each side, rising abruptly to steep cliffs, gently levelling to a plateau. The Germans occupy the higher north side shielded by dense thicket. The French are to secure the Eastern tip at Chemin des Dames. In the stillness of the night, under cover of thick fog, we are ordered to move forward to cross the River Aisne any way we can, on pontoons or partially demolished bridges, to advance up very narrow paths to the plateau. We make good progress, so our spirits are high."

Joe squirmed in his chair as he continued, feeling decidedly uncomfortable. "Suddenly, as we reach the plateau the morning sun breaks. It is shining bright. The mist clears, leaving our position exposed. We shout in fear, realising that our platoon of men is nothing more than sitting ducks for the enemy. There is no cover to speak of and no protection. The horror of it all overwhelms me. I watch friends fall. Seeking shelter, some run back the way we came. Systematically, we are being slaughtered, mercilessly raked by crossfire. As the bullets fly overhead, my bad feeling intensifies."

"I cry out for Dorothy, for my God. I am hit, once in the stomach, arm and head. I feel no pain. My spirit is free... my peppered, blooded lifeless body falls to rot in the stinking mud. I leave behind carnage, horror and a mass of fresh discarded corpses. From a distance, I can clearly see man's folly – the utter futility of war!"

Joe took a sharp intake of breath as his eyes fell to the floor. As he glanced up again with sadness in his eyes, the picture settled, softened and was still. Feeling emotional, anxious and angry, he looked across at the Master.

Standing up to his full height he faced the Master shouting and screaming. "Why did I have to watch that? It was horrid. They didn't even have a life together."

After tears broke free, he sat down and sobbed. The Master waited patiently for his outburst to subside.

"You see, Joe," he began, "what you just witnessed was you in a previous lifetime. You had dreams and ideals. You were brave and fearless, especially marrying the lady you loved in such dreadful unpredictable circumstances."

"Yes, I know, but I died young. We never had a life."

"I agree, but you shared something special. There is a saying in your world 'It is better to have loved and lost than never to have loved at all.' Joe how many people do you feel marry for the right reason – marry because they feel they have found a special soul-mate, a missing someone they have unknowingly been searching for?"

Joe swallowed hard, his face wet with tears and cheeks crimson. His jumper sleeve was wet with mopping up tears. Looking directly at Joe, the Master continued, "In spite of all the difficulties, distance and obstacles, you married Dorothy because you truly loved her. You gave the lady your heart; you took a risk. Remember too, Joe, that you loved her so much you implored her to find a new love and life in the event you didn't return. That took great selfless courage."

"I know, I know, but it still makes me sad. You made me sad yesterday, and sad and miserable today."

Joe sobbed as deep uncontrollable emotions bubbled to the surface. His red rimmed eyes were swollen with heartfelt tears. They sat in silence. The Master watched, guiding Joe's thoughts and reaction. Eventually, Joe settled.

"Joe, do you understand why being here with me has been so important for you?" he asked quietly.

"I am not sure," replied the young man, feeling calm and receptive.

The Master continued, "You were so unhappy when we first met. You were on a collision course to nowhere. The build up of anger had to be quenched and sadness dispersed. It is essential for you to see the person you truly are."

"You have learned the lesson of isolation and now understand the true meaning and depth of love. I can now tell you that within a short space of time, when complete healing has taken place, you will leave this estate with a plan. You will have the opportunity to study, meet someone special and live your life to the full. Although you will have no recollection of what has transpired these past two days, you are now free to follow your destiny and live a fulfilling life."

"Everything is now in place. You will, as you have already experienced, encounter many injustices, unkindness, greed and deceit. You will recognise these in others. More importantly, you will now have the courage and insight to rise above them."

The Master approached Joe, placing his hand on the top of his head. "My child, you will lovingly guide others in this lifetime by example. Now go, for Avani is waiting to take you to the Healing Room. Stay as long as you wish. Allow the energy to revitalise, rejuvenate and refresh your higher self."

Feeling wobbly, Joe looked up at him. Erratic emotions had quelled. Now Joe realised how fortunate he was. Kissing the Master's hand he uttered with joy, "Thank you! Thank you! I will, I will. I understand."

"I know you will Joe. You have been given a life, so live and enjoy every minute of every new day! Treat every problem as a challenge to overcome."

Avani stood waiting. Taking Joe by the hand, she gently and slowly walked him to the Healing Room. Joe swayed as he felt for the chair, the energy already affecting his vision. "Sleep and rest," said Avani. "I will come for you later." The door closed – and she was gone.

17

JOE SLEPT, THE MEMORY of the past few weeks merging into a blur of swirling emotional images. He felt safe, sensing he was climbing a small flight of wooden steps, a brilliant white light ahead of him forcing him to lower his gaze.

Upon reaching the top, he found he was facing a small arbour shaded by a canopy of rainbow coloured silk set in the middle of a meadow awash with colour and fragrant summer flowers. To the left, stepping stones straddled a fast flowing stream, bordered by weeping willows. To the right was a field of early barley, poppies and cornflowers.

Although he felt an intruder, the arbour beckoned him to step inside, greeting him with waves of uplifting inspiring silence. Empty, apart from two small high backed white wicker chairs, there was also a small round white wrought iron table, on which sat two glasses. Frenetic energy of brilliant white light bounced on and off the canopy, causing him to feel slightly off balance yet calm and content. Joe's immaculate dress suit and shoes were a brilliant white. Instinctively, he removed a creamy white top hat, in keeping with the nameless unfamiliar occasion, and placed it carefully on the table. He subconsciously felt the need to sit down to wait for the unknown.

After what seemed like a lifetime, he watched a beautiful demure young girl with flowing dark brown hair, sparkling blue eyes and pink cheeks climb the steps. She was dressed in a long, white, high-necked gown and carried a white parasol. The girl curtsied. He bowed his head in greeting, pulling out a chair, inviting her to join him. They smiled at each other. Thoughts passed between them for what seemed like an eternity.

In unison they each picked up a glass containing sparkling clear liquid, toasted the occasion and sipped until the glasses were empty, staring into each other's eyes. Suddenly and unexpectedly everything around them changed.

The mysterious haunting silence was broken by the distant sound of mellow birdsong, a warm light breeze gently caressing the folds of canopy silk.

In an instant their attire changed as if by magic to modern day dress. Their voices were a mere whisper. Glancing into one another's eyes, they rose, smiling knowingly, and then hand in hand, they walked slowly down the steps disappearing into the sunshine.

*   *   *

Joe's breathing became slightly laboured and out of rhythm. He gasped and opened his eyes. Glancing around the room, his mind slowly surfacing to reality, he watched Avani harness healing energy with her hands, her nimble angelic fingers drawing pictures on the wall. Dancing and twirling to a silent song, she proceeded to outline bigger and bigger loops and whirls. She was having fun. Their eyes met and she laughed.

"I always have a sense of thrill when I do this," said Avani joyfully. "It reminds me of when I was a budding angel. I would decorate the classroom with rainbow lights. The others failed to master it, so the Archangel always knew it was me."

She chuckled recalling mischievous happy thoughts, glancing across at Joe. "How do you feel?"

Joe looked down at his hands, and then his feet. "Actually," he said smiling, laughing out loud. "Actually....I am good."

"I am so very glad for you. You will be fine now. You know that, don't you?"

"Actually..." he said with a belly laugh. "Yes, I do. I know I have a future. I also know that my past has given me the strength to find it."

Avani clapped her hands in delight.

"Joe, stand up. I want to give you a special hug. You are one of the nicest people I have met in a long, long time. You deserve to be happy you know."

"Actually," said Joe, giggling, "I will."

"Let us go now."

Joe glanced back at the Healing Room. Avani read his thoughts. "You know Joe, you only have to close your eyes and you can visit this room any time you wish."

Joe squeezed her hand. "I know."

As Joe left the Hall his step had a light spring in it. He no longer felt angry, heavy and unhappy. He looked up at the brilliant blue sky and the birds flying high. His step quickened and then suddenly stopped.

"Thank you, thank you to whoever you are. A million thanks!" he shouted at the top of his voice. "I am so glad to be me!" Then he ran at a fast pace to find Pip.

Avani waved to Joe, who was oblivious of her presence. She smiled with relief.

"Great!" she uttered silently as she did a hop, skip and jump pretending she was playing hopscotch before returning to the little blue room at the end of the hall.

Sitting quietly, she sensed that Ellie was thinking of her. Jumping up, she flew up the stairs to talk with the Master in his quiet room, the small lantern lit by his side. The flame flickered then brightened as Avani entered the room.

"Forgive the outburst, Master." Avani spoke with a sense of urgency.

"I know, I know," he said. "Ellie?"

"Yes," said Avani. "She is thinking of us and someone called Sam. Does that mean anything to you?"

"Oh yes, the name certainly does. He is our next charge and a real challenge."

The Master looked tired and more than a little troubled.

Avani spoke quietly. "Tomorrow when you have rested?"

"Yes, tomorrow would be good, late morning as usual. Will you arrange it?"

"Of course. Leave it to me."

*　　*　　*

Ellie was restless. The book she had just retrieved from a pile at the bottom of the sitting room bookcase failed to inspire any creative thought. Her mind drifted. She was tired. Her eyelids drooped and she slept.

When she woke, the afternoon sun had moved, leaving her to feel chilly. Even the cats had moved from her side, further into the middle of the room where the late sun was still warm. Ellie heard the phone ring in the distance, stop and then ring again. Sleepy and disorientated she made her way to the hall.

"Hi Ellie, it's Sam. Sorry I haven't been in touch. As usual, I have been away working. Got your message though."

"Well," said Ellie, "it's really hard to explain, but to keep it short, there is someone I would like you to meet, or should I say, someone would like to meet you. Someone I know will sort you out."

"Sort me out? You cheeky toad!"

"Seriously Sam, you are so volatile sometimes and in your more amenable moments you have often told me you are fed up with life."

Ellie sighed, waiting for a reply, becoming agitated during the long uncomfortable silence.

"Yeah, you are right there, though everything seems okay at the moment."

"Just okay?" interrupted Ellie.

"Well yeah, just okay," answered Sam. "Who is this person and what did you have in mind?"

"Well," continued Ellie, "that's really a long story, too long to chat with you over the phone, but are you up for it?"

"Let me consult my diary," replied Sam hesitantly, playing for time.

"I am not joking, Sam," continued Ellie. "We have known each other for over five years now. Although you can be good company, you must admit that every twist and turn of your life seems an uphill struggle, especially where ladies are concerned."

"Laydees," joked Sam. "They are just a hobby. I certainly don't let them interfere in my life plan now."

"Okay Sam, delete that last comment."

"I will... Anyway, we must get together some time soon."

"Yeah, good idea. I'll give you a call!"

Feeling cheated, Ellie replaced the receiver. She told the Master she knew Sam needed help; she did her best, but obviously it was not meant to be. Annoyed and frustrated, Ellie returned to the kitchen to check on a lamb casserole slowly cooking in the Aga. A few moments later as she proceeded to peel potatoes, the phone rang. It was Sam.

"Hi Ellie, it's me again. I feel a complete fool and an utter idiot. You are right. I don't know what you have in mind, but I am up for it. Don't tell me any more. Where do I go and what time?"

With her confidence restored, Ellie excitedly gave Sam clear instructions of where to meet.

"I will take you, but won't be able to stay. Is that okay with you?"

"Course it is. I am a big boy you know," answered Sam, now in more cheerful voice. "See you there."

Ellie waited for Sam at the top of Fountains Hill, announcing out aloud that she was bored with mundane routine, happy to use any excuse to put work on the back burner. Her thought pattern changed with seeing sight of Sam moving through the copse, waving madly to her.

Laughing uncontrollably, she watched Sam clamber up the slope. Poor Sam was considered by many to be a bit of an oddity and a sad clown by others. She knew there was a sensitive side he rarely allowed others to see, becoming adept at keeping a close guard on his feelings.

Sam was a lumbering giant of a man, 6ft 6ins in height, with broad shoulders, long legs and body, with big feet, emphasised by his choice of footwear. He insisted on wearing a certain American style shoes. "My dear, they are so comfortable they are worth the trouble and expense." He was extremely fit, but with a bit of tummy. His steel blue eyes bored into you when he was concentrating, which some found unnerving. Highly intelligent, borne out by his strong wide forehead, he had a square friendly face, broad smile and hair thinning on top. Witty, Sam had an infectious laugh, was good intellectual company and a loyal friend.

Together they clambered down the bank. Sam chatted and chatted, so much so that in the end Ellie told him.

"Sam, for goodness sake shut up! You talk too much."

They walked in step, side by side, following the contours of the long high wall.

As they approached the huge stone pillars, Sam's eyes widened. Scratching his head in amazement, unconsciously touching the gleaming wrought iron paintwork, he looked across at Ellie in complete bewilderment. Putting her fingers to his lips, she whispered, "Shsssh. All will be revealed."

The huge heavy iron gates slowly opened, giving them just enough space to walk through, and then slowly closed behind them. Sam glanced back, dumb stricken. Glancing at Sam's expression, Ellie whispered, "Don't ask."

The neat grass borders and shrubbery in full bloom complemented the curve of the long winding drive. They hurried, feet noisily scrunching the pea shingle as they made their way to the Hall. Ellie hoped Avani would be waiting for them.

As they turned the corner, they looked at one another, trying to disguise a sharp involuntary intake of breath as they were greeted by the stature and gleaming cream masonry of the Hall. An array of sparkling windows adorned with crafted wooden blue shutters was in the middle of the centre wall, which had a magnificent curved central turret.

Sam's eyes welled with tears in disbelief as he scanned the unique architectural design of the building with its splendid porch and canopy. Lost for words, the vista of the Hall, lake and rolling gardens took his breath away. Ellie sensed emotions rising and slipped her arm easily into his for comfort and reassurance.

Suddenly Sam spotted a lithesome female form moving towards them. "Wow, who is she?" he asked excitedly. "She is truly beautiful!"

Ellie smiled, looking up at Sam's excited face.

"I am sure that is Avani."

"Gosh! You must introduce me." Ellie laughed.

Avani ran to greet them. "Hello Ellie. How are you?"

"I am fine thanks. Avani, this is Sam."

Sam looked at Avani in disbelief. Her breathtaking beauty and knowing look suddenly made him feel gawky and shy.

Ellie sensed the awkwardness. "I can leave you now, if you wish," she offered.

"Are you sure?" answered Avani softly.

"Oh yes. Good to meet you again."

With that, as Ellie turned to go, Avani called out to her. "Ellie we will spend some time together very soon."

Ellie sighed with relief, knowing the hidden meaning behind the words, feeling content and happy to visit again very soon, but this time for herself. Running down the drive in spurts of newly found energy, she mischievously made as much noise on the shingle as she could muster. The gates opened and closed behind her. Continuing to run full tilt down the road, scrambling easily up the bank, she climbed to the top of the hill, choosing to go the back way home. Inexplicably, she felt a little apprehensive and excited for Sam, thrilled she had a special visit to look forward to.

18

Feeling slightly apprehensive, Sam watched Ellie disappear. He looked back at Avani, wondering what he had let himself in for. Avani sensed his anxiety. "You wanted to come?" she asked.

"Oh yeah, I suppose I did."

"Do not be concerned, Sam. We only have your interest at heart."

Sam gulped, feeling uncomfortable with people taking an interest in him. Having spent the last forty-five years paddling his own canoe, why should today be any different?

"Did you want me to bring anything?" he asked, quite perplexed.

"No," said Avani. "You have brought yourself. That is enough."

Sam relaxed a little, although still concerned at what he might be asked to say or do.

"You are," Avani beamed, "very tall and quite handsome in a rugged sort of way."

Feeling a little foolish, Sam responded, "Yeah, I get it from my father's side of the family. They were country folk – strong, hard working and resilient."

"Yes, I know," replied Avani. "Let's not waste any more time. Please follow me."

"Where are we going?" asked Sam, who was reluctant and wary to move any further into unfamiliar territory.

"Going to meet the Master, of course," answered Avani softly with determined overtones.

Sam refused to move. "Hang on a minute – meeting the Master? I didn't agree to any hocus-pocus."

Avani smiled. "Do you trust me?"

Sam remembered the telephone conversation with Ellie. "Yeah."

"Well," continued Avani giving Sam a steely stare. "Please, follow me."

In complete contrast to the brightness of the late morning sun, the light in the hall appeared quite dim. Sam reluctantly followed Avani up the stairs and onto the top landing, gasping in amazement at the collection of beautiful pictures and tapestries adorning the walls.

"It is a great house," he could not resist commenting. Avani ignored the comment putting her finger to her mouth, indicating him to "Shsssh."

Sam felt annoyed. It was the second time in a short space of time he had been told to be quiet. Glancing in disbelief at the pulsating light creeping under the first door, clenching his fists, he was keen to ask her how, but thought better of it. When they reached the second door, Avani stopped.

"Are you ready?"

"Well," replied Sam, adjusting his shirt, "as ready as I'll ever be."

The door slowly opened and Sam was greeted with a dazzling array of brightly coloured pictures in a room full of luminous white light. For a moment, standing motionless, he unconsciously cocked his head to one side to see how the pictures would look from a different angle and then stood upright as he saw the Master standing waiting to greet him. Avani nodded to the Master, saying in a whisper to Sam, "I will collect you later."

As she closed the door, Sam's eyes followed her, his level of anxiety increasing, rising so rapidly that he felt he would explode.

Out of his comfort zone, he felt a little afraid of the unknown yet not comprehending why. Used to pedantically standing up for what he believed was right, Sam found this environment unsettling and disturbing as he glanced around the vibrant colourful room. It was roughly ten feet by ten feet, with two small high windows breaking up the main wall. Pictures graced three walls and there was a highly polished wooden floor. He also noticed two high-backed chairs and a small wooden table on which stood a small lantern. Glancing across at the Master, he relaxed his unfounded irrational fears.

"Sam, please sit down," the Master invited, gently pointing to a chair.

"Thanks," Sam whispered awkwardly. "Ellie told me to come."

"That is correct. I asked her to invite you."

"Oh I see," answered Sam, although he didn't see at all.

The silence ate into him after a while. He felt unable to contain burning questions any longer.

"Why do they call you the Master?"

"Because that is what I am."

"Don't you have a name?"

"I do, but people seem to be content to call me the Master."

"So what is your name?" insisted Sam.

The Master looked at him for a few moments before speaking.

"Do you really want to know? Is it important?"

"Of course, otherwise I wouldn't have asked," replied Sam somewhat defiantly.

"It is John Joseph... Satisfied?"

Realising he had been offensive and extremely rude, Sam muttered "Sorry" under his breath.

"Apology accepted," replied the Master with a glint in his eye. "Now Sam, let's knuckle down to why you are here."

"Yeah, okay," Sam replied grudgingly.

The Master settled into his seat, watching Sam's every move. Sam knew his argumentative self was winning. He swallowed hard, clenching his jaw and fists to restore equilibrium.

The Master began gently. "Well, Sam, I have been following your progress on this life journey and it would appear that the core of you is deeply unhappy. If I may say so, at times you can become quite demanding, difficult and challenging."

Sam stared into space, feeling embarrassed and uncomfortable. The Master continued.

"Do you remember the night you returned from visiting friends in Norfolk when you headed off the motorway and got lost?"

"Yeah," muttered Sam.

"You were so angry that night that the wildlife hid. The energy vapour you left behind took two days to completely evaporate."

Sam sat rooted to the spot. "I didn't see anyone," he protested. "I was alone."

"That was your perception that night. I can assure you the incident has been recorded."

The Master sat, allowing Sam time to collect his thoughts.

"Does your temper get you into hot water often?"

Sam wriggled in the chair, looking down at the floor. "I suppose so. It has got me into trouble at work, but I am so good at my job, they turn a blind eye."

"How does that make you feel?"

"I guess angry and hurt. They don't understand."

"What don't they understand?"

"They don't understand that I can't help it."

"Oh, I see," commented the Master. "Is it important for them to understand? Would you like them to empathise with you?"

"Of course I would. Do you take me for a fool?"

"No Sam, I do not, but you are a big fool, a fool to yourself. Whether you admit it or not, you are your own worst enemy."

Sam stood up, this time really annoyed. "I did not come here to be insulted you know. Ellie told me it was important. I think it is time for me to leave."

The Master spoke gently, "Sam, isn't getting yourself right important?"

Sam sat down heavily. "Yeah, I guess. I have got so used to getting frustrated that losing my temper has become part of me."

Sam's body shook with angry heat and frustration. He desperately tried to stem his quickly rising temper.

The Master ignored his predicament, adding, "Sam, your life is a self-inflicted perpetuating pattern, which deep down in your being you hate."

Tears flowed. Sam felt a complete and utter idiot blubbing in front of a total stranger. Standing up, this time he was determined to leave.

The Master spoke with conviction. "Sam, you may leave if you wish, but before you do so, think on this: we can change the pattern, if you wish. It has to be your decision."

They sat in stony silence, leaving Sam feeling very edgy.

The Master broke the mood. "By the way Sam. Would you please indulge me and select a small crystal from the wooden box to the right of your chair?"

With angered frustration Sam tossed the crystals around in the box and then selected one. "What colour is it?" asked the Master.

"It's deep red with an orange thread," answered Sam in a cantankerous, grouchy voice. "Why?"

The Master smiled. "I thought it might be."

Sam turned the crystal over and over in his hands, inexplicably feeling calmer. The build-up of annoyance and frustration slowly dispersed.

The Master chuckled. "How about it Sam? Shall we try to explore why you feel the need to let your temper fly on occasions?"

Feeling remorseful, Sam looked at the twinkling blue eyes of the wise fragile being. "I am so sorry for being rude. Yeah, please, that might be a good idea."

"Right Sam," said the Master delighted his charge was responding. "Relax and trust. Is the crystal still in your hands?"

"Yeah and it feels kinda hot. I can feel it vibrating in the palm of my hands."

"That is good. Now Sam, let's begin. You chose the red crystal. Will you now please turn and focus on the red picture. Tell me what you see and feel. Just talk to me."

Sam smiled at the Master, adjusting his posture and looked straight at the red block of colour.

"What do you see?" quizzed the Master.

"Just a red blob. The colour looks somehow deeper in the centre."

"Excellent Sam! You are doing well. Look deep into the picture with the crystal in the cup of your hands. Share with me. What does the picture reveal to you?"

Sam focused until he felt as if he was going cross-eyed, then in a hoarse voice whispered, "It's changing. It's changing! How weird."

"Yes, Sam. The picture will reveal truths."

"Will I understand?"

"Sam, it is your beginning. Drift, trust, watch and explore your feelings. Your awareness will forget you are sitting in this room. Be mindful, as the picture will accelerate from time to time. When it does, just close your eyes for a moment and relax until the image settles."

"Yeah, okay."

The Master sat back in his chair, tired but satisfied.

Eyes glued to the block of red, Sam relaxed willing to see what he guessed he was supposed to see, silently hoping to become part of the scene which eventually revealed a moving darkness. It was warm and safe. A rhythmic beat was accompanied by a mixture of swishing gurgling sounds. The space appeared small. Suddenly Sam shrieked, seeing a tiny form stretching and turning somersaults in the darkness. Peering deeper into the void, he noticed another slightly smaller form. Uncontrollably he blurted out, "There are two of them, both male. How cool is that they have each other!"

As Sam watched he sensed a change of energies, clearly understanding that the boys, although identical, had different personalities. One appeared to be a deep thinker and was eager to achieve, travel and explore while the other boy seemed quite content to let life unfold.

"This is really weird," whispered Sam.

"No Sam, not at all. You are looking at yourself in the womb. You are a twin. So often with twins, even identical twins, one will assume the dominant role and be ambitious, practical, possessive, loyal and stubborn whereas the other twin chooses a more passive personality and is protective, sensitive, security-seeking and maternal. Although conceived at the same time, they each develop their own distinct personality."

"Does that really influence who we are?"

187

"Yes, Sam. It is how the world sees you, the way you project yourself to the world. How do you feel?"

"I am thrilled to have a playmate, a brother. I feel happy and content."

The picture accelerated. Sam waited and then continued excitedly. "The tunnel has turned dark red. The tiny form is surrounded by noise and frantic movement. It's being squashed and pulled into the light. Hey, it's a healthy baby boy! He's crying lustily. Fat fingers clear his mouth, wipe his face and eyes, and then wrap him tight in a blanket. They close a tag on his arm and foot. He's placed on his side in a metal cot."

Sam sniffed, preventing a flow of tears. "I can see a nurse wheeling the cot next to a lady in a huge bed. There are machines bleeping, and nurses checking tubes and charts. The patient doesn't look well. I feel sorry for her. She appears very weak and is sobbing hysterically. I don't understand why she is crying."

"Look again Sam. What is missing?"

"I am not sure… my playmate, my brother. Where is he?"

Convulsed with tears, Sam glanced at the Master. "He didn't make it, did he? Is that why I am alone?"

Sam pulled an enormous handkerchief from his trouser pocket and sobbed, "I knew it; I knew it." He howled in grief, rocking to and fro.

The Master spoke softly. "Sam, accept that you are alone, painful though it is. What else do you see?"

"I don't want to look!"

The Master emphasised, "Sam you must. You are only part of your beginning."

Sam looked up in amazement, believing the scene was all about him. He focused on the lady in bed, realising she was critically ill. Her prognosis was poor.

"Sam, she loves you, and needs you to be healthy and strong. She will be unable to have any more babies, so you are very precious." The Master spoke firmly. "She is grieving for the child she lost, believing it was her fault that he did not survive. She is struggling to deal with deep-driven guilt."

Feeling his heart would break, Sam's eyes filled with tears. For the first time in his life, he was forced to explore unresolved pain.

The picture accelerated again,

"What do you see, Sam?" asked the Master.

"I see a room where the sun shines on the cot and walls are decorated with circus animals. I see lions, clowns and coloured balloons. The room is painted blue, yellow and white."

"From your description, it sounds like a nice friendly cosy room."

"Yes, it is. The cot-bed seems enormous. I see a white wicker nursing chair, a linen box where clothes are stored, a bookcase full of books and a few toys. The house is so quiet; I cannot quite believe a baby lives there. Out of the window I can see fields, cows and sheep. The home is in the country."

"I see a baby in a rocking cradle surrounded by people in the sitting room. There's a lady who coo's a lot, has shaky hands and is very old. A man, who appears at the end of the day, sleeps in the next bedroom to the baby. Oh, and there's a father who works away a lot."

"Sam, tell me. Can you see the mother?" asked the Master gently.

"Yes, she always seems to be busy, spending her life working in the kitchen cooking."

"Sam," the Master continued, "how do you feel?"

He thought long and hard. "Strangely odd, alone, isolated

and desperate for communication."

The picture accelerated. "The child seems to spend hours on his own, alone in his bedroom playing with a variety of crayons and boxes, transforming them into a garage, fort or farm. The household regime seems orderly and disciplined. My impression from watching the boy is that he seems anxious, toes the line, is seen and not heard. Understandably, he spends a lot of time on his own in his room."

Sam wriggled in his seat. "He hums a lot, as singing makes too much noise. I would say he's happiest at bedtime when spending time with his mother. She reads to him for hours, playing 'I Spy' and sharing playful cuddles, and then she goes downstairs to do ironing and more housework."

"The father visits the bedroom occasionally, but always seems to be preoccupied with work. The other two rarely come upstairs. The child's life seems to revolve around the mother. It's weird. She is the disciplinarian and yet spoils the lad to extreme."

"Explain Sam," interrupted the Master.

"I notice that the boy only has to squawk and his demands are met. He eats lots of sweets and biscuits. I sense his frustration. After all, it's only natural for a four-year-old to want to shout, run and explore. Instead, he is persistently told to play quietly."

"The garden is huge. I would imagine it's fun to explore, but not alone. The only visitors appear to be adults, who visit the old lady. The man goes out in the morning and the child has to be good to avoid upsetting the old lady. I guess he learned from a young age the right buttons to press to get what he wants. He is like an artful monkey, knowing he is the pinnacle of his mother's world, using this knowledge wilfully."

Sam sighed. "How sad and what an insular life. A child needs to scream, shout, play in mud, get dirty, be cheeky and play with other children. He reminds me of little Lord Fauntleroy, a child who on the surface had everything yet in reality had nothing of true value or importance."

The Master smiled, saying, "All the goods in the world never compensate for the time spent with friends of the same age. It is a valuable time when children learn to share, to care for one another and discover who they truly are."

Sam sat in silence, his inner voice confirming why memories of his early years were nothing less than a blur, which he had conveniently chosen to forget.

The picture accelerated. The Master jolted Sam out of his meditative state, saying, "Please continue Sam, although it is painful. You are doing extremely well."

Sam shuffled, adjusting his position again. "I see a new school uniform at the bottom of the bed. The moody child is pouting, and resisting dressing. It's his first day at school. He's throwing temper tantrums. His exhausted mother is close to tears, pleading with him to be good and bribing him with sweets. At the school gates another tantrum erupts. Other children look on in disbelief."

"The experienced teacher wins after having her shins unmercifully kicked. Sensing this will be a difficult child to tame, she's wise enough to realise that although he's intelligent, his school years will be hindered by being an indulged spoilt child. It is becoming more and more obvious that his early life has been surrounded by adults, his every whim being met. The mother leaves. She is crying."

"I see the child squatting, sullen and angry in the corner of the classroom. He is so horrid that classmates create a distance between him and them."

The Master sensed Sam's lapse of attention. "Sam, share your impressions with me."

"I don't exactly know what to say except that the child is spoilt rotten. No wonder the children find him hateful."

"Continue," interrupted the Master.

"Well," answered Sam, "I truly feel sorry for the lad. It seems he's suffering from lack of spontaneity; no child is goody two-shoes. Being cheeky and naughty is surely part of being a child, not constantly being bombarded with, 'Be good, be seen and not heard'."

"And your thoughts?" asked the Master.

"Well," answered Sam, getting a little irate, "the poor lad should have had friends, been invited to birthday parties, toddlers groups, etc, etc."

He looked down at his feet, mumbling, "I suppose it was nobody's fault. The father worked away and the mother…" he whispered, tears in his eyes. "In today's society, she would be regarded as a saint."

Sam's heart ached. Finally he found his voice. "I suppose with three generations living in one house it's understandable that the child was spoilt. His intelligence may have helped in some ways yet in others might have been a hindrance."

"Let us continue," said the Master.

The picture accelerated. Feeling pained, Sam spoke with emotional exhaustion. "I see him at a new Junior School, a chubby lad with glasses, pubertal and prime for a spot of teasing. He appears equally uncomfortable with his peer group. In fact, I would have said slightly worse. He's a perfect target. He looks miserable, dragging his feet when moving between classes and with a tendency to look dour and aggressive. It is obvious he hates girls, who taunt and tease him. He reacts quite beastly to their girlie games, and excels academically."

The picture accelerated. "He seems a little more comfortable at Grammar School where there are no girls. His intelligence shines, earning respect from teachers and peers. He's enjoying lessons, apart from compulsory Physical Education and Games, which he hates, cleverly wriggling out of taking part. Consistently shining in exams, he's top of the school academic year, passing entrance examinations to university with flying colours."

The picture accelerated.

Sam excitedly shrieked, "I can see his University Certificate! He got a first. Good for him!"

The Master smiled, "Sam, you have done well. We will stop there."

Sam glanced up at the windows. The light was fading. The length of time spent with the Master suddenly registered. "Gosh, have I been here all that time?"

"No matter," answered the Master. "You must be exhausted dredging up childhood memories." Sam looked sheepish after years of choosing to suppress unpleasant emotions.

"As painful as this is Sam, I need you to listen and understand what I am about to say."

"Of course," replied Sam listening intently.

The Master spoke with resolve. "Sam, really listen. Do not switch off, a habit you have mastered. The reason for this meeting is for you to fully appreciate and understand your beginning. Only then can you go forward in life with a happy heart."

Sam squirmed, resurrecting a memory of being chastised by his mother. The Master read his thoughts.

"I am not your mother, father or any authoritative figure. I am your friend. I speak the truth."

Feeling uncomfortable, Sam blushed, realising that this wise figure knew everything about him, understanding every little idiosyncrasy, and there was no escape.

"Sam, you are here to unmask the old Sam, to smash the brittle shell you have erected around yourself and to help you destroy the self-imposed placard, 'Leave me alone'."

Feeling clammy and uncomfortable, Sam swallowed hard, almost choking in the process. He wanted to go to the loo, his favourite ploy to escape pressurised quick decisions, but thought better of it. The Master closed his eyes, allowing Sam time to regain his composure.

19

SAM SAT STILL IN the silence, a feat he found extremely difficult, never having tried before. He was battling with powerfully destructive and unrelenting demons, wishing to leave this merciless encounter yet ingrained propriety dictated that it would be discourteous and rude. He reluctantly had to admit that the Master's words rang true. He did possess a soft, giving side to his nature, though it was very selective. When he chose to do so, it was on his terms.

The Master looked tired. For the first time, Sam experienced an unfamiliar overwhelming feeling of remorse and empathy for the fragile, perceptive being, gradually acknowledging the enormous energy expended in trying to help him, a mere stranger, come to terms with the many facets and complexities of his character.

He was feeling increasingly uncomfortable in the unfamiliar stillness and silence, an exploitation he did not understand. Unexplored thoughts triggered submerged emotions. For no plausible reason, his body began to overheat and he felt nauseous. Fiddling, focusing on the crystal in his hand, he grasped the reality that he could be selfish, arrogant and self-centred. His sweaty frame crumpled deeper into the chair.

The Master sensed Sam's change of mindset. Smiling warmly, he asked, "Are you ready Sam?"

With moist eyes, Sam whispered, "Yeah, I suppose I am."

"Difficult though it may be for you to comprehend Sam, you chose your life path."

Sam swallowed hard, feeling naked and vulnerable. His wounded stare returned the Master's steady gaze.

"You met with the gathering of the higher echelons to discuss whether to return to the earth plane, choosing your parents as the foundation stone for the lessons you agreed to learn. Remember that this life time and the lessons therein were your choice."

Feeling extremely awkward, Sam flushed, his cheeks glowing crimson as he wriggled, pulling his shirt away from his clammy torso.

"As you will eventually discover from a previous lifetime, you chose the entity to embark on the journey with you. Viewing your early years, when you shared your thoughts and feelings with me you were compelled to confront raw truths. In playback, there seemed to be only one person uppermost in your mind – yourself."

Sam squirmed; he no longer wanted to be part of the process. The feeling to flee grew stronger. The Master continued, "Sam, your twin's demise was mutually agreed. You took on the mantle of achiever, the intelligent one, a hands-on academic, an avid student and a respecter of knowledge. You will at some point meet your twin again."

"Oh!" exclaimed Sam, shocked at the thought. Fully aware of Sam's senses and screaming nervous system, the Master continued. "The lessons you chose to learn this time around are tolerance, unselfishness and compassion. When you were young, never once did you try to understand the pressure your mother was under by keeping a household of mixed generations."

"Did you ever once try to comprehend the impossible

position and the promise to care for her mother and sibling she gave to her father before he passed? You never once showed true kindness and affection to your uncle or father, who were desperately trying to battle with their own uncertainties and responsibilities. You just wanted your world to revolve around you and your mother."

Sam wriggled, crossing and uncrossing his legs. Hoping the bombardment of words would stop, he avoided the Master's gaze.

"Be mindful. You chose this incredibly difficult situation for a very important reason, the rationale for which is for you to discover. You were granted the gift of high intelligence, tinged with sensitive creativity, which is a complex combination. You chose to ignore this rather than seek a harmonising solution. Instead of discovering your life's purpose, you created a wall of self-centred indifference and a barrier of anger."

"Over the years, you created enraged resentment towards your mother, blaming her for the absence of a brother or sister. Despite the deep love bond between you, not once did you take the time to sense her needs, private difficulties and personal pain. You were only concerned with your need for attention."

Sam sat speechless, feeling like a hungry spoilt two-year-old in a temper, shouting for food and attention.

"Rest assured Sam, you are not completely to blame for manipulating people and situations. Unfortunately, you cleverly mastered that trait in the mix of circumstances you found yourself in."

"You now need to understand that the loss began in the womb; one babe chose to survive, the other babe choosing not to touch the earth. Over the years, these suppressed emotions created a unique way of sensing and feeling – a bit like a short circuit in your emotions. Accept that you have lived in this self-imposed pattern for so long that the habit is ingrained. Yet it does not have to be."

"Have you ever considered how your mother coped emotionally with having to care for three generations, two she pledged to care for? How your father felt not being able to have his family unit to himself? How privately distraught and guilty your grandmother must have felt burdening her daughter?"

"The withdrawn, sad figure of your uncle was privately dealing with unrequited love – a much-loved girlfriend who chose to emigrate with her parents to New Zealand, grieving for the support and love of a lost father."

"The opportunity of growth was there for you to take when you went to school. On three occasions the hand of friendship was extended. Each time you chose to reject them. Did you ever consider how those people felt, especially the boy who invited you to his eleventh birthday party and you told him to go and stuff himself?"

Sam slid down in the chair, wishing the floor would swallow him up. His mouth opened, but no sound came. The Master continued, despite the silent angry protestations to stop coming from Sam.

"I am not being harsh. I just need you to understand that you do not have to live the rest of your life in the bubble of protected indifference you have created. Find the courage to burst the bubble! Live your life before it passes you by."

Sam's face turned deathly white. His fists were clenched tight, explosive anger building as he glanced at the Master's tall slender frame. As he tried to leave, an unexpected powerful wave of energy moved through him.

The Master smiled. "Your higher self is trying to guide you, Sam. Please listen. You do not have to be so unhappy. You are loved more than you will ever know by both worlds. Begin to love yourself."

Sam emotionally collapsed in a heap. This was not what he anticipated. Feeling heavy in the chair, he did not know where to turn or what to say. In a whisper he asked, "Was I really that horrid?"

The Master spoke gently. "The circumstances were ripe for you to thrive as a spoilt brat… and that is what you became. The indiscretion, if there was one, was that instead of looking outside your box to see the real world where people of all walks of life live, work and play you chose to retreat inside a self-imposed prison of unhappiness and discontent. This was so much so that towards the end of your school life, your parents found it extremely difficult to communicate with you. Your indifference scarred them because of their deep love for you."

Sam's emotions erupted. Inconsolably blubbering like a baby, he spluttered, "I never meant to hurt anyone. I didn't know. I cannot possibly know or understand!"

"That is untrue," replied the Master firmly. "You can – and I know you will. There is a bright future waiting for you Sam. However, you will not recognise or embrace it until you let go of the self-exiled exclusion capsule you have created."

Sam's shaking damp frame unconsciously shifted deep into the back of the chair, his shirt wet with a toxic blend of sweat and tears. His head throbbed with pain, slowly releasing suppressed emotions. Suddenly he crouched on the chair, knees up under his chin like a scolded child.

Avani appeared. Smiling at the Master, she took Sam's hands. "Stand up, Sam. Come with me." Like a meek child, Sam obeyed, leaving the room without a backward glance at the Master.

Slowly they made their way to the Healing Room. As Avani

opened the door, the pulsating lights overwhelmed Sam. He wept. Avani held his hands tightly, ushering him to the little wooden chair. Frightened to let go, Sam gripped her hands as if his life would depend on it.

Avani smiled. Her eyes met his and he relaxed his grip. Her gaze was both reassuring and soothing.

"You will be fine," she said in a calming tone. "You have built up so much anger and resentment inside you over the years that it had to explode. Let go now rather than keep it within."

Avani smiled as he stumbled towards the little wooden chair, reminding her of a three-year-old child. "Be still now Sam. Rest, sleep, cry and sob if you want to. I will come for you later. You are safe. Just let go!"

The room filled with pulsating healing light, dancing and darting around the walls, ceiling and floor. Sam clutched the crystal tight in his hand. As he did so, the pulsating energy quietened to a smooth, comforting, gentle rhythm. Exhaustion took over and he slept.

20

THE INSTINCT TO PANIC overwhelmed Sam as he woke in unfamiliar surroundings with a feeling of weightlessness, as if his head and body were bizarrely disconnected. He was surrounded by invigorating, pulsating, swirling crystal energy-emitting healing rays, which were restful and soothing. Surprised to see his chosen crystal still cradled in the palm of his hand, Sam noticed the dark red colour inexplicably change to rich burnt amber, the orange thread still clearly visible.

"What a bizarre whacky place!" he whispered silently, gradually acclimatising to reality and very aware of a smiling Avani sitting on the chair opposite.

"How do you feel?" she asked gently.

"Er, I feel fine," stammered Sam feeling out of touch with reality. "Yeah, I feel fine I suppose." He tried to stand, wobbled, felt disorientated and then sank back heavily in the chair.

Avani laughed. "You certainly slept."

"Yeah, I must have crashed. I didn't realise how tired I was!"

Avani chuckled, her laughter echoing like a clear tinkling bell. "When you feel ready we can leave. There's no rush. Take your time."

Sam looked up at the window. Light was fading. Darkness would soon fall. "Have I been here all this time?" Sam stuttered.

"Yes," smiled Avani. "You needed to experience peace, rest

and healing."

Sam sat staring at the crystal, then murmured, "Yeah, I suppose I did."

"Are you glad you came?" asked Avani enthusiastically.

Sam laughed, contentment resonating deep within. "What a ridiculous question! At the moment, I just feel spaced out. Ask the same question later and I will be able to answer you."

With a smile and twinkle in her eye, Avani moved towards him. Taking his hands in hers, she gestured for him to stand. Looking deep into his eyes, she then asked him to close them. Slowly, Sam's balance steadied, his solar plexus calmed and his stature relaxed.

"You can open your eyes now," said Avani.

Their eyes met. Sam regained his posture. "Thanks," he assured her. "I feel better now."

Letting go of his hands, she whispered reassuringly, "It is time to go now."

Slowly, taking small baby steps, they left the room. Sam descended the long staircase as if he was experiencing something new, repeating softly, "I feel really weird, really, really weird."

Avani smiled and assured him, "You will be fine very soon."

As she opened the huge front door, Sam sighed with relief at the welcome figure waiting for him. Avani spoke reassuringly, "Ellie will take over from here."

Hesitating, she said, "Sam, the Master would like to see you tomorrow at eleven. Are you willing to come?"

Ellie's eyes searched Sam's bewildered face. She nodded and Sam responded, "Yeah. I will be here."

Ellie clasped Sam's arm as Avani closed the door. Sam glanced back and then focused on Ellie. "How did you know I would be ready and how did you manage to get through the gate?"

Squeezing his hand, Ellie smiled, "Avani arranged it. I don't know how, but she told me to come. She has a clever way of transmitting her wishes through a form of thought transference. I was shopping in Torchester when I received her message. I just stopped what I was doing, jumped into the car... and here I am!"

She continued chatting, enjoying having the upper hand. "If you agree, I think the best plan is to take you to Nestledown. We can chat over supper, then I recommend an early night for you, my friend. The guest room is ready, so there is no problem."

"How weird. She read my mind!"

Sam tried in vain to eat a light supper of creamy chicken risotto, eagerly prepared by Ellie. "Can't manage any more," yawned Sam. "I am so sorry. You were right. I feel so tired that I just want to crash."

Ellie giggled, seeing the normally controlled Sam awkward and helpless. Although they were good friends, over the years he somehow always took control of any meeting, dictating the venue, time and frequency of chatting on the phone.

"Your room awaits you, kind sir." She curtsied, giggling as she showed him the room.

Sam took one look at the bed, scarcely giving himself time to take off his shoes and disrobe before falling into it. He pulled the duvet tightly to his chest, falling easily into a deep sleep with total relaxation overriding his constantly analytical active brain. Thoughts of the day's events were muddled. His highly intelligent logical mind was befuddled, unable to comprehend the day's happenings. "No matter," he yawned, grinning sleepily, echoing the Masters words. "No matter!"

Sam slept so soundly that he failed at first to hear Ellie call as she knocked on the door, clutching a steaming mug of freshly ground coffee. "Wakey, wakey, sleepy head! You just have time for a shower and quick brekkie before we head back to the Hall."

Blearily, Sam opened his eyes, squinting as the sunlight hit his face. "Yeah, okay. Will be with you soon, I promise."

"Don't go back to sleep or I will pull back the duvet…"

Sam's grin revealed wicked thoughts. "What a shame! What if…?"

They both laughed. Ellie left. Sam drank his coffee slowly, wondering what the day would reveal. Nervous apprehension built up, resulting in a dry throat. With his heart missing beats and a thumping head, Sam remembered his work diary and the numerous important phone calls he had to make, plus attendance at a hastily arranged morning meeting. He immediately resolved the dilemma by forwarding messages and apologies to voice mail. Relishing time in the hot power shower, he quickly made his way downstairs where scrambled eggs and bacon were waiting for him.

"This is becoming a habit," he commented cheekily. "You knowing my every move!"

"Kind sir, your wish is my command," replied Ellie in good humour. Warm and content, the well-fed cats, curled up together in a tight ball by the side of the Aga, amused Sam.

"I guess I wouldn't mind being a cat next time around," he said.

"Only if you are loved and have a good home," shouted Ellie from the hall.

"Yeah, I guess you are right."

Chatting light-heartedly, arm in arm they walked at a fair pace, soon reaching the top of Ellie's favourite walk to Fountains Hill. Stopping for a while and sitting in silence, they watched the frenetic populace moving through the day, bemused at a stream of cars patiently waiting for traffic lights to change. Ellie was blissfully content in her private heaven.

"I love it here, Sam," she said. "It helps me forget all my worries." Sam looked across, detecting a flicker of fear in her eyes. Instinctively putting his arm around her for protection, he asked, "Ellie, are you okay? Somehow you look troubled and unhappy, as if you have seen a ghost."

She wriggled into the comfort and safety of his chest, stroking his worried face. "I'm okay, really," she replied. "Just thoughts."

Sam's concerned demeanour softened as he cradled her close in his arms. Standing up, Ellie shouted so the world could hear,

"On a clear sunny day one can see for miles and miles. Sitting here with you makes me feel good to be alive!"

"I suppose it does," replied Sam wistfully. "I never thought of walks and hills in a positive uplifting way."

Ellie recounted the tale of the ramblers, their interest and intensity in geographical history.

Sam laughed. "Still, it keeps them fit," he commented.

"Yes," she grinned spontaneously returning the hug, "and we will both be ultra fit climbing this hill every day."

"Let's do it," said Ellie, looking at Sam and pointing to the Hall.

"Yeah let's," replied Sam as they scrambled down the bank. The intimating high wall was as majestic as ever.

"Have you noticed, Ellie, that when we jump down we never meet anyone or hear as much as a car engine. It's almost as if we are completely alone."

"Yes, it is strange. But if the truth be known, this whole scenario is completely whacky!"

The huge gates slowly opened as they approached the entrance, just wide enough to allow someone to edge through. Ellie stayed back. "This time Sam, I'm going to let you to do this alone. I will wait for you as before."

With a wave of her hand, she turned on her heel and ran, disappearing into the distance. Sam suddenly felt empty. Everything seemed okay when Ellie was by his side, but inexplicably fear and panic enveloped him yet he couldn't possibly explain why.

Sam's feeling of being like a trapped caged animal heightened as the gates clinked shut. Without knowing why, he felt sick. With nervous tension rising, he broke out into a cold sweat. His thought process momentarily debated whether he was being totally irrational, acting like an overgrown wimp. A burst of determination increased his stride as he made his way up the drive in record time, oblivious and blinkered to the hive of activity surrounding him. Sensing he was being watched, Sam chose not to look or to detect anyone in the shadows. He felt somewhat nervous, afraid of what the Master would say during this visit. Rounding the corner, suddenly coming face to face with the towering turret of the Hall, Sam's unfounded fears heightened, but were dispelled when the welcome sight of Avani lifted his spirits.

She smiled, sensing his apprehension. "It is a beautiful day Sam. The lake looks absolutely wonderful!"

Sam looked just to appease her. His heart thumping, he wanted to get on with whatever he was here for today. Looking at lakes was definitely not on his agenda. "Can we just get on with it?" he responded rudely.

Avani ignored the question. "Shall we walk down to the lake Sam? It would be good to see the cygnets and ducklings."

Sam's annoyance melted as he glanced at Avani. As she extended her hand, he took it and they made their way down the steps.

"I just wanted you to see the Hall and grounds in their true glory. You didn't have time yesterday."

They strolled down to the lake arm in arm, like two coy lovers who had just met. Sam felt strangely calm and glad he had time to spend with Avani.

"You are truly lovely," he said with genuine feeling. "Thank you, Sam. It is nice to hear."

Sam blushed, finding paying compliments difficult. They sat watching ripples moving slowly to the edge of the lake and spied a small shoal of fish moving towards them, with ducks paddling furiously.

"I guess they think we have food," Avani commented quietly.

"Then they will be disappointed," said Sam.

"Not for long. Pip and Joe will be along later to feed them."

The pair sat in peaceful silence, relishing the beauty and harmonious peace of the moment.

Avani stood up, saying, "Sorry Sam to break the mood, but it is time to go."

With some reluctance, Sam glanced back at the lake. "Oh, what a shame. I was enjoying myself just sitting and doing nothing."

Avani responded with enthusiasm. "You should enjoy being with Mother Nature more often. It would do you good. I love it here."

As they walked towards the Hall, Sam could not resist asking, "Do you always travel with the Master?"

"Not always," answered Avani softly. "But I did ask if I could come. He is so very special, so wise, and one of the few who have eternal wisdom and knowledge."

"Oh..." uttered Sam, speechless.

Avani continued, "There is much work to do; I only play a small part." She skipped up the steps, then twirled at the top to meet Sam's lumbering frame.

"I am so glad to have met you!" he shouted.

"Me too, Sam. These couple of days will always be special to you."

The two enormous bronze dogs guarding the entrance porch glowered at them as they approached. Sam struggled to recall seeing them. As the door opened, shafts of sunlight lit up the colourful tiles of the outer hall. Sam's eyes quickly observed every gracious architectural curve.

"I would love to look around this house some time!" he said excitedly. "Who knows?" answered Avani quickly. "Perhaps one day you will. The Master is ready for you. Would you like me to take you or are you happy to go up on your own?"

Suddenly, Sam felt insecure like a small child. Gripping her hand tightly, he replied, "Please take me."

"Okay," replied Avani, blending with his thoughts and feelings. "Follow me."

With a hesitant Sam trailing behind Avani, they climbed the stairs, his eagle eyes absorbing the vastness and vibrant energy of the staircase and upper landing. Passing the door of the first room, the pulsating, dancing colours reminded Sam of his previous visit to the Hall. Avani sensed his reaction and turned around, giving him a reassuring smile, squeezing his hand to give him courage. She knew what was to come.

As she opened the door to the Chakra Room, the Master stood up to greet Sam with a "Good morning, young man." Sam winced, for he did not regard himself as young. The Master extended his hand. "Please sit down Sam. Avani, my dear, thank you once again for looking after our young charge. We will meet later." Avani put her hands together gesturing love and respect to the Master, and closed the door quietly.

The Master confronted Sam. "How do you feel after your adventure yesterday?" Sam responded with a sense of urgency.

"Well, to be honest, I don't feel too bad. In fact, I feel quite good, although I have to say I was extremely nervous coming here today. It may sound silly, but that is how I honestly feel."

The Master looked directly at Sam. "I understand. Do not concern yourself with doubts and fears, as it is all part of the journey. Tell me – were you able to process the events as you understood them yesterday?"

Sam's thoughts raced. "Yes, on reflection the content of our meeting did make sense, although I must confess to not feeling too enamoured with my past."

The Master glanced at the little burning lantern, returning his gaze to the crestfallen, uncomfortable, unhappy person sitting opposite. "The past is the past, young man. Let's leave it there just for the moment."

Sam sank into the chair; sensing what he had to do. "Shall I pick another crystal?"

The Master laughed. "Sam, one of your gifts is high intelligence."

"Yes I know. Sometimes it's great and sometimes a curse. I get irritated with people very quickly. I have little tolerance and definitely don't suffer fools or people full of their own self-importance."

"I know!" said the Master with a chuckle.

The Master settled into his chair, slowly and deliberately rearranging his fine apparel. Sam became irritated and started fidgeting, fiddling with his hands, and crossing and uncrossing his feet several times. His angry frustration was obvious. The Master was keenly aware that his charge was becoming more and more agitated.

Eventually the Master spoke. "Sam, do you get frustrated easily?"

"Yeah, I suppose."

"It seems to me you have no patience or understanding either with yourself or others."

"No, I suppose not."

"Tell me, after the events of yesterday are you now aware that everyone's energy vibrates on different levels?"

"Yeah, I suppose."

"The reason for this, Sam, is that some human beings are very old souls. You have incarnated the earth many, many times. Hence, sometimes your vibration oscillates. There are those around you who are young and vibrant, where the understanding of being impulsive, impatient and intolerant have not yet been included in their life path curriculum."

Sam glared at the Master in amazement, as if he were a little unhinged.

"I know what you are thinking," the Master added. Sam flushed with embarrassment.

"It appears to me, Sam, that although you do not fully comprehend my words, you must try sometimes to put yourself in other people's shoes."

Shaking his head, an aggrieved Sam answered, "Ugh, I would hate that!"

The Master looked at Sam with sadness in his eyes. "I know you would. Well, Sam, yesterday was yesterday. Today we are going to explore something quite different – a lifetime you have purposefully chosen to forget."

Sam's eyes opened wide, his heart skipping a beat. His head thumped as he tried to rationalise what, if anything, he had done wrong in the past.

The Master smiled reassuringly at him. "Relax, young man. You are now here with me for a very important reason. You have been chosen."

"Me... chosen?"

"Yes Sam. You were given your intelligence for a purpose. Sadly, your earthly, spiritual, emotional, mental and physical elements are out of balance, perpetually fuelled by explosive anger."

Sam froze, not taking kindly to judgemental criticism, especially from a stranger. He made a move to leave yet felt unable to do so.

The Master continued. "We must explore why you have these frightening outbursts. You may feel habitually comfortable with them, but observers find them terrifying."

Aware he was being challenged, Sam shouted in annoyance, "Do you believe I like them?"

"Listen Sam. Over the years, you have got so used to living with the build-up of energy that in some strange way it has become an uncomfortable pattern you have cultivated. The rise and fall of accumulated frustrated energy results in explosive volatile outbursts."

Sam sank heavily into the back of his chair feeling guilty and ashamed. Excuses evaporated, ugly truths registered, he understood. Retorting antagonistically, he said, "But I can't control it! It's the way I am."

The Master spoke firmly, looking directly at Sam. "Yes, you can... and you will!"

"But..." stammered Sam

"No buts. You have listened to far too many people in this short lifetime of yours. Now is the time for you to listen to your inner voice."

Sam crumpled, feeling like a chastised three year old child, instantly recalling an incident when his mother had scolded him, sending him to his room, sobbing until she came to tuck him into bed.

"Yeah, I suppose."

The Master hesitated, looking directly at Sam. "There is no 'suppose' about it Sam. You just need reprogramming."

Sam's annoyance grew. "But, but…" his infuriated words faltered. Tears streamed down his face, his body convulsing in waves of deep-seated unhappiness, wounded by truthful words cutting deeply.

Ignoring his obvious distress, the Master continued. "Sam, you need to understand you are loved by many here on earth and in the Higher Realms. Remember what I said?" Sam looked up. "You have been chosen."

Sam warmed to these words, releasing a series of deep sighs, his physical shaking settling. "Yeah, I suppose."

The Master smiled at him. "Right, Sam. Are you ready for another peep into your past?"

Sam's embarrassed look fell to the floor, then searched the room – the paintings, their intense blocks of colour, the Master sitting comfortably in his high-backed chair, the two little windows. His gaze finally fell on the little lantern, following the rise and fall of the flame. As he did so, it brightened and grew in height.

The Master followed his stare and smiled. "All is ready."

Sam looked back at him, "Yeah, okay. I am as ready as I'll ever be."

"Sam, the purpose of today is to explore where this deep-rooted anger began." Sam gulped. "It is a fearsome energy you have carried for many, many lifetimes. I am sure you would like to release it so you don't have to live with it any more."

Sam's astonished face said it all. The Master continued. "Right Sam. Please select a new crystal, then wriggle until you feel comfortable in the chair with your feet flat on the floor."

Sam smirked at the last comment, silently acknowledging, "I suppose he is okay!"

The Master tracked his thoughts, adding, "Laughter is the best medicine when tensions rise." Sam looked back at him in agreement. The Master smiled, delighted that Sam looked ready and more relaxed.

"Rest assured Sam that every situation experienced in a lifetime is a valuable lesson undertaken under the watchful care of a Guardian. Human beings have been given free will. Therefore, it is their choice whether to follow a pathway of light or a pathway of darkness."

With closed eyes, Sam's fingers caressed the small box of crystals, turning them over and over in his fingers, trying blindly to distinguish the colours. Eventually, he settled on one that felt smooth with few indentations. It had a rough hewn triangular shape.

"You can look at it Sam."

Sam's eyes shone with delight. It wasn't red or amber, but deep amethyst. Sam felt pleased.

"Are you ready, young man?" queried the Master.

"I am ready."

"Focus on the block of purple colour."

Sam felt encouraged, turning the crystal over and over in his hands, concentrating on the picture. The colour appeared effervescent, with shadings of deep purple light at the top and bottom.

"I can't see anything!" he proclaimed in a disappointed tone.

"Sam, please relax. Breathe deeply, focus and move deep into the colour."

"I thought purple was a spiritual colour."

"Sam, it is."

"Oh…" answered Sam quite perplexed.

The more he focused, the heavier and drowsier he became. Sam's eyelids closed as his breathing settled into a shallow rhythm and his body became still. The Master protectively observed.

"Although your eyes are closed Sam, you will clearly hear my voice." Sam nodded. "In your own words, tell me what you see, sense and feel."

Sam's words resounded and were crystal clear. "It is very dark. I cannot see anything."

The Master spoke reassuringly in soft tones. "Allow your eyes to become accustomed to the dark as you explore. Tell me what you sense and see."

"I am in a world of darkness. It's cold and dank as if there is no flow of air."

"Sam, describe where you are."

"I am in a stone building. It feels a bit like an old castle of sorts. I am at the end of a long dark corridor. There is no light. I can just about make out a smallish dark door. It is solid and appears to be extremely heavy, with huge iron studs driven into it. The wood is very dark, almost black. The door has two huge iron hinges, an ugly lamp bolt and latch. There is no window. I can now feel a huge round keyhole, which feels cold, sinister and almost evil."

"Does the door open?"

"No, it is locked. I have tried to move it, but it won't budge."

"Sam, why do you think you are there?"

"I'm not sure. I believe I'm being followed. I feel anxious and scared. I want to turn back."

"No Sam. You must continue."

"Okay, if you say so… Hey, wait! I see a key on a tiny stone ledge to the right of the door. It fits. The key turns easily. As I push open the door, a horrid damp smell hits my nostrils. Ugh! It is so strong that it makes me want to retch. I need to hold my breath."

The Master spoke firmly. "Sam, attune your mind to the experience."

Sam stood rooted to the spot, his courage building.

"My eyes are now accustomed to the dark. Just ahead, I can see a small level space about four foot by four, then a flight of steps leading down. I seem to be at the top of a spiral staircase enclosed in a small circular room like a tower. I don't know how far down it goes; I cannot see the bottom. I am petrified, really frightened."

"Breathe deeply, Sam. Control your breathing. Move through the experience, no matter how painful."

"I need to discover where this leads and what is at the bottom. The stone steps are narrow and small. I can just about put my foot safely on them if I turn my foot slightly to the right as I descend. There is no rail, so I will lean my body against the curve of the wall for stability. I feel scared yet compelled to explore."

"As the staircase spirals down, the smell is putrid. I am holding my hand to my mouth to avoid inhaling the awful stench. My eyes now see the stone steps clearly. I have just noticed that I am wearing some kind of tunic. I presume I'm a soldier of some kind. I have a double-edged sword in a close fitting scabbard on my right hip. The hilt and cross guard are smooth and beautifully forged. The touch of the sword gives me courage and strength. The air is vile and the walls wet and slimy. Shall I continue?"

"Yes, please."

Despite laboured breathing Sam's experience continues. "Pools of water sit on the steps as I make my way down. This turret, tower or whatever it is must be near water. All the steps are sopping wet. I feel as if I have descended about thirty or forty feet. I can now hear water dripping. The sound echoes; it's eerie and frightening. I'm nearing the bottom. I have now reached the bottom step."

Sam wailed, "Oh my God! I don't believe it. I am now in a dark, dank, cold circular room. All the walls are dripping wet with slime. I can hear the constant drip, drip, drip. It is really scary. There is a huge wooden chest in the middle of the room. To the left is a smaller chamber with a grille in the centre of a heavy iron studded door. Oh, I feel ill! I don't want to investigate any more."

"Be brave a little longer. Explore, Sam," persuaded the Master, fully aware of his fearful distress and erratic heavy breathing.

"Oh my God! In the prison cell, for that is what it is, lies an emaciated figure huddled in the left hand corner. He's obviously been dead for some time. I think he must have been a soldier. I recognise the tunic. It is the same as the one I am wearing!"

Sam wailed so loudly that the Master cringed.

"Oh, my dear Lord, why? Who would do such a thing?"

Sam's face glistened. Sweating profusely, tears trickled down his cheeks, his shoulders and torso heaving with repulsion.

"I must return. I have an aversion to revulsion and cruelty. It is horrid down here."

"Sam, look inside the chest," the Master urged him.

"Oh, yeah, the chest. It is like a strong old trunk. It's quite big and of the same dark wood as the door. It is secured with four rusting iron bands. The rusty lock is huge. I don't know how to open it. I don't want to look. I want to leave."

Sam turned to climb the steps. The Master's voice was firm. "Sam, look around."

"I just want to get out of here... Hey, I have just noticed that my sword is gleaming. What incredible craftsmanship! There is a Latin inscription and crest on its hilt. I will try to see if leverage will break the lock, so I can open the lid. I need to get out of here."

The presence of the sword enabled Sam to overcome his deep-rooted fear, in the process discovering in amazement long-forgotten strength and determination to expose hidden secrets. With ferocious force, he vented pent-up frustration and anger on the lock. The blade split the lock in two. Using the tip of the sword, with trepidation Sam forced the trunk lid open.

Peering into the darkness, with one hand over his mouth and nose to avoid breathing in the stench of decomposition, he let out a terrified bloodcurdling scream, which ricocheted off the chamber walls. Uncontrollable shaking took hold as aghast, he stared in horrific disbelief at the sight of the bloodied remains of a young woman. Dark, wavy long hair covered part of her face. Her hands and feet were bound together with coarse cord. A grubby red cloth was forced down her throat. Sam stamped his feet in anger, shrieking in explosive temper at the top of his voice, "Who would do such a dreadful thing?"

He fell to his knees, shaking in desolation and fear, screeching, "Why? Why?" The Master spoke softly. "Sam," he said. "It is up to you to uncover why..."

21

Slowly Sam's awareness returned to the Chakra Room. Sitting crumpled in a heap, he felt exhausted and drained, as was obvious from his blank expression and posture. He questioned the validity of this disturbing roller coaster, asking himself if the reward was worth the price.

The Master's soft, clear voice interrupted his flow of thought. "Do not despair Sam. Be humbled. You normally shy away from facing up to difficult situations, so be proud of your achievement so far."

Sam shuddered, visualising in graphic detail his horrific findings in the circular room. The vile, evil depraved stench still permeated his nostrils.

Visibly distressed, agitated and upset, after thought-provoking silence Sam spoke. "Did I really have to go through that awful experience? Do I need to discover the truth of the demise of those poor people?"

"Well, it is like this," replied the Master. "If by conquering your deep-seated fears and phobias of the past you are then free to follow your true destiny, isn't it worth taking the risk?"

"Yeah, I suppose so," answered Sam, shuddering at the prospect of yet more cruelty and horror being thrust in his face.

"Sam, before we embark on that journey, perhaps I can explain why discovering the essence of who you truly are is so crucially important to your future wellbeing."

Resting his head on his knees, a comforting posture assumed since childhood, Sam looked at the Master with fresh eyes. He yearned to receive wisdom, understanding and clarity, knowing in his very being that deep-seated unhappiness was preventing him from achieving inner peace and reaching his full potential. Admittedly he didn't feel safe in the world where he lived. Clutching the little crystal tight in his hands, he adjusted his posture, ready and willing to listen intently to every word the Master uttered.

The Master smiled lovingly at his complex, despondent young charge. "Divine Intelligence exists in the universal consciousness. In essence, a human being is the blending of three functions – body, mind and spirit. The soul contains the vast source of all spiritual knowledge and earthly experiences. The mind accesses this valuable wealth of wisdom and experience through the power of thought."

"Despite scientific and technological breakthrough in your world, mankind has still yet to discover the incredible power of thought. Every human experience of this and past lifetimes can be experienced through the powerful majesty of thought. When it happens, 'Awareness' will be a true Eureka moment, a breakthrough for mankind."

"The physical form you chose to inhabit is merely a vehicle to enable human beings to recognise one another. Through the power of thought, they have the ability to dictate their inner world, to create happiness or conflict on Mother Earth. The Higher Realms replenish spiritual sustenance when sought with sincerity and humility. In essence, the soul dictates its own journey."

"There are seven main spiritual centres located within the

human frame. When accessed and aligned correctly, they enable the soul to attune easily to the Higher Realms, where one can reach wisdom, inspiration, creativity, guidance and support to move through every difficult and troublesome experience. These precious energy centres enrich and illuminate the soul. I believe in your culture you refer to them as chakras. No matter what the choice of name, they are in essence one and the same."

"These powerful energy centres enable human beings to link with their higher self – the inner voice – and connect with the Higher Realms. A truly wonderful feeling of inner peace can be derived from allowing the physical, mental, emotional and spiritual to blend as one."

Sam sat mesmerised. The Master continued: "Every soul has its own blueprint, a pattern forged before the first incarnation, or should I say born, into earth time. When humans are in touch with their higher self and listen to the small, still voice within they can achieve what, to their perception, is the impossible. Many humans inflict limits on their potential. They have yet to understand that all they need do is simply open their hearts and minds to the infinite possibilities that await them."

Sam sat transfixed, swallowing hard, the little crystal digging into the soft flesh of his palm as his awareness and concentration heightened.

"Soul growth occurs through many lifetime experiences. To this end, memories of previous lifetimes are temporarily erased during a chosen earth lifetime. Sadly, the chosen lesson sometimes may not be clearly apparent for many years. Once acknowledged and accepted, choices may or may not impact on whether that lesson has been mastered. The time span is dictated by the lesson and choices made."

"Depending on the circumstances, occasionally a flashback

of a past lifetime is granted. I suppose you would liken it to looking through a fine muslin cloth where a fragmented image is sometimes visible. With focus, this can give insight into a previous existence. This brief peep may be pleasant, sad or happy depending upon the lesson and circumstance of the particular incarnation."

"Your earth plane is so complex, so inextricably interlinked. The animal kingdom has not been given the same wonderful opportunity of choice as human form. Their patterning is about survival, breeding and nurturing yet their existence is vital to the continued existence of humanity. Much can be gained from understanding the patterning of the animal kingdom. It enhances your planet."

The Master smiled, his knowing gaze directed at Sam's bewildered open face. "You will incarnate on your earth plane until you have nothing else to learn. Then you will progress to becoming a higher spiritual being. To climb out of this entrenched pit of unhappiness, you need first to listen to your higher self, your wise inner voice, to understand and accept the essence of who you are. Your parenting gave you your unique foundation stone."

"Remember that a lesson not understood and mastered may be presented again in another way or another lifetime until the core of the lesson is learned. In essence, planet earth is merely a classroom. You can pass your exams with flying colours or prefer to play truant; the choice is yours. Humans have been given free will. Whether you choose wisely to enhance soul growth is up to you. The key of this teaching is for you to keep in mind that every action has a reaction."

Exhausted, Sam sat wide-eyed, as if a heavy multifaceted university lecture had just come to an end. He looked down at the floor, up to the little windows and then to the brightly flickering lantern.

"I never knew," he stammered, feeling sad, confused and mortified. "I didn't realise. So the gist of what you are saying is I will not find contentment until I have the courage to search for the unfathomable painful missing link."

The Master laughed. "Sam, young man, this day you have made a very old Master very, very happy!" They laughed in unison. A difficult hour had passed without tears and tantrum. The Master sighed with relief.

Sam sat deep in thought and then found his voice. "Well, I am ready. I know it will be difficult. I might want to shout and kick off, as I have done so often in the past, but I promise I won't allow it to happen."

"Wait and see, young man," the Master answered gently. "Let's just sit quietly for a few moments."

The Master closed his eyes. Sam joined him and their energy blended, replenishment essential to them both. Avani woke them, pouring refreshing rose petal water.

"Thank you, my dear," said the Master. "We would have slept on if you hadn't been kind enough to tell us it is time."

Avani smiled, glancing across at Sam's pale rested face. "I will come for you later," she said. Sam nodded in agreement.

"Right Sam, this part of the journey is vital for your continued wellbeing. Just trust. Allow yourself to become part of the scenario. You are safe in my care and protected, so no harm will come to you. Hold in your heart and mind that you are merely exploring a previous lifetime, a life span where your incandescent anger and guilt began."

Sam felt scared out of his wits, realising somehow he had been given a life-line to inner peace and contentment. He wriggled in his chair until he felt comfortable.

"I am ready."

"Sam, take courage in both hands to explore your emotions. Rest assured that I am your journey's guardian."

"Yeah, okay, I will, I promise."

The Master sighed with relief, acknowledging this voyage to the past would be tough. He caressed the top of the lantern lovingly, the flame responding by its brilliance. Sam clutched the dark amethyst crystal in his cupped hands and was entranced by the hue of purple. He allowed strange hypnotic sensations to overpower his awareness as the picture swayed, the depth of colour swirling and whirling faster and faster in a circular motion until he felt consumed by the energising colour.

Unexpectedly, he awoke to find his chilly frame sitting in the middle of what appeared to be dense woodland, the trees so tall he could barely see the darkening sky. Thick lush grasses brushed against his legs. The undergrowth was so overgrown that he felt lost and alone. Trying to get his bearings was a challenge in itself. There was no clue as to the season or point in time. Distrustful of his predicament, Sam broke off a small branch as a staff to create a passage through scrub. Eventually, he came across a narrow forest path. Apart from wildlife stirring, there was no sight or sound of activity.

Sam noticed for the first time that wearing fine cut leather boots and leggings was surprisingly comfortable. His distinctive attire was made up of a white surcoat with a red cross and a white mantle, recognisable as the mantle assigned to the Templars of the Council of Troyes in France. The brilliant scarlet cross was the symbol of martyrdom. The Templars were schooled that to die in combat was a great honour and an assurance of a place in heaven. The cardinal rule of the vow was never to surrender unless the Templar flag fell to the enemy, pledging to regroup and fight alongside knights of a neighbouring Christian order.

The magnificent sword he used so swiftly in the tower by his side furnished him with confidence, courage and strength. Instantly, he sensed he was not merely a lone soldier in the heart of a forest, but an elected soldier of Christ, one of the revered Knights Templar. In fear and awe, he fell to his knees in prayer while rocking gently and mouthing, "Oh, my God, my God! I don't believe this!"

From historical writings he understood that the Knights Templar were regarded as being among the most skilled fighters of the Crusades. They had the bravery of heavily armoured knights on warhorses, fulfilling their mission to charge the enemy in an attempt to break opposition lines during vicious battles. At the battle of Montgisard, five hundred Templar Knights helped to defeat an army of more than 26,000 soldiers. Suddenly, an unmistakable feeling of pride overwhelmed him as he respectfully smoothed his uniform, sensing that he wasn't an accomplished skilled fighter. Although the primary mission of the Order was military, he recalled that analytical and statistical skills were crucial in managing the financial infrastructure.

Why was he here and who was he? Did this woodland lead to somewhere or nowhere? A memory of the past surfaced – he was of aristocratic descent, a nobleman who willingly placed all his assets under Templar management, journeying to the Holy Land. Yet why was he here now?

Wandering through the greenery he recalled acts of treachery by those he trusted. Many close friends were persecuted or imprisoned with trumped-up charges from heresy to fraud in the hope of learning their guarded secrets.

Suddenly tripping headlong over a vine hidden from view,

he swore in French, as he painstakingly followed the meandering path, remembering comrades who suffered arrest and torture to make false confessions. They were then burnt at the stake. With hands clasped in prayer, looking up to the darkening cloudless sky, he thanked God for his life.

With instinctive stealth he meandered through the woodland, relieved at last to see a small cluster of homes. A fire crackled in a makeshift fire basket. The smell of food filled his nostrils. Bread and meat were cooking side by side. The place appeared deserted as he approached. He hastily took the opportunity of drinking from a discarded water flagon to quench his thirst.

At the sound of heavy footsteps marching towards him, he quickly hid behind a rough sturdy dwelling, witnessing a bedraggled group of villagers armed with staffs and knives. They looked saddened and angry, and were shouting obscenities to a lanky lad at the back.

"I thought I told you to keep an eye on her."

"I did!" he yelled back.

"You couldn't have done otherwise she would still be there."

The voices grew closer, louder and more hostile.

"We have been duped. The noblesse won't like this."

As they approached, Sam moved position, furtively running to an adjacent barn where two horses, oblivious to the drama, were tethered, contentedly munching hay. After a sigh of relief, getting his breath back, he was safe for the moment, concealed in the shadows of a dark corner. He frantically tried to assimilate the situation, feeling an unwelcome intruder. Suddenly, as if from nowhere, an elderly lady appeared. Dressed from head to toe in black, her wispy, straggly greying hair was drawn tightly back in a bun. She was barefoot, an ugly protruding wart on the side of her nose. She spotted him.

"Shsssh... please don't tell them I am here!"

The old lady glared back in surprise at the obviously shaken and disorientated young man cowering in the corner. Debating whether to call the others, recognising the uniform she decided against it. Their stares locked in disbelief.

After what seemed a lifetime, she whispered, "Stay hidden. I will come back for you later."

Sam had no choice, but to trust her.

The villagers' mood changed as they ate, drank and chatted with intervals of raucous laughter. Eventually, one by one they fell asleep by the hot fire embers. As dusk fell, under a starless sky the old lady returned, somewhat agitated and bewildered.

"What are you doing here?" she demanded to know. "They will set upon you and lynch you if they know you are here."

Sam rose to his feet, facing her. "I am a man of honour. Doesn't my mantle stand for something?"

"It did," she replied huskily. "Come with me."

Together, they silently crept out of the barn into the depth of the forest where the old lady lived comfortably, quite content in her untidy ramshackle home. Pouring a drink, she handed a rough hewn mug to Sam, who, despite misgivings, drank to avoid this woman's possible displeasure. It tasted bitter. He shuddered. The effect was like a kick from a mule. He slumped to the floor, unable to stand.

"You are safe here, for a while anyway. You are close to Mayenne, not far from the coast of Normandee." Facing Sam, she took another swig of her liquor.

"A group like you passed by some time ago, fleeing from Paree." She looked down at the cluttered woodland floor. "We, that is the villagers and me, thought we could trust them."

"Oh great..." stammered Sam.

CHAPTER TWENTY-ONE

The woman glowered, "No it isn't."

"What on earth do you mean?"

"We have been living here in this little setting for over ten years now. We pay our dues to the Monsieur Lemassey – that is what we call him." She grinned. "He is reasonable and never bothers us. It works just fine."

"So why the intrigue? What is the problem?"

"Well, a group of men dressed like you appeared one day and because of what you stand for, were made welcome."

She sat heavily, slurping another mug of 'still,' starting to shake with uncontrollable anger. "We believed them... it.... was..."

Sam asked her to speak slowly so he could understand.

"Well, it is like this. There was fighting over the hills and we thought the Crusaders were on our side. He..." She rose to her feet, making a sign of the cross on her brow and chest.

Vented anger overcame her. "They were nothing but bloody conspirators out to fleece us! They took all our money."

Suddenly she was convulsed in floods of tears. She looked up at him, shouting in between sobs. "Bloody swines! They repeatedly raped the women unmercifully and beat young girls who wouldn't co-operate."

Sam sat on the floor, shocked and still in disbelief. "Did they really wear our mantles and handle our swords?"

"Oh, yes. We weren't to know."

Sam felt outraged and was incandescent with anger. "Where have they gone now?"

"To Chateau Rouget Blane. Do you know it?"

"No, but point me in the right direction. I cannot stand by and let our reputation be maligned and tarnished by a group of ruffians!"

The old lady looked relieved to have the opportunity to outpour her distress.

"Tell me," said Sam. "Were any children witness to this and where are they now?"

The old women recoiled, looking frightened. "You're not going to kill them?"

Sam fell on one knee, looking deep into her eyes. "Look, my dear lady. Look at my sword and the inscription."

"I cannot read!" she sobbed. "The letters mean nothing to me."

He knelt, looking into her eyes. "Trust me, dear lady, when I say I am who I say I am."

"Let me look into your eyes. Let me have your hand."

Sitting on a stump of wood, she held his hand tightly, squinting as she did so. His handshake was firm, the lines on his hands revealing he was speaking true.

"When we realised what was happening we quietly gathered the children together, only fourteen of them, aged from ten months to fifteen years. We hid them in the old flint cave by the stream, about a mile from here."

"Is that what the men were shouting about?" quizzed Sam.

"Yes. We left Marianne in charge. She is a good, sensible girl able to keep the little 'uns quiet. Jed was supposed to keep lookout when Marianne went down to the stream to collect water. Stupid fool! He went off to see if he could catch rabbits and when he came back she was gone. Her pitcher and shawl was all he could find."

Sam felt rising anger. How dare anyone betray the pledge and hide behind what the Knight's Templar stood for? How could they rape and pillage a small community, beat and abuse women, and terrorise children?

"I will stay tonight. You have my word. Tomorrow I will track them down."

The old women looked relieved, offering a plate of rabbit stew. "I am glad you came by."

Sam felt dispirited and was unsure of what to do. Still puzzled over unfolding events, he soon picked up the trail. Something didn't feel right. What in the end did these vagabonds achieve, easing carnal lust, and filling their bellies and coffers? It just didn't make sense.

After a heated early morning debate, he reluctantly agreed to ride the old lady's faithful dappled mare to hasten his quest, promising to return the faithful animal, when it was no longer needed.

"Don't fret, my friend," said the old lady. "She knows the way home."

Approaching the grasslands surrounding the Chateau, Sam heard loud drunken voices. He dismounted, pushed the horse into the cover of trees and spied two or three men falling about laughing, snorting and drinking. Creeping slowly forward on his belly and taking care not to be seen, he stopped, pulling back in horror. Ahead was a small group of bedraggled sniggering men. Dressed as knights, their swagger and behaviour was evidence that they were impostors.

Tying the horse securely to a tree, he climbed it, resting on a large bough. Under the cover of laden branches, Sam observed the shenanigans from a safe distance. Shedding angry tears in mortified disbelief, he watched the unbelievable unexpected scene being played out. Several times he was in danger of losing his foothold as his concentration wavered, forcing him to grasp an overhanging branch to prevent crashing headlong to the ground.

Once down, struggling to recover his equilibrium, he

recognised the face of the obvious ringleader as Pierre, a childhood friend. The men pledged their oath to the cause together as young men. Shaking uncontrollably, sick in his stomach with unexplained despair and disbelief, Sam silently continued to watch the charade from the safety of a thicket.

He had heard the rumours. Pierre was a turncoat, falsifying records, stealing donations and narrowly escaping death. Fully aware that there were enemies of the faith, Sam was unable to believe and accept what his eyes were revealing.

Alongside Pierre were two men dressed as sergeants. Wearing black tunics with a red cross on the front and back, and a black mantle, they were drinking heavily, jigging and shouting drunken coarse expletives. A short distance away, were five terrified young women, he guessed in their early teens, tied up, huddled together, their feet and hands bound. Feeling powerless, he needed to formulate a plan. Watching the group carefully and monitoring their moves, he desperately tried to discover if any of the men were fallen knights.

He decided that his best plan to wait until nightfall and move under the cover of darkness with the element of surprise. Deliberating that if the girls remained tied together he could cut them loose, where could they run? He guessed that if it was possible to escort them to the chateau, they would be safe, so decided to remain still, waiting for his chance to act.

22

A MOONLIGHT SKY lit the way. The knight loosened the amiable mare with appreciative strokes of her shaggy mane, allowing her to trot home through the trees, fearing that any unexpected invasive sound would announce his presence.

Wrapping his thick surcoat around him for warmth, watching safely from a distance, he patiently waited for an opportunity to move forward to attract the girls' attention. The hours ticked by, heavy mist hanging in the night air as midnight approached. Unhurriedly, the spread-eagled group of drunken loud-mouthed men slowly wandered away from the girls, trudging haphazardly towards the lights of the chateau, leaving a safe reasonable distance for him to approach undetected.

Tentatively squatting, crouching low, he was finally in sight of the terrified girls. Cautiously he gestured them to be silent and approached as a friend, their rescuer. Shaking with relief amongst outbreak of tears, the frightened group acknowledged his presence, silently responding in gratitude.

As clouds concealed the moon, he took his chance, imploring the girls to be deathly quiet, to follow his lead and do as he asked. He first released their bound feet, then cut the ties that held their hands, indicating for them to lie flat on their stomachs, lie low and close, and mimic his every move. Snivelling with relief, they all nodded in agreement.

Despite aching limbs and bleeding wounds where the rough ties had cut into their flesh, they obediently followed, slowly wriggling forward, dragging numb, battered limbs in the wake of their unknown liberator. They dreaded that any cry or outburst would alert the drunken louts of their impending escape. Several times they had to stop, lying flat and motionless as a swaggering slurred voice broke the evening silence. Slowly, the girls inched forward until hand in hand, they followed Sam, running for their lives to the shelter of dark shadows close to the chateau grounds. So far, so good. Sam felt relieved.

Once inside the intricate wrought iron double gates, the chateau fort towered majestically before them, slightly eerie in the sporadic moonlight. The twin turrets were starkly silhouetted against a sombre sky. The main block and its outbuildings linked by balustrades were arranged symmetrically around a dry paved and gravelled central courtyard. Tucked close behind the central building was a formal garden, with park land beyond, graced by clumps of trees and two small lakes. Sam sensed the building was familiar yet could not fathom why.

As they approached the chateau's inner courtyard, his hopes sank as he heard voices. He ushered the women to crouch down close together behind a low stone wall.

Unbeknown to Sam, Pierre's training had kicked in. Unbelievably, in the courtyard entrance to greet them they were ambushed and surrounded. Pierre took control, grinning malevolently with victory.

"Hello my old friend," he sneered. "Just to let you know that we were here first!"

Sam stood firm, the girls cowering close behind him, the tops of their heads just visible.

"Stand aside! We wish to see the owner."

Pierre gestured in defiance, bowing maliciously. "You mean, dear knight, Sir Jacques Levaye?"

"I do. Please be kind enough to ask one of your men to inform him we are here and seek his sanctuary and hospitality."

"Really?" smirked Pierre, enjoying his controlling position. "Well now, dear knight, that will be very difficult. You see, the family and entourage are no longer in residence. They have gone – or should I say fled!"

Deflated, Sam stood facing his adversary. How could a single knight possibly defend these girls now against a group of immoral, ruthless, brutal fellows? Had he inadvertently increased the danger they faced, exchanging one form of hellish misery for another? The sword by his side unconsciously reinforced his stance. Somehow he had to try.

The quick-witted girls' sense of survival overtook fear. Seeing the rest of the men approach, they took a chance. In unison, they rushed at Pierre, knocking him to the ground. Sam followed, drawing his sword. The girls ran with him in hot pursuit, disappearing into the comparative safety of the open doorway before Pierre could stop them. Slamming the entrance door behind them, they left a furious Pierre shouting obscenities. They were all safe for the moment, lost in a maze of breathtaking luxury.

The inner wooden panelled hall was wide and long. In the centre gallery was a magnificent highly polished twin marble staircase. The girls hid behind a pillar, holding on to one another for comfort. Petrified and shaking, their pale cheeks were wet with tears. Sam ushered them into a small anteroom while he investigated the ground floor, struggling to devise a plan of escape. Drawing on undiscovered formidable reserves of strength, he instinctively identified a way out through the servant's quarters, believing from there that an escape route could be found.

He was suddenly taken unawares when a dainty, feisty, pretty young woman, with doe-like brown eyes and auburn hair falling down to her waist stepped out of the shadows. She approached Sam, saying, "My name is Marianne. I will look after the girls. Please, please just find a way out of here!"

Moving to the safety of an enormous intricate carved overhanging alcove, she explained how Pierre and his associates descended on the village late one night, seeking shelter.

Drawing close to Sam's ear, Marianne sheepishly whispered, "Big Lou, as we affectionately call him, because he is tall and cuddly, is the one we look up to when a decision has to be made that affects us all. Under duress, he was forced to give permission for the strangers to stay in the barn with the horses. However, at the time, many questioned why they chose to visit our little homesteads when we live miles away from the fighting."

She paused for breath, relaxed and sat on the floor beside Sam. "Mid-morning when they woke, we realised the true reason for their visit. They drank our mead and ate our food. Out of their skulls with drink, they then set about raping women, irrespective of age."

Marianne burst into tears, her slight frame shaking as she recalled the villagers' fear, helplessness and horror. Looking up at Sam with pleading eyes, she continued.

"When the louts were out of sight, Big Lou took control. We gathered the children and ran and hid in an old flint cave. I love the little 'uns, so I offered to go. We believed they were noble like you." She wiped tears with her dress.

"Oh… why did they come?"

"I don't know," answered Sam reflecting on her tale.

"It doesn't make sense. Knights are proud to take the pledge, an oath to be Fellow Soldiers of Christ and the Temple of Solomon."

"Oh…" Marianne answered somewhat bewildered.

Sam sighed, realising his words meant nothing to her. Although as pretty as a picture, Marianne hadn't been graced with nobility and education. Looking into her eyes, with a reassuring hug, he whispered, "Find somewhere for you all to hide and be safe. Trust me. I will find you."

Spontaneously undoing a yellow ribbon from her hair, insistently handing it to Sam, Marianne said, "This is for you, so you don't forget us."

Emerging from the alcove, Sam smiled with satisfaction as he watched the girls, under the capable care of Marianne turn on their heels, disappearing into the gloom.

Furtively, Sam searched the interior, moving through the luxurious rooms with a stealth skill any marauder would have been proud of. Slowly, he descended a small flight of stairs, the tread quite narrow. Upon rounding the corner, he suddenly heard voices. With nowhere for him to hide, his presence was detected. Abruptly manhandled by two scruffy men, he was pushed into the small room, dumbstruck at the gathering before him.

A stunningly beautiful young woman with exquisite features, dressed in aristocratic finery of deep scarlet and gold, sat on a wooden stool, laughing and chatting with two of the men. His face was ghastly pale as their eyes met.

"Well, well!" jeered a malicious Christina. "Didn't expect to find you here."

Sam squealed like a pig about to be slaughtered.

"Why, why are you cavorting with these so-called men?"

Before she had time to answer, Sam's mouth dropped open in disbelief as two men grabbed him. Obviously enjoying the control, they sat him down facing the young woman.

The female poked Sam's chest with her manicured finger, the venomous force like the tip of a knife. Sam panicked, wanting to throw up, his body sweating profusely.

"Why?" shouted a bewildered Sam. "Tell me why!"

"That is for me to know," Christina laughed, jeering at his obvious fear and discomfort.

Sam's legs gave way, the shock reverberating at an alarming rate through his system. His head threatened to explode. He consciously dug his fingernails into his hand, biting his cheek to avoid an unprecedented emotional outpouring. This cold-hearted, cruel, mean-spirited woman was once his childhood sweetheart. He was unable to comprehend he was facing the same person.

Sir Jacques Levaye had two beautiful daughters, whom he hopelessly indulged. Christina, the eldest by two years, was an energetic, feisty young lady, an enchantress to suitors, proffering passion and adventure. Meanwhile, Adrianne, quiet and demure, was happier in the garden sketching, reading, and embroidering. Christina was fun, charming, a natural horsewoman, a fantastic dancer and outrageous flirt. Her wicked, spirited streak fascinated him.

"Why? For God's sake tell me why!" asked Sam again, regaining some composure.

"Because," she laughed, parading provocatively, enjoying the taunting, "because I got fed up with being good. My loving sister took that role. I was bored with life. I could say bored to death until I met Pierre."

Sam stared into space. Christina's eyes blazed with excited fury. "I found him one night hiding in the parklands."

Sam remembered with anguish that she loved walking alone

in the moonlight, often barefoot. She was sensuous and loving. His forgiving heart raced with tender memories of loving, heart-stopping intimacy.

"Pierre is bad, wild and exciting," Christina added. "I seduced him and we have been lovers ever since. He, too, was totally disillusioned with his role of relying on other people's donations to survive. I offered to share everything I had to have a life of wicked passion and luxury."

Her eyes flashed with vindictive excitement.

"But he was a fearless knight. We…!" Sam blurted.

"He still is," said Christina as she swung round on him with anger, venom in her eyes. "He is my knight now. I have shown him another life, another way to live. Life is for living, enjoyment, taking risks and having fun."

Sam's eyes dropped to the floor. His heart ached, betrayed by memories and a fellow member of the Knight's Templar.

"Where is Adrianne now?" he queried.

"Oh, Pierre sorted her out. He asked one of his henchmen, a knight like you, I believe, to take her to Aunt Jeuy in Ariege. She would have spoilt our fun if she had been here!"

Finding great difficulty in grasping the unfolding scenario, Sam looked at her in disbelief.

"Your parents," enquired Sam. "Why aren't they here? Where are they?"

Christina continued to flounce, answering without a flicker of emotion. "They fled to Saint-Nazaire with all their devoted servants."

Her scorn was evident, her face twisted with hate. Sam found it impossible to believe the change in someone he thought he knew so well, someone he once loved so much. Christina taunted him further.

"Sam, I played a game and schemed to make you believe I was madly in love with you. You were so innocent, gullible and easily manipulated. In the end, it was no fun at all. You were boring, a mere plaything!"

Tears of hurt and anger gripped Sam's heart. His handlers had bound his wrists tight.

"You are our prisoner now," she laughed mockingly. "But, dear Sam, I wouldn't want you to be on your own. You will have company!"

Sam's eyes grew wide. What exactly did she mean? He realised in that moment that Christina was capable of anything,

Being manhandled didn't suit him. Sam struggled as they marched up the small flight of steps, down a long, dark corridor, turning left, right and then left until they faced a dark heavy studded door.

Sam was forced into the darkness, the door closing with a thud. Apart from his laboured breathing of anger and fear there was silence. Sensing company, his sight gradually became acclimatised to the gloom. Several pairs of terrified eyes stared at him. Accustomed to the dark, aware of intermittent sobs and sighs. Sam realised that the eyes belonged to the group of girls he left safely in the capable watchful eye of Marianne.

Recognising him, Marianne moved forward, grasping his arm, weeping and whispering, "Thank God you are here!" Hugging him tightly in desperation, she then collapsed on the floor.

Sam comforted Marianne on the floor, bit by bit recalling that this situation was familiar. He had somehow been in this predicament before with its memory of vile odours, the persistent drip, drip, drip of water and the stone staircase spiralling down. Sensing that the girls looked to him for a way out, he uttered reassurance, despite being unconvinced.

"We will get away from here," he promised. "Just give me time to formulate a plan."

The girls screamed and sobbed, begging him not to leave them. Peering at them in the gloom, Sam pulled out of his mantle the little yellow ribbon Marianne had given him earlier.

"You will be safe. They will not bother you now. I promised I would return and I did. I must go. I need to check something."

The girls huddled together for warmth. Sam steadily descended the spiral staircase. His heart in his mouth, his head thumping, he reaffirmed that he was a knight of honour, his soul protected by the shield of faith. The compulsion to uncover what was in his mind was growing yet he feared what he might find. Sam knew in his heart that he would never be able to rest until he investigated and satisfied his curiosity. He prayed for strength and courage.

The steps were wet and slippery, the air dank and vile, as ghastly as he remembered. With strong unwavering determination with every step he took, Sam eventually reached the bottom step. There before him was the circular room.

Leaning against the wall for strength, he steeled his quaking frame for answers. First, Sam moved towards a dark, dank chamber to the left of the room. The moisture in the sour air hit the back of his throat, making him wanting to retch. Then came the grim task of studying the emaciated huddled figure in the corner. He recognised the angle and boot of one of the legs. Crying out in dismay, he realised it belonged to Knight Paul. Sam threw his heavy bulk against the slimy wall in abject horror.

Paul and Pierre were brothers who had fought alongside one another. Looking again, he thought perhaps he was wrong. Yet searching the hollow face, he knew for certain he was right.

Feeling enraged and nauseous, Sam felt compelled to

continue searching for answers and to discover the identity of the slaughtered prisoner in the trunk. Displaying painstaking craftsmanship, the roughly hewn wooden chest was still in the middle of the room. The sword easily severed the lock. In fear and hesitation, Sam pushed open the lid, holding his hand to his mouth to avoid inhaling stale, putrid air.

Terrified and fearing what he might see, his eyes searched the gloom, detecting a decomposing bundle of rags. Slowly realisation dawned. The bundle revealed a small female frame. The hands and feet were tightly bound, a dark coloured rag forced into the mouth. Standing back from the trunk weeping, he was unable to take in any more. After a pause for breath, Sam raised nerves of steel from every fibre of his being for one final searching look.

Gently sweeping aside long wavy locks from the face with his sword, he fell back in repugnant abject horror, a bloodcurdling scream of painful despair reverberating around the chamber. He recognised the rotting remains as Adrianne, Christina's sister. Removing his sword, which was holding open the heavy trunk, the lid shut tight with a thud. Sam leaned against the wall to steady his balance, tears of incandescent disbelief trickling down his face.

The drip, drip, drip of water echoed in his ears as he dragged himself up the spiral staircase, finding it impossible to believe what he had just witnessed. He questioned whether Christina was aware of his gruesome discovery.

As Sam reached the top of the stairwell, the girls were still huddled together, shivering with cold and fear. Sam knew he had to search deep within to escape this tower of horror and find an answer to their dilemma.

He remembered the little ledge with the key and then recalled that it was outside the door. The girls sat in silence, praying and wondering if they would ever see daylight again. Resigned to their fate, they looked to the knight for a miracle.

Assimilating the circumstances, Sam sat on his haunches, questioning what makes people change and act as they do. What on earth turns an intelligent, adventurous female into one of selfish self-centred cruelty, a cold heart replacing wit and warmth? The girls sobbed silently, clutching each other tightly for comfort, fearful of dying. Marianne continued to whisper words of faith and hope.

Suddenly, in shock they heard light footsteps approaching, they stopped, then – nothing. They recoiled back into their wretched imposed prison. Very slowly the door opened. A face appeared, with fingers to the mouth, gesturing them to be silent, to utter no sound.

They looked from one to another in amazement. Was she an apparition? The female figure was small, no more than five feet tall, dressed in pale blue and wearing tiny black shoes. Blonde hair flowed freely on her shoulders. Again she reinforced the need for silence.

Stepping inside the gloom, she whispered, "My name is Paulette. Please follow me quietly."

Unable to believe their good fortune, Sam and the girls followed closely in single file. Closing the door after them, and replacing the key to the ledge, Paulette led them downstairs, along a dark empty corridor, where lots of furniture and boxes were piled high. Dawn was about to break, so they had a clear indication of how long they had been imprisoned.

Although they were exhausted, with painful limbs screaming for attention, she urged them to hurry, for they had to reach safety before daylight. Following silently, in crocodile fashion through a maze of corridors, they finally reached the basement. At the end of an unimportant half-moon bay was a small wooden door divided in half. Opening the half door, on the right Paulette pointed to a thick hedge surrounding the outer courtyard.

"Please," she pleaded urgently. "When you move, keep your heads down or you will be spotted. The hedge isn't high, but you should make it if you curl into a small ball and run in a crouched position. That way you should be able to escape without being seen. At the end of the hedge there is a hollow. Wait there until you feel it is safe to run across the open parkland. When you reach the woods you will be safe."

The girls wept with joy, hugging her tightly, tears blocking words of thanks. "Thanks not needed," Paulette whispered. "Just make your escape."

In single file, the girls left the safety of the basement. Marianne, the tallest, chose to be last in case any of them fell. Sam motioned her to go on, promising that he would follow.

Before making a bid for freedom he needed to ascertain from Paulette how she knew where they were. She explained that the family watched Pierre and Christina become lovers, terrified at the influence he had over her, and how the household lived in fear. Adrianne suspected they were plotting something. Paulette sobbed as she explained how the parents became so unhappy. Unable to cope with having Pierre in the house, they were frightened and feared for their lives.

It was a death-defying decision, telling Christina they were visiting Louis Pierre, his brother in the Loire Valley. In fact, they were leaving to seek help, believe it or not, from friends of the Knights Templar. Sam lowered his gaze in shame, quickly sharing Pierre's demise with Paulette.

"I couldn't believe it when I recognised Pierre," said Sam.

"He always was a true adventurer, though I would never have believed he could stoop so low as to renege on his pledge."

Paulette winced. "Christina was always flighty. The whole situation is so out of control. None of the servants knew what to make of it all. Sadly, we may never know the truth. I merely watched from the sidelines as instructed by Adrianne, and when she disappeared I was heartbroken. Never for one minute did I believe the story that she followed her parents. I know because she left her favourite locket behind, a present from her beloved maternal grandmother. She wore it every day. I discovered the ghastly truth when I overheard them boasting during a drunken brawl."

Sam stood for a minute in silence. "You are very brave."

"Not at all," Paulette responded. "When I joined the family as personal maid to the younger sister, I pledged my allegiance to Adrianne and her family – and here I stay until they return. I know that with help they will return soon."

"Where will you live until they return?" queried Sam.

She laughed. "I know this chateau well and its little secrets." Paulette touched her nose with her finger. "I will be okay. Go now before the morning light gets too bright."

Sam bade her farewell with a hug of thanks and respect.

"My heartfelt thanks for your bravery and for rescuing us."

Paulette pushed him out of the door. "Go now before it is too late!"

Sam ran. Paulette shut and locked the door, disappearing to her safe hiding place.

Crouching low, Sam reached the girls, who were safe in the hollow. Marianne spoke with concern. "We are not quite sure which way to run and what to do now. The light is getting brighter."

"I have a plan," announced Sam. "When I give the signal, you all run towards that clump of trees to the right. I will crouch down and run in a zig zag pattern to the left. If my movements are spotted they will run after me, as I am bigger. They will be so interested in catching me that hopefully you will be outside their line of vision."

Marianne hugged him. The exhausted girls looked up, speechless and wide-eyed. They waited until they felt ready and ran. The plan worked. They were all safe.

Sam languished in his chair, drained. The Master glanced across at him, sighing in relief.

"Sam," he said quietly, "when you are ready it is safe to open your eyes."

Sam's movements were slow, his vision disorientated. The swirling purple was dancing in his head. Familiar faces appeared and then disappeared. Wiping tears from his face, his breathing settled. Opening his eyes in disbelief, Sam felt exhausted. He had witnessed events he could not begin to describe. He pinched the flesh on his inner arm to check he was alive. He felt unable to share with anyone where he had been, his experience or how he felt. He was devoid of feeling.

The Master asked again, "Sam how do you feel?"

"I don't know. I can't explain... I don't know!"

"What don't you know Sam?"

"Well..." stammered Sam, "I cannot comprehend what I have just seen. It was a bit like watching a movie except that I played a role."

"That is correct," answered the Master. Sam sat perplexed, still reeling from the experience.

The Master asked Sam to close his eyes. Sam hesitated.

"Trust me Sam. You will not go back into that experience.

CHAPTER TWENTY-TWO

Close your eyes for a little while to regain your equilibrium."

Sam did as he was asked and they sat in silence. Slowly, Sam's breathing settled to a gentle rhythm, his energy harnessed in a completely different way. They sat looking at one another. Eventually, Sam spoke.

"I believe I understand now."

"Tell me, Sam. Share your thoughts with me."

"Well, strange to say, my anger has subsided."

"No Sam," replied the Master firmly. "Your anger has been dispelled."

"You see, I believed my anger has always been directed at me," said Sam. "I now understand it was because I felt inadequate and needed to prove myself. The journey, horrid though it was, helped me see everything clearly. I now understand the parallels between the past and now. I know I have put myself in impossible situations, as if to punish myself. How could I possibly prevent something that already happened?"

"Quite so," smiled the Master.

"I now see that I also felt guilty for not matching up to Christina's ideal man. Watching that scenario made me see she wasn't worth it anyway."

"Quite so!"

In comfortable mode, Sam continued, "So in essence, Pierre's betrayal of what we both believed in and fought for enabled me to find the true me, to help me understand that I am worthy of just being me!"

"Quite so!"

They sat in silence. "The point you are missing, Sam," the Master continued, "is that you need to be content with the person you are, to realise and accept that no one is out to hurt you. Recognise that people come into your life for a reason. They are not all the same. Although there is badness in the world, there is also goodness. There are many genuine people who really care for others, often putting their own lives at risk in the pursuit of helping, encouraging and guiding their fellow man. These people are special. The desire to help others outweighs any doubts or fears they may possess."

"What you have been living with, Sam, and carrying with you over many, many lifetimes, is fear. Fear of failure, fear of not being recognised for the qualities you have, fear of being rejected, ridiculed by someone you love, fear of being loved. Instead of acknowledging this mirage of fear, you systematically turned negatives on yourself in the hope that people will hate you to justify this fear."

"Hate and mistrust are destructive. If Paulette hadn't stood by, willing to risk her freedom and her life to set you all free, where would you be?"

"The thought is too unpalatable to even consider," replied Sam.

"Quite so!"

Sam sat ruminating over the day's events, feeling different. His head was lighter, not so irrational and argumentative. Sensing it was time to leave, he tried to stand, but felt dizzy and fell back in the chair.

The Master stood, taking Sam's hands. "Remember young man that you have done well today. Be very, very proud of the courage you have shown."

Sam blushed, feeling like a child winning his first race. Avani appeared. Assisting the Master's needs, she then turned and took Sam's hands. He looked at her with light in his eyes.

"Come with me Sam," she said. "I am sure healing is called for."

The Master relaxed, glancing at Avani with an expression of completion. Avani led Sam to the Healing Room, where she knew all his energies would be reorganised and freed from guilt and anger.

Sam sank into the chair, the purple crystals still in his right hand, the crystal energies moving and dancing in between the walls and ceiling. Whirling, swirling colours blended in harmony. In disbelief he saw Indigo blend with a honey pink.

Murmuring, "What a funny combination!" he drifted into a deep, peaceful sleep.

23

SAM OPENED HIS EYES, feeling like a different person, finding great difficulty in locking into his habitual agitated energy. Feeling uncomfortable and disorientated, he gripped the arms of the chair. His fragmented thoughts drifted towards work pressures, wondering why he didn't feel at all guilty or frustrated for having avoided important meetings.

He was content to sit and watch Avani, who was sitting opposite. She was a joy to behold, enjoying catching imaginary butterflies, her slim legs swinging free. She truly was beautiful. Shafts of sunlight streaked her hair with golden lights. She looked up smiling.

"How do you feel?" she asked teasingly. "You have been asleep for ages."

Sam stretched. "Yeah, actually I feel quite good."

Looking directly at him, she asked in more serious vein, "No more explosive tantrums?"

Sam's face flushed, looking down at his feet in shame. "Yeah, I suppose I have been a bit of a menace."

Jumping easily down from her chair, slowly Avani moved towards his bewildered frame. "You know, you are so lucky to have spent time with the Master. He is only here for a relatively short time."

"Yeah I suppose, I mean…" whispered Sam. "I am truly so

very grateful."

"Before we go downstairs to meet Ellie…" she began.

"Ellie's here?" stammered Sam.

"Sam, listen to me," replied Avani, a little annoyed.

"You must try to really listen to what people have to say. Trust more. Give them a chance! Ellie promised to be there for you, and true to her word, she is waiting for you downstairs."

Sam's face responded to the sharp words. "I will try!"

"No!" said an infuriated Avani. "That's not good enough! Change your attitude. Let gratitude be your new mantra, then before you know it, you will discover how wonderful and rich your life can be."

Sam's face shone with admiration for Avani as he became conscious of the truth of her words.

"The Master is resting now," she added in a slightly calmer tone. "He asked me to pass on this simple message."

Anxious to absorb every important word, Sam adjusted his posture.

"Your present work involves safety?"

Sam thought long and hard. "Yeah, I suppose it does."

Avani continued with a tone of insistence in her voice.

"Apparently, something isn't quite right. There are short-cuts to do with saving money. You have voiced concerns."

Sam's face lit up. "You are right there."

"Well Sam. You will now have the courage and clarity of mind to resolve this issue in a calm responsible manner."

"I am not sure," said Sam. "My firm insists on keeping shareholders happy and squeezing savings where they can."

"Sam please listen. Trust what I have to say."

Sam squirmed in his chair, aware that his thoughts were beginning to drift.

Looking directly at him, Avani continued, "Be resolute! Remember that yesterday is yesterday. Tomorrow is another important day!"

"Yeah, okay. Please continue."

"You have been concerned about seepage and weakness in the bedrock."

Sam's face shone. "Got it! I know what you are talking about now."

"Hurrah!" rejoiced Avani.

"Detection and resolution will begin within the next couple of months, finalising within two years. Your courage and dogged determination will eventually save many lives, protect the environment and in the long term save money."

"Wow!" stuttered Sam wide-eyed, his cheeks pink with excitement.

"You are highly qualified in your field. Believe in your findings from now on. Stand your ground."

Sam looked amazed. "And when you have accomplished matters to your satisfaction, you will be approached by the UN in Geneva. Do not hesitate. Accept their offer – your destiny awaits!"

Sam sat staring into space, and then looked across at Avani's sombre expression.

"Do you know? In some strange way, I understand."

She took his hand, whispering softly, "It is time for you to go."

Fully aware of his clenched fist, Avani murmured, "If you like, you can take the crystal with you. It will be a permanent reminder of your time here."

They slowly descended the staircase, Sam lovingly caressing the beauty of the wooden banisters as they did so. Standing in the entrance porch stood Ellie, looking tanned and happy. Her face lit up when she saw him.

"How was it?"

In reply, Sam went over, giving a huge hug, lifting her feet off the ground.

"Ellie, you are wonderful!" he said tenderly. "I cannot thank you enough for everything."

Avani looked on, smiling as she closed the door behind them.

*   *   *

The Master sat by the lake, enjoying the tranquillity of a beautiful day, the sun's rays warming his fragile figure as he watched geese dip and dive for food. A mallard's antics illustrated nature's magic at its very best. It was comical, fascinating and incredible. Avani joined him. In harmonious silence they sat by the water's edge, her fingers trailing in the water, creating circles.

"I do love it here," she whispered.

The Master looked across at her, smiling. "Yes, it truly is beautiful. The Higher Realms did us proud."

Avani continued to look up at the birds flying in a cloudless sky, to the lake, then across to the Master, smiling and sighing with delight.

"What a wonderful place to be, even though it is for a short time."

The Master returned her gaze with appreciative affection.

"Will you report back soon?" enquired Avani.

The Master thought long and hard. "I regularly keep the higher echelons abreast of my findings, though I fear my final report may be dispiriting. They will not be pleased, but it will be as they suspected.

"I must confess," he sighed, "that I have found this mission far harder than I believed it would be."

"Why?" asked Avani seeking to understand.

"The people I have met in their own right were interesting. I assisted their ability to focus on their life path and encouraged them to embrace their future with positive enthusiasm entwined with love."

Avani smiled.

"More importantly," he continued optimistically, "I was able to give them insight into their very existence, a glimpse of the spark of divine that they are."

Avani looked up smiling, continuing to stir the water with her fingers. Thoughtfully she answered, "I know they are grateful."

"Yes," said the Master with meaning. "They were, although it will take some time before they realise the importance and full impact of our meeting."

"I agree," replied Avani.

The Master's thoughts drifted. Eventually, he spoke with elation.

"I have to tell you Avani, that the idea of placing the portal stone inside the old lantern was a brilliant idea. It enables me to carry it with me everywhere."

"The higher gatherings are so clever," replied Avani astutely. "They think of everything."

"Yes, my dear. You understand my needs so well. I am so glad you agreed to join me. You somehow make my task seem so effortless."

Avani smiled, giving him a fleeting kiss on his cheek. "Master, I cannot love you any more than I do. I have learned so much just being here with you."

Glancing up at her, he sighed. "Thank you, my dear. This precious little lantern is a bridge of light, a vital energy between the two worlds, enabling me to connect with the higher echelons. My journey to the earth plane has been challenging but fulfilling."

They grinned in unison, enjoying the stillness. "And yet," the Master continued poignantly, "I always return feeling empty. I do wish *they* would listen."

"*They?*" enquired Avani.

The Master sighed, "'*They*' meaning human civilisation."

"Oh, I now understand. In essence, *they* are the reason for your visit here to Planet Earth."

The Master stared beyond the far reaches of the lake in deep thought. "My dear, there are pockets of humankind scattered around the planet where people live by a natural spiritual code; following inherited instinctive principles, completely unaware that they co-exist alongside those who do not follow a spiritual code of growth and understanding.

"*They* have become greedy, dissatisfied, discontent and unknowingly disillusioned. *They* are oblivious that every thoughtless action of desecration and destruction has drastic reactions. *They* must learn to move forward using natural gifts bestowed on them by Divine Intelligence. Depressingly, I fear that this time they may have gone too far."

They sat staring at the water in silence.

Releasing exhausting deep sighs, the Master continued.

"Do you know, Avani, I am astonished by the diverse power of magnetic negative energy vibrating through continental land masses. Fragmented waves of disharmonious conditions are visible to the Higher Realms, clearly evident when nature's natural flow is traumatised. The reverberating protective energy field is influenced by their actions. *They* forget that everything moves cyclically. Seasons are witness to this fact. Spring always follows winter. Every stage of growth has its own unique purpose.

Everything interlinks. *They* forget that Mother Earth is a celestial universal body."

Adjusting his robes, he added, "Come Avani. We need to pray. Mother Earth needs our help. She is rebelling."

"Oh, you make me feel really unhappy when you talk that way."

Tired, dispirited, frustrated and exhausted with the day's events, he looked into her devoted compassionate eyes.

"How can we make them see?"

Avani took hold of his arm as they made their way back to the Hall, his room ready and waiting for him.

"I am sorry, my dear," said the Master a touch wearily. "I am not melancholic. I have high expectations and pray there will be some good news to report back. I know there is a great spiritual transformation taking place here on the planet. *They* will be given due warning, which hopefully they will observe, understand and take notice before it is too late."

He nearly stumbled while wiping a tear from his eye. Avani clutched his arm for reassurance. "*They* must discover the simplistic essence of blending hearts and minds for the common good of humanity. To respect living forms, to understand wildlife and to acknowledge that the animal kingdom interlinks with their very existence. If not, I fear *they* will be brought to a point of facing conditions and circumstances which are out of their control."

With tears falling, he looked at Avani's pure, beautiful radiant smile.

"I do so pray that humanity will embark on accepting, believing the Higher Realms hear their plea for guidance. Unwittingly, *they* turn their back on the powerful meaning of love. Instead they gravitate to revering influential status, wealth and power. They are so misguided. Through eons of time, humanity never has – and never will – be able to control or harness the changing powerful energy of their planet."

"Depressing and distressing though it is, it seems only catastrophes make them stop in their tracks and assist them in re-evaluating the meaning and sanctity of life. In time, global conditions will alter, obstacles to their growth will be cleared and a new pathway will unfold to enable them to move forward with ease. *They* will then accept the true value of life, love and trust."

They walked in silence, Avani supporting the Master as exhaustion weakened his movement.

"Come Master," Avani answered with a new found lightness. "Return to your room. No journeying tonight or tomorrow night. You need to rest."

With gratitude he touched her reassuring hand. "Thank you, my dear. I fear I may have failed in igniting the flame of truth and revelation."

"You have not," said Avani thoughtfully. "You are just exhausted. You came here to report back your findings, not to take humanity's selfishness and the world's burden on your shoulders."

He raised a smile. "You are right. I was told exactly the same statement a couple of nights ago by my spiritual teacher."

"Right," said Avani. "So listen. You are very special and will, I know, leave an indelible mark on this planet when it is time for you to return to the Higher Realms."

The Master squeezed her arm in grateful appreciation as she settled him into his chair, the lantern by his side, the flame flickering gently.

"See they are ready for you, to inspire, replenish and reinvigorate your energies. Now rest. I will come for you when I am instructed by my archangel."

He smiled, closed his eyes and slept. Avani crept out of the room, allowing the cloak of protection and replenishing healing energy to surround him. She ran quietly downstairs, to resume her position by the lake.

Joe was lost in his own world, feeding the wildfowl and fish, and failed to see Avani approaching.

"Hi Joe," she called to him. "What a beautiful day!"

Joe looked up. Avani smiled. She liked Joe. "How are you?" she asked.

"I am well," stuttered Joe, a little embarrassed and unable fully to meet her gaze. "Do you know, I feel so much better since I saw the Master."

Avani laughed. "He has that effect on people."

"Pip has noticed that I smile more, am happier and more positive. I wake up looking forward to each new day."

"I am so very glad," smiled Avani, trailing her fingers in the water.

"Do you know," continued Joe, "strange as it seems, I am so glad I found the courage to run away. If I hadn't done so, I wouldn't be here. I wouldn't have met Pip, the Master or you!"

"Joe, do you believe in destiny?" asked Avani. "I believe you call it fate."

"I guess I do," Joe stammered. "Why?"

"Because," continued Avani, "you climbed over the wall..."

His eyes fell to the ground. He didn't know anyone, but Pip knew how he came to be at the Hall believing it was their secret. Avani looked at him with a knowing smile.

"It is all right Joe. Remember that everything happens for a reason. Sometimes we are led to a place, but are unaware of the reason until we get there. You could call it an inevitable course of events."

Joe's face glowed with pride. "He, I mean the Master, told me I have a destiny."

Avani laughed. "Sure you do, Joe! Your learning was thrust upon you as a small child. Never forget your roots, for they are your foundation. You have mastered many lessons for someone so young."

Joe listened intently, then asked, "Is that why the Master is here, to help people?"

"Partly," replied Avani, not wishing to voice the revelations shared by the Master earlier that day.

"The reason I ask..." Joe hesitated, "is that I feel so good. I met someone the other day who I know needs help, although she would never admit it."

Avani listened, enquiring, "Who is this person?"

Joe looked at Avani, a little embarrassed. "It is Lottie. Well, we call her that," he grinned. "I mean Charlotte Harrold. Apparently, she used to visit the Hall often, since she was a girl of twelve, if I remember rightly. Her Ma knows Nanny Su, the old housekeeper. She still pops in from time to time to see Pip. Pip knows her too."

"Oh, I see," said Avani, trying to make sense of the conversation. "Do you really believe the Master could help her? More importantly, do you think she would be willing to come?"

"I do, I do! She is really nice yet..." his thoughts drifted, "there is loneliness and a sadness in her eyes which I cannot describe."

"Quite an observation for a young man," teased Avani.

"Do you think it possible?" Joe asked excitedly. "Please, say it would it be possible!"

"Well, I am not sure," replied Avani. "When is she due to

visit again?"

"I am not sure," replied Joe. "She lives the other side of Torchester."

Avani sat quietly, closing her eyes. Joe sat in silence, watching. Slowly Avani opened her eyes, looked at Joe and then spoke.

"She will visit on Friday, early afternoon. We will meet then."

"How?" quizzed Joe.

"Never mind how, Joe. We will meet with your lady Lottie."

Joe sat quietly, throwing the last bits of food to the gathering ducks.

"She is really nice and so pretty," he said. Avani glanced at him and Joe blushed.

After an awkward silence Avani asked, "Do you like water Joe?"

"I do, I do. I love the colour change, especially when the clouds block out the sun, then the water alters its mood."

Avani spoke with conviction. "Joe, if in the future you are given the chance to row or sail, please accept it. You will excel and enjoy the experience."

Joe looked wistfully at the water, imagining being on a huge sailing yacht with a light wind moving the vessel swiftly through the waves, salty sea stinging his face.

Looking up at Avani, his heart pounding, he said, "Do you know Avani, I have learned so much since I came here. I feel so lucky."

Avani gently touched the tousled top of his head. Then lifting his chin she said, "Joe, my lad, you have far to go. Your journey has just begun."

Joe jumped up, tears of joy in his eyes. "Thanks Avani. See you!"

Clutching the fish food container in his hands, he ran to join

CHAPTER TWENTY-THREE

Pip to continue his day's work.

24

PIP AND JOE WERE taking a break from work, slumped lazily under the shelter of a huge gnarled apple tree, munching an old-fashioned Ploughman's Lunch, their stomachs full to bursting.

"Why is it called a Ploughman's Lunch?" asked Joe, yawning.

"I suppose," laughed Pip, "it's because a hunk of bread, a wedge of cheese and a dollop of pickle was a quick, easy way for farmers' lads to enjoy lunch. I don't know, Joe. You ask the most bizarre questions."

"No, I don't" replied Joe. "And old fashioned?"

"Aye," laughed Pip, imitating a craggy country accent. "I suppose so, because we are swilling it down with ye olde apple cider."

They both cracked up laughing dozily in the hazy hot sun. Their day had begun just before seven.

Pip murmured contently, sprawling flat out on the grass, watching birds high in the tree, a spasmodic gentle breeze brushing leaves in the midday sun. He was amused to hear the odd friendly scrap in the hen house close by, oblivious to life's, every day cares and worries.

"'Tis better to start early young 'un, and finish early before the sun gets too hot."

Joe saw the shoes first, bright red patent, with three-inch stiletto heels. They were T-bar court shoes at the end of long, tanned, well shaped legs, the perfect finishing touch to a tailored close fitting skirt in pillar box red, and a long red and black dogtooth fitted jacket. A crisp white cotton blouse, black leather clutch bag and diamante brooch completed the outfit.

Joe squinted in the sun, trying to make sense of the confident figure standing at his side. A coiffure hairstyle framed a strong, intelligent face with immaculate make up. With a heady perfume filling his nostrils, Joe sat up, nudging Pip.

Taking a few moments to adjust to the strong sunlight, they stood up.

"Lottie!" welcomed Pip. "What a surprise! Great to see you. How are you?"

"I am fine thank you. How are you and Joe?"

"We are good too, and could play this game all day long," chuckled Pip in buoyant mood as they ambled towards the cottage.

"Would you prefer cider or tea?" he asked mischievously.

"Well," replied Lottie teasing, "surprise me!"

Pip emerged with a tray of three small ciders. "I have only poured you a little one, Lottie, as it is my own brew and a strong one! Gotta think of you driving home."

Pip looked at Joe, who sat giggling.

"This really is a lovely surprise Lottie. What brings you to the Hall today?"

"Well," replied Lottie, taking off her jacket and adjusting her blouse, "I finished work early. My last appointment was cancelled, and as I was close by, I thought I would pop in to see Nanny Su. She is great company you know, a mine of information. She always keeps me informed of all the goss, if you know what I mean."

Pip nodded.

"In fact, it was she who suggested that if I had time to visit the Hall, I should check out the new gardens. She tells me you have made many changes."

Pip nodded again. Lottie chattered, drinking her mug of cider and feeling more relaxed by the minute.

"I must say Pip that I couldn't help but notice the woods teeming with colour and wildlife as I walked through. It brought back many childhood memories."

Lottie continued to sip her cider, lost in thought. "Pip, I must congratulate you on your hard work. The grounds look magnificent. They do you credit, especially the fragrant flower borders by the kitchen garden wall. You have surpassed yourself this year. The grounds haven't looked so colourful since Lady Lillian was in residence."

"I did some too," interrupted Joe, wishing to be part of the *tête-à-tête*.

"Tell me," said Lottie, "The Hall is different somehow. Everything looks clean and fresh. Has the old solicitor instructed a maintenance company to spruce things up?"

Words failed Pip.

"In a way," stammered Joe quickly. "It's great though, don't you think? The Hall has visitors too. They are kind and pleasant. You would like them."

"Would I?" retorted Lottie, a little annoyed. "I asked about the Hall, not who was staying there. Anyway, are visitors allowed?"

Pip found his voice. "Hey Lottie, come off your high horse! Joe was trying to say that the visitors have been enormously supportive and helpful."

"Oh, I am sorry guys. Don't take any notice of my grumpy mood. I've just had one of those irritating bad weeks."

Joe and Pip looked directly into her discontented eyes. "We

understand!" Lottie felt foolish. She straightened up, returned their gaze and asked, "Have either of you time to show me around the rest of the grounds while I am here?"

"Of course we have," Joe answered quickly. "Can I do it Pip?"

"Sure you don't mind?"

"No not at all," replied Joe, delighted to have found a way to get Lottie to himself.

"I will catch up with my work later Pip, I promise."

"Oh, tomorrow will do, lad. You worked hard this morning. Go and enjoy the rest of the day."

The three sat reminiscing, the cider helping Lottie to unwind. Eager for her to finish her drink, Joe asked as casually as he could, "Are you ready?"

"Gosh, you are keen!"

Lottie sighed, smiling at his excited enthusiasm, all signs of frustration and annoyance dissolved. The pair waved madly to Pip as they left him busily contemplating the following day's task of re-laying a small path.

"See you two later!"

Joe proudly showed Lottie the new alpine garden with its two interlinking ponds and fountains. Sitting together at ease on Joe's favourite wooden bench, mesmerised, they stared at rainbows dancing through the fine fountain mist.

"It is so peaceful here," remarked Lottie. "I'm sure if the Hall was my home, I would never want to leave."

"I know how you feel," Joe responded. "I have only been here a short time, but I feel safe. I love the comforting silence."

In the distance, he saw Avani walking by the lake. Lottie noticed her too. Pointing, she asked, "Hey, Joe, who is that?"

"Oh, she is one of the visitors," Joe remarked.

They watched Avani cross over the rustic wooden bridge

on the far side of the lake and then disappear behind the trees. Lottie's inquisitiveness eventually got the better of her.

"Can we go down to the lake?"

Joe cleverly concealed victorious mirth. "If you would like to."

The lush grass by the lake was dense under the trees, like an expensive carpet you sank into. Lottie took off her shoes and walked barefoot. Instantly, the formidable successful business mask dissolved, revealing a carefree amiable young woman. Avani saw them and waved.

"Gosh! She's really pretty stunning," sighed Lottie, walking towards her.

"She is that," replied Joe proudly, "but so are you!"

He blushed, his face and neck glowing a deep crimson. Avani walked to greet them. Joe stood tall, coyly introducing them, feeling unsure of what to do next. Avani suggested they sit by the lake, watching the geese and ducks.

"They never fail to amuse me," she began. "They are so comical. Real comedians, they remind me of characters in a play."

"Yes, I suppose they do," replied Lottie.

Sitting close together in a semi-circle on the grass in silence, they were content in each other's company to let time slip by, observing the clowning around of nature's waterfowl. Avani was joyfully content.

"I feed the ducks and fish every day," remarked Joe. "It's one of my duties here. In fact, I will soon have to run back and get food for them."

Avani caught Joe's eye. He understood. Lottie paddled, splashing her bare feet in the cool refreshing water.

"You know, Avani, I just mentioned to Joe that I would never want to leave here if this was my home. This place holds special memories for me."

Avani and Joe nodded, exchanging a knowing look.

Joe sat for a little while longer, then scampered back to find Pip. Lottie relaxed, using Avani as an unconscious sounding block.

"It's strange Avani. Clive Burton, my last client, never cancels appointments. He's known for being a stickler for time, is a difficult client to deal with. I couldn't believe it when he rang really annoyed saying that his train was delayed leaving London, so regretfully he had no choice but to cancel the meeting."

"Really!" commented Avani, appearing to be half listening, intent on creating more and more circles in the water with her hands.

"I am so glad I came, though," said Lottie. "I always feel as if my batteries have been recharged when I leave here."

"Do you need your batteries recharging often?"

Lottie sat in silence, unsure of how to answer. The exposures of a raw nerve highlighted her vulnerability. She stood up.

"It was good meeting you. I think I will go back to join Pip now."

"Whatever," replied Avani nonchalantly.

"Whatever?" replied Lottie smartly. "I hate that word."

Avani stood up, meeting her gaze without being intimidating.

"Lottie, I know what that word means to you. I also know the real reason you are here. I know of your deep guilt and unhappiness."

"Trust me when I say that you can't possibly know!" Lottie swung round on her. "I came just to see the garden as Nanny Su suggested."

Avani ignored the bristling defence.

"In part, and if my understanding is correct, your impulse to visit the Hall today was far greater than the opportunity to go home early."

Lottie glared into her soft gaze, wary of this stranger. Weary and beaten, she collapsed in an undignified heap on the ground. Reassuringly, Avani brushed her hand, crouching down to her level.

"If you carry on persecuting yourself as you have been, living your life with blinkers on, everyone involved will eventually irretrievably suffer."

Lottie burst into tears, rocking to and fro like a small child.

"I know, I know, but I don't know how to undo what I have done."

Avani spoke gently, waiting for her emotions to subside. "If there was a way, would you take it?"

Lottie looked shocked, wary and apprehensive of this beautiful knowing stranger intruding into her private closed world. Her righteous indignation exploded.

"How dare you challenge me?" she exploded. "You don't know anything about me."

Avani sat quietly, allowing Lottie time to gather her thoughts and feelings. Sitting in uncomfortable silence, eventually she continued.

"Lottie, I do know someone who can truly help. I have to say that meeting him is the true reason you are here now at the Hall. It's an opportunity to put matters right."

Lottie's slim frame shook through a window of tears. She met Avani's gaze with a tortured expression of fear, guilt and sadness.

"I guess there is truth in your words. Do you truly believe you can help me?"

Avani took her by the hands. "Lottie, come with me. I would

like you to meet someone very special. It is vital you right wrongs. Do you realise how many people's happiness and future are in your hands?"

Lottie gazed at Avani in awe, all her defences smashed. With tears streaming down her red swollen cheeks, she whispered, "I don't know why, but I believe you."

Slowly, the two figures sauntered to the Hall. The huge entrance greeted them with a blaze of light, the heat haze clearly visible on the backs of the two huge bronze dogs on guard. Lottie's demeanour altered. Depleted of antagonistic energy and fight, she meekly allowed Avani to take the lead. Fresh tears flowed as they set foot inside the entrance hall, as vivid memories surfaced. Lottie froze.

"Avani, I don't think I can."

Avani took her hand firmly, ignoring the protestations. "Lottie, trust me. You can... and you must."

Lottie's body locked in fear. She was terrified that long held suppressed emotions would finally split open the controlled hard shell she had painstakingly constructed over the years.

Her hands touched the rich polished wood of the familiar wooden banisters with tears welling in her eyes. Approaching the top landing, pulsating coloured lights danced brightly. Lottie pointed at the coloured lit floor in amazement.

"How... where are they coming from?" she asked in a bewildered fashion.

Avani ignored her questions, leading her firmly towards the second door. A soft white light was just visible under it. The landing, although familiar, was somehow different.

Avani opened the door, but Lottie pulled back, hesitating, unsure of whether to enter or not. The Master stood to greet her. His compassionate smile fixed on Lottie's sad face and was then directed towards Avani.

"Avani, my dear. Thank you for kindly bringing Lottie to me."

Avani nodded, promising, "I will return later."

"Lottie, please sit in the little chair opposite me."

Lottie followed the instruction as if in a trance. "You know my name?" she snapped.

"Of course, my child," said the Master. "I know everything about you."

Lottie's swallowed hard, nearly choking, an embarrassing discomfort resulting in her body over-heating. Perspiration trickled down her shoulder blades and between her breasts. Her contrived cool exterior was suddenly exposed.

They sat in silence. Lottie's eyes circled the room. She was feeling strangely reassured. The two small windows let in just enough light to brighten the room. The collection of pictures obviously modern art, were probably painted by some off-the-wall, hippie-type artist from the local commune.

"How odd electing to hang those blocks of colour in huge beautiful patina frames," said Lottie. "Each one must have cost a fortune!"

Intuitively respectful, with unspoken admiration for the mysterious strange inquisitor sitting opposite, Lottie was instinctively comforted by the Master's loving influence. Inexplicably, she was here in the Hall, sitting before an indescribably imposing fragile yet powerful energy. Looks belied his wisdom. His flowing draped robes were of a different era. It was like stepping back in time. The graceful shape of his hands and feet fascinated Lottie further. His strong chiselled face was kind, wise and compassionate. Noticing the little lantern, Lottie observed its flame oscillating from burning brightly to a mere flicker.

CHAPTER TWENTY-FOUR

"How do you feel now?" asked the Master.

Lottie sniffed, drying her tears, trying to regain some composure. "I feel sort of odd, as if I want to cry yet I feel unable to do so."

"You can cry real tears," answered the Master.

"Yes, I did... I do, but..." Lottie stammered, "not what I call real tears, where afterwards I feel a wreck, as if I have been purged in some way."

"I understand, my child. Have no fear. I arranged for you to come and visit to enable me to help you."

Lottie sat shock still, digesting this remark.

"Let me ask you a question. Do you believe in angels?"

Lottie thought long and hard before answering, wondering if this was a test or trap. "Yes, I suppose I do."

"I know you do. You prayed hard as a small child."

Flinching, Lottie shied away from him. She had forgotten.

"Let me explain, then this might help you to understand. Guardian angels are spiritual beings that assist the soul during its earthly journey. They have the power to inspire and fine-tune intuitive awareness to those whose need is greatest. A life journey on Mother Earth is merely a platform for experiences, enabling a soul to learn and grow. Spiritual experiences are constant reminders that there is a purpose to every earth life."

Lottie sat in silence. The Master continued. "Would you agree you have experienced a roller coaster of emotions during this lifetime?"

Lottie glared at him, sensing barriers being demolished.

"Your progress has been observed since you were a young child. We tremble as we monitor your feelings of loneliness, guilt and regret, and watch you zip around in your little car. I am sure you will not be surprised to learn you were not alone when you visited your favourite inlet cove recently, unburdening your emotions on the incoming tide."

Lottie sat transfixed, staring in disbelief. She was in tears yet her incensed emotions had quelled. Interpreting her distraught expression, the Master asked, "Are you ready to begin?"

Frozen but magnetised by his presence, Lottie still doubted his well intentioned interference.

"Are you really able to help me?"

"Of course, my child. My assistance is the reason for our meeting. Though be warned: the insight will be distressing and reveal hidden painful truths. Secrets can harm you."

Lottie sat perplexed, shaking, knowing in her heart that she had done wrong.

"Please help me. What do I have to do?"

The Master smiled reassuringly. "In essence nothing. Just observe and share with me truthfully what you see and feel."

"It sounds really simple."

The Master smiled and was relieved, gesturing for Lottie to choose a crystal from the little wooden box to the right of her chair.

"Untruths, for whatever reason, mask truths. Over time, those truths surface, wound, fester and destroy unless they can be captured in time."

"I think I understand," whispered Lottie.

The Master touched the little lantern for the surge of wisdom and energy he needed, asking, "What crystal have you chosen?"

"I believe it is amber. It is a deep dark yellow, one of my favourite colours."

"That is fine," answered the Master, who was pleased. "It is essential for you to be comfortable. Please focus on the yellow picture."

Lottie felt puzzled. The Master spoke firmly. "Lottie, as you focus the colour will change. Please allow yourself to be drawn into the colour. In essence, be part of the picture and tell me what you see and feel. Remember Lottie that you are safe, protected here with me."

His words impinged on her solar plexus, accepting this journey would be extremely tough. Lottie stared at the yellow block of colour until her eyes streamed, the crystal cradled in the palm of her right hand. She was finding the shade strangely magnetic, drawing her deeper and deeper into the depth of colour. It slowly changed, swirling and whirling into tighter and tighter circles of dark and light shades of burnt amber.

As she focused, her eyes closed, the colour eventually revealed the silhouette of a small girl. It remained just long enough for Lottie to recognise the face. Instinctively shrinking back in fear, she realised that the image resembled her as a three-year-old, drawn by an artistic family friend. Suddenly and unexpectedly the image reappeared, changing to bold colour. Feeling panic rising, she glanced at the Master, seeking reassurance.

"Lottie, you must focus. What you see will not hurt you. It will reveal truth in its raw true state. It cannot hurt you now. It is the past!"

Lottie sighed, reluctantly resuming concentration. Slowly her eyes closed.

"Rest assured Lottie," the Master whispered, his voice trailing way off in the distance. "You will see pictures on the screen of your mind. Though you cannot see me, you will hear my voice."

She nodded, sighing heavily, her shoulders dropping into relaxing mode.

Lottie observed a confident, pretty fair-haired young girl celebrating a fifth birthday in extravagant style. She was an adored indulged child, playing on an elaborate garden swing. Seeing the girl push the swing higher and higher, an anxious mother was monitoring every move. The girl resembled the mother, a fine-looking woman in her early thirties, and an epitome of elegance. An affluent lifestyle was afforded by a devoted husband, who jetted to and from the States, sacrificing time with his family to give them the best money could buy. Classed by friends and family as a workaholic, the father was respected by all who knew him, and loved and adored by his family.

Feeling remarkably elated, Lottie watched a taxi stop outside the house, then pull away. She watched the man drop his suitcase at the side gate and run to the back garden where the family would be waiting. Lottie smiled as he threw his coat and briefcase haphazardly to the ground, an American "First Class" tag swaying. Scooping the girl up into his arms, he embraced his wife with deep affection. He was home.

The imposing bespoke, architect-designed house was created in a peaceful setting abutting the river, pristinely maintained by husband and wife, gardener and housekeeper. Side and front walls were adorned by wisteria and honeysuckle. The landscaped two-acre garden gently sloped to the riverbank, where three wooden steps reached the river water's edge.

Most afternoons the family sat watching wildlife while slow moving houseboats, motor boats and the odd barge made their way to Gloucester Docks. A magnificent old weeping willow graced the river bank, and was a sanctuary to water fowl and precious water voles. It was a magical place in which to fantasise.

The picture accelerated. Lottie sat back in surprise.

The garden looked different. The sun appeared not as bright; the swing was motionless. Now seven, the young girl was sitting alone on the riverbank steps, crying. Surveying the garden, close to the house Lottie noticed a shiny coach built Silver Cross pram, sun shade tassels gently swaying in the breeze.

The baby cried. Mother ran to pick it up, looking drawn, tired and sad. After a few moments, the exhausted, harassed father approached with a wide stride and gaunt face, which was drained of colour, concern etched into deep lines. He hugged the mother and baby. The young girl ran towards them, desperate to be included in the embrace.

Sensing underlying tensions, Lottie wriggled. Her heart warmed to the young girl, who was obviously shut out, sensing her desperate need for love and affection as the inconsolable chubby baby screamed, demanding attention.

Lottie watched in rapid speed the weeks and months unfold. She observed with poignancy the poor interaction between mother and child, both inescapably locked in an unfortunate intricate web of isolation and fear. The father's despondency was forcing his decision to spend more and more time away from home. Visibly bewildered at the turn of events, he was unable to understand or comprehend where love had gone. What had gone so horribly wrong in their lives? His frantic, solitary, heart-wrenching search was to restore happiness for his family and to meet his beloved wife's expectations.

"I don't want to see any more!" announced Lottie, leaning forward. "I find watching this drivel distressing and – I might add – quite boring and unnecessary."

"Do you really? Dear child, I am impressed how observant you are. Please humour me for just for a little while longer."

The Master shook his head, praying he could somehow penetrate Lottie's formidable wall of defence.

Aggrieved and irritated, Lottie sat back in her chair. She turned the little crystal over and over in her hands.

Reluctantly, she watched an emotional battle unfold between mother and child. Despite trying her best, the girl was unable to please her exacting mother. Every day, niggles, problems and worries were directed her way.

Biting her lip, she cringed, watching the mother fawn over the baby. Lottie despaired watching the rejected girl burdened by more and more daily tasks in order to ease the mother's day. With father absent on business, the girl's days were peppered with arguments, periods of sullen silence and tension, resulting in bitter unspoken tearful unhappiness for them both.

Lottie watched the heartbreaking scene of the girl constantly seeking her mother's approval for every task undertaken, struggling to be the daughter she perceived her mother wanted. She winced, understanding the girl's desperate need to seek her mother's relentless reassurance.

"Whatever?" she heard the mother's scornful comment over what appeared to be an insignificant incident. The girl had split a bag of flour she was carrying to the kitchen table.

"You are such a clumsy loon! Whatever I ask you never seem to do it right. Whatever…. Whatever..?"

Lottie sobbed. The girl spent more and more time alone, sitting by the river bank or in her bedroom. The mother's growing resentment of the girl was clear to see yet Lottie failed to understand why.

Over the months, the girl withdrew into a world of books, believing she was wicked, deserved to be punished and didn't merit happiness. A remark was reinforced daily by her mother's stinging words. "Whatever you do in your life, young lady, you will never amount to anything!"

The outburst came suddenly. "She can't do anything right!" screamed Lottie. "What a cow! She is nothing more than a horrid bitch!"

The wall of tearful pain collapsed, years of pent up unhappiness forcing the dam of restraint to flow free.

"I hate her; I hate her!" wailed Lottie. "She always spent time with Harriet and never wanted to spend time with me."

The Master listened.

"I loved my father!" she shouted angrily at the top of her voice. "He was a nice man, a good man. It's not my fault he had to work away."

"Do you love Harriet?" quizzed the Master.

"I don't know," wailed Lottie, blubbering in between words. "I suppose I care. She is my only sister, after all, but why did I always seem to be in the wrong? I could do nothing right. When I got good marks in my tests at school, Mum never seemed happy for me."

The torrents of angry unhappy tears flowed. "I could never please her. If I was late coming home after being out with friends, I was in the wrong. If I was home early, I was in the wrong. If I was home studying I was ridiculed for being a book worm!"

The Master allowed her to rant. "Shsssh, Lottie. Dry your eyes and watch."

"I don't want to! She made my life hell when she was alive."

The Master took her hand. "Lottie, listen. Your mother loved you very, very much. Sadly, she was not as strong as you."

Lottie looked at him in wide-eyed disbelief. "She was," the Master continued, "a desperately unhappy lady, a victim of her own circumstance."

Lottie sat bolt upright, full of enraged indignation. "What do you mean?" she demanded.

"You are doing so well, Lottie. Please bear with me for a little while longer. Tell me, are you still focusing on the colour?"

"Yes, yes!" replied Lottie impatiently.

"Good. You have already experienced a change in energies. This time it is important you experience feelings and emotions in order to grasp how unexpected circumstances unleashed a change of events."

Lottie sat quietly. "I do understand," she answered, instinctively aware that this meeting was more than a psychological session of prying.

"Lottie, listen to me. You are strong, my child, in character and health, with the gift of a positive attitude to life, regarding everyday problems as challenges which you face head on."

"During your young life, you showed courage. Your mother's upbringing was entirely different. She was spoilt. From time to time, children who never have to strive for anything find the harshness of real life daunting and frightening. Your mother was like that. She came from a privileged background, with impeccable credentials."

Lottie's mouth dropped open. Eyes open wide, she relaxed. The Master adjusted his robes, looking Lottie in the eye. "Your mother used to be a happy, carefree young woman that is until the age of thirty-five."

Listening intently, Lottie gawped. "When you were nearly six, an episode in her life turned her world upside down. Your father embarked on a three-month business trip to Virginia in the States. During his long trips away, you and your mother stayed in a holiday apartment near Weymouth where you spent many happy days together, swimming, shopping and visiting St James's Park nearby. Do you remember?"

Lottie nodded. "I remember vaguely."

"During one of these visits, you fell off a high slide, landing on your left arm, ending up in the local Accident and Emergency

Department where it transpired you had sprained your wrist quite badly. In fact, you were lucky not to have broken it!"

Lottie nodded, remembering the incident clearly. "I recollect I was brave," she laughed. She recalled the memory of an enormous plaster cast on her left arm, the nursing staff drawing squiggles and faces, distracting her from pain and discomfort.

"While you were waiting to be discharged, a dark-haired young man with a goatee beard, an old boyfriend of your mother's, bumped into you while visiting his mother, who earlier that week had been admitted with kidney problems. An urgent call summoned him from South Africa to resolve nursing care for his widowed mother. Jeff naturally took compassionate leave from his mining job to be close at hand."

"Waiting to see the consultant, and worried for his mother's future health, he was delighted to share concerns with an old friend, visiting the town together, reminiscing over coffee and cake. Do you remember?"

Lottie nodded. "Worried about you, your mother was also lonely and vulnerable. At that time, your father was lecturing at a series of seminars, for old friends to support one another during a stressful phase and to catch up on old times. It was a natural sequence of events."

Lottie smiled, recalling bumping into Mike Lovell, a colleague from her old company. A chance meeting over dinner, he was someone she regretted losing touch with.

More relaxed, Lottie absorbed the Master's words with renewed interest.

"Jeff Humberstone was an only child, an honourable, clever young man your mother met through friends in Bristol when just eighteen. He was your mother's first love. They were long-standing friends with time on their hands. It seemed reasonable and quite natural to spend time together. In fact, young lady, you were spoilt rotten."

Lottie grinned, snatches of memories returning. "Do you remember visiting the Tower of London and getting lost on the London Underground? Spending time at the Kennington Hotel, Chiswick? Paddling in the sea off Padstowe in Cornwall?"

Her posture relaxed as she relived happy memories. Glancing across at Lottie with relief, the Master continued. "Loving feelings were inevitably rekindled, romance blossomed and they fell deeply in love. It is important to acknowledge that during this time you and your mother were very close."

Lottie closed her eyes and remembered.

"Completely out of the blue, one day Jeff announced that he had been recalled to South Africa, returning at the end of the week. Failure to do so signified losing his job. He had no choice. Your mother was distraught by the news. In her mind, the arrangement worked well. Jeff was there for you both; your father was working hard on the other side of the Atlantic. Over the weeks they spent time together, your mother accomplished a way to compartmentise the two relationships. Convinced she could easily pick up the threads of married life when your father returned, the three of you were having fun."

Lottie snuggled deeper into the little chair. The Master continued, relieved that she appeared to be taking these revelations so well.

"Your mother's idyllic world was torn in two as she finally grasped Jeff's return to South Africa was imminent. She became hysterical and panic stricken. Jeff pleaded for her to go with him.

"Unable to deny your father the family he cherished and worked so hard for, the daughter he worshipped, her head ruled her heart. Heart-broken, she and Jeff agreed to do the right thing and part, vowing to sever all ties, never to contact one another again. Sadly, this was the beginning of your mother's deep unhappiness."

Lottie listened, seemingly unperturbed. "For a short while, your lives returned to a form of normality. However, your mother was unable to come to terms with turning her back on Jeff, the man she truly loved, until the full impact of this romantic encounter erupted – she was pregnant!"

Lottie watched the block of colour, observed her mother's distress, her loss of weight and irrational behaviour, electing to sleep in the guest quarters. Night after night, she paced the floor, over the coming weeks becoming more and more isolated from friends and family. Late one night, conscious realisation struck hard. Her beloved daughter was the only witness to her clandestine encounter.

Lottie wriggled, feeling strangely ill at ease.

"Your mother shared her condition with no one, choosing to isolate herself more and more from people," said the Master. "She was ashamed and aware that conception didn't coincide with your father being home. Suffering self-imposed torment, she was racked with anguish."

"Just over twelve weeks into the pregnancy, alone in the early hours of the morning, drenched in blood, silently screaming in agony, she miscarried. Her physical and emotional suffering took place in private."

"Followed by an overwhelming relief, her secret would remain just that. The following days and nights were replaced with pangs of unrequited love, guilt and fear, which, over time, bore deep into her soul."

"Your father returned from a three-month stint in the Far East oblivious to events. He was shocked and devastated to face a beloved wife who was unwell, depressed and tearful, and an emotional reclusive daughter. Unable to comprehend events, he sought medical advice, took time out from work and booked a two-month holiday in Cornwall, your mother's favourite county, in an effort to turn back the clock."

"In fact, he booked a hotel suite overlooking the sea a few miles up the coast from Padstowe. Ironically, it was just a fifteen-minute walk from the very hotel you holidayed with Jeff. Unbeknown to your father, for your mother the choice of location was an utter nightmare, fearing you would unknowingly betray her secret. Irrational fear clouded common sense."

"The following year, Harriet was born. Your father was proud and elated. Sadly, a few days after her birth, your mother's deep-seated problems began. The self-imposed guilt of losing her clandestine love child, reinforced by the birth of a healthy baby, tainted her joy."

"In her mind, the child had been conceived in guilt, not love! Compounded by the complexity of daily life, the weight of remorse grew heavier over the years, so much so that day-to-day living became impossible. She mentally shut down."

"Your mother loved you dearly, but feared your knowledge. Her only way of releasing guilty shame was to control and manipulate the one person who could betray her secret. Wickedly and very cleverly, she prevented husband and daughter from forming any loving meaningful relationship, thwarting painful truths bubbling to the surface."

"Cleverly influencing emotional interaction within the family, becoming unwittingly devious, she ignored your heavy-hearted father's wish to understand how life had soured through his wife's change of personality. Tragically for all involved, in order to survive, your mother became brittle and an accomplished actress."

"In denial for her actions and feelings, she transferred the blame for this romantic interlude onto her daughter, convinced that if she hadn't stupidly fallen off the slide, the encounter would never have happened. In her mind, the sequence of events was all her daughter's fault. Over the years, she became more and more embittered. Deeply unhappy, she inwardly resented seeing couples in love and families happy in one other's company."

Lottie looked up at the Master with red-rimmed eyes. Sitting in silence, she sobbed. Her throat, rib cage and heart ached. Slowly she released deep, heart-wrenching emotions. The Master watched as years of hurt and pain released their hold.

25

THE MASTER WATCHED Lottie's pain slowly dissipate as the healing rays enveloped her, replenishing their energies. It was a difficult, exhausting journey for them both.

Lottie sat forlorn, emotionally drained. The Master smiled, knowing the worst was now behind her. The door opened and Avani peeped around the door. She handed the Master a glass of rose water, then gently roused Lottie. The Master nodded, relieved and sighing with satisfaction. With one process completed, he closed his eyes and slept.

"Come with me," Avani whispered. Lottie looked up, silently weeping and obediently followed Avani to the Healing Room. Avani understood and helped her to the little chair, pointing to the vibrant swirling, iridescent streams of powerful healing energy bouncing around the room.

"Lottie my dear, you must rest," she said quietly. "The process has left you empty. Your energy centres need balancing."

Lottie nodded, relieved that Avani was taking control. Giving in to emotional exhaustion she slumped into the little chair, holding the crystal tightly in her right hand.

"You will be revitalised very soon," whispered Avani. "Just allow the crystal healing energy to build. It will revitalise your being with love and light. The Master requests you to be still and to rest. Allow the healing energies to replenish, heal and uplift you."

Lottie complied, feeling as weak as a new-born kitten. Every facial expression was an effort. Her physical frame felt weak.

"You are safe here, Lottie. Please give yourself permission for healing to take place. It is sorely needed. I will come for you when it is time."

Lottie collapsed like a rag doll, suppressed embers of distrust and resentment disintegrating into the ether. She momentarily glanced around the immense room, dispersing energy flowing from the blocks of nature's precious gems. Her befuddled mind struggled to rationalise the experience. Her inner core more at peace, Lottie's erratic breathing settled into a gentle, shallow, rhythmic pattern. She was drowsy, drifting into deep sleep, completely unaware that she would soon be bombarded by powerful rays of revitalising healing cleansing energy.

As dusk fell, Lottie stirred, her waking awareness focusing on the Hall and recent events. Through muzzy thoughts she recalled an unexplained compulsion to view the Fosseway gardens. Did she really see them? Her floating conscious mind searched to connect fragmented unrelated jigsaw pieces. She recalled meetings, a London hotel, important contracts and Clive Burton. Her sharp logical mind seemed totally incapable of forging any connection. She was flanked by a roller coaster of illogical events while drifting in and out of a surreal mindset.

Avani sat patiently, waiting for Lottie to sense her presence and wake to the here and now, to be greeted with an amazing warm smile.

"Hello sleepy head. How are you feeling?"

Lottie stretched her arms and wriggled her toes.

"I feel different. I don't feel so ... um... disconnected. Does that make any sense?"

Avani moved towards her, squeezing her hands.

"I am so relieved. The Master was really concerned that you were so low. He saw your life force draining away in front of his eyes."

"Oh," replied Lottie, trying to remember how miserable and exhausted she felt. Holding Avani's hand tightly, she murmured softly, "It was very emotional!"

"I know. Sometimes it is necessary to lance a boil to release the poison to allow the wound to heal."

Lottie grinned. "You sound just like Nanny Su!"

"Guess what," chuckled Avani. "I heard her say that to young Joe a few days ago when he had an infected splinter in his hand. It's a brilliant analogy.

"Lottie, the Master asked me to put an important question to you. Please stop to think before you answer."

Lottie sat perplexed, wondering what response she would need to consider.

"The Master would be greatly relieved if you could stay within the grounds of the Hall tonight."

"Oh," replied Lottie in surprise.

"He is anxious for you to remain within the protection of his energy until the process is complete. His far-reaching energy stops at the boundary of the Estate and he needs to spend time with you tomorrow."

"Oh!" shrieked Lottie, taken aback. Avani read her thoughts.

"Believe me Lottie, the worst is now behind you."

Lottie sighed. "I do hope so."

Avani continued, "Am I right in assuming that your family are not expecting you back tonight, as you planned to stay overnight in London?"

"That is correct," answered Lottie warily, wondering what

was coming next.

"Good," said Avani. "That's settled. I am so relieved."

Lottie looked at her, completely baffled. Avani was pleased with herself, excitedly skipping and twirling, delighted with her clever arrangements.

"I have spoken to Pip. It is all arranged. He has made a bed up for you in the little attic room."

"Oh really?" Lottie replied, a little aggrieved at not being consulted.

Oblivious to her annoyance and bewilderment, Avani continued. "You are in for a treat tonight. I believe Pip is making his famous venison stew in your honour."

Lottie burst into laughter at Avani's excited expression.

"Do you know Lottie. It is marvellous how sometimes everything works out just perfectly."

Lottie understood the reasoning. "Yes, Avani. On reflection it makes sense. I must admit I would have found it extremely difficult to leave and then return. I give in. I am happy to go with the flow and do as the Master asks."

"Good!" whooped Avani.

The attic room reminded Lottie of visiting her grandparents in Kent. The patchwork quilt was reminiscent of spending hours watching Grandma Connor patiently and meticulously sorting squares of fabrics into a pleasing shape and design. Lottie's pride and joy at that time was mastering "Cat's Cradle" and French knitting with a large wooden cotton reel. She felt strangely cushioned as she approached the cottage, laughing male voices reinforcing the decision. The venison stew was as Avani had promised a delicious succulent treat with tender vegetables and "Oh to die for!" dumplings.

Lottie woke early to the familiar sound of Schubert the

cockerel announcing it was time everyone was awake.

"I am going down to the lake before breakfast Pip. Is that okay?"

"Sure thing," answered Pip.

Lottie ran all the way, with a new-found spring in her step, beyond caring that her clothes were creased. It was good to be free, which was a long forgotten feeling.

Glancing at the morning sky, everything looked bright, fresh and alive as she viewed the wild fowls' early morning ritual of flying high, oblivious to material pressures. Ambling back to the cottage, she spied the Master in the distance. Lottie started to run after him and then instinctively stopped, realising that this was his quiet time.

Pip and Joe were just finishing breakfast when she burst through the door.

"Avani asked me to meet her at the Hall about eleven o'clock," said Lottie. "Is that okay with you guys?"

"That's fine. We plan to tackle the far side of the orchard today. I reckon Mr Fox was on the prowl last night as Jess found feathers on the ground."

"One of the hens?"

"No," responded Pip from deep inside the larder. "My guess is that it's one of the guinea fowl. The fox family must be starving."

Lottie tucked into a hearty breakfast of eggs, sausages and beans. "Delicious scrummy breakfast, Pip!"

"Cooked it myself," volunteered Pip playfully. "The sausage mess is my secret recipe. Nanny Su showed me how."

"Yes, she's brilliant at sharing new ideas."

"How long have you been visiting the estate?" asked Joe.

"Since I was about twelve," said Lottie. "My mother was a close friend of Nanny Su. They often worked together preparing for visitors when Sir Alf entertained shooting parties and the like."

"So you knew the family well?"

"I suppose I did," replied Lottie wistfully.

"You must have met David?"

"Yes, I did," answered Lottie quietly, who quickly changed the subject.

Sitting under a cherry tree, she idled time watching the two men work. Lottie found viewing others working a kind of mischievous therapy. By choice, her lifestyle was frenetic, making sure she was always on the go with no time to think or worry. It was pure bliss to watch others work. Lottie wished that next time around she would like to return as a lazy duck on the lake.

"You work well together," she commented.

"Yes we do," shouted Pip from high up in one of the trees. "Hard work never hurt anyone. Great company, fresh air and a beautiful orchard. What more could a man want?"

"Yes, indeed," Lottie sighed. "What else? It's nearly eleven, so I'm off now boys. See you later."

"Maybe. Not sure where we will be later today, so feel free to use the cottage. Enjoy today!"

"Hmm," muttered Lottie to herself. "I do hope so. I wonder what revelations the Master has in store for me today."

The hazy sun was hot, too hot for comfort. Rushing to the welcome shade of the entrance porch, she found Avani sitting sunning herself, a daisy chain on her wrist, nimble fingers plaiting long grasses.

"Hi, Lottie! The Master is ready for you. Are you happy to go up or would you like me to accompany you?"

Lottie hesitated, pleading, "Please take me. Somehow you give me courage."

"Me give you courage? Come on Lottie, you don't need courage, but just a good dose of honesty."

Feeling embarrassed, Lottie looked down, keenly aware that Avani could see right through her improvised bravado.

Climbing the stairs, Lottie felt sick, anxious and light-headed, her solar plexus working overtime. She looked to Avani for reassurance.

"Come on Lottie! You met the Master yesterday. He is wise, gentle and keen to help you."

"I know," sighed Lottie, wiping away uninvited tears. "I admit to being a ridiculous scaredy cat."

Comfortable in his chair, the Master appeared refreshed. The Chakra Room seemed vibrant, with shafts of sunlight streaking the floor and walls. The lantern was more significant than she remembered. The flame seemed brighter and taller than before.

Standing up to greet her, the Master smiled.

"Come my child, sit with me. Thank you for coming and for staying within the boundaries of the estate. I fear I would have lost you if you ventured outside my protective field."

Lottie nodded. Avani signalled to them both she was leaving. "I will come back later."

Their eyes followed her departure as she closed the door. Lottie's gaze returned to the Master.

Plucking up courage, she said hesitantly, "Avani told me that the worst is behind me."

"Really?" commented the Master. "I suppose it all depends on what you define as 'the worst'!"

Lottie swallowed hard, realising that this meeting wasn't going to be as easy as she had first hoped.

"Lottie," said the Master. "I feel it is my task to implore you to take your responsibilities seriously."

CHAPTER TWENTY-FIVE

"I do, I do – and I work really hard!"

The Master shook his head. "Lottie, I do not mean responsibilities as in earning a living or caring for others. I mean responsibility for your actions."

Lottie looked down at her shuffling feet, as if they were going to speak on her behalf. She knew deep in her heart that the unspoken message was instigating a feeling of being exposed and naked, fully aware that deceit eventually harnesses deception and misery. Up to now she had successfully convinced herself that little could be achieved by self-recrimination and tears.

"Lottie, it is vital for everyone concerned for secrets to be revealed to prevent any more destructive unhappiness. In essence, it is time to set the record straight."

Feeling like a naughty chastised child in front of a feared headmaster, Lottie stared into space. The Master read her thoughts.

"The Higher Realms know you did what you thought was correct at the time for what you perceived to be the right reason whereas we suspect you knew almost immediately, deep in your being, that you took the wrong course of action and have been suffering for it ever since."

"I know! I know!" yelled Lottie, sobbing and shaking with remorseful self-imposed guilt. "No one can possibly guess how miserable I am."

"Lottie, you have a specific role to fulfil this lifetime. Trust me when I say that together mountains can be scaled, but only if you believe it can be so. The past cannot be altered, but you can change the present and future by a change in attitude. Meet life and its challenges in a positive rather than a negative way. Accept that unkind people are under the spell of illusion, believing what they want and say is right."

Lottie sat transfixed as the Master caught her gaze. "Please choose a crystal from the wooden box to your right and hold it in your hand as before. Now focus on the chakra pictures surrounding you. What colour are you drawn to? Choose carefully and sense the vibrations. How do you feel? Select one that resonates with your emotions."

Lottie selected a small piece of green calcite, which was soft and smooth to the touch. Looking first to the Master, she focused on the block of bright green until her vision blurred to a fuzziness of muted greens. Eventually, her eyes closed. In the far off distance she heard the Master's voice.

"As before Lottie, you will hear my voice. Describe what you sense and feel. This is important. This past life memory had a bearing on choices and decisions."

The colours swirled into swathes of green, spiralling faster and faster until Lottie felt they would whirr so fast that they would spin into oblivion.

Suddenly everything went black, becoming enveloped in a blurred world of darkness. There were indistinguishable sounds, moving, tumbling, tugging and then silence. Brightness was followed by bloodcurdling screams of agony and fear, anxious words, then cold crisp air.

The picture accelerated. Lottie saw a village church with a notice board proudly announcing, "St Stephen's Church, Roegate. Vicar: Rev Herbert Bridgman. Everyone welcome." The Gothic arch church porch had handcrafted benches. The solid studded oak door was a symbol of protection, one which offered reassurance to those seeking comfort and answers.

A sprinkling of fresh snow slowly coated lovingly tended graves, the afternoon air cold and crisp. It was mid-December. Surrounding trees dressed in white Chantilly lace depicted an early Christmas scene.

Suddenly, the still silence was shattered by the excited chattering of a noisy school party on their way to a nativity service. Approaching the porch, soft whimpering cries could be detected and then faded. As the children lined up in crocodile fashion waiting for the teacher to catch them up, one lad heard a muffled sound.

"I guess it's a cat," suggested a boy.

"It might be hurt," shouted a self-assured young man of twelve.

"Boys, don't be so silly!" replied a tall affected girl, who was dressed from head to toe in blue, with a white muffler. "It is probably the vicar's dog."

As the walking shuffled to a halt, the sound seemed closer. The twelve-year-old saw it first. "Hey, someone has left a basket on the porch bench. It might be kittens!"

As he removed the covers, he drew back in astonishment and surprise. Concealed beneath a thickness of coverings, lay a tiny new-born baby. The children shrieked as one "A baby!"

The teacher arrived, irritated and demanding to know what all the fuss was about.

"I thought I told you children to be good, to be quiet and to respect where you are."

"Yes, but…" The twelve-year-old pointed to the basket.

"Oh my God!" replied the harassed teacher.

Faced with the contents of the basket, he felt the baby's hand, which was barely warm, the tiny face blue with cold. Opening the church door and beckoning for the vicar to come, he ordered the children to go in single file and sit quietly in the pews until he returned. Carefully carrying the basket, he ran to the adjacent vicarage, quickly explained events to the vicar's wife. He handed her the precious bundle and then ran back to the church to take control of his charges, who sat silent and motionless awaiting his return. Their eyes followed his entrance, eager to know if the baby was all right. "All is well," he motioned with his lips and hands.

"Wow," whispered one of the smaller girls. "Why would anyone leave a baby in the church porch?"

The picture accelerated. Mrs Bridgman, a lovely soul with a big heart, stood just over five feet tall, was well rounded, homely in a motherly way and anxious to support her husband's career in every way. She found time to visit the sick and needy. Her jams and bottled fruit were quickly snapped up at the local village socials. Mrs Bridgman married late, so children were out of the question. She and her husband met whilst helping dysfunctional families cope with post-war problems in London.

After great deliberation, with much excitement and delight she willingly agreed to care for the infant until its mother could be found, deciding to call him Stephen. After all, he was found in the church porch.

Despite lengthy enquiries, the authorities drew a blank. After much contemplation regarding a permanent placement, it was agreed that the Bridgman's could care for the child. If over the years, the mother came forward, a decision would be made as to whether they could continue caring for him until he became an adult.

Lottie watched the joy this child brought to their lives, enriching it overnight. Mrs Bridgman took every opportunity to proudly show off her new addition, thrilled to relay the story of how the little infant had been found in the church porch.

"Someone must have loved the child a great deal," commented Violet Atkins, a willing well-wisher. "He was left where he would be found."

"Yes, yes!" Mrs Bridgman replied, thrilled to be centre of attention for the first time in her life. "But the most amazing part of it all is the letter."

"A letter?" asked the middle-aged woman.

"Yes," replied Mrs Bridgman enthusiastically. "It's a bit of a mystery really. It simply read, "'Love this bairn and please do not let him suffer'."

In-depth questions revealed no further clues to the baby's origins. Mrs Bridgman continued, "He was well cared for, you know. The basket and covers were real quality. I am convinced that the mother of this beautiful child was accustomed to the very best."

"Well, I never," thought Violet.

The picture accelerated. Lottie settled into her chair, enjoying the lightness of moving into the green chakra picture, relieved she was not viewing distressing gloom and doom. She watched the child grow strong, happy and healthy. Starting school, he warmed to his adoring guardians, who proudly marked every milestone reached, recognising that the bond between the three of them grew stronger every day.

The lad showed a natural leaning towards music. Singing solo, his beautiful clear voice lifted the vibrations of church services with the choir chanting the chorus. The Bridgman's watched him grow to be popular with his peers, for he was both kind and considerate. The admiring Mrs Bridgman's keen observation noted the importance of encouraging Stephen's friends. Groups of lads visited the vicarage after school whenever they could to indulge in mutual interests.

The picture accelerated. Lottie observed Betty Bridgman lose weight, become depressed, reclusive and then pass away.

The young man returned from university in Scotland, devastated at the loss of the woman who loved him, showing by example the right way to conduct his life. With heavy heart, he returned home to grieve with his beloved Herbie, the Rev Bridgman. The young man achieved the efficient transition of moving Herbie to a one-bedroom flat close to the vicarage, then returned to his studies.

The Rev Bridgman's faith kept him buoyant. Alone, he often recalled Betty's fear when Stephen decided to study medicine in Edinburgh.

"I feel as if my heart will break, Herbie. He has been the centre of our lives for so many years."

Fragile as he was, Herbie Bridgman's faith enabled him to see the best of every situation. "Betty, my dear. We are now coming to the end of our lives. Stephen was a wonderful gift, but he was on loan to us. We were given the opportunity to nurture him and in return he gave us great joy. It is time for us to wish him well and to allow him to fulfil his dreams."

Lottie saw Stephen graduate with honours and fall madly in love with a pretty young Scottish lass. She sensed his great reluctance in sharing his future plans with the man who showed him love and kindness. Lottie also sensed Herbie's depth of disappointment and his hesitant acceptance that the lad he loved and nurtured was moving away for good.

"We will come and visit often Herbie. We promise."

"You do that young Stephen. Never forget that Betty and I loved you as if you were our own. I cannot begin to describe the wealth of joy you gave us over the years."

Lottie cried as she watched the two souls shed and share heart-wrenching tears. Both men knew that this parting would be the last.

"Before you go Stephen, remember that your birth mother loved you very much, so much so that she put your life in God's hands."

Stephen's eyes welled. With all the gratitude, love and gentleness he could muster, he hugged and thanked the man who loved him and taught him so much."

The picture faded and was replaced by a block of emerald green. Lottie sat back in the chair feeling emotional, but relieved.

"Thank you Master. Avani was right; the worst is behind me. What a happy outcome."

"Any questions Lottie?" quizzed the Master, looking directly at her bright shiny face.

"I suppose Stephen was lucky. Good folk cared for him."

"Yes, very true. Cast your mind back to the circumstances."

"Oh," replied Lottie, a little stunned. "You mean abandoning the baby?"

"Quite so my dear. Are you telling me that is an everyday event?"

Lottie sat upright feeling marginally uncomfortable. "I suppose I was thinking of Stephen, not his mother."

"Quite so," answered the saddened Master. Lottie was silent, disturbing thoughts whizzing round her head.

"If we are nit-picking," she threw at him, "what is this to do with me?"

"Everything," replied the Master. "Everything!"

26

The Master patiently permitted Lottie's explosive frustration to erupt. "Why put me through all this?" she demanded, confronting him rudely, with an air of arrogant indignation. "What do you want from me?"

Unruffled, the Master quietly asked, "Why do you believe you are here?"

Crestfallen, Lottie's guilt overwhelmed her unease. She knew deep in her heart what the answer was, realising that the emotional build-up was leading to a situation she chose to ignore.

"How can I possibly put things right after all this time?" she implored.

"There is always a way," answered the Master gently. "There is always a solution to any problem if it is sought with the right intent."

Looking up at him, Lottie fiddled with her skirt, smoothing imaginary creases. Seizing the moment he continued. "Are you willing to peer into yet another scenario to help you fully understand the depth and power of love, which, sadly is so often misused in your world?"

"Will it be distressing and painful?" replied Lottie trembling, now in a more controlled frame of mind.

"Lottie, that is for you to judge."

Wriggling in discomfort, clutching the green calcite tight in her right hand, she adjusted her position to gain a clear view of the block of green, her posture remaining awkward and clumsy.

She watched intently as the block of green swirled around and around. Uncontrollably, once drawn deeper and deeper into it, she felt slightly nauseous as the shading colour spun faster and faster, seemingly spiralling out of control. She retched, momentarily losing consciousness in another dimension.

The green picture depicted a scene from the 1920s. She observed a young woman, who was hurrying, waddling strangely and furtively. A thick woollen shawl was pulled close to her head, covering her shoulders, shielding a lost, drawn, worried face with its frightened coal black eyes and pinched lips. Her face was framed by dark wavy locks, her long skirt and coat sweeping the ground as she hurried. Her worn buckled shoes were dusty with walking many miles. A small but heavy tapestry bag was clutched tightly in her left hand.

The warm summer evening encouraged groups of people to loiter, laugh and chat aimlessly, excitedly waiting for the music hall doors to open. The woman was slinking close to the walls and shop doorways as she approached, desperately trying to be invisible. She saw the doorway and with a cautious backward glance entered the building.

Thick smoky air tinged with greasepaint hung like wet sails in a ferocious ocean. The heady cocktail of stale sweat and booze made her giddy and unsteady on her feet. The woman felt nauseous and gasped for breath. Trying to avoid inhaling more of the intoxicating theatrical concoction, she covered her mouth with her right hand. Slowly, she manoeuvred herself further into the maze of corridors.

Head down low, her face partly covered in fear of being

recognised, she ignored dancing girls in costume cavorting with brilliant coloured feather boas, trapeze artistes in leotards twirling coloured hoops and tap dancers rehearsing their routine. Stopping exhausted outside a cluster of dressing room doors, she was desperate to rest, but anxious to view nervous unsuspecting artistes as they passed by. Tapping on a parade of doors calling "Lily?" the muffled reply always the same, "Not in here, dearie! Further down the corridor."

At last she found Lily. Elegant in a long, dusky pink satin dressing gown trimmed with ostrich feathers, she was touching up eye make-up. When their eyes met, the young woman burst into tears, collapsing on the floor with sheer relief and exhaustion. "Lily, thank God I found you at last! I need your help."

Lily helped the young woman to a garish gold covered chair, kneeling down on one knee to address the weary visitor.

"Violet, what on earth are you doing here? You look dreadful! What brings you here? What's happened to you?"

Violet opened her coat to reveal a swollen torso. "Lily, I'm pregnant and need your help urgently."

Lily gasped in utter amazement, quickly gathering her thoughts. "I am due on stage in five minutes, so can't talk now. Stay here. I'll put a note on the door to stop anyone coming in and will be back soon."

With a display of professionalism, Lily quickly changed into a gold and black Charleston dress with matching headband, black patent silver buckle shoes and was gone. Feeling drained, Violet sat shaking, clutching her stomach, but relieved that she had successfully tracked down Lily.

Lily returned with a glowing look on her face. "I was brilliant tonight!" she exclaimed. "The audience was in fine voice and showed their appreciation by applauding two encores."

Violet acknowledged her excitement, then anxiously and meekly asked, "Can we talk here?"

"Not really, it's a bit difficult. I have to be on stage for the finale in fifteen minutes, then we can go to my digs. Is that okay?"

"Thank you," whispered Violet, trying to keep awake.

Time dragged. Minutes seemed like hours. It was a long wait. Violet was hot, sticky and uncomfortable, with the foetus pressing down on her bladder increasing her discomfort.

After a quick change, the two women left covertly by the side door, busy stage hands oblivious to their plight.

"My digs are just round the corner Vi. It's not far. They are quite basic, but suit me, as they're close to the theatre."

In the safety of Lily's room, hugging a warm mug of sweet tea, Violet poured out her tale of woe.

"This babe," she began, lovingly stroking her swollen stomach, "was conceived out of love and deserves a life. I do not want him to suffer, 'cos he wasn't wanted and born out of wedlock. Against all the odds, he's growing inside me and I pray he'll survive."

"What on earth are you talking about?" asked Lily, concerned and a little frustrated. "And how to do you know it's a boy?"

"Trust me Lily, I just know. I knew from the moment of conception. I remember laughing with elation and shouting, 'I am pregnant!' until reality hit me." Her face paled as tears welled in her eyes.

"I need your help Lily. I haven't got long. My system has been out of sorts for weeks now. I came to you because I have no one else to turn to."

"What do you mean, Vi? What are you trying to say?"

"As you know, at eighteen we lost touch for ages. Much to Ma's annoyance you left home to dance in London, always saying you would follow the lights. It was pure fluke that I found you.

I glanced through a local paper left on the train and recognised your face."

"My face in the paper!" shrieked Lily with excitement.

"Yes," continued Violet. "I was amazed but not surprised to see that you had changed your name from Kathleen Beccles to Lily May."

"Well, I had to," replied Lily giggling. "Can you imagine a successful artiste by the name of Kathleen Beccles?" Vi shrugged.

"Any regrets about moving to London?" asked Vi, manoeuvring her bulky frame to a more acceptable position.

Lily glowed at the flattery and numerous advances thrust upon her by admiring suitors while living her new life.

"No regrets. I'm so very glad I fled the drudgery of life up North."

"Yes, yes, I understand, but please listen to me," urged Violet, adjusting her heavy size. "Please listen."

"Go on. You have my attention. I am all ears."

"I left home shortly after you, had a few jobs as maid to various households. Eventually, I secured the position as lady's maid to Lady Foshelm, up at the manor house on the west side of Hatchet Green, not far from the common. I'm happy there. She's a gracious lady, and they treat me well."

Her gaze dropped to the floor whilst reminiscing. "It's all a bit bizarre really. I don't quite know how to explain. Lady Foshelm has three sons, all of them serving abroad. Her eldest, Freddie, came home unexpectedly from his regiment. The Lord and Lady were away in Paris... and one thing led to another. I'm not a good-time girl Lily, you know that. This is the result," sighed Violet, stroking her swollen, stretched abdomen.

"It just happened, it was..." she stammered emotionally, words tailing off to a whisper, "as if... we knew each other before… We were meant to be together!"

"So what do you want from me, Sis?"

Violet smiled, looking at her with deep sibling affection. "You haven't called me that for years."

Feeling remorseful and a little ashamed, Lily eventually responded. "I know. I am sorry. Being in London is a completely different way of life. It's exciting with a real buzz. I just want to leave the past behind."

"I understand," murmured Violet, feeling unimportant and a little hurt.

"I need somewhere to have this babe – if I survive. I say that because I know it will be an ordeal. Somehow, I feel the babe is laying the wrong way round, so I'm not expecting an easy birth."

"Oh err…" answered Lily, lost for words.

"When it's all over, I'll return to the manor as if nothing had happened. If not, we must talk of a plan."

Lily listened, worried and shaking.

"If I don't manage to get through this, I beg you to arrange for my body to be buried in the cemetery close to Snuff Mill Woods. Freddie and I used to walk there. It's our special place and reminds me of him."

"Where is he now?" asked Lily, struggling to contain her emotions.

"He was recalled to his unit in India. He knows nothing of the babe. If the family got to hear of the pregnancy, well you know what they would have done – kicked me out and possibly taken me to that dirty old gal in Lambeth. You know, the one reputed to sort out tangled knitting!"

She shuddered at the thought. "Some survive, but most die. I wasn't going to do that. I concealed it pretty well, don't you think?"

Lily looked on in disbelief, pondering how her older sister had managed to conceal her swollen figure from her employers.

Violet continued, easing her expanding torso again. "This little lad."

"You really know what sex it is?" asked Lily in astonishment.

"No, but I got a good feeling and know I'm right. Anyway, I promised this little one he would not suffer for my foolishness. I lost my head and that's about it. Tell you something, though. Being in love is a kind of mad all-consuming magic. Words cannot describe how I feel just to hear Freddie's voice. Just being in the same room as him is enough." She blushed, trembling. "My heart flutters and I go weak at the knees just thinking of him!"

When they started, the contractions came strongly at regular intervals. Alone in Lily's dingy room, the little lad was born, oblivious to the secrecy and strife concerning his existence. Lily was regarded by artistic colleagues as being superior and unapproachable. Her childhood roots had instilled practical common sense, so she dealt with her sister's complicated labour in a cool, efficient manner.

"I have been thinking, Vi. I feel it's best to resolve this matter as quickly and easily as we can."

Vi wept as she hugged and kissed the precious gift lying on her breasts. He fed vigorously.

"In the morning, I will find Mrs Mann. She is known to be the local gossip and midwife round these parts. I need to ask her advice."

Violet and the babe snuggled together. The birth had been difficult, but was quick at the end. Violet ignored the bleeding.

Lily returned anxiously. "I have a resolution, Vi. Apparently, Mrs Mann knows of a woman in her late thirties who has just delivered her fourth child. She's willing to take your baby and bring them up as twins if that is what you want."

"It is not what I want, but what I must do," Violet howled. "I have no choice."

"Good, that's settled," answered Lily, who was firmly in control of the situation. "Mrs Mann will come for him late tonight and your secret will be safe."

Vi clung to the child all day, feeling as if her heart would break. Lily stroked her head tenderly. "Vi, it is the right decision." Violet nodded.

"I need you to promise me something," she pleaded. "Promise me that the thirty- something mother will love and look after him."

"Of course," Lily retorted, drained of the responsibility of dealing with her sister's hopeless situation. She felt disagreeably annoyed at being forced to make difficult decisions.

"And you. What will you do now?"

"If you walk with me to Snuff Mills Woods, I can slowly make my way back to the manor without being seen."

"Okay, that's what we will do at nightfall," replied a relieved but worried sister.

The infant was taken from her as agreed. Both sisters were numb for different reasons. They both had red-rimmed eyes, puffy with heart-wrenching emotion. Holding Vi tightly around her waist, Lily clung to her distressed sister, who leaned against her for support. Together they made slow progress to the woods.

"Will you be okay Vi if I leave you now? You are still bleeding quite a bit."

"Thank you, I'll be fine. And thanks for being there for me, Sis. Although we lost touch, I never forgot you."

The sisters hugged and kissed through farewell tears.

Suddenly, in what seemed an eternity, Vi was alone. Her heart ached for the new-born infant, her torn uterus screamed for attention. Moving unhurriedly through the woods, the outline of the manor loomed in the distance; she was nearly there. Vi knew that the housekeeper had a compassionate heart, despite presenting a hard exterior. Hanging on to the knowledge that she could soon rest, Vi longed to receive the care and attention so urgently needed.

With legs of jelly and a pounding head, clutching her aching stomach, Vi whispered words of encouragement to her traumatised body.

"Vi, keep going! Just a few more steps. You can see the lights in the distance. You are nearly there!"

All of a sudden, her world spun at an alarming rate. Disorientated, losing her footing, she managed to clamber up the bank and leaned against a tree trunk for support. Light headed, trees seemed to be spinning like a top. Streaks of brilliant light cascaded from above. Vi fell again, enveloped in a pool of blood, the expected haemorrhage ending her plans.

The Master calmly watched tears stream down Lottie's cheeks.

Angrily she screamed, "Why show me that horrid image? It was awful!"

Looking directly at her, he asked "No, Lottie. You tell me why."

A cloud of venomous anger overwhelmed her sense of reasoning. "She didn't have to die!" screamed Lottie. "Anyway, what does she have to do with me?"

"As mentioned before Lottie – everything."

Lottie pouted, indifferent, sulkily drumming her fingers on the arm of the chair in abject defiance.

CHAPTER TWENTY-SIX

"Tell me, does the image ring any bells?"

"What on earth do you mean?" responded Lottie.

In exasperation, the Master coloured his words. "Lottie, please sit round and face me."

Lottie did as she was told, pondering that each vignette illustrated the meaning and depth of love.

"Obviously your residual memory is very faint," said the Master, "because in both lifetimes you were the baby."

Lottie sat shell-shocked, her body contorted with unexpressed feelings. Emotion engulfed reality. Slowly, she understood the root cause of her melancholic, discontented existence, which resonated loudly in her heart and head. The compulsion to visit the Hall was now painfully clear.

"Please forgive me," she pleaded.

"Lottie, you have to find a way to forgive yourself."

Smarting, she felt rejected. Silence reigned. Lottie sat still. Closing her eyes, she hoped that the two disturbing images would disappear.

"Please help me to understand!" she implored. "I did it, I decided..."

"For who?" interrupted the Master.

"I did what I did because I thought it was right at the time, but I now see I was being selfish."

"You were not only being selfish," said the Master calmly. "You were also self-centred and dishonest, convincing yourself that the decision you made was perfect for you, not at any time prepared or willing to address the consequences of your actions."

Lottie sniffed, wringing her hands, transferring the crystal from one hand to another in a semi-trance. Looking up at the Master, her painful anguish slowly began to ease, inner strength rising up from deep within.

"You are correct. I will put matters right. I cannot carry on living this lie for much longer. It makes me feel that I do not want to carry on with just existing."

They faced one another in silence.

"Well done, my child. Put matters right. Do not hold back now. Although there will be tears, remember that it is impossible to find true peace and happiness through other people's misery. Dishonesty feeds misery."

Avani appeared, on cue as always.

"You are incredible!" Lottie commented. "You always appear when needed."

Avani smiled. "That is why I am here. I am merely a link in an integrated inexplicable chain of events."

Lottie laughed at the convoluted answer.

"Remember," added the smiling Master, "to take courage in both hands. Love is often a misunderstood powerful emotion."

With some trepidation Lottie allowed Avani to settle her in the Healing Room, drained, but emotionally relieved that her secret had at last been shared. Now more at peace, she sat with her eyes closed, physically calm, the green calcite in her lap. Her mind was now determined to put matters right.

Lottie sighed with relief. For the first time, she was willing to see the far-reaching unhappiness and incomprehensible repercussions manifested by her actions. Now that they were transparent, the way forward was unmistakably clear. Breathing deeply, focusing on her intended mission, Lottie revelled in the emerald, gold and pink light enveloping every fibre of her being. She was aware of fearful guilty concerns being slowly dispelled in this sacred healing place.

Avani allowed her to rest for more than an hour, longer than Lottie intended. The difference was clearly evident. Lottie's eyes were bright, alive with hope and excitement.

Lottie hugged Avani. "Thank you so much for everything. I feel strong now. I can do it. Believe me when I say everything will be okay."

Avani escorted her to the Hall entrance. Squeezing her hand, the earth angel murmured, "Remember Lottie that the hardest part of any decision-making is the indecision. Once made, the easy part is carrying it through."

Lottie returned the embrace. "My thanks again Avani. I will never forget you."

Lottie left the Hall, running and skipping all the way back to Pip's cottage. The boys were still in the orchard. They had worked hard and were resting, a half-full glass of cider on the grass beside them.

"Hiya!" said Joe. "Everything okay?"

"Fab!" replied a smiling Lottie.

"Before I leave Pip, can I run something past you?"

Pip looked at her out of breath flushed face. Standing up to face her, he said, "Well my dear, ask away!"

"Pip, I guess you know the Jenkins family better than anyone around here."

"As well as any, I reckon. Why?"

"I need to get in touch with David and Lady Jenkins. Can you point me in the right direction?"

Pip thought for a moment with a knowing twinkle in his eye. "James McGoonan, Lady Jenkins' family solicitor in Torchester, might know. I believe he is still in contact with the London legal beavers."

"Thanks a million, Pip," answered Lottie, hopping up and down, eager to get home.

"For what?" asked Pip.

"For just being you, Pip!" Lottie shouted, laughing as she disappeared into the woods.

Smiling, Pip scratched his head. "Joe, this world gets crazier every day!"

Lottie's little red sports car glided into the circular drive of an ostentatious modern four-bedroom home, which was situated on the affluent side of Torchester. At the front door to greet her was a bewildered, suited, mild mannered, bespectacled man, standing a little over five foot eight tall.

"Darling you are home at last!" he said. "I tried Clive Burton's office and was rather taken aback to hear that your meeting was cancelled. Where have you been? I've been worried sick and thought that you might have had an accident. Couldn't raise you on your mobile."

"I'm fine," answered Lottie, giving him a quick peck on the cheek. "Yeah, that's right. The meeting was cancelled."

"Hey Paul, it's great to see you! Just off to have a quick shower and then we must talk."

Paul glanced at her in astonishment. He could never describe their relationship as affectionate, so the spontaneous display of warmth left him reeling. Opening the patio doors, he poured two large gin and tonics and then sat waiting for Lottie to join him.

Lottie appeared, dressed in white trousers and a blue striped T-shirt. She greeted him with a curious smile. Her face was free of make-up. Lottie's combed hair was still a little damp, all visible signs of the past thirty-six hours had been removed.

"G and T?" asked Paul.

"Yes, I cannot think of anything nicer. Have you had a good day? The garden looks good this year. I can't remember seeing the shrubbery looking so vibrant."

Paul stared at her. This wasn't the Lottie he knew – soft,

reflective and interested in him.

"Are you sure you are feeling all right? You look somehow different."

"Yes, Paul, I am, but I need to talk and come clean."

"What do you mean 'come clean'?"

Paul looked at her, puzzled, worried, confused and agitated.

"Before I launch into my impromptu monologue," Lottie uttered nervously, "I just want you to know you are one of the finest men I know. You're dependable, patient, caring, good-hearted and always championing the underdog."

Paul downed his drink. "I presume you mean like an obedient puppy dog." He promptly got up to replenish his drink with a double and then sat down.

Lottie continued, looking directly at him. "I know this may come as a shock, but I have to confess that I have been living a lie. Or should I rephrase that? We have been living a lie."

Speechless, Paul took a gulp, wondering what was coming next.

"Sorry Paul, but there is no easy way to say this."

Lottie knocked back her drink. "Do you remember fifteen years ago when you asked me out on our first date? I seduced you."

Paul remembered. He was excited but embarrassed at the memory.

"I seduced you for a reason. I was already pregnant."

Now shaking in total shock, Paul finished his drink, and then poured them both another large one.

Eventually finding his voice, he asked, "Are you trying to tell me that Tristan isn't my son?"

"That's correct," continued Lottie, ignoring emotional protestations, rising indignation and anger.

"You see, Paul, I was in a relationship with someone I loved very deeply before I met you and the feeling was mutual."

Paul's dry mouth opened to speak, but no sound would come. Lottie continued.

"When I realised I was pregnant, I panicked. You were keen on me and the rest is history."

"But…" said Paul, desperately trying to salvage his manhood. "The dates?"

Lottie laughed. "Conniving women can always manipulate dates to fool a man. In actual fact, Tristan was early, which helped make the deception even more credible, so much so that over the years I convinced myself you were his biological father."

Head in his hands, Paul sat shaking. "So what you are telling me is that our whole marriage has been one big sham?"

"Paul, I care for you deeply. You are one of the best friends any girl could have. I trust you implicitly. I love you, but I am not in love with you, and to be honest never have been. There is a difference."

Paul got up from the chair, praying his legs would support his body. "Okay, if that is so, why now? Why all this sudden wonderful pretence of affection?"

"I am truly fond of you, but for years I've been denying my true feelings. I just cannot do it any longer, and the truth has to come out for the sake of everyone involved."

Puce with anger, Paul screamed, "Don't you bloody care what happens to Tristan and me?"

Lottie swung round on him, defending her words. "Yes, I do care! For all our sakes, I need to tell Tristan the truth you are not his biological father, but also to reiterate that you have loved and nurtured him since the day he was born. He couldn't have asked for a better father."

Paul convulsed in tears, desperately trying to make sense of the outpouring, trying to rationalise the timing of this excruciating revelation.

Drinking heavily, they sat in silence. There were no words of recrimination or anger. They both knew that their relationship was built on acceptance and mutual respect. Intimacy was a topic never voiced or challenged by either of them, silently accepting it didn't exist, so wasn't important in their relationship. Both accepted that their needs were not met. Separate bedrooms reinforced infrequent intimacy.

"May I ask who the father is?" asked Paul, by now a little more composed.

"Of course. In a way it is your right," Lottie answered as gently as she could, relieved that her secret had surfaced at last.

"It is no one you know Paul, but someone I know you would like if you did meet and I pray one day you will. Let me explain."

Paul sat wide-eyed, a little light-headed after consuming alcohol on an empty stomach. Finding the truth unpalatable, he inwardly knew it answered many searching questions.

Lottie continued, her voice husky as nervous energy took over. "As you know, Nanny Su and my mother were always good friends. When I was sixteen, I accompanied my mother to Fosseway Hall to help with a summer fete, which, incidentally, was a great success."

"It was a wonderful hot, balmy summer. Lord and Lady Jenkins were great sports, not a bit snobby. During my time there I met a cheeky chappie, full of fun a crazy dynamo. Looking back, I suppose, we were both mischievous. His name is Davy – David Jenkins. I have to confess I did not know at that time he was their son otherwise I don't feel I would ever have had the nerve to speak to him let alone flirt with him."

Paul sat in silence, staring into space.

"Anyway," continued Lottie, "we got on so well, spending many days and hours together. I would trump up some excuse to visit with my mother when she was needed at the Hall. Over the months we became great friends, often meeting in secret."

Lottie's face lit up like a beacon as she recalled happy, carefree moments.

"One idyllic afternoon, after a picnic in Dorcas Wood, we made love. Although both virgins, it just felt right, as if we were made for one another. David's touch made me feel alive. My body responded as if I had emerged from a deep sleep. Emotions cascaded like a waterfall. We lay close, lost in time."

Paul's faced crumpled in pain. Lottie's words pierced his heart like a succession of knife wounds.

"Sorry Paul, I didn't mean to go on so. We arranged to meet a number of times after that, but everything changed when David's father was killed. It was difficult for us to meet. David was bereft. I felt like an outsider, unable to make contact let alone comfort him. I understand from Nanny Su that university life for him was a let down, a bit hit and miss, so much so that he lost heart in his studies."

"Did you tell him you were pregnant?"

"I couldn't. I knew straight away. Believe it or not, it is true what they say: you just know, as if a little switch is clicked in your head, saying, 'You are now about to nurture a new life, you must take extra care. You are soon to be responsible for another human being.' This knowledge freaked me out.

"David was grieving for the loss of his father. How could I tell him he fathered a child when no one knew we were seeing one another? We were, and still are, from different social backgrounds. I certainly wouldn't have been his family's choice and didn't feel I was good enough for him."

"So he doesn't know?" insisted Paul.

"No, Paul. Sadly he doesn't."

Paul screamed so loud that Lottie put her hands to her ears to block out his incandescent anger. "Lottie, how could you possibly hope to sweep this under the carpet and get away with it?"

"I know, I know! I have no right to ask you to stand by me, but I need to tell the truth now, to put the past behind me, and to try and make everything right. Telling you has been really hard, but it's the first step. Believe me – despite everything, I really do care for you. You truly are my best friend, the brother I never had."

Paul sank into the sofa, with his head in his hands. He loved Lottie deeply, and always had from the first moment he set eyes on her. He got up, pouring another large drink for them both, feeling inexplicably calm.

"Somehow," he mumbled, "I don't feel Tristan will be too surprised when he learns the truth."

"Why do you say that?"

"Because he has often asked who he takes after in the family. He is tall, dark, slim and artistic whereas I am bigger in build with fair hair and shorter in stature. The lad is naturally musical, creative and intent in protecting the planet's wild life. In fact, he has many qualities we do not posses. Unbeknown to you, I passed off his probing questions by joshing around, saying he took after Uncle Larry."

Lottie smiled through salty tears. "Yes, you could be right, but who is Uncle Larry?"

"A fictitious uncle who fitted the bill!"

"Oh, I see. How thoughtful."

Through sobs and tears Paul looked directly at Lottie.

"Although it hurts me to say this, I must confess I have known for years that your innermost feelings were for someone else, though I never guessed who. Words are not always necessary. Touch and tenderness reveal all, and you haven't wanted to be close to me for years."

Lottie got up, giving him a huge hug. "Paul, you deserve someone special. Someone who is worthy of you, someone who can love and really appreciate you."

They held each other close, safe in the understanding that for the first time they were being honest with one another, aware that the painful, heart-wrenching truth would set them both free. Walking arm in arm into the garden, Lottie nuzzled her head into Paul's chest for comfort.

"What are your plans now?"

"I am not sure Paul. This painful unravelling is something I have to face head on. I have to explain myself fully to those I unintentionally hurt and try and make amends to those whose lives have been affected. May I ask you to promise me that until I have achieved this my unburdening must remain between us?"

"I agree," replied Paul, feeling close to Lottie for the first time in years.

"I will start with making an appointment to see the Jenkins' local solicitor, Mr McGoonan in Torchester. He must have a forwarding address for Lady Lillian. I don't believe anyone knows where David is, but I know a way will be found."

"How can you be so certain?" quizzed Paul.

"Because," said Lottie calmly, "I met someone recently who made me see the error of my ways. He showed me to trust the power of love and how faith in one small flake of integrity creates an unstoppable avalanche."

27

Despite her mind being in a whirl, Ellie completed the writing assignment easily. She was pleased with the outcome and felt that congratulations were in order for having the knack of embellishing any simple wisp of news. Grant's words echoed in her head – "You have to find a way to make mundane news interesting to the reader." She had succeeded. Another project was completed.

Humming contently, with the cats at her feet, she stirred creamy scrambled egg, her favourite, and pondered on recent events at the Hall. Ellie was curious to understand how and why she had somehow become so caught up in events yet she was thrilled at the same time.

Pleasant faraway thoughts were disturbed by what she thought was a distant high-pitched noise. Curious to find out, she peered out of the kitchen window hoping to gauge its direction. Listening hard to distinguish the sound, she then gave up, slightly irritated at the interruption. Returning to the breakfast table a little put out, Ellie resumed eating her now slightly soggy warm breakfast with less enthusiasm.

A few moments later the shrill call seemed closer. Again she peered out of the window, finally stepping outside the back door, looking to the sky for any aircraft that may be in trouble. Hearing the call again, she shook her head in disbelief. Singing loudly to drown out the sound, she resumed her morning chores, suspecting wild imagination was working overtime. Yet the vibration was familiar. The call came again, this time clearer. In a split second of lucidity, Ellie recognised the call as Avani.

"She obviously needs me," she thought. "I wonder what she wants. Something must be wrong."

Without any further hesitation, Ellie rushed upstairs, showered, fed the cats, locked up and hurried to the Hall.

"Why would Avani want to see me?" she mused. "Thanks to the Master, Sam is sorted. I do hope everything is OK and that no-one is ill."

Ellie sensed urgency. The visit important otherwise Avani wouldn't have invaded her thoughts. Quickening her pace as she approached the Hall, again she heard the clear strains of Avani's soft tones calling, "Ellie…Ellie."

"I must hurry," she thought. "Perhaps something dreadful has happened to the Master. Oh, I do hope not! He is so kind."

Stopping to catch her breath, she felt slightly agitated and uncertain, recalling conversations the last time they met. Avani had promised that they would meet before the Master left. Debating the sanity of dropping everything on a whim and a hunch, she was rushing to answer a call she believed she heard, but which her common sense questioned.

White clouds flitted across the sky. Ellie's warm fleece was ideal for keeping out the morning chill. Her feet barely touched the ground as she ran. Reaching the entrance gates in record time, her heart was beating rapidly. She was puffing like an old stager, emphasising the fact that she needed to get fit, so she slowed down in order to pace herself for the visit ahead.

The gates opened, allowing her to slip through. She was surprised to see Avani in the distance, half way up the shingled drive. Avani appeared equally astonished to see her.

"Hi Ellie!" she said. "Enjoying the crisp morning? What brings you here today?"

Feeling utterly foolish, Ellie uttered, "I am not sure now. I thought… I guessed you wanted to see me."

Avani nodded. "Yes, I suppose I do. You are part of my plans. I know the Master is keen to see you before we leave."

"You are leaving?"

"Yes. Our time here is nearly at an end."

Ellie looked shocked and inexplicably lost, voicing that she would miss her visits to the Hall, which had been a remarkable interlude in her life. They stared at one another in silence lost for words.

Avani smiled, lifting the mood. "Don't look so worried. I am really pleased to see you. The Master is out walking. He looked very tired and weary earlier on today, but his early morning meditation, communing with the Higher Realms will, I am sure, replenish his energies a little."

Ellie looked up in surprise, feeling selfish, never once giving a thought to the energy expended by the wise being.

"I guess you linked into my thoughts earlier on Ellie," said Avani. "I must confess to thinking of you. We do care for our charges." Ellie blushed.

"Let's go and walk around the lake, though it's not very warm this morning. Do you feel the cold?"

"I will be fine. I have my fleece, which is cosy and warm. You don't appear to notice the change in temperature."

"No Ellie, I don't. I am not of human form. I present this physical side to you to enable you to recognise me. We understand human beings need to see a solid form, as many find our etheric body disturbing and unsettling."

They circumvented the lake slowly in silence. Ellie's mind was whirling, frantically trying to rationalise their meetings and the vibration call she had heard. Vivid images in her mind were building, merging and then dispersing until she felt quite giddy. Avani supported her arm.

"You will be okay, young Ellie," she promised. "You need to listen and trust more!"

"I will be so sad when you leave. I have grown accustomed to your presence. In a very short while you have become my special confidant, if such a relationship can exist between an earthling and angel."

"Of course it can. Do you have many good friends?"

"Yes, I am lucky to have so many yet I know they are not close enough for me to be open. Talking with you feels comfortable. I feel I could share anything with you and you would not judge or criticise me."

"Could that feeling be anything to do with the past?" Avani queried.

"Yes, I suppose it all has something to do with the past. I lost a dear friend many years ago, someone I really cared about. Her demise was my fault."

"I wonder if that is the reason you are here? Do you believe the Master can help you?"

Ellie contemplated the remark before answering. "I truly believed you called, so I ran. I really did – all the way to the gates!"

Avani understood, taking her hand. "Unless they can be identified, understood and released, nightmares can haunt and preoccupy thoughts day and night."

"I suppose so," answered Ellie, breaking out in a cold sweat, recalling waking in the middle of the night in a blind panic with a sea of enraged faces glaring down at her screaming, "Get rid of her! String her up! She let us down."

With the ground spinning beneath her feet, Ellie leaned against one of the lake's seats.

"I must confess I do need to know why. I don't experience the same nightmare every night, but when I do the angry, hostile pictures remain with me all day. They really terrify me. I find the images shocking and terrorising. I cannot begin to share them with anyone. When I try, the words jumble into nonsense, making no sense at all."

Ellie's pleading dejected look reminded Avani of an animal ready for slaughter.

"Are you able to help me? Would the Master be able to help me? I have been having similar nightmares, the same images since I was little. Mum didn't understand when I tried to explain, believing they were growing pains, the result of eating too much chocolate or perhaps watching too much television."

Ellie's bottom lip trembled. "Nana Jack understood!"

"Can you imagine, Avani, going to sleep at night, waking in the middle of the night and seeing angry faces, screaming that they want to lynch you?"

Avani shook her head. "I am sure the Master will help you unravel the puzzle, for I am sure that is what it is. Let's go and find him. I will ask if he feels able to meet you today."

Although weary, the Master welcomed Ellie to the Chakra Room. "I knew you would come. Your undisputed urgency impressed me for days."

"I am sorry for burdening you with my worries. Thank you for seeing me and for your time."

"Ah yes, time …. Tell me Ellie. What is time?" Ellie sat dumbfounded, unable to give a coherent answer. "You are quite complex, young lady. On the surface you appear confident, amenable and happy go lucky yet within you tremble with trepidation of what tomorrow will bring, concealing deep, dark fears remarkably well."

Head bowed, Ellie responded quietly, "Years of practice. I don't want anyone to know or to regard me as being weak."

"Weak? I never heard such poppycock." The Master laughed at his own statement, adding, "I must say you have some extraordinary sayings in your world!"

Ellie relaxed, lightening up to the wit of the wise being.

"Well Ellie, let me ask you a question," the Master continued. "Do you really want to delve into these so-called nightmares of yours?"

"But they are! They are nightmares. I wake up with palpitations, sweating and feeling sick. They happen often."

"I know, dear child. Please accept and understand that every fear, irrespective of how it manifests, has a beginning. If you so wish we can explore it and perhaps harness an ending."

"Oh yes, please."

Ellie sat in a chair finding the Chakra Room safe, inviting and a little exciting. Relaxed, the Master sat back resting his head, comfortable in his high-backed chair.

"You understand the purpose for sitting, my dear?"

"Oh yes."

"Relax, be open to receive and you will receive. May I please ask you to place your hand in the wooden box beside you and select a crystal. Choose one that feels just right in your hand."

Ellie did as she was asked, her fingers searching texture, size and shape. Some were cold to the touch, others smooth and slightly hot.

"Here it is!" she announced proudly, holding up the smooth,

glassy volcanic stone.

"My dear, you have chosen wisely. The Black Obsidian will serve you well."

Ellie wriggled in her seat, apprehensive, relieved and energised.

"Now relax my dear. Cast your eyes around the room. Which block of colour are you drawn to?"

"That's easy! Without a second thought, the purple one please," Ellie smiled, thrilled with her choice.

"Excellent." The Master chuckled knowingly, enjoying the moment.

"Right, my dear. Please make yourself comfortable, relax and focus on the block of amethyst."

Ellie did as she was asked, struggling to keep her eyelids open, eventually resisting no longer.

"During this process, I want you to describe in clear tones what you see and how you feel. Trust! All will be well."

Ellie struggled to harness her nerves, apprehensive pangs of panic rising from deep within, dreading what she might be forced to see.

"Ellie, you are here to seek and search. Now is the time to speak your truth."

She felt a cold sweat envelope her. The thought of the continuing frightening nightmare disturbed her focus, knowing she had this one opportunity to face her fears and dismiss dark terrifying shadows.

Ellie drifted in and out of consciousness until she eventually settled into a breathing rhythm. As her eyes became accustomed to the gloom, she saw a pretty young woman with long dark hair tied loosely at the nape of her neck, a hand embroidered blue cotton collar peeping over the top of a black laced up bodice.

Her long dark grey skirt barely covered wooden clogs. The young woman's legs were clothed in thick black stockings. Her glistening dark, frightened eyes darted from side to side, vigilant, watching every sudden move by the angry crowd. Cowering behind a heavy wooden cart, an amiable horse was absorbed in munching grass. Persistent angry voices reverberated in her head as incensed terrified faces moved closer and closer. A mirage of angry faces taunted until she could stand it no longer.

"Please leave me alone!" she begged. "I tried to help. I didn't mean any harm."

"We will hound you until you die," screeched the angry mob. "You are to blame."

"No, No… I'm not to blame. It was a mistake… I didn't know… I did what I thought was best!"

"Yeah, you knew, you knew!" shouted a bereaved, angry young father.

"We trusted you and you betrayed everyone here. We protected you and kept you safe, and this is the way you repaid us!"

"No. No. No. It wasn't like that!"

The mob moved forward, manhandling her and ignoring her screams for mercy and forgiveness. She had no choice but to sit in the midst of them. Her hands were loose and her feet bare. A rough rope was tied tight around her waist with the other end wrapped around the heavy pole of the village well.

A group of older women looked on in disgust. To the right of the well, four or five bewildered tutting children sat behind the group. Though believing in her, they were helpless against the fury of the disenchanted rabble. They tried hard to be heard, reiterating to the townsfolk that they believed she was genuine and had the power.

Ellie noticed an old woman with scraggy grey hair tied up

on the top of her head. She was dressed from head to toe in black with an enormous crucifix on black beads dangling from her neck.

"She did right by me when I was retching," she shrieked. "I thought I was a gonner. My Bert can't thank her enough. My family would be lost without me."

"I know," yelled the elected spokesperson of the group. "I hear you."

The chilly evening sunset was dropping quickly behind the trees. Soon it would be nightfall. Blaze, the dog, lay hidden in a thicket, head on his paws, ears alert, heart racing and bewildered. The confined woman willed him to stay hidden, fearing he would betray his position should he move. If they tortured her she would give in and die gracefully. If they hurt Blaze as punishment, she would fight like a tigress to the bitter end, unable to bear the thought of seeing him suffer their angry brutality.

Wood smoke from the fire irritated her eyes. She spluttered, gasping for breath. The mob glared, making no move to help or offer water. Momentarily shutting her eyes, she recalled memories, gratitude and a welcome when she was fifteen.

The young lad was terrified and panic stricken when she spotted him, screaming in agony after falling against a wasp nest while climbing trees. "Thought there was honey there, Miss."

Invited with warmth into the small community, her powerful healing gifts helped cure afflictions, enraging many, who viewed her as an enchantress, living among the elementals, fairy rings and folk lore. She reassured the bereaved that their loved ones never die, but live on in a better world. She diagnosed ailments, creating potions from the abundant pharmacy of Mother Nature gathered from fields, hedgerows and woods.

Built on results, her reputation spread. Many from afar

sought her out, trusting her diagnosis, treatment and cure.

The gathering brooding group continued shouting obscenities like a bunch of hooligans, suppressed emotions erupting and unprovoked anger gathering momentum. She remained still, searching hostile faces, aching, huddled in a half sitting crouching position, waiting for reprisals. Terrified the mob rule would explode, she silently prayed for a resolution.

"Let's string her up!" yelled one.

"No!" screamed another.

"That's too good for her. Let's starve her!"

"Throw her down the well!" yelled a third.

Amidst the racket, a young girl no more than eighteen, struggling to hold onto a sickly month-old baby, cried out, "She tried to help me when no-one else could!"

"Yeah, but she let us all down," screamed Len Baxter from the back row.

"She did her best," echoed a group of young lads from the far side of the group.

"Yeah, but she let us down badly. We believed in her."

"We did that," they echoed. "What shall we do with her?"

"Let her suffer like we did!"

"I don't rightly know. I am sure she meant no harm."

The terrified pretty young woman crouched low, with a sleepy pale baby lying awkwardly in her lap. "How could she know?"

Heart pounding, her body wet with sweat, Ellie observed angry eyes bearing down on the confined woman. Praying for clemency, she saw vengeance in their eyes.

"They don't understand," she whispered silently. "If only they would listen."

"Let's string her up on the old oak!" screeched an old man, swilling mead. "It will be quick!"

CHAPTER TWENTY-SEVEN

"We don't want it to be quick!" someone screamed. "We want her to suffer."

The heated words grew louder, seeking reprisal and revenge. The heat of the roaring fire overcame the need to remain alert. With head swimming and glazed eyes, the young woman fell forward a mere foot away from the edge of the burning embers. In an instant, Ben Penn broke ranks and ran forward, dragging her away from the flames.

Ben, a farmer's son, was hardworking and shouldering the responsibility and burden of providing for his mother and three siblings since his father's untimely death.

"Enough!" he screamed angrily. "Were we not taught to believe that there is good and bad in everyone? Isn't this the motto we live by? There are savages in the world who do not believe in the sanctity of life, who destroy, cheat and steal. Surely we are not like them yet we are acting like them."

The mob quietened. "Yeah, we know what you are shouting, lad, but we believed in her."

"Yeah, yeah. String her up I say!"

The momentum increased and the volume grew louder. Betty, the eldest of the inhabitants, stirred. Raising her hand, she whispered hoarsely, "Can I speak?"

The hollering grew louder.

"Shall we give her a chance?"

"No! String her up!"

"Nay," shouted Bill Sherman, rising to his feet. "Let her have her say and then we will deal with her."

"We could tie her up and leave her in Mangot's Barn to rot."

"Yeah, yeah. Let's do it!"

The mob's anger reached fever pitch, simmered, but then quietened. The rabble was exhausted, dispirited and defeated, and at a complete loss how to handle the situation.

Ben helped Jessie on to a log by the side of the fire, handing her a flagon of water, which she slurped down. "Please let the lass have her say."

Clutching the round stone hanging around her neck, a cord fraying at the knot, the girl recovered her composure enough to address them.

Huskily she whispered, "Please let me speak."

Hostile glares faced her, intent on judging every movement, mannerism and word.

Face stained with tears, she pleaded softly, "Can I have another drink of water?"

She drank eagerly.

"I have lived amongst you in the heart of the forest, where I am happiest, since I was young lass," she began. "My Ma, as you know, was always sickly. I looked out for her until she died."

Glancing down at the clearing grassland floor, she choked back tears, remembering difficult, heart-wrenching days.

"I couldn't save Ma. She was too sick. While she was alive I learned from her the way of the woods, watching birds, animals, understanding why they eat some plants and not others, preferring some habitats. I learned why some creatures die and others survive. You call upon me when you're worried about your animals. I give you herbs from the fields and woods to make them well."

"Yeah, that's right. You made my old nags better when they couldn't eat."

The crowd turned, acknowledging the craggy voice.

"You young ones," she said, pointing to the young woman with the sickly baby. "You call upon me when you need advice, before the little 'uns come and after when they don't settle."

"We have done."

"Yeah, I agree."

Clutching her stone tightly, she continued. "I vowed when me Ma died and I couldn't save her that I would do my best to pass on my knowledge, the old way, you understand, not this new fangled way. Me Ma had the knowledge and so did her Ma, so it's in my blood."

"Yeah, we know," screamed a voice from the back.

Jessie stood up. Turning to face the group, she took time to look into every pair of accusing eyes. "If you want to torture me then kill me, so be it. I am ready to face the consequences, but let me have my say."

Ben stood facing the others. "Do we all agree?"

"Yeah, yeah," the group muttered, then settled down, paying attention.

Jessie gasped, grateful for a few moments to collect her thoughts, knowing that Blaze, her beloved life-long companion, was only a few feet away. She had nurtured him to life, after finding him abandoned as a dying pup, the runt of the litter. Crossing her hands across her chest, she sat facing them.

"When Jim Spenlow came to see me those weeks ago, saying his family were ill with a fever, I gave him a cure, believing the remedy would work within a couple a days." Jessie lowered her eyes. "I was shocked and saddened to learn that the two-year-old was retching uncontrollably, had a fit and then died."

"When he came to see me again, saying Mary, Ellen and Toby were also sick, Martha, his wife poorly, was unable to care for the little ones, I went to see what could be done. Sadly, when we arrived little Toby was out of it. There was nothing we could do, but watch and wait."

"You should have done summat," a sobbing voice called from

the back, a bewildered middle-aged woman who, at a loss what to do, wrung her hands.

Jessie's gaze dropped to the floor. "I knew my concoction was right for the symptoms, but when I saw Toby dying I realised that this would be a difficult problem to solve. Being stronger, Jim seemed able to shake off the symptoms, though I must confess that he looked ghastly. Martha was just about holding her own."

"What did you do?" whispered a little lad, sitting cross-legged between his grandfather's legs.

Jessie smiled. "I went back to my roots. I told the family to drink or eat nothing apart from drinking cow's milk direct from the cow."

"Did that work?"

The group sat listening, anxious to hear her revelations. "I spent many sleepless nights, I can tell you. Jim and I worked together on eliminating the cause. We checked everything. He and I scrubbed the cottage inside out, but found nothing suspicious. My dowser confirmed there was a problem close by, so it was up to me to find the source.

"Then we heard that little Mary had died. That is when you pounced on me and Blaze at our little home. I still can't grasp why you all reacted as you did, accusing me of harming the family. I have lived here for always in these parts, me Ma and Granma before me. I adore my work and the way I live. I'm passionate about my beliefs and knowledge. In your hearts you must know that I wouldn't hurt any creature. You call me your Wise Woman, a name I'm proud of. If you want to harm me that is up to you, but please, I beg of you, don't hurt Blaze. He is not responsible for the Spenlows' problems."

Jason Cretbury burst through the clearing, sweating profusely, his lumbering bulky frame moving clumsily with fatigue. "Hey you folks!" he shouted incoherently, his face etched with worry. "Stop, stop and please listen!"

Ben ran to support his friend. "Jason, sit. What on earth is the matter?"

"It's my young'uns. They are sick, like the Spenlows. It can't be anything Jessie has done. Please stop. We're acting like daft things!"

"How are the young 'uns?" asked a concerned middle-aged woman.

"They are really sick, though I pray they'll pull through. Doc Bamber is with them. He's doing some tests."

The muttering crowd settled. The gathering began to grow ashamed of their hostilities.

"We thought?"

"I know what you thought, but you are wrong."

"I am so sorry the little 'uns are poorly," Jessie interrupted. "We need to get to the bottom of this. I do believe I can solve this problem, but I will need your help and support, and then if you like I will leave the area for good."

The mob sat in stony silence, ashamed of overreacting. Murmurs reverberated around the group. "Have you an answer?" asked Ben.

"I believe I have the answer, but I cannot do it alone. It's up to you."

Now fully behind her, they waited for instructions. "Where are we going?"

"Having eliminated everything else, I believe it must be something to do with the water. The young 'uns play in the water all the time and also bring it home for the washing."

"Yeah they do," someone shouted, "sometimes getting water from the stream."

"We need to check that the flow of water is running free and isn't fouled. The timing is perfect. We need to spread out. Start where the river line is high, where the stream breaks into two. We need to search, check the pools carefully and walk the stream until we meet here in the clearing at daybreak. Checking at night might give us a clearer idea of what is going on. Please note any tell-tale sign of rats. Although no one's seen them, they could be the cause."

Now in amenable mood, they set off in parties of four, their unspent energy directed at the job in hand. Starting where the weir tumbled into a clear stream, small groups walked either side of the water channel, chatting in a more conducive mood.

They walked, finding nothing odd to report – no signs of foxes, voles or the odd badger. Disheartened, to their left they suddenly heard a voice shrieking, "We've found something!"

In a nearby deep pool adjacent to the meandering stream lay a deer's rotting carcass, its stripped skeleton protruding through its ugly torn hide. This was a sure sign that scavengers had completed their work. The surrounding water was pungent with an overpowering stench. The carcass blocked the flow of water, causing a build-up of rotting vegetation, in effect creating a dam. To the right were the telltale signs of rodent trails.

"I reckon there is the source of your problem," shouted Bill Baines.

"I wouldn't have believed it if I hadn't seen it with my own eyes. Deer don't usually travel this far inland. Maybe one got frightened and lost its bearings."

"What we need to do now is to drag it out of the water and bury it, poor thing."

"Oh, I can't look!" yelled one of Ben's brothers. "It's horrible."

"Sadly, son, it is nature's way."

"Yeah, we must get the news to Jessie and let her know the source of the problem. Who would have believed it – dirtied, fouled water? The Spenlow children must have been poisoned."

"Makes sense, though."

"Yeah, perfect sense. It will take a while to clear, though, eventually the little 'uns will be able to play there again. Guess we need to check all the pools and ditches from time to time."

"Good idea."

"She must hate us."

"Jessie is wise and compassionate. She'll understand our fears, though I admit we are all guilty of overreacting and jumping to conclusions. I suppose we just needed to point the finger!"

Unable to assimilate the images, Ellie sat trembling. What dreadful deed did she imagine she was guilty of? Was she innocent and – if so – of what? What guilty conscience had been playing on her mind?

The Master looked across at her anxiously as Ellie squirmed in the chair, her expression distorted with twisted emotion.

"I am here Ellie," he soothed. "You are safe."

"But I don't understand."

"What don't you understand?"

"I understand why they wanted to hound Jessie, but why do I feel they want to persecute me?"

"Through your young life," said the Master, "all you have been doing is merely reliving a past lifetime memory where you believed you let people down and were responsible for their misery, wretchedness and misfortune. For years, your mind has been trying to clarify events, which you can now clearly see were out of your control. A freak of nature created a chain of events. Unfortunately, you were caught in the middle, your subconscious unwilling to visualise the scenario to the end. You feared facing circumstances too horrifying and unpalatable to delve into."

"I see. So I have been stupid?"

"No… not at all. You just allowed your mind to play tricks, your conscious mind a willing participant."

Ellie sighed. "I wonder if this has anything to do with why I always feel I have to justify my actions to everyone, to prove myself all the time and to be the best."

"Possibly, but that is for you to determine."

They sat quietly, the Master lightly touching the little lantern with relief.

Avani appeared with some rose water. "Are you okay?" she asked a little anxiously. "You both look exhausted."

The relieved Master sighed as Ellie whispered, "I'm fine Avani. Thank you for everything."

28

RELISHING THE SERENITY, Ellie sipped the rose water. "Avani told me earlier that you will be leaving soon."

"That is correct," said the Master kindly. "I have completed my mission. You have been a great help."

"Have I?"

"Most certainly. You enabled me to gain deeper insight into the human psyche. We sometimes struggle to understand human frailties, and pray for peace. Remember, Ellie, that no matter where you are or what you're doing inner peace is always possible. All it takes is a subtle shift in awareness and peace will follow."

"I do feel lighter inside me, although that sounds weird somehow," she smiled, relieved to understand the significance of her so-called nightmare.

"Have you unravelled the complete puzzle and now understand your purpose in this lifetime?"

"I'm not sure. I do try to understand people's motives, but some situations just leave me reeling with total disbelief"

"Why is that?" the Master queried.

"Oh, it would take too long to explain. Looking back, if I am honest I wish some situations had been different and I could turn back the clock."

"You can be nothing but honest in my presence. Talk to me."

"I know I can. Well, I feel responsible and guilty for someone's death. I have replayed the circumstances over and over in my head, arriving at the same conclusion. I reacted when I shouldn't have done. In consequence, a life was ended."

"So you learned the lesson that every action has a reaction," the Master commented, "and that every unkind word taints or maims someone somewhere."

"Yes. It's a bitter pill to swallow and digest. You commented earlier that I am a complex character. I suppose I am, but surely all humans are?"

"Yes, but some more so than others. The secret is to listen for possible hidden meanings, a clue to the exact opposite of what is being conveyed. Do you understand?"

"I think so."

Avani smoothed her hair. "Ellie, allow the Master to help you while he is here. We will be gone tomorrow." Ellie felt panic rising, suddenly realising how much she would miss their influence in her life.

"Oh, no! What will I do when you are gone?"

"Don't fret, my child. We will only be a thought away. Now that the connection has been made, you will still be able to communicate with us."

Avani took Ellie's hand. "Trust what you see and feel. Open your heart. Clear and cleanse your mind from needless clutter."

Ellie laughed at the simplicity. "Hey ho" she laughed. "Here we go again."

The Master gestured for Avani to leave.

"Before we explore the far reaches of your mind, it would be beneficial and advantageous to your future happiness to highlight your purpose this lifetime."

"Oh, yes, please!" said Ellie with a tone of excitement.

"When our meeting is at an end, I want you silently to go

with Avani to the Healing Room. Release every doubt and fear, look deep within and sweep away the many lessons you have learned. Then leave quietly, closing the door behind you. Do you recall that I described you as being special?"

"Yes," Ellie gulped, feeling embarrassed.

"Although I am not prepared at this time to reveal the intricacies, I need to inform you that your purpose this lifetime is to be an ambassador for peace. Not in war zones, you understand. That would be too easy."

"Easy?" answered a bewildered Ellie, pondering what revelation was coming next.

"You will discover a simplistic way to reach the hearts of mankind. A flame of hope, magnified when carried by millions, can ignite your planet. In time to come, people will be fearful for their future, growing to be unpredictable, searching for guidance and a way forward. You will be one of the chosen to light their way."

"How…will…?"

"The how is not important now. The timing is not right. Your bond with Avani will grow stronger over time. She will guide you."

"Will I see her again as I do now?"

"Very occasionally, though you will hear her voice clearly. She will be your link between the two worlds. As I said before Ellie, open your heart and mind. Trust."

Ellie wriggled, speechless, the glassy volcanic stone still in her clammy hand.

"Look into its mirrored facet," the Master instructed. "What do you see?"

Ellie did as she was asked, finding it difficult to contain her excitement. Slowly a picture emerged. "This is incredible and astounding! I can clearly see mountains, trees and what looks like an enormous lake."

"Now look again. What do you see?"

"Just a reflection of me."

"That is because you expected to see a certain image. Ellie, learn to free your mind. Trust your higher self and listen to your inner voice. It will never let you down."

"I see," replied a somewhat bewildered Ellie, unsure of what to say.

The Master stretched, adjusting his robes.

"Right, Ellie May."

"How did you know my name?"

"I know *all* about you." A humbled Ellie shrank back in the chair.

"Shall we try to unravel that dark conundrum persistently countermanding the huge personality hiding beneath a cleverly constructed shell? As before, focus on one of the pictures. Share your thoughts and feelings. Allow the colour to draw you into the centre."

The swirling colour instantly affected Ellie's balance. She swayed before eventually settling.

"Friends are important," she began. "I seem to collect friends as some people collect shoes. The difference is that when they try to get too close, I tend to freeze emotionally, feel suffocated and push them away."

"Why is that?"

Her deepest inhibitions exposed, Ellie burst into tears. Reticence revealed deep-seated anguish.

"Ellie, talk to me," the Master continued, but she just sat there, her hands loose in her lap, staring into space.

"Although regarded as being clever, I just couldn't settle into a job. Brilliant as they are, my parents failed to notice or ask why I always seem to be disgruntled and dissatisfied with certain aspects of my life. It was easier to pretend everything was great whereas in fact it was the complete opposite."

"Before going to university, I was offered a fabulous job as personal assistant to a new company, securing the interview through my close friend Julie. I was fluent in French, had good personable skills and got the job. It was only after I started working that I learned Julie's parents had invested heavily in the business. Chris and Julie had been married for three years."

"Why did that concern you?"

"I don't know. I just had an uneasy feeling and was sort of unsure of accepting the job, although I had no foundation for my fears."

"After three months, seminars were planned across the country. A prime location was selected for the launch of a new business, using sales marketing skills, plus good contacts I made in Scotland and Ireland. The offices in London were located on the top floor of a five-storey office block with breathtaking views across the city skyline."

"With Chris at the helm, five entrepreneurs invested in Star Roles, an exchange restaurant cookery school for people wishing to open high class restaurants. A groundbreaking team trained for all levels – chefs, sous chefs, maitre d', waitresses and front of house... It was an innovative concept."

"Over time, I got to know Chris Mahoney quite well – a hunk of a man with dark, thick wavy hair and warm, brown inviting eyes. He was tall with broad shoulders and handsome in a rugged sort of way. He oozed public school charm and dressed for the part, sporting a new car every year. He offered me a good salary with lots of perks. In essence, it was a wonderful opportunity to spread my wings, though from the outset I had reservations about Chris. Julie loved him, so who was I to cast aspersions to the wind, but there was just something I couldn't put my finger on. I told Julie I was amazingly happy."

"Travelling home by train one weekend, I enjoyed the luxury of a carriage to myself, which was pure bliss. I absolutely adore the soporific sound and motion of the train wheels on the track. It takes me back to childhood. Sorry... I digress."

"At the next station, a scruffy old man in his late seventies carrying a bundle of newspapers got into the carriage. At first, I must admit to being apprehensive. He appeared grumpy and inebriated, and peered at me through thick glasses. Initially acknowledging my existence by raising his trilby hat, he then proceeded to complete crossword puzzles, murmuring out loud as he did so. Although I had a book, I found it very difficult to concentrate. Eventually, he folded the newspapers into a neat pile on the small table and we chatted. Actually, he was interesting company, with roots in Glasgow. We talked happily about everything and nothing."

"As the train approached his stop, he doffed his hat and mumbled, 'Young lady, I need to pass on a message: don't incite the raven's scorn!' I thought him slightly batty, and found his demeanour and words more than a little disturbing. Pooh-poohing his bizarre ramblings as nothing more than alcohol-induced cryptic rubbish, though I must confess they did unnerve me."

"The provincial launch at Tunbridge Wells was a three-day event, with a professional four-man team fulfilling a brilliant sales marketing pitch in Castle Carrack. This was a five-star hotel set in six acres of parkland. It was a perfect venue with a conference hall seating two hundred and fifty people. Video links were set up for restaurateurs unable to attend in Scotland, Wales, Ireland and France.

"It was a resounding success for all involved… and a bonus for the sales team made it financially worthwhile! Chris was thrilled with the level of interest. Firm sales and agreements were signed in UK and France, so we were mentally planning to research other countries."

"Over a celebration dinner, I remember telling Chris that in my opinion success was rushing to his head which, as you can imagine, went down like a lead balloon."

"My remit at the launch was to sort out the paperwork trail, which I did at the end of the conference room. Tucked in a corner and hidden from view, I had space to systematically sort everything in piles. I work best that way. Although I was given free time to shop during the day, I chose to oversee events. Just after the conference ended, I noticed a change in Chris's manner. By chance, I was privy to his inappropriate behaviour with a pretty young blonde waitress, who had been flirting with him all day."

"I was so angry that I marched up to them, verbally tearing them apart. I didn't care that Chris was my boss. In my book he should not be fraternising with hotel staff. I was so upset that my deep-held, uncomfortable suspicions were justified. I was infuriated for Julie, who, oblivious to unfolding events, was at home with her elderly parents and six-month-old daughter."

"The ensuing heated exchange alerted the porter. My impassioned angry words were obvious to guests and staff, who were all justifiably embarrassed. We elected to go to Chris's suite to discuss the incident, which in hindsight was a big mistake."

The Master raised his eyebrows. "Is this going anywhere?"

"Oh yes – Sorry, I got carried away."

Ellie relapsed into the block of colour, becoming totally immersed in the core of swirling energy. She continued cautiously, reliving the tale as an observer.

Over drinks in his suite, a contrite Chris explained. "What you saw was a mistake. You misconstrued the situation."

"No I didn't. You were all over her like a rash."

"You misread the signals; I was simply thanking her for all the attention to detail."

"No, it was inappropriate behaviour. You wouldn't have acted that way if Julie had been here."

Still reporting events as if watching a film, Ellie revealed that Chris had then sidled up close to the woman, touching her breasts while caressing her bottom.

"Come on! You know what this is all about. You have been giving me the 'Come on' on and off ever since we got here."

"I have not!"

Then it happened. Chris pinned the woman against the wall, so close that she could hardly breathe. He tore at her clothes, sexually assaulting her. She retaliated with the cunning agility of an angry cat, scratching his face, fighting him off.

"Chris, stop!" she shrieked. "You don't know what you are doing!"

"Come off it! You fancied me ever since we first met. I know what you want!"

"You've got it wrong! Your wife Julie is my closest friend. You have let her down."

Grimacing with satisfaction, he muttered, "No one will know unless you tell. Why did you have to interfere? It was only a bit of fun. After all, I am a hot-blooded male."

As she broke free, upset and fighting tears, her mobile rang.

"You had better retrieve it from your bag and answer it

pronto. Officially you are still on duty."

"Hi, it's Julie. Is everything okay? I tried to ring Chris, but got no reply. How did everything go today?"

"Yes... It was a great success," mumbled the distressed woman.

"Are you okay? You sound strange and upset."

"I'm fine," she answered, lying through her teeth. "Just a bit tired. I'll phone tomorrow and catch up then."

"Okay. I'll phone Chris."

"Okay. I'm not sure where he is, but I'll ask him to phone you."

Feeling distraught, she left Carrick Castle in a quandary about what to do and unsure of what action, if any, she should take. Driving home like a demented fool, anger overrode exhaustion. "He's a monster," she muttered loudly, "and a womaniser. He doesn't deserve a wife like Julie! Do I tell her or just keep quiet?"

The woman stood in the shower for over an hour, allowing the comforting water to cascade over her. With tears streaming down her face, she washed away the memory of the last few hours. "One reads about situations like this in magazines," she thought. "How can it have happened to me with the husband of my dearest childhood friend? How on earth did I get in this mess?"

The exhausted woman clambered into bed, determined to rest, and deciding to hide and stay close to base for the rest of the week.

Julie insisted meeting for coffee, leaving numerous messages on the Ansaphone.

"Are you avoiding me?"

"No, of course not! I'm fine."

"Chris tells me you have been off sick since returning from

the launch in Tunbridge Wells. Are you really okay? Come on. Talk to me. I know there's something wrong. Please tell me. Doesn't being friends since the fifth form count? Don't you trust me?"

"That's not the issue."

"Come on. I'll ask my neighbour Helen to have Daisy. Let's meet for lunch at the Cricketers tomorrow lunchtime at one. I won't take 'No' for an answer, so be there or I will come and get you."

At the usual table by the inglenook fireplace, the beautifully presented lunch at the Cricketers was spoilt by misgivings, as Julie pressed for answers.

"Please tell me what is going on! I have never seen you look so drained and stressed. I tell you, I won't leave you alone until I know. I'll extract the truth from you somehow!"

The women faced each other in silence.

"Not here, Julie. Let's walk."

Linked arm in arm, Julie held tight on to her friend's hand. "Okay. Let's walk over to those trees across the green – and for goodness sake smile! Whatever it is, it can't be that bad."

Ill at ease, the woman blurted out, "Julie, there is no easy way to tell you. I don't know how to say this, but Chris is fooling around."

Feeling uncomfortable and out of her depth, Julie swung round on her. "He wouldn't! He loves Daisy and me. You've got it all wrong!"

Tears welling in her eyes, the woman murmured, "I'm sure he does. Perhaps he can't help himself. You know what some men are like."

By now in tears, Julie responded angrily, "I hear what you are saying, but not my Chris. He is a good hard-working man. You are mistaken."

They walked, a distance between them, both feeling awkward. An infuriated Julie continued. "I don't believe a word you are saying. Chris is at the office. I will sort this out once and for all. Don't worry; I won't drop you in it!"

The woman looked upset, hurting for her friend, fearing the outcome.

"That's not my concern. I only share this with you because of our long-standing friendship. I care for you. He doesn't deserve someone as lovely as you."

"That is for me to find out, don't you think?" screeched Julie with a face like thunder. "Perhaps you are not the true friend you purport to be. After all, I have what you always wanted – a husband, home, baby and successful business. All you have is you! Chris always said you would end up an old maid."

Incensed with the news, Julie marched off, exasperated, angry and smarting at her friend's revelation.

The lift took ages. Julie tapped her fingers on the rail in anticipation of a fight. "I can't believe my best friend would double-cross me," she muttered angrily. "She only got the job because of me!"

Oblivious to events, Chris sat relaxed behind an enormous desk in his plush executive suite. Like a proud peacock, he was bathed in success, which was reaffirmed by numerous congratulatory phone calls and faxes.

A seething Julie stood in the doorway. Chris stood up to greet her. "Hi! Long time no see. I was just about to leave. You come to congratulate me?"

"Hmm, yes, I suppose so," replied an annoyed off guard Julie.

"First, I need you to clarify something. I have just had lunch with your PA, who informed me, a little scathingly, that you've been cheating on me, 'fooling around,' to quote her words. What do you... By the way, what is that awful mark on your face?"

Touching his scratched face, Chris's thinking moved into overdrive. "Oh this? I forgot my razor and borrowed one from the hotel with this result. It's a right mess. Perhaps I ought to sue."

"Forget the jokes, Chris. This isn't a joking matter. Is there any truth in her statement because if there is, I can assure you that you will go out through that window head first. I am ready for a fight!"

"Listen, my treasure..."

"Don't 'treasure' me! There's an old saying that 'There's no smoke without fire' or something like that. What the hell is going on?"

"Julie, please sit down. I'll explain."

Still seething, Julie sat, resenting the conversation and drumming anxious, infuriated fingers on the highly polished desk.

Composed and adept at formulating answers in record time, Chris replied, "Actually, it's the other way around. She came on to me and I... well, I rejected her and I suppose I hurt her pride. Can't you see that she's jealous of you, of what we have, our love for one another and our future?"

"But if that's the case, why bring it up now?"

"Possibly because she is lonely, unfulfilled, envious of our success and what we share."

Unconvinced, Julie watched Chris's mannerisms. Moving quickly forwards, she pushed him hard against the frame of the open window, incensed strength manipulating the move. Chris's back forced hard against the sill, his bulk precariously vulnerable as he desperately tried to keep his balance.

Julie continued seething, poking him in the ribs. "After all that I and my parents have done for you, if you have cheated on me, I promise I will destroy you and mutilate your manhood. You will be finished. Either way, Chris Mahoney, your card is marked. From now on I will watch every move you make!"

Chris took his chance swiftly, pushing Julie hard against the edge of the desk, holding her arms so tightly that she squealed in pain. As he tried to kiss her, she turned her face away in fury, yelling. "Let me go! I didn't expect this reaction from you. I'll get Daisy. Be home about seven and no later. We can talk then!"

Chris stopped her before she could reach the door. "Don't be angry, my treasure. You know you are a maniac on the road when you are angry."

In the doorway, Julie exploded. "Angry isn't the word! I'm fuming and humiliated. Losing a best friend is one thing, but questioning my husband's love is another. We'll sort this out later."

As Julie slammed the door, the window vibrated. Chris sighed, wiping his brow with a monogrammed handkerchief. Reaching into the top drawer of his filing cabinet, he fumbled for the gin bottle and tonic. Trembling with relief, his shaking hands poured a large drink. He gulped it back and poured another, slouching in his chair, calling a number on his mobile.

"Hey, it's only me. You okay. Phew, that was a close call! See you later at the usual place?"

Locking the office, Chris sprinted down the stairs, avoiding the reception desk. Grinning and punching the air with glee, he made his way to the underground car park.

"Yep, Chris old boy. Though you didn't see that confrontation coming, you got away with it again."

Rushing to his latest acquisition, a gleaming British racing green convertible, as usual he got ready to pose with the top down. Armed with chocolates and flowers, he arrived home very apologetic in record time. Despite a tear-stained face, Julie, elegant as ever, was waiting to greet him with outstretched arms. Oblivious to the unfolding trauma, Daisy was safe in the vast kitchen content in her high chair, chewing on a teething rusk.

Julie opened the conversation. "Chris, I have calmed down since our heated argument. Thinking about things on the way home, you are right – I have a turncoat for a friend, though I wouldn't have thought it possible. On reflection, you are right; our lifestyle is so very different to hers. I suppose she just wanted some excitement in her life. I will never, ever forgive her for all this upset!"

Grinning and giving Julie a big bear hug, Chris replied, "Yep, I am sure you are right."

A little calmer, Julie squeezed his hands. "Supper will be about an hour. Is that okay? Do you want to shower and change before spending time with Daisy?"

Relieved, Chris took her in his arms, kissing her softly on her forehead. "Tell you what. I have a better idea. Why don't I pop out and get a bottle of celebratory champers?"

Crestfallen, Julie answered with pleading eyes. "You don't need to. I am sure we have bottles in the cellar."

"Not the bottle I have in mind. Tonight is special. I'll leave the shower till later. Depending on traffic, I'll probably be about half an hour."

"Okay. Take care."

Doubts crept into her mind as Julie closed the front door, watching Chris move towards his beloved car.

"Don't be a silly goose Julie! He's a bit of a wine buff, perhaps he knows of an extra special Champagne to celebrate the launch."

Jumping into his car, Chris muttered under his breath while waving madly to Julie. Quickly inserting the key in the ignition, he smugly told himself, "Old boy, you should be awarded an Oscar for your performance today!"

As the car glided effortlessly out of the drive, Chris punched the air again with glee while turning the volume up on the radio. "Chris, my boy. How the hell did you wriggle out of that one? What a day!"

The rush hour traffic was heavy. Chris drove out of town the back way, through the countryside, meandering along leafy lanes, steering the car with his knee while texting. "Hi. Got away with it! See you five minutes. Usual place."

A group of lads from the local football club who were out jogging witnessed the crash. Shocked and stunned, the group stopped in their tracks.

"Hey, you guys! Did you see that?"

The tall fit lad voiced their thoughts.

"I don't believe what I've just seen! Instead of taking the bend, the bloke in that posh car seemed to accelerate straight into that old oak tree!"

*   *   *

Sobbing like a child without its favourite comforting toy, Ellie faced the master. "So he was a rotten cheat after all!"

The Master monitored Ellie's reaction. "It would appear so. Tell me: do you still hold yourself responsible for the family's misfortune and loss of life?"

"No, I guess not. Viewing the episode as an outsider, I see clarity in the chain of events. Julie had a lucky escape and I would say Chris got poetic justice. The old chap on the train knew what he was muttering about after all."

The Master smiled. "Ellie, you are on your way. Remember to listen and trust your inner voice."

"I will."

Avani escorted a shattered Ellie to the Crystal Room. Admiring the powerful brilliant energising crystals, she asked, "What will happen to these rooms when you leave?"

"They will be dismantled and kept safe, perhaps for another time," Avani answered poignantly. "Who knows? Harmonious love will remain. As you know, love knows no boundaries, can never be extinguished and never dies."

Ellie rested, soothed by the swirling powerful uplifting healing energies.

"I bid you farewell, Ellie," Avani whispered. "I must join the Master. Leave when you are ready."

With her awareness heightened, Ellie glanced around the room before tip-toeing down the stairs, closing the door quietly behind her.

She woke among a pile of cushions on the Chesterfield to find Truffles and Wynchester, content and curled up together on the sofa beside her. How long had she been there? It was now nightfall, time for bed.

After a quick shower, Ellie jumped into bed, snuggling under the cosy, warm duvet. "What an extraordinary day!" she pondered. "Somehow I feel I have travelled many miles, though admit I have never felt better, and glad to be alive."

Jumping up, Ellie drew open the curtains a little to enable shafts of sporadic moonlight to dance on the ceiling before snuggling back into bed. She lay content to drift, staring at the moving streaks of light, considering the enigma, "How can we really be sure that what we dream isn't real and what we believe or perceive to be real is merely a dream?"

About the author

REBEKKA CARROLLE is a published author making her debut in fiction with this compelling novel with philosophical overlays. It is a story of warmth, pathos and revelation, skilfully drawing the reader through hoops of emotional issues, leaving them questioning.

Rebekka continues to help those who yearn for peace, need to find their right path, by giving powerful insight into their lives.

After many years in the Health Service, Rebekka now pursues her passion for writing, approaching life's difficulties from a reflective perspective, enabling the reader to experience the journey that unfolds in this book.

The powerful uplifting energy within the New Forest, where she now lives, continually inspires Rebekka's enthusiasm for exploring life and its many diverse challenges through inspirational eyes.

Bridge of Time, the sequel to *The Fosseway Lantern* is still to be published. The magical *Truth Teller* soon to unfold.

For more information visit her website:
www.rebekkacarrolle.co.uk

BRIDGE OF TIME
Sequel to
THE FOSSEWAY LANTERN

Where does forgiveness begin?

Love is often a misunderstood powerful emotion
as a guilt ridden seeker discovers to her cost, in her
quest to undo the web of deception she wilfully
wove years ago.

The search begins with a visit to a cautious
suspicious family solicitor, where she is greeted with
mistrust and scepticism.

No one hides or runs for ever. An unexpected
encounter with a remarkable stranger encourages
a bitter, angry man to fulfil a seemingly impossible
promise. Walls of hostility and distrust tumble, as he
struggles to uncover the truth.

Facing impossible tasks makes perseverance
and determination stand firm against walls of
indifference. Despite many blind alleys, persistence
wins through, but all is not as it seems.